T0366146

CHALKBOARD JUNGLE

One Teacher's Struggle to Survive
in the American Public School System

BARBARA MARIA KOVACS

iUniverse LLC
Bloomington

CHALKBOARD JUNGLE

ONE TEACHER'S STRUGGLE TO SURVIVE IN THE AMERICAN PUBLIC SCHOOL SYSTEM

iUniverse books may be ordered through booksellers or by contacting:

iUniverse
1663 Liberty Drive
Bloomington, IN 47403
www.iuniverse.com
1-800-Authors (1-800-288-4677)

Because of the dynamic nature of the Internet, any web addresses or links contained in this book may have changed since publication and may no longer be valid. The views expressed in this work are solely those of the author and do not necessarily reflect the views of the publisher, and the publisher hereby disclaims any responsibility for them.

Any people depicted in stock imagery provided by Thinkstock are models, and such images are being used for illustrative purposes only. Certain stock imagery © Thinkstock.

ISBN: 978-1-4917-1200-9 (sc)
ISBN: 978-1-4917-1202-3 (hc)
ISBN: 978-1-4917-1201-6 (e)

Library of Congress Control Number: 2013920941

Printed in the United States of America.

iUniverse rev. date: 11/13/2013

This book is dedicated to my dear mother and father, and also, to the educators of America

CHAPTER 1

It was Brenda Connor's graduation day. She awoke early that morning with the realization that it was the last day of her old life. All her years of schooling had finally come to completion, and today she was going to receive her degree in education. She had dreamed of being a teacher since she was a small child. When she was only four years old, her mother had bought her a chalkboard, complete with an eraser and a box filled with multicolored chalk. Much to her mother's surprise, Brenda had cherished this toy above all others. She had transformed her bedroom into a classroom and had given every toy she owned an assigned seat, along with explicit instructions to sit quietly while she scribbled away on her board. On some occasions, her mother and father had passed by while she was teaching, and according to her whim, she had pulled them in and required them to attend her class. And once they were inside, she had expected her parents to sit side by side with her stuffed animals and pay close attention while she conducted her class.

Brenda recalled these early memories of her childhood with fondness and smiled at the thought of things to come. After hitting the snooze button on her alarm clock for the second time, she decided it was time to get out of bed and begin dressing herself for this special day. She selected an outfit that complemented her graduation robe and decided to wear her hair down. Her grandmother had lent her a stunning pearl necklace with matching earrings, and her sisters took charge of her makeup. When her makeover was finally complete, she took one last look at herself in the mirror, grabbed her graduation cap, and headed downstairs.

As she descended the stairs, she found herself assaulted with flashing lights from family members who were waiting in the wings with cameras to take her picture. Although she hated having her picture taken, she smiled politely and posed willingly with everyone who wanted to be in a photograph. After her family had photographed her from every possible angle, they finally left Brenda alone and gave her a few moments to immerse herself in her thoughts. As everyone bustled around her, she tried to eat a little breakfast, but she found that she had no appetite for food. She was dealing with a wide array of emotions, feeling excited and terrified all at the same time. After today, she would no longer be a college student; she would be an actual teacher, working with children at the middle-school level. Originally, Brenda had wanted to work with younger children, but following the advice of her college adviser, she had decided to expand her marketability and become certified in the area of math. This had turned out to be a wise decision, as few jobs were available at the elementary level. As a student just out of school, Brenda was lucky to have found a job at all. The present economy was one of high unemployment rates, and people were losing their jobs every day. However, Brenda was not afraid and felt that the current economic climate was in no way any threat to her. She was confident and almost haughty in her belief that she would always be employed. After all, according to the state of Florida, she was a highly qualified teacher in a critical shortage area. As far as she was concerned, loss of employment would surely never be an issue for her.

As Brenda secretly commended herself for choosing the right path, her mother began yelling, instructing her to hurry up, as the ceremony would soon begin. Since this was a momentous occasion, all of Brenda's family had been invited, as well as numerous neighbors and close friends of the family. Brenda felt somewhat embarrassed to have so many people attend her graduation, but her parents had insisted, and Brenda had reluctantly relented. Once they all reached the college campus, Brenda left her family and friends behind and took her assigned seat on the stage.

As Brenda looked upon the campus for the last time, she couldn't help but feel remorseful. After all, this place had been her second home for the last four years, and the people who were graduating alongside her had been like her second family. Brenda had gained more than just an education at this university. She had developed friendships, discovered her strengths and weaknesses, and actively participated in many school activities. She had carved out a comfortable little niche for herself, but now everything was about to change. She would have to leave her old life behind her and embark upon a new adventure. As Brenda looked at the smiling faces of her classmates, she wondered if deep down, they were sad too. Perhaps she should have concentrated more on the happiness of the day, but all she could think about was how radically her life was about to change. She wasn't sure if she was ready to leave the comforts of campus life and face the challenges of the working world. And while the valedictorian gave his speech and the students went up to receive their degrees, Brenda contemplated her future—and anticipated everything that could possibly go wrong.

Once the graduation proceedings were over, Brenda and her guests left the campus and drove to a nearby park. With so many people in attendance, it made perfect sense to hold the celebration outside, but it was the rainy season, so Brenda's family made sure to rent a space that provided a pavilion in case there was a storm. Nevertheless, when Brenda looked up at the sky and surveyed the clouds, she felt fairly certain that the day would turn out to be a perfect Floridian day. However, although it wasn't raining, it was still a hot and humid day. And because the weather was so unbearable, Brenda decided to take off her graduation robe and join her mother under the pavilion. They had much to do, and Brenda busied herself by setting out the silverware and sorting out the food. Since there was such an overabundance of food, she decided to keep half of it under the pavilion and take the other half outside to the picnic tables. However, as she attempted this task, she suddenly heard a nasty scream come out of nowhere, forcefully criticizing her actions and aggressively instructing her to do otherwise.

"No! No! No! You can't take the coleslaw and potato salad outside! Don't you know that you have to keep perishable foods in the shade or else they'll spoil in the sun? Do you want your guests to get food poisoning? Honestly, Brenda! How can a college graduate be this stupid?"

Brenda didn't even need to turn around. She instantly recognized the voice and knew exactly who was reprimanding her. Not wanting to make a scene, she turned around and responded as calmly as she possibly could.

"You're absolutely right, Aunt Margery. Would you like to help me set up the food?"

"What I would like is for you to use some common sense! What did they teach you in that fancy university anyway?"

Aunt Margery continued to rant for quite some time, but Brenda, having had enough, quickly walked away and rejoined her guests. Who the hell did her aunt think she was, talking to her that way? Why did Aunt Margery have to go and put a damper on Brenda's special day? Had it been left up to Brenda, Aunt Margery would never have been invited to her graduation. Aunt Margery was her mother's youngest sister and was by far the most miserable woman Brenda had ever met. Nobody in the family liked her, but because she was family, they tolerated her and invited her to all of the family functions. To say that she was bitter was a huge understatement. In the course of her entire life, Brenda had never heard one positive thing come out of her aunt's mouth. Aunt Margery's entire disposition reeked of anger and resentment, and her mere presence was enough to send people running in the other direction. Like the rest of her family, Brenda was careful to keep her distance, but she couldn't help wondering what propelled her aunt's hostility. Perhaps her unhappiness stemmed from the fact that she was alone.

Or perhaps she was disgruntled in her job as a schoolteacher. Whatever the reason, it was rumored that she hadn't always been this way. At one time, her aunt had been the polar opposite of who she now was. Brenda couldn't believe it! If this was indeed the case, then why had she changed for the worse? What terrible things had she experienced in her life to cause such a metamorphosis in her character?

Well, today was Brenda's day, and Aunt Margery's self-loathing was her own problem and not Brenda's concern. Whatever questions she had about her aunt's past would have to remain unanswered until a later time. Right now, she needed to focus on her guests and finish setting out the food. As Brenda carried out the last of the trays, she heard her mother call everyone over to eat. Brenda proudly took her seat at the head of the table, and her guests gradually congregated around her, strategically selecting their seats. Brenda looked over to her right and noticed that the children had chosen to sit together far away from the adults but close to the fence that enclosed the nearby pool. To her left was the pavilion, where the elderly sought protection from the sun. The day was getting hotter with each passing hour, and some of her relatives had serious health conditions that could be exacerbated by the sun. Lastly, Brenda looked at the people who sat at her own table. She was pleased to see that her sisters were nearby, and her fiancé, Joseph, was seated right by her side. However, one seat at the table still remained unoccupied—until Aunt Margery sat down and claimed it for herself.

"Why is there only one basket of rolls at a table that sits sixteen? Who made the undercooked roast and overcooked vegetables? It would have been better if you had just had the whole thing catered!"

As her aunt continued to critique and criticize everything in sight, Brenda noticed that the people at her table were slowly leaving one by one. Some tried to be considerate by making excuses, while others slipped away without any explanation. Brenda's trepidation was compounded by the realization that eventually, she would be left all alone to deal with her aunt. As she had predicted, her aunt cleared the table within five minutes, with the exception of her fiancé, who remained faithfully by her side. However, it didn't take long for Aunt Margery to chase him away too.

"So what do you do for a living? You're not a bum, are you? You look like a bum to me. I thought my niece had better taste in men than this."

Joseph withstood the insults as long as he could but, like everyone else, could only take so much and eventually walked away, leaving Brenda to fend for herself. Brenda glanced sorrowfully at the empty table and wanted nothing more than to speak up and put her aunt in her place. However, Brenda was not without filial conduct, and her proper upbringing prevented her from speaking her mind. Therefore, she restrained her emotions as best as she could and listened to what her aunt had to say.

"So I heard that you accepted a job in the public school system. I certainly hope that you didn't just take the first job that was offered to you."

"Actually, I attended a job fair and made my selection based upon what I was told by the recruiters."

"What! How could you have been so stupid? Don't you know that those recruiters are nothing but a bunch of liars? Their only focus is to get the positions filled. Did you even bother to do your own research?"

At these harsh words, Brenda stammered slightly before she answered. "What type of research are you referring to?"

"Did you bother to ask about the demographics that you would be working with? Do you know where the school is located? Are you going to be working for a Title I school? Do you know if the school has made adequate yearly progress?"

"What difference does any of that make? I'm a teacher, and my sole purpose is to educate and nurture the minds of children. It doesn't matter who I teach or where I work. Unlike you, I became a teacher to make a difference."

Brenda suddenly felt ashamed of herself for yelling at her aunt. She could see by the expression on her aunt's face that she had spoken too harshly. She hadn't meant to hurt her feelings. She had simply wanted her to understand that she knew what she was doing and that she had her life under control. Was it too much to ask for her support and validation? Here she was, graduating with honors and fortunate enough to have a job right out of school. So many of her classmates had sought employment but were still out of work. Why couldn't her aunt be proud of her? Why couldn't she just be happy for her this one time?

"Brenda, you have no idea what you're getting yourself into. I've been in this profession for nearly three decades, and

I can honestly say that over the past few years, things have consistently gotten worse. I'm at the stage of my life where my career is coming to an end; however, you're just at the beginning, and it would behoove you to listen to someone who has more experience."

Brenda thought about this last comment and wondered if maybe her aunt was right. Maybe she needed to listen and learn from someone who was already in the field. However much she despised her aunt, she could not deny the fact that her aunt had seen many things throughout the duration of her career. What real harm existed in seeking this woman's guidance? It was likely that her aunt would disparage her, but then again, maybe she would offer her some valuable advice. After giving the notion some thought, Brenda decided to take a chance. She would risk another tongue-lashing in exchange for some help. She would ask her aunt to elaborate on her previous comments and share her views on the educational system. However, just as Brenda was about to ask a question, her family and friends suddenly whisked her away and threw her into the festivities of the celebration.

CHAPTER 2

Brenda enjoyed her graduation party immensely and was overjoyed with the presents that she received. Her friends and family had collectively given her enough money to cover two months' rent on her new apartment, with plenty left over to purchase a wardrobe for her new job. However, Brenda found the prospect of shopping for new clothes somewhat disheartening. Upon graduating high school, she'd had an athletic build and boasted a near-perfect physique. However, once she had entered college, her eating habits had changed for the worse, and the pounds had quickly piled on.

Although Brenda could have done her part by exercising a little more restraint, her ever-expanding waistline wasn't entirely her fault. After all, who could resist the buffet style of eating that was offered by the college three times a day? And what about the invitations that she received from her friends? Somebody would always call in the middle of the night, inviting her to a diner or bar, and how could she be rude and refuse to go? Lastly, her fiancé, Joseph, lovingly wined and dined her, not thinking of the repercussions that she would have to face later on.

The consequences of her indulgent behavior had soon caught up with her, and by the end of her first year of college, she had gained more than the average freshman fifteen, and she had steadily continued to gain throughout the course of her four years. Although she exercised on a daily basis, Brenda still continued to gain weight, because she refused to moderate her eating. During her senior year, she had mustered the courage to step on a scale and had nearly fainted when she saw the number staring back at her. It had been far worse than she had expected, and as she had never had any weight issues in the past, she had been at a complete loss as to what to do.

Since exercise had failed to work, Brenda had decided to accept her new size and the health consequences that came along with being overweight. One of the results of her weight gain was that she was forced to trade in her stylish outfits for more-comfortable clothing. Pants in general were out of the question, and Brenda had spent most of her college years in loose-fitting skirts and dresses. Now here she was, overweight, with nothing appropriate to wear for her new job. She enlisted the help of her mother and grandmother, and the three of them set out together for the neighborhood mall. Her grandmother suggested they start the shopping spree by looking for shoes. Upon hearing this, Brenda's spirits suddenly rose. She loved shoe shopping! No matter how much her body expanded, the size of her feet always remained the same. Once they reached the store, Brenda immediately headed toward the section that displayed the latest styles of shoes. However, before she could try anything on, she heard her mother's voice beckoning her to come back and reconsider her decision.

"Why don't you come over here and take a look at these shoes instead?"

When Brenda walked over, she discovered a dismal collection of dark and tan-colored shoes. Most had little or no heels, and all were completely lacking in style. Some of them even looked like the orthopedic shoes that her old teachers used to wear. After closer inspection, Brenda cringed as she noticed that many of the shoes fastened with Velcro.

Brenda's mother sensed her disgust but replied, "These shoes may not be the most attractive, but they're practical and appropriate to your new position. You can expect to be on your feet most of the day, and comfort should be your number-one priority."

Brenda's grandmother nodded in agreement. "Your mother's right. In my day, teachers dressed sensibly and were expected to set a positive example for the children. How do you expect the children to respect you if you don't respect yourself?"

Brenda could see that arguing with her mother and grandmother was futile, as they were strongly united on this matter. She grudgingly selected three pairs of shoes of varying colors and then made her way over to the clothing department. Brenda looked around her, unsure which direction to take. The choices of clothing were daunting. She had no idea which style of clothing might flatter her new fuller figure while still being appropriate to her new job. Interestingly enough, her mother went in one direction, while her grandmother went in another. It seemed that her mother's preference was for pants, whereas her grandmother leaned more toward the dresses. Instead of taking sides, Brenda decided to try on some of each. Her fear of pants subsided once she saw that many of them had a comfortable elastic waist and were made of a stretch-based material. Many of the dresses also turned out to be forgiving and complementary to her figure. All in all, Brenda's fears turned out to be unfounded, and she left the mall that afternoon with a wide array of outfits for her new job. Once she had paid for all of the items, she parted ways with her mother and grandmother and decided to head back to her apartment. With the ordeal of shopping finally behind her, Brenda could now focus on making last-minute preparations for her new job. It was Sunday night, and Brenda was expected to report to work promptly at 8:00 a.m. the next morning. She carefully selected one of her new suits and placed it gently next to her new workbag. Her workbag had been a present from her parents, and Brenda loved its deep maroon color and faint scent of leather. At some point, her new bag would hold lesson plans and tests for her to grade, but for now, it would hold only her identification. She needed her driver's license and social security card to finalize the application process, and a copy of her transcript, along with her teacher's certification, would be placed in her personnel file and would serve as proof that she was indeed qualified to teach in the state of Florida.

As Brenda put these things in her bag, she remembered the afternoon at the job fair, when she had tried to negotiate her salary with the recruiters only to discover that salary was nonnegotiable with the school district. After careful investigation, Brenda had discovered that the school system followed a salary schedule involving the use of steps. Since

Brenda was a new teacher, she would naturally begin at the first step, which would start her out at the lowest salary. Although Brenda had been negligent in researching schools, she had thoroughly studied the salary schedule. It seemed that with each passing year, a person could elevate by only one step. Furthermore, a person's salary hardly increased from one year to the next. Teachers had to work at least ten years before they saw any significant increase in their pay.

Brenda knew that as a general rule, teachers throughout the country were severely underpaid. Yet this system seemed particularly unfair, as the starting salary in Florida was well below the national average, while the cost of living was one of the highest in the country. However, on a brighter note, Brenda saw that besides the salary schedule, the school system offered various supplements, incentives, and bonuses. If she pursued a graduate degree and regularly attended in-house trainings, she could expect to see a slight increase in her salary within a few short years. Besides these perks, there was also the union that bargained for a cost-of-living increase each year, and the state offered a loan-forgiveness program to teachers who taught in the areas of reading, math, and science.

The salary aspect of her new job was certainly disappointing, but Brenda hadn't chosen this profession to become wealthy. All she had ever wanted was to make a difference in the lives of children. It would take years before she would be financially comfortable, but at least she would be doing what she loved. In due time, she would make her big money, but meanwhile, she would have to pay her dues and accept the system for what it was, no matter how flawed it might be.

After Brenda finished packing her workbag, she set her alarm clock and tried to get some sleep. Unfortunately, she spent many hours tossing and turning in her bed, full of anticipation, her mind racing at the thought of things to come. At precisely 6:00 a.m., her alarm went off, and Brenda awoke, startled by the noise. She was not a morning person and could not even remember the last time she had gotten up this early. In college, she had been careful to schedule only afternoon and evening classes so that she could study for exams late into the night. She felt exhausted and was tempted to sleep in a few minutes longer, but she quickly reconsidered since she didn't want to be late on her first day of work. As she leaned up against the shower wall, the warmth of the water against her body felt rejuvenating, and she slowly began to wake up. After she finished showering, she looked in the mirror and wondered what she should do with her hair. This portion of her morning routine would definitely be the most time consuming, as her hair was unmanageable and difficult to tame. After arranging her hair in various styles, she finally settled on a French braid. Her clothes and shoes were sensible, so she figured her hair might as well be sensible too. Once her transformation was complete, Brenda took one last look at herself in the mirror and then bolted out the front door.

Fussing over her hair had cost Brenda a few valuable minutes, causing her great concern that she might be late for work. She had done a test-run during the weekend and found that she could complete the commute in just under an hour;

however, her estimate proved to be inaccurate during rush-hour traffic. She merged onto the highway and found herself at a complete standstill. She attempted to swerve around the halted cars to no avail. There was an accident on the road, and nobody was going anywhere anytime soon.

Because there was nowhere to go and nothing to do, Brenda fidgeted anxiously behind the wheel, wishing that she had left a few minutes earlier for work. She watched helplessly as one minute passed after another, and she grew angry at the situation that was completely out of her control. *Will my morning commute be like this every day?* thought Brenda to herself. Then an even more terrible thought entered her mind: if the morning rush hour was this bad, the evening rush hour was sure to be equally bad, if not worse. And as it was tourist season, accidents were likely to occur on a daily basis. During the tourist season, thousands of people migrated to Florida to escape the winter cold. The tourists, who were comprised mainly of the elderly, were responsible for many of the accidents on the road. In the future, she would have to wake up earlier and leave herself more time to get to work.

As Brenda squirmed around in her seat, the cars suddenly began to move, and she began to pick up momentum once again. She could have gone even faster if the people in front of her would've concentrated on the road rather than slowing down to view the accident. Still, she exited the main highway with a few extra minutes to spare and continued on through the back roads until she reached her final destination.

Once Brenda exited the main road, she found herself in the heart of Miami. She knew that when people thought of Miami, they likely thought of the crème de la crème spending endless hours lounging on their yachts upon the pristine waters of the Atlantic. Or perhaps they envisioned people residing in homes with breathtaking oceanfront views and partying the nights away at the endless nightclubs along South Beach. However, this lifestyle was a reality for only a lucky few. Not long ago, Miami had been a booming city; however, the downturn of the economy had left many people unemployed and even homeless. Evidence of this existed throughout the residential neighborhoods, and although she was pressed for time, Brenda drove ever more slowly, astonished by the poverty that surrounded her.

The first thing that caught Brenda's attention was the large number of homeless people walking aimlessly throughout the streets. Some were still asleep, having sought protection from the sun by lounging under the palm trees, but others had already awoken and were hard at work begging from every car that crossed their path. Brenda tried to rationalize what she saw by acknowledging the fact that homeless people tended to congregate in large cities; however, she could not rationalize the large number of police cars stationed at every intersection. She looked around to find justification for their vigilance but could find nothing amiss. It was almost as if they were waiting in case something should happen. As Brenda sat in her car, she began to wonder. Why did this neighborhood require this magnitude of security? Then a thought suddenly entered her mind: the children she would be teaching were a product of this neighborhood. Would she also have to be vigilant and act as a police officer in her own classroom?

Brenda could not dismiss what she had seen even as she entered the Twin Palms Middle School parking lot. When she had accepted this job, she had known that she would be working in an inner-city school. She had felt that she could make the greatest possible difference within this particular environment. However, she had never worked with inner-city children before. In college, she had completed a semester of student teaching but had done so in a small private school in the suburbs. Brenda had found the experience to be most rewarding and wondered whether it could be duplicated in a school such as this.

As Brenda stepped out of her car, the first thing that caught her attention was the fencing around the school. Both the field and the parking lot were completely enclosed. Why did the administration feel the need to cage the children like animals? Were they afraid that the children would try to escape? Then there were the surveillance cameras. There were four cameras strategically placed to monitor every angle of the parking lot. With the fencing and the cameras, the place seemed more like a prison than a school. As Brenda stepped through the main entrance, she paused briefly to gaze upon the landscape. She could see maintenance people cutting the grass and trimming the hedges in preparation for the first day of school. Other workers were repainting the walls. This particular task was of special importance, as the county allowed each school within the district to be painted only once a year. As Brenda walked by, she couldn't help noticing that the painters were sweating profusely as they struggled to conceal the graffiti left over from the prior years' students.

Brenda wished she had more time to explore the campus, but all the teachers were expected to report to the media center for a meeting to review the schedule for the remainder of the week. Upon entering the media center, Brenda immediately noticed how the other teachers were dressed. She remembered how much she had agonized over her own appearance and felt somewhat confused as she looked upon her fellow coworkers. Nobody was dressed as professionally as she was. Most everyone wore jeans, sweatpants, or shorts, and a few even appeared to be in their pajamas. Brenda had read the employee handbook and recalled that there was no formal dress code. However, in one week, these people would be standing in front of a classroom full of children. Was this the impression that they wanted to make? Brenda felt herself blush with embarrassment as she realized that all eyes were suddenly upon her. Just as she was judging those around her, these people were judging her in return, and their eyes clearly reflected their disapproval.

Never mind them, thought Brenda to herself. She was proud of her appearance and refused to feel ashamed for having high standards. Since the meeting was about to commence, she rushed to the front of the room in hopes of acquiring a good seat. Surprisingly, rushing was entirely unnecessary. It seemed that most of the teachers were of the opposite mind-set and were in search of seats located at the back of the room. Once seated, the teachers opened their laptops and took out their cell phones. Once again, Brenda felt like the awkward one as she sat in the front row, anxious to take notes, while everyone around her navigated the Internet or checked text messages. However, this display of detachment did not go unnoticed by the administrators. One of the assistant principals caught sight of what was going on and, with great agitation, attempted to herd everyone back to the front of the room. The teachers moved, but they did so reluctantly. All around her, Brenda could hear people moaning and complaining about having to forgo their seats. As the teachers moved to the front of the room, one person sat on Brenda's left side, while another sat on her right side. Much to her surprise, they began conversing as if she wasn't even there. Although she felt uncomfortable eavesdropping, she did so anyway because she wanted to gain some perspective on how they felt about the school. The colloquy that followed sounded something like this:

"How was your summer?"

"Not bad but, as usual, way too short."

"So where did they stick you this year?"

"Looks like I'll be teaching eighth-grade math."

"That's too bad. I had those kids last year, and the majority of them are a bunch of assholes."

"Well, they can't be any worse than the morons I had last year."

Brenda was flabbergasted! How could people say such things about innocent children? She wanted to say something in the students' defense but quickly reconsidered and decided to switch seats instead. However, no matter where she went, the conversation was always the same. Disgruntled teachers throughout the entire room were badmouthing the children and complaining about their jobs. It was shocking and horrifying to hear how much these people hated their work. They hated the children, the parents, and even the profession itself. Even more disturbing was the universality of the sentiment. Most everyone felt this way, and Brenda suddenly felt relieved that she had not spoken out earlier. Once everyone was seated, the principal came out and began the meeting by introducing himself. Mr. Jenkin was his name, and as it turned out, this was his first year as a principal. After introducing himself, he proceeded to introduce his three assistant principals, who, coincidentally, were also new in their positions. After the introductions, he turned his attention to the staff. He welcomed everybody but took extra time to give a special welcome to the new staff and allowed each person to introduce him—or herself individually. Brenda was delighted at the opportunity and took full advantage of her allotted time to speak extensively about her background. After she finished, there was nothing left to do but wait until everyone else had his or her turn. This turned out to be the longest portion of the meeting, as the majority of the staff were also brand-new recent college grads like herself or transferees from other schools.

As the meeting concluded, Brenda couldn't help wondering why there were so many new teachers at this school. Why had this school experienced such a high rate of turnover? She recalled her childhood and remembered how the teachers at her middle school had seemingly never left. As a matter of fact, she and all of her siblings had had the same teachers all the way through high school. When she was growing up, teachers tended to stay in the same schools for the duration of their careers. In fact, they not only stayed in the same school but also often stayed in the same grade and sometimes even in the same classroom. This school was nothing like the schools that she had attended, and Brenda felt that the loss of so many teachers was yet another omen of bad things to come.

Although long and somewhat tedious, the meeting actually turned out to be quite informative. Each teacher was issued a "week one" folder that contained the schedule as well as a wealth of other information. Although Brenda had remembered to pack her personal identification, apparently she still needed to fill out other paperwork—a lot of it. She leafed through the paperwork and discovered that the entire week was jam-packed with meetings, trainings, and time for classroom setup. The first week of school was known as the training week and was basically a time for teachers to set up and prepare before their students arrived the following week. After the principal reviewed the schedule, the teachers took a short break and then broke into groups based upon their grade level.

Since Brenda had been hired to teach sixth-grade math, she joined the other sixth-grade teachers in the administration office and waited to meet her new assistant principal. Each grade was assigned one assistant principal, and her assistant principal was a woman by the name of Mrs. Harrison. Mrs. Harrison followed the principal's example by introducing herself and then allowing the staff members to introduce themselves. However, she also took a few extra minutes to discuss the structuring of the school. Like other middle schools in the state of Florida, Twin Palms Middle School educated sixth-, seventh-, and eighth-grade children, but in this particular school, each of the three grade levels was further broken down into three specific categories. Each grade level had a Gifted, Montessori, and Traditional program. Brenda had been hired to teach within the Traditional program, which typically dealt with the lowest-level children. Each of the programs had two teams consisting of five teachers per team—one teacher for each subject area. To differentiate things even further, every team was named after a bird, and according to Brenda's roster, it appeared that she and her students would be known as Mockingbirds for the remainder of the school year.

Brenda was glad when the meetings for the day were finally over. According to the schedule, the teachers were to spend the second half of the day setting up their classrooms. She removed the map of the school from her packet and discovered that her classroom was located in the 900 wing of the school. The wing was in the shape of an *L* and housed ten classrooms, ranging from 900 to 909. All ten classrooms belonged to Traditional teachers; five of the ten belonged to teachers on Brenda's team, and the other five belonged to the teachers on the Seagulls team. Once Brenda found her classroom, she tucked the map under her arm and searched for the key to open the door. With great exhilaration, she turned on the light, slowly entered the room, and took a moment to examine her surroundings.

The classroom was rectangular in shape and fairly large in size. By the door was a huge window decorated with typical Floridian plastic pink blinds. The side parallel to the window was the closet area, which, from where Brenda was standing, also seemed quite large. The final two sections of the classroom contained the boards. On one wall was a basic whiteboard approximately twenty feet long, while on the other wall was a technological marvel known as a Promethean board, which connected to an overhead, television, DVD player, and her laptop computer. The board was the size of a small movie screen, and speakers were built into the ceiling to provide for surround sound. Unlike the whiteboard, the Promethean board could not be written on with markers. Instead, a special magnetic pen was used to gently tap the board to navigate and access information. Erasers were also unnecessary, as a simple computer command erased the entire board. This setup, otherwise known as a SMART classroom, was extremely costly and available in only three other classrooms on the campus. All in all, Brenda was quite pleased to have such a special classroom, but a part of her couldn't help missing the old days of blackboards and chalk.

The center of the classroom contained the desks, and at present, there were twenty-five desks scattered throughout the room. Brenda wondered if this meant that she would be assigned twenty-five students in each of her classes. She looked at her roster and saw that she would be teaching five math classes a day, with one free period for planning and another free period for lunch. The roster also listed the names of her students and the classes to which they would be assigned. Coincidentally, her smallest and most advanced class contained only fourteen students, whereas the largest class, which contained her lowest-level students, listed a whopping thirty-eight students.

It seemed that the school used an *A* through *E* lettering system to group students by FCAT (Florida Comprehensive Assessment Test) level. The FCAT was a Florida standardized test that graded students by range. Based upon the range in which he or she fell, a student would be scored a level one through five-five being the highest a student could achieve, and one being the lowest. Brenda looked at her roster a second time and saw that more than half of her students had scored a level one on the previous year's FCAT. These children had been placed in her *A* and *B* classes, while students who had scored a level two had been placed in her *C* and *D* classes. Her most advanced class, otherwise known as the *E* class, was not really advanced at all, consisting of students who'd scored only a level three on the prior year's FCAT. As a Traditional teacher, Brenda would never know the luxury of teaching children who had scored a level four or five; those children were in the Gifted and Montessori programs. However, Brenda didn't mind. She was so thrilled to finally be a teacher that she didn't care what level of students she would have to teach. However, she couldn't help being concerned about her students' low FCAT scores. In college, she had learned about the No Child Left Behind Act and the ramifications that came along with low scores on the state's standardized test. However, she had no doubt that she would be able to raise FCAT scores. After all, she had been born to teach and felt highly confident that her students would thrive academically under her guidance.

After Brenda finished reviewing her roster, she set upon the task of rearranging her classroom. At present, the room was in complete disarray, and Brenda couldn't decide what to do first. Fortunately, at that moment, another teacher entered her classroom and introduced herself as Mrs. Clifford, Brenda's NESS coach. NESS, otherwise known as New Educator Support System, provided mentors to new teachers to help them get through their first year. Brenda felt a sudden rush of relief when she saw this woman walk into her room. Back-to-back meetings and an endless stream of paperwork had left Brenda feeling confused and overwhelmed. Throughout the day, she had often wanted to ask questions but had felt ashamed to raise her hand. At last, now she could ask her questions without the fear of chastisement hanging over her head.

"It's a real pleasure to meet you, Mrs. Clifford. I'm so relieved that I have someone to go to for help! How do you think I should set up this classroom?"

"I would definitely start by putting posters up on the walls. You also have four display boards that need to be covered in decorative paper and framed with a border. You'll need to decide which of these boards you will use to display student work and which boards you will use as your word walls."

"I don't have anything to decorate the classroom. Who should I go to for supplies?"

Mrs. Clifford laughed. "Don't you know that schools all over the county are in a budget crisis? There's no money for supplies!

If you need something, you're just going to have to go out and buy it yourself."

Brenda's heart sank. Graduating from college had left her in terrible debt, and in six months, her grace period would be over, and she would have to start repaying her student loans. In addition, she and her fiancé, Joseph, had recently become engaged and were discussing the prospect of marriage. Brenda was anxious to get married and start a family, but at the moment, it was financially impossible for them to do so. Her salary was disappointingly low, and Joseph didn't fare much better in his profession. She currently lived in a studio apartment and saved every penny that she could, but at this rate, it would take at least two years before she could have the wedding of her dreams.

Paying for supplies was simply out of the question. She needed to find alternative ways to acquire the materials that she needed, or else she would sink further into debt. Mrs. Clifford, sensing her frustration, attempted to console her and offer an explanation on the current budgetary crisis.

"There was a time when teachers were given money for supplies. However, over the last few years, the state has severely reduced the budgets of the schools, and teachers now have to pay out of pocket for everything that they need."

"Why has the state taken money away from the schools?"

"The main reason is because the children are not meeting the proficiency requirements mandated by No Child Left Behind. Every year, a minimum standard is set in the areas of math, reading, writing, and science. If the children don't reach this standard or at least show gains from the previous year, the government reduces funding to the schools and cuts the budget for the following year."

"Why aren't the children meeting the standards? Is it because the teachers aren't doing their jobs?"

At this, Mrs. Clifford became angry. "Why are you so quick to blame the teachers? Can you even fathom the pressure that we must endure because of NCLB? Do you have any idea how unfair this law is? The goals set by NCLB are insurmountable, and when those goals aren't met, the teachers are the only ones who are held accountable."

Without meaning to, Brenda had hit a nerve and had inadvertently caused her mentor to turn against her. She had not meant to be insulting; she was only trying to understand the complex machine that was the educational system. In the future, she would have to choose her words more carefully. For the moment, Mrs. Clifford was her only friend, and she desperately needed this woman's help. She needed to find a way to fix this situation—and fix it fast—because if she didn't, her new mentor would abandon her, and then she would be left all alone to fend for herself.

"Truly, I meant no offense, and I apologize if I've upset you. Do you think that we could just start over again?"

Must to Brenda's relief, Mrs. Clifford accepted her peace offering, and her yelling eventually subsided. Once she calmed down, they once again revisited the discussion regarding school supplies.

"If you don't have the money to buy classroom supplies, there are other ways to acquire the things that you need. For instance, I suggest that you introduce yourself to your teammates and see if they'll lend you some of their posters and decorations. As for obtaining supplies for the children, my recommendation is that you create a wish list."

"What's a wish list?"

"On the first day of school, send home a list of the supplies that each child should have for your class. This will help eliminate a lot of unnecessary spending on your part."

Brenda's mood brightened when she heard this. Just like that, her problems were solved! She would follow Mrs. Clifford's advice and send home a letter to the parents on the first day of school, listing the supplies that each child needed and saving herself a considerable amount of money in the process.

"However, you need to take into consideration the population of students that you'll be working with and be realistic with your demands."

"What do you mean by 'population of students'?"

"Well, many of our students are socioeconomically disadvantaged. It's likely that they won't be able to afford many of the supplies on your wish list."

"I like to think that if their parents take an interest in their education, they'll find a way to pay for the supplies."

"What's wrong with you? Are you seriously this naive? Don't you know that the majority of our students don't come from a two-parent household? Many of them don't even have one parent. These children are being raised by relatives or neighbors or have been placed in group homes. Nobody cares about their education! Furthermore, the last thing that these people are going to want to do is spend their money on school supplies."

"Well, surely the children value their education. Perhaps they'll take the initiative to spend their own money on supplies."

"Is that what you think? You really believe that children come to school to learn? What do you think will happen when you're standing in front of a classroom full of children? Do you think that they'll be sitting quietly, hands folded on top of their desks, obediently following your instructions? You'd better think again! You better brace yourself for the misery that's coming. The war begins promptly Monday morning with your first-period class when your students arrive and doesn't end until sixth period on the last day of school when your students leave. Each and every day will be a struggle, and if you don't toughen up fast, you won't even survive the first week."

Brenda sat frozen with horror as Mrs. Clifford continued to prattle on. She should have spent what little time she had setting up her classroom, but instead, she spent the remainder of the afternoon listening and learning from one who was more experienced than she. Brenda was appalled yet also mesmerized by everything that Mrs. Clifford had to say. It was difficult to discern how much of the information was actually true and what Mrs. Clifford might have added for embellishment; however, Brenda listened respectfully and was careful to keep her opinions to herself, lest she infuriate this woman a second time. Listening to Mrs. Clifford speak made her realize that although she was an educator, she herself was in need of an education. And what an education she was receiving! Brenda couldn't believe what she was hearing. Were things really as bad as Mrs. Clifford said? Wasn't there anything positive to be said about the teaching profession? Brenda wished that this woman would stop talking, but much to Brenda's dismay, Mrs. Clifford continued to ramble on. Just when Brenda thought that she could take no more, the dismissal bell finally rang, and Mrs. Clifford left her alone to digest everything that had been said.

With Mrs. Clifford finally gone, Brenda had the time to set up her class, but now she lacked the desire. The events of her first day at this school had been discouraging, to say the least, and the stories her mentor had told her kept circling around in her mind. Brenda had the utmost respect for the educational system, but the events of this first day had revealed that the system had cracks. Just how deeply the cracks ran, Brenda could not yet tell. She could have worked in a private school, but against the advisement of all those around her, she had chosen this path instead. It was too late to change jobs now. She had signed the employment contract and was obligated to fulfill her end of the bargain. School would be starting in less than a week, and she needed to get prepared. She had to brace herself for the worst of it and prove to everyone around her that she had what it took to survive.

CHAPTER 3

Brenda was amazed how quickly the preparation week of school flew by. Brenda knew there was a misconception that a teacher's sole responsibility was to educate children, when in fact, a teacher had a myriad of responsibilities. No sooner had she completed one task than another was thrust upon her without warning. She recalled how anxious she had been to bypass the training week and just start teaching. However, the superfluity of work quickly changed her tune, and she was regretful that she didn't have an additional week to get everything done.

What Brenda found most difficult of all was prioritizing her work. Every time she attempted to work on her classroom or make sense of the paperwork, the loudspeaker would interrupt her, beckoning her to attend yet another meeting. Meetings pertaining to this or that monopolized far too much of her time, and Brenda wished that she could just hide out in her room and ignore the stern voice blaring over the intercom. Attendance at meetings and trainings was mandatory, however, and a sign-up sheet was always present to ensure that the teachers showed up. And because the administrators frowned upon tardiness, Brenda always made sure that she arrived a few minutes early, positioning herself in the front row, where everyone could see her.

Out of all the meetings she was forced to attend, Brenda found the technology training sessions to be most beneficial of all. When she was growing up, there had been no computers, and all of her teachers had done their grading and lesson plans by hand. However, that time was long gone, and now everything was computerized. At her first training session, she was introduced to Mr. Gold, who was the technology specialist, and issued a laptop that would be hers for the duration of the year. Brenda had worked on computers in college but had never had a computer that she could call her own. However, when she opened the computer, she was disappointed to discover that the letters on the keyboard were faded and some of the buttons were missing. Why couldn't the school buy new laptops for the teachers? Why were teachers forced to use someone else's hand-me-downs? Brenda thought back to her conversation with Mrs. Clifford and realized that the computer situation was one of the many budgetary cuts that she had been talking about. Along with the computers, the teachers received computer cases, and inside were numerous handouts on how to navigate the various programs. At this point, Mr. Gold could have left the teachers to fend for themselves, but to Brenda's surprise, he took the time to review each and every handout in a calm and patient manner. Typically, computer experts did not make the best teachers, but this man was the exception to the rule. He was so thorough that by the end of the training, Brenda walked away feeling significantly more confident then when she had first walked in.

If only everything could have run as smoothly as her training with Mr. Gold! Brenda was not so lucky when it came time to obtain textbooks for her students. According to school policy, every child was to be issued two textbooks— one to be kept in the classroom and the other to be sent home. Administrators had created this policy because disgruntled parents had complained over the heavy backpacks their children were required to carry to and from home. Unfortunately, there weren't enough books to go around. Each year, damaged books were discarded, and lost books were not replaced, and because there was a shortage of textbooks, some teachers simply had to do without. When Brenda went to the book depository, she found that a system had been put in place to distribute the books to the teachers; however, she saw that the system lacked organization and, more importantly, speed. It didn't take long for impatient teachers to break protocol and for a frenzy to break out. Courtesy and polite behavior soon went out the window as teachers began to push and shove, all in a desperate attempt to make their quota of books. However, not all of the teachers participated in this chaos. Those who were cowards stood a safe distance away from the turmoil, anxiously watching for any scraps that the others might leave behind.

Because Brenda was nonconfrontational, she decided to wait, but she sorely regretted her decision once she saw the number of books that remained. She needed over two hundred books for her students, yet she could find only half that amount. Besides this mishap, there was also the issue of transportation. Her classroom was located at the other end of the campus, and carrying those heavy books was completely out of the question. She noticed that the other teachers were using small carts to transport their books, and she decided to do the same. What a nightmare that process turned out to be! The rickety old carts were designed to hold overhead projectors and had never been intended to hold anything heavier. So when Brenda loaded her cart to capacity, the poor cart squeaked in agony throughout the hallway. As the cement ground was uneven, it was a struggle just to get the cart rolling. Once the cart gained momentum, she made every effort to keep it going. Brenda was not opposed to physical labor, but transporting these books was sheer misery. No assistance was provided to facilitate the task, and teachers all over the campus sweltered under the hot August sun, cautiously maneuvering textbooks back to their classrooms.

After dropping off the first load of books, Brenda took a short break to review the schedule for the remainder of the day. What masochistic person had devised this agenda? There was just too much to do in too short a time. According to the agenda, another meeting was scheduled in less than an hour. Brenda sighed as she realized that she would have to stay late yet again to finish her work. It was frustrating to have to stay late every single night, when it seemed as if everyone else around her was leaving promptly at 3:30 p.m. She attempted to call her mentor, but Mrs. Clifford always claimed that she was too busy to help. Brenda couldn't understand why her NESS coach was giving her the cold shoulder. What had she done to deserve this kind of treatment? After giving it some thought, she concluded that Mrs. Clifford had not entirely forgiven her for the

35

comments she had made on the first day of school. If anything, Brenda's candidness had permanently marred their relationship, and try as she might, there was nothing she could do to repair it. She had apologized immediately after it happened—and many more times since—but the damage was done. Things would never be the same between her and Mrs. Clifford ever again. It was unfortunate to no longer have the guidance of a mentor, but Brenda had learned a valuable lesson. In the future, she would have to keep her thoughts and questions to herself. Little did she know, the answers that she yearned for would all be revealed to her in due time.

According to the schedule, the next meeting that Brenda was required to attend was a departmental meeting. The head of the math department was a woman named Mrs. Johnson who taught the gifted children. The position of departmental head was a thankless job that only added more responsibility to an already overwhelmed teacher. Through a democratic election, one unfortunate person within each department was elected and assigned to this position. Because of the budgetary crisis, no additional compensation was provided, but for the sake of necessity, someone had to step up and assume the additional workload.

The purpose of the departmental meeting was to review the curriculum map for each of the three grade levels. The curriculum for each subject area was clearly outlined for the entire year and could easily be downloaded directly from the county's website. As an added benefit, the system could be manipulated to break the curriculum down daily or weekly.

Brenda saw both an advantage and a disadvantage to the design of this curriculum map. On the one hand, a teacher would always know exactly what to teach on any given day. On the other hand, the curriculum was exceedingly difficult, paced far too aggressively, and, worst of all, left little to no time for review. How would her low-level students ever be able to keep up? As it was, they were coming in with low grades and low FCAT scores. How would she ever pull this off? Even with the combination of her teaching abilities and the absolute dedication on the part of the children, adherence to the curriculum map was still inconceivable. Anyone with a pair of eyes could see that the curriculum encouraged higher-order thinking and was geared specifically toward the higher-level students. However, the government mandated that all students, regardless of background, follow the same curriculum and take the same FCAT test. As if this weren't bad enough, all students were expected to make gains, and the lowest-level students were expected to make the greatest gains of all. Apparently, when low-level children made gains, it benefited the teacher greatly— and, for that matter, the entire school. However, if the opposite occurred, all involved were forced to suffer the consequences. The school itself risked losing funding from the government, and teachers were at risk of being transferred or, worse, stood the possibility of losing their jobs.

Brenda sat dumbfounded as she absorbed all of the information being thrown at her in the departmental meeting. She was finally beginning to understand why so many of the teachers were bitter. Children and teachers alike were caught up in a system that doomed them to failure. The NCLB, which was signed into law in 2002 under the Bush administration, was created to close the achievement gap, and it demanded that all children be proficient in the areas of math and reading by 2014. However, the law neglected to take into account the many extenuating circumstances that could contribute to a child's failure. There could be any number of reasons a child might fail, and not all of these could be pinned directly upon the teacher. The curriculum itself was the number-one culprit. Brenda remembered learning in college that curriculums were designed with the proverbial "mile wide and inch deep" philosophy. This philosophy was evident within Brenda's own curriculum. It appeared that she was required to teach over eighty different topics within the course of the year. This averaged out to approximately one topic a day, with a few days left open for tests and review. With so much to learn and so little time to learn it, how could anyone achieve mastery of the material?

And so this was the challenge that Brenda was in for. Like so many other teachers before her, she was caught up in a system that capitalized on teaching to the test. This new millennium had brought the NCLB into existence and, with it, a plethora of unrealistic expectations. The concept of a well-rounded curriculum had become an obsolete and outdated idea. Today's children were inundated with lessons that coincided with the FCAT, and woe to the teacher who dared to deviate from it! The current educational system cared nothing for nurturing the love of learning, nor did it strive to encourage creativity. Instead, it was an unstoppable juggernaut that mercilessly ground both student and teacher to achieve the highest possible test results. It cared not for the struggling or disadvantaged student. It was a cold and heartless machine that relentlessly raised the bar a little higher each year, forever condemning those who got left behind.

As terrifying as all this was, Brenda took comfort in the fact that she was not alone in the struggle. Teachers all around her were in exactly the same predicament. After the meeting concluded, the math teachers were divided into three groups— one group for each grade level. Brenda joined the sixth-grade teachers, and although she listened to everyone, she paid particularly close attention to what the veteran teachers had to say. There were only a handful who remained, and hearing them speak nearly brought tears to Brenda's eyes. These teachers had known a time before the NCLB, and it had been their great fortune to experience a golden age of teaching. Unlike all of the negativity she had heard thus far, the attitudes of these teachers were positive. They still loved their jobs and held on to the belief that someday things would change back to the way they used to be. However, Brenda was doubtful and hung her head remorsefully with the realization that she would never know this kind of gratification within her own career.

After a while, Brenda could no longer listen and had to walk away. However, just as she was about to exit the room, she bumped into another new teacher who happened to teach on the Seagulls team. As luck would have it, he was located in the classroom right next to hers. His name was Mr. Fisher, and interestingly enough, he was not a certified teacher. Instead, he was transitioning into the profession from another field. As it turned out, such transitions were not uncommon. It seemed that the majority of new teachers at Twin Palms Middle School had noneducational degrees. Under the umbrella of a Statement of Eligibility, people were permitted to teach for a period of three years with the understanding that they complete all of the required coursework and pass all of the state exams. Listening to Mr. Fisher explain the process made Brenda thankful that she was already a certified teacher. She couldn't imagine being laden down with the additional stress of fulfilling the certification requirements on top of all her other responsibilities.

This chance encounter with Mr. Fisher brightened Brenda's day. She found consolation in speaking to another person with concerns similar to her own. Needless to say, on that day, a friendship was formed. They agreed to help each other navigate the treacherous waters of the school system and promised to support each other through both the good and the bad. For the first time that week, Brenda felt optimistic. She had found someone she could rely upon—someone who would be there for her through thick and thin. As Brenda thought more about it, she realized that having the support of others would be essential to her success. If she could make one friend, then surely she could make others. But with such an abundance of work, where would she ever find the time?

Fortunately for her, the schedule had secured a block of time for just this purpose. By the end of the week, she had completed all of her work and could relax and collectively meet with the other members on her team. The meeting took place in the social studies classroom, and as Brenda entered the room, she found that the other teachers were already there. She quickly sat down and, just as she had done at every other meeting, listened intently to what was being said around her.

Every meeting that Brenda had attended thus far had revolved around the curriculum, policies of the school, or expectations relating to the FCAT. This meeting differed in the sense that it focused solely on the children. For the most part, Brenda could run her classroom however she wished, but she was still obligated to collaborate with her teammates and create a set of team rules. The school had put this procedure in place not only to show unity among the teachers but also, more importantly, to help the children. Every day, a child would have to sit in six different classrooms with six different teachers, and this procedure eliminated the need for a child to adjust to six separate sets of rules.

Besides creating a list of rules, Brenda and her teammates also had to come up with a list of rewards. Some of the teachers suggested giving candy and stickers, while others suggested class trips and free time on the classroom computers. In the end, Brenda was forced to veto every suggestion. Financially, she was in no position to spend money on the children and could not agree to any reward that took time away from the curriculum. With the impending FCAT, she would need every available minute of class time if her students were to make the necessary gains.

The last portion of the meeting was by far the most interesting of all. The team leader distributed a disciplinary matrix to each of the teachers and explained that the entire school system was required to follow this matrix when disciplining the children. As Brenda reviewed the matrix, she discovered that a child could be disciplined any number of ways. Methods of discipline included warnings, time-outs, parental contact, team interventions, and, finally, as a last resort, a referral for suspension. Before actually writing the referral, a teacher would first have to exhaust all of the other disciplinary methods. If a teacher still had no success after implementing these methods and backing up the disciplinary problem with extensive documentation, then—and only then—could he or she write up a referral.

The disciplinary matrix was an extensive document that Brenda found completely unnecessary. Why the need for so many interventions? In her day, when a teacher told a student to do something, he or she did it, and that was the end of it. Once, when Brenda was eight years old, a teacher had told her to stop talking, but against her better judgment, she had snubbed the teacher and continued to talk anyway. This mild infraction had resulted in a phone call to her parents, and when she got home, she'd found her father waiting in the doorway with a wooden spoon in hand. For a brief second, she'd considered running in the opposite direction, but then she had realized that at some point, she would have to take the beating. So she had taken it, trying not to cry and praying that it would be over quickly. The next day, Brenda had limped to school and shown off her bruises to all the kids on the playground. Needless to say, Brenda had never disrespected a teacher again, and neither had her classmates. By current standards, Brenda knew that form of discipline would be considered child abuse. However, Brenda had never blamed her parents for beating her. If anything, she was grateful to them and believed that the beatings she had received as a child had helped mold her into the successful adult that she was today.

When the meeting was over, Brenda finally had the opportunity to meet the other teachers on her team. The team consisted of five teachers teaching in the areas of social studies, reading, math, science, and language arts. The sixth teacher, who taught the elective class, was not present at the meeting. Elective teachers were not part of any one team but were instead in continuous rotation. Brenda looked about her and tried to read the new faces that surrounded her. The social studies teacher, Mr. Morrison, was by far the most outgoing. Although he wasn't the team leader, he took it upon himself to conduct the meeting and did the majority of the talking. The reading teacher, Ms. Spencer, was new to the school but had over fifteen years of experience. She was pleasant enough, but she fidgeted constantly. When she spoke, her voice was high pitched, and her overall demeanor exuded a kind of hyperactivity. The science teacher was quite the opposite. Like Mr. Morrison, she was outgoing, but unlike Ms. Spencer, she was well composed and considerably calmer. Mrs. Kane was her name, and she was in her second year of teaching and was one of the teachers working toward certification under the Statement of Eligibility. Brenda already knew this teacher because she had heard her name mentioned throughout the week. She was known throughout the school as the fun teacher. The students loved her, and because there was no sixth-grade science FCAT, she was free to pace her class slowly and engage the children with movies, games, and other fun activities.

Then there was the language arts teacher. He refused to participate in the meeting and even elected to sit by himself in the back of the class. Brenda sensed that he was agitated, but she could not guess why. He shamelessly alienated the entire team and added insult upon injury by talking on the phone while the meeting was in session. Brenda also couldn't help noticing that the alienation was not one-sided. The entire team kept their distance from him as well. Brenda found this to be curious and decided to approach one of the teachers for an explanation.

"Mr. Morrison, may I speak to you for a moment?"

"Hello, Ms. Connor! What can I do for you?"

"I was just wondering about the language arts teacher. I couldn't help noticing that he appeared somewhat distant during the meeting."

"Oh, you're referring to Mr. Richard. Take my advice and stay away from him."

"Why?"

"Well, I hate to be the one to tell you this, but Mr. Richard is not to be trusted. Nobody wants to work with him, because he has a reputation for running to the administrators and spreading lies about everyone. All I can suggest is that you watch your back and try to keep your distance."

"Why do the administrators tolerate this? Why don't they put a stop to his gossiping?"

"Actually, they encourage it. And to make matters worse, he's also a sycophant."

"A what?"

"You know, a person who does whatever it takes in order to gain favor with the higher-ups. When school starts, you'll see Mr. Richard answering phones in the office, assisting with hallway duty, and participating in after-school activities."

"How does he have time to do his own work if he's picking up all of these additional responsibilities?"

"Who knows? All I can say for sure is that the administrators love him. Everyone knows that he's a poor teacher, but he's protected because of his additional contributions."

"How did he get to be this way? Was he always this malicious?"

"I can't say for sure, but rumor has it that Mr. Richard was originally a law student. He comes from a prominent family of lawyers that have a very successful practice in South Florida. Apparently, he completed law school but failed the bar exam."

"Why didn't he just take the bar exam again?"

"He did retake the exam. He actually ended up taking it fourteen times and failed it every single time."

"I suppose I can understand his frustration, but it still doesn't explain his behavior in the workplace."

"You have to understand that failing the bar exam made him the black sheep of his family. He was expected to take over the family business, but when he made the decision to go into teaching, his family disowned him completely. He's been trying to prove himself ever since. He wants to show his family that he can become successful in a career other than law. Therefore, he's taken every measure to elevate within the school system. He aspires to be an assistant principal and then a principal and, in the future, will likely work one day for the school district."

Brenda listened to this explanation without much reaction. She had encountered people like this before in her various part-time jobs. These were people who elevated professionally at the expense of others. Often, they weren't even the best workers but were considered assets because they could be depended upon to betray their fellow colleagues. Their actions were despicable, but even worse, they were dangerous. They would toady to the management and, in exchange, would be guaranteed job security. Brenda could already see that this man was going to be a problem, but what could she do? It was too late to request a transfer to another team. She would just have to heed Mr. Morrison's advice and proceed with caution.

This particular situation was unfortunate, but Brenda's entire week had been filled with misfortune. On her first day, she had entered Twin Palms Middle School full of energy and enthusiasm. However, the events that had transpired throughout the week had changed her entire view of the profession. Here she was, only one week into her new job, and she was already full of uncertainty. Would she be able to meet the expectations mandated by the state? Would the children be able to keep up with the curriculum? It was horrific to think that her entire career depended upon the success of these children. If they didn't make the necessary gains, her job could be at risk. This thought constantly haunted Brenda's mind. What would she do if she lost her job? As it was, she was drowning in debt, and the ever-increasing unemployment rate significantly diminished her chances of finding another job anytime soon. Such were the cruel terms upon which Brenda began her life. In her private moments, she found herself contemplating the unfairness of her circumstances. She was scared and, at times, became terrified at the thought of the challenges that lay ahead. In the end, she decided to turn to a higher power and pray for help. In her desperation, she prayed for the children to succeed and for herself to remain employed. To defy the odds against her, she would need a miracle. She would do her best, but ultimately, she would have to put her faith in the Lord and hope that he would answer her prayers.

CHAPTER 4

On Monday morning, Brenda woke up an hour earlier than usual to go to work. Today she would meet her students for the first time, and she was determined to not be late. Getting an early start turned out to be a wise decision, as Brenda soon found herself stuck in bumper-to-bumper traffic. Surprisingly, Brenda wasn't overly concerned with the delay. Her mind was preoccupied with other thoughts. Would the children like her? Would they enjoy being her students? She was exceedingly excited to meet the children, and all that had happened thus far no longer seemed to matter. Today would be her first day as a real teacher, and she felt completely confident that meeting her new students would provide the silver lining that she so desperately needed to brighten her cloudy outlook.

As Brenda drove through the school gates, she was suddenly jolted out of her daydreaming by what she saw. All around her, children were running amok without any adult supervision. Some were climbing the fences that enclosed the campus, while others were sitting and jumping on top of the cars parked in the faculty parking lot. Brenda was horrified at the scene that unfolded before her eyes. These children were completely out of control! The school employed three security guards, but they

48

were nowhere to be found. Brenda could see that the security cameras were on, but what difference did that make? The children thought nothing of the cameras and fearlessly continued with their deviant behavior. As Brenda circled the parking lot, she realized that at some point, she would have to park her car. But where could she park it without having it vandalized? The only other parking available was by the side of the building; however, this was a considerable distance away from the main entrance. After careful deliberation, she decided to choose safety over convenience. Knowing that her car would be secure compensated for the additional time it would take her to get to her classroom.

As Brenda walked through the parking lot, she couldn't help but notice how different the school seemed now that it was filled with children. The route that she took to her classroom necessitated a shortcut through the teachers' lounge, which then funneled her directly into the student cafeteria. She then made a beeline for the administration office and picked up a folder that contained the procedures for the first day of school. As Brenda reviewed these procedures, she realized that no actual teaching would take place that day. It seemed that the first day of school was devoted entirely to reviewing the rules, rewards, and consequences of the classroom, as well as distributing packets of paperwork to the students. Brenda read through everything meticulously but paid special attention to the explicit guidelines for taking attendance.

Teachers had to take attendance every day at the start of every class, but the first day's head count was especially important and could not be miscalculated. Brenda had been issued her roster of students during the planning week, but the roster was subject to change. Some children simply wouldn't show up, and others would show up unexpectedly. The final tally of students—or student count, as it was called—ultimately determined the amount of funding a school received. However, the quantity of students was not the only thing that mattered. Apparently, labels also played an integral part in school funding, and the child with the greatest number of labels paid out the most. For example, if a child was on free lunch, additional money would be given to the school. If that same child also had a learning disability, even more money was given to the school. And if by chance the child had all of the labels, then the school hit the financial jackpot.

However, unlike the administrators, the teachers were actually hoping for the lowest possible enrollment. Class size was a huge issue for the teachers, and it was the one topic that had continuously come up during the planning week. Although the state of Florida had enacted a class-size amendment, few schools actually honored it. In truth, it was quite easy to circumvent it. If a teacher complained that he or she had too many students in his or her classroom, the administrator would pacify that teacher with a reminder that many students dropped out during the first two weeks of school. If the teacher was still argumentative, the administrator would say that it wasn't the individual class size that mattered but the overall class average. If the teacher was still obstinate and invoked the amendment as his or her defense, then that teacher might find him—or herself out of a job.

However, at the moment, Brenda wasn't even thinking about class size. She was more concerned about surviving the first day of school. It was now nearly nine o'clock, and the children were released into the hallways and directed to find their homeroom classes. The returning seventh—and eighth-grade students were already familiar with the layout of the campus, but the sixth graders were completely lost. They roamed aimlessly up and down the hallways with maps of the school in hand, approaching any adult with a Twin Palms Middle School badge. The teachers were expected to stand by their doors during every class change, herding the children into their classrooms and monitoring the hallways until everyone was safely inside. Brenda wasn't pleased with this arrangement and wished that she didn't have to waste her time standing outside her door. She needed those few minutes in between classes to set up her activities and organize her materials. Unfortunately, the administration deemed it necessary to have constant coverage in the hallways. Interestingly enough, the teachers weren't the only ones expected to be present in the hallways. The administrators and guidance counselors were also expected to stop what they were doing, leave their offices, and assist with every class change. To Brenda, it seemed as if a whole lot of people were being unnecessarily inconvenienced repeatedly throughout the course of the day. However, the school's motto was Safety First, and the administration had put this procedure in place for good reason. Apparently, fights were apt to break out, and rumors were already circulating that this year's sixth-grade students were the worst children the school had ever seen.

Brenda stood in her doorway and watched as her students entered her classroom. She greeted each and every child with a "Good morning" and waited patiently for the children to reciprocate. Much to Brenda's astonishment, most of the children ignored her. A few looked in her direction, and some grunted, but the vast majority didn't even acknowledge her presence. *How incredibly rude!* Brenda had never behaved this way with any of her teachers. When she was in school, children had been expected to acknowledge their teachers upon entering and exiting the classroom. As if her students' dismissal of her greeting wasn't bad enough, the children refused to accept her seating arrangement. Brenda had painstakingly created a seating chart for each class and had developed a numerical system for the children to follow. Instead of following her system, the children took it upon themselves to select their own seats. Brenda watched with amazement as the children pushed the desks together and flung their schoolbags recklessly onto the floor. She couldn't believe it! These children had absolutely no consideration for her classroom. She had worked so hard, and now, within a matter of minutes, everything was ruined. Who did these children think they were? How dare they rearrange the desks in her classroom! As soon as everyone was inside, she would put a stop to this nonsense and show her students who was in charge.

Once everybody was inside, Brenda locked the door and took her place at the front of the class. She assumed that her mere presence would be enough to quiet the children down, but despite her stance, the talking and horseplay continued. Brenda needed an alternative plan to attract their attention and decided to implement one of the strategies she had learned in college. Besides positioning herself directly in front of the children, she also attempted to give her students her best "teacher's stare." The teacher's stare was a particular look a teacher gave a student when he or she was misbehaving. All teachers had this stare, whether they realized it or not. Some had even perfected it to the point where children would freeze instantaneously when they saw it. Essentially, it was a look that scared children into behaving themselves. During the planning week, the veteran teachers had encouraged Brenda to work on her stare. In college, her professors had emphasized it as a strategy for maintaining classroom control. However, Brenda's stare still needed some fine-tuning. Despite her efforts, the best that she could muster was a look of annoyance. It would take time—and some practice in front of a mirror—before she would be able to master this look to her satisfaction.

Even with her glaring at them, the children refused to settle down. Brenda was now starting to panic. She had never seen children behave this badly before. During her brief stint in private school, she had taught only well-mannered children who understood how to behave in a classroom. Brenda's students, on the other hand, behaved liked feral children and had absolutely no classroom etiquette. Ten minutes into the class, the children were still ignoring her and were now beginning to take out their cell phones and other electronic devices. She glanced through the window and could see the administrators moving about in the hallways. At any moment, somebody could walk into her classroom and witness her complete lack of control. The only other thing that Brenda could think of doing was yelling at the children. This was by no means the way she wanted to conduct her class, but what other choice did she have? Therefore, she took a deep breath and starting screaming until the children finally settled down.

Much to Brenda's dismay, she was forced to yell for the full forty-five-minute class period. She knew she was dealing with low-level children, but did that mean she had to deal with poor behavior too? In her mind, yelling did not constitute good teaching, but it seemed that these children were incapable of responding to anything else. In between her fits of rage, she took a closer look at the children and couldn't help noticing that many of them had come to her classroom unprepared. It was the first day of school, and half of her students had arrived without pencils or notebooks. The absence of school supplies was of great concern to Brenda. She had followed her mentor's advice and created a wish list, but based upon what she was seeing, she felt fairly certain that her students wouldn't buy the necessary supplies. As Brenda mulled over the situation, a terrible realization suddenly came over her: If these children refused to bring pencils and notebooks to class, how would they complete their assignments? The responsibility would ultimately fall upon her to provide them with everything they needed. This was completely out of the question. She couldn't afford to buy school supplies for over one hundred children! She leaned up against the wall and took a moment to consider her options. Perhaps she could call their parents. Or maybe she could discuss the issue with her administrator. In the end, Brenda decided that for the moment, she would just bide her time. She would remind her students daily to come to school prepared and would hope that over time, her persistent persuasion would somehow resonate with the children.

Another one of her concerns was the age of the children. As Brenda looked around the room, it seemed that some of the children were too old for sixth grade. A number of them stood well over six feet tall, and Brenda could have sworn she had seen a few of them drive past her in the parking lot. She decided to double-check her roster, and sure enough, a handful of children in her class were fifteen and sixteen years old. How could this have happened? How could these children have failed this many times? What made this realization all the more disturbing was that this wasn't even her lowest class. This was her *C* class, which, in theory, should have contained average-level children.

Brenda forced herself to regain focus and revisited her roster. Time was flying by, and she had yet to take attendance. Part of the first-day procedures involved printing out the attendance roster for each class and calling out the name of each student listed on the sheet. Brenda located the first-period attendance roster and began calling out the names of her students, one child at a time.

"Ecstasy? Is there an Ecstasy in this class?"

"What up?"

Brenda cringed as she heard the first student respond. She wasn't sure which troubled her more—the response of the student or the name to which the student responded. It was baffling to think that some parent had actually named his or her child Ecstasy. With a name like that, how would she ever be taken seriously? Furthermore, when she grew up, how would she ever land a job? Unless she was planning on being a stripper or a prostitute, who would ever consider her for employment?

However ludicrous, the name a parent chose for his or her child was none of Brenda's business. Therefore, she shrugged off the absurdity of the child's name and continued to take attendance.

"Litinmilife? Is Litinmilife present?"

Brenda wasn't even sure if she had pronounced this name correctly. It appeared that the child's name was Light in My Life, but instead of spelling it properly and separating the words out individually, her mother had mishmashed the phrase into one incorrectly spelled word. Once again, Brenda couldn't understand why somebody would do this to a child. Against her better judgment, she couldn't resist asking the child for the origin of her name.

"May I ask where you got your name?"

"I dunno."

"May I call you Light for short?"

"Whatever."

As Brenda continued to take attendance, she encountered the same scenario time and time again. She would struggle with the pronunciation of some ridiculous name and, in return, receive some form of rude response. Why did parents burden their children with such names? What was wrong with giving a child a normal name, such as John or Emily? Furthermore, how would she ever memorize all of these ridiculous names and say them with a straight face?

Incidentally, the next name on her list was the pinnacle of ridiculousness, and Brenda had to turn her back until she could contain her laughter and compose herself in front of the children. She looked at the attendance roster one more time to make sure her eyes were not deceiving her. The name on the list must have been a typo. Or perhaps one of the veteran teachers was having some fun at her expense. Regardless, it took her quite some time to regain her composure and call out the little boy's name.

"Shithead? Is there a Shithead in this class?"

"It's pronounced Shiheed!" yelled the little boy defensively.

"Well, according to the attendance roster, it's spelled Shithead."

"I don't care how it's spelled! My name happens to be very common in my culture! As a matter of fact, I was named after my father!"

"So what you're saying is that your father is the big shithead and you're the little shithead," called out one of the students.

At this, the entire class burst into laughter. Brenda felt bad for the poor little fellow. She knew that she was in a multicultural school, and she should have been more sensitive to the multifarious nationalities of students sitting in her classroom. From there on out, she would limit questions regarding the pronunciation and spelling of names and do her best to avoid embarrassing any of the other children.

Brenda finished taking attendance just as the dismissal bell was about to ring. However, before she could properly dismiss the children, they all jumped out of their seats and bolted out the door. Why was she even surprised? It wasn't as if the children had followed any of her other directives. Why should the dismissal procedure be any different? All she could do was jump out of their way, hide behind the door, and avoid getting knocked over. These children were not only tall but also powerful. It wouldn't take much for one of them to injure her or, worse, put her in the hospital if she didn't get out of the way.

Brenda was relieved when her first-period class finally left; however, that relief didn't last long, as the second group of children began to pile into her classroom. This class coming in was her one and only advanced class. Within the first few minutes, Brenda could already see that this group was going to be far more manageable than her last group. All of the children came prepared, took their assigned seats, and sat quietly without her having to tell them. Brenda was grateful to have the privilege of teaching children of this aptitude; however, the luxury of teaching advanced children came at a high price. Making gains with advanced children was difficult because they were already coming in with high scores. What if their scores went down? What would happen then? At the very least, the children had to maintain their high scores, because even the slightest drop could put her job in jeopardy.

Brenda had barely finished reviewing the classroom policies and procedures when the bell rang for lunch. She couldn't believe that it was lunchtime already! She had this group for only twenty-five minutes, and the period was practically over. How was she supposed to complete a lesson in twenty-five minutes? As she was lining the students up, she reexamined the schedule. It appeared that the time that was lost during the second period was added back onto the final period. This meant that Brenda's last-period class would not be a standard forty-five-minute class but would instead be a sixty-five-minute class. And as it turned out, her last class was the *A* class, which contained some of the most badly behaved students in the entire school.

Brenda put the schedule away and lined up the children for lunch. She had to get the children safely to the cafeteria, show them to their assigned seats, and, with what little time remained, inhale her own lunch. As lunch was only thirty minutes long, Brenda urged the children to walk quickly to the cafeteria. As Brenda exited her classroom, she noticed that the other sixth-grade teachers were also making their way to the cafeteria. Like her, the other teachers lined up their students and directed them to walk in a straight line. However, unlike her, the other teachers were unable to control their students and keep them in the required formation. Brenda could not blame these teachers for their lack of control. By sheer luck, she happened to have a small class of fourteen children—and well-behaved children at that. The other teachers had many more students to contend with, and the behavior of their students closely resembled the behavior of the children she had fought with earlier that morning. Suffice it to say, guiding these children was a complete nightmare. Even though the distance to the cafeteria was a mere fifty feet, the majority of the children could not walk in a straight line—or rather, they refused to. Many of them ran through the grass or dodged their line in favor of another. Then there was the issue of how the children walked. When Brenda had been in school, children had been instructed to walk quietly with their arms glued to their sides. Unfortunately, these children were incapable of following such simple instructions. Somebody was constantly getting pushed or tripped, and what was the teacher supposed to do? As Brenda had done earlier, many of the teachers resorted to yelling. However, even the strongest-willed teacher gave up in the end. The students significantly outnumbered the teachers, and unless a teacher wanted to raise his or her blood pressure and risk a possible stroke, it was easier to let the children act like animals until they reached the cafeteria.

Although the majority of the classes behaved horrendously, one class in particular stood out above all the rest. This class contained thirty-eight students and was being escorted by the social studies teacher, Mr. Morrison. It didn't take long for Brenda to realize that this was the dreaded *A* class, otherwise known as the repeater class. These children seemed to take delinquency to a whole new level. Mr. Morrison did everything humanly possible to coax them into walking, but fights still broke out along the way. What started with pushing and shoving quickly evolved into student-on-student combat. The violence escalated to the point where Mr. Morrison had to call for backup, and Brenda immediately took notice of how quickly every single available adult came running in an attempt to restore order. Even the administrators, the counselors, and the new principal came to provide assistance. Brenda paused momentarily to catch a glimpse of all the excitement but then quickly moved on. There was no way she was going to risk her safety or the safety of her class by becoming involved. However, she lingered just long enough to witness two teachers, two security guards, and one administrator become seriously injured by the brawling students.

Brenda found it absolutely fascinating that children were capable of behaving this badly on the first day of school. Brenda had actually expected the children to enter their new school with timidity and a desire to make a good first impression. However, these children didn't seem to care what anybody thought. The only reason they came to school was because the government forced them to. The law required every child in the country to attend school, and Brenda's students were no exception to the rule. The fact that they lacked social skills or respect for authority was immaterial. They were protected by the law and were therefore entitled to receive a free public-school education regardless of their behavior. The way the laws were written didn't seem fair to Brenda; she felt that if children didn't want to behave, then they shouldn't be allowed to go to school. As far as Brenda was concerned, education was not a right but a privilege. However, until the government saw things her way and put a reform in place to revamp the disciplinary system, the disciplinary matrix would be the only tool at Brenda's disposal.

Brenda entered the cafeteria, led her class to their assigned table, and stayed with them until the administrators arrived. According to the union handbook, a teacher was entitled to a duty-free thirty-minute lunch. However, despite this stipulation written in the handbook, the reality was that a teacher rarely ever received such a luxury. The so-called thirty-minute duty-free lunch could easily be reduced by any number of circumstances. For example, the administrators could be running late due to meetings, parent calls, fire drills, or, as was the case that day, student fights. Brenda was fairly shaken by what had just happened and desperately needed a break, but she was not permitted to leave her students unattended. There had to be constant adult supervision, and if coverage for the cafeteria was unavailable, then the teachers simply had to forfeit their own time to supervise the students. Brenda repeatedly checked her watch and grew angry as the minutes steadily passed by. What was taking the administrators so long? Hadn't they broken up the fights by now? As Brenda wondered what was going on, the administrators started to trickle in, finally giving the teachers leave to eat their lunches.

Even though Brenda had packed her lunch, she decided to examine what the cafeteria had to offer. The majority of her students were on the free-lunch program, and Brenda was grateful the cafeteria provided nutritional meals to help nourish the minds of her children. Unfortunately, the only nourishing food she could find was a basket full of rotting fruit that the children were apt to wince at and then quickly bypass. Contrastingly, sugary drinks and highly processed foods were plentiful. The day's main attraction appeared to be chicken fingers smothered in instant mashed potatoes, with a side of canned green beans. A poster displaying the nutritional pyramid hung prominently on a wall near the checkout line, allowing the students to educate themselves about proper nutrition while waiting to pay for their food. After carefully studying the poster, Brenda failed to understand how the food in the cafeteria fulfilled any of the nutritional requirements listed on the pyramid. What the school was passing off as food was essentially just an edible form of poison. Indeed, the food was consumable, and perhaps even filling, but nutritious it was not. Brenda asked one of the cafeteria ladies for a chicken finger and nearly choked when she tasted it. This faux food might have been engineered to taste like chicken, but Brenda was relatively certain that no chicken had actually died to provide lunch for the students at Twin Palms Middle School that day.

Brenda was horrified to see what the school system was passing off as food. In her mind, it was almost healthier to encourage hunger rather than to force a young child's growing body to digest what was only a semblance of food. If anything, food such as this would most likely hinder a child's intellectual and physical growth rather than promote it. A steady diet of this fare would eventually lead to the onset of diabetes, heart problems, and obesity. As Brenda scanned the cafeteria, she couldn't help noticing how many of the children were overweight. Some were only mildly overweight, while others fell into the category of morbidly obese. Brenda had battled her own weight issues but had never been heavy as a child, and as an adult, she would never allow her weight to soar to such dangerous extremes. For some children, their obesity was so severe that just walking required considerable exertion. Brenda was grateful that she wasn't a physical education teacher. There was tremendous pressure to meet the math FCAT requirements, but at least she wouldn't be held liable if a child suddenly dropped dead in his or her tracks while attempting some form of physical activity.

Brenda checked her watch and realized that she had only fifteen minutes left until she had to pick up her students. She left the cafeteria and entered the adjoining room that was designated as the teachers' lounge. Brenda wasn't really hungry, but she knew that if she didn't eat now, she wouldn't have another opportunity until the end of the day. As she took out her sandwich, three teachers sat down at her table and immediately began discussing the fight that had just broken out.

"Can you believe what just happened in the hallway?" asked Mr. Fisher.

"Actually, I'm not really all that surprised. We were warned in advance about this group of sixth graders and told to brace ourselves for a miserable year," replied Mrs. Kane.

"I've dealt with challenging children before, but I've never seen behavior like this in all the years that I've been a teacher. I'm beginning to think that I made a big mistake coming to this school," said Ms. Spencer.

"Well, at least we're not elementary school teachers. If they have a rotten class, they're stuck with the same group of children all day. Fortunately for us, we're in constant rotation, and most of our classes are no longer than forty-five minutes long," said Mr. Fisher.

"That's easy for you to say! You don't have to teach reading! Did you know that our new principal decided to double-dose reading for the *A* class by extending the class from one period to two periods? That means that not only do I lose my planning period, but I also have to find a way to control the *A* class for a full hour and a half!" exclaimed Ms. Spencer.

Brenda thought about this last comment, and although she felt sorry for Ms. Spencer's plight, she felt relieved that the principal had decided to double-dose reading instead of math. The administration desperately counted on the low-level children to make the greatest gains; however, they failed to realize that these children needed to be tamed before they could be taught. The principal thought that adding an extra period of reading would increase test scores, but any experienced teacher knew that a child mentally checked out after about twenty minutes of instruction. A more experienced principal would never have forced a teacher to forgo his or her planning period or punished a child by taking away his or her elective. However, Mr. Jenkin was a brand-new principal, and with his new position came a flagrant display of arrogance. Only five feet two inches tall and thirty-two years of age, he had every attribute of a Napoleon complex. Those who were more experienced offered him advice, but did he listen? Of course not! He did whatever he pleased without giving any consideration to the consequences of his actions. And as a result, if a teacher had a mental breakdown, then so be it! The public school system did not tolerate weakness and quickly discarded causalities and replaced them with fresh recruits who were capable of withstanding the torture.

It was truly disheartening to have a principal like Mr. Jenkin leading the school. To some extent, Brenda could overlook his age and even his lack of experience; however, she could not overlook his lack of ethics. It was rumored that he had a long history of sexual indiscretions related to his time as an assistant principal, and as a principal, he had violated school policy by enrolling students who were considered out of boundary. Brenda found the details of his sexual exploitations alarming, but the situation regarding enrollment nearly made her collapse with anger. She had heard the teachers whispering about how he had accepted students outside of his jurisdiction just to maximize the school budget. It was no accident that this year's sixth graders were the worst group of children to ever attend Twin Palms Middle School. These multilabeled children were a financial gold mine for Mr. Jenkin, and the teachers were already speculating as to how he might spend the extra money. Brenda figured that he would spend his newfound wealth on educational resources, but instead, he chose to spend it elsewhere. It appeared that a remodeled office was of greater importance than investing in the education of the children.

While Mr. Jenkin was sitting pretty in his newly remodeled office, Brenda and the other sixth-grade teachers were the ones faced with bearing the burden of his decisions. Lunch was now over, and Brenda went to pick up her children. The first thing she noticed was that a significant number of children were missing. It seemed that the chief instigators responsible for causing the fight had been pulled out of the cafeteria and thrown into detention. Brenda was shocked to discover that an offense of this magnitude received so mild a punishment. As far as she was concerned, those children shouldn't have been slapped on the wrist with a detention. They should have been suspended or, better yet, expelled. The administration should have made an example of those children so that no one would ever step out of line again. However, the disciplinary matrix dictated that other interventions first be explored before a child was suspended. Interestingly, if the situation had been reversed and an adult had struck a child, the adult's punishment would not have been so lenient. Any teacher who assaulted a child faced certain termination and possible revocation of his or her teaching license.

Brenda made it back to her class just as the bell was about to ring, and she braced herself for the next group of children. This was yet another low class, but at least her next period would be a student-free planning period. She went through the rules, rewards, consequences, and other details, just as she had with her first two classes. This was the third time she was reciting this information, and she could feel herself droning on without enthusiasm. She found it tedious to be so repetitive, but this was the job. Brenda was required to teach five math classes a day, and she was to teach each class exactly the same material. She could differentiate her lessons to meet the varying needs of her students, but at the end of the day, she still sounded like a broken record. The only benefit to this type of schedule was that she needed to create only one lesson plan per day. Elementary school teachers, on the other hand, were never repetitive, because they taught five subject areas to only one group of children. However, that also meant that they had to create five separate lesson plans every single day. Therefore, during the course of their careers, all teachers had to make a decision. They could have a day filled with variety but be bogged down with endless hours of planning, or they could deal with the monotony of teaching one topic all day long and have virtually no planning at all.

Brenda was pleased to see how quickly the period flew by. It was now fourth period, and the next forty-five minutes were hers to do with as she pleased. Her first thought was to collapse at her desk and take a nap, but an overabundance of work forced her to push through the fatigue. She surveyed the aftermath and saw that her classroom was in complete disarray. As she was obsessive about cleanliness, she set upon the task of piecing her classroom back together. In truth, she hardly knew where to begin. Desks were out of alignment, textbooks were scattered everywhere, and trash was all over the floor. Brenda couldn't understand how only three classes of students could have caused this kind of a mess. These children clearly had no respect for the school facilities. Here they were, sitting in a SMART classroom that had cost the school well over $20,000, and some child had stuck gum on the Promethean board. Mrs. Clifford had been right. These children did not appreciate the free education they received, nor would they ever appreciate the resources provided to them.

It took Brenda nearly the entire period to recapture the original appearance of her classroom. By the time she was finished, she had only a few minutes left to run to the restroom. The faculty restrooms were located in the teachers' lounge, administration building, and media center. None of these were near Brenda's classroom, so she grudgingly resorted to using the student restrooms. As she walked through the 900 wing, she couldn't resist peeking into the classrooms of her teammates. As she passed by, she saw that some of the teachers were working at their desks, while others were absent from their classrooms. However, when she reached Ms. Spencer's room, a disturbing spectacle met her gaze. Ms. Spencer did not have the pleasure of spending her time working peacefully at her desk or engaging in idle indulgences. Instead, she was the only teacher on Brenda's team forced to teach a class during her planning period. At the moment, however, no actual teaching was taking place. Instead, Ms. Spencer was staring out the window, hands pressed up against the glass, tears streaming down her face.

Brenda could have easily walked by and ignored the obvious cry for help, but her conscience would not allow her to do so. Therefore, she took a deep breath and knocked on Ms. Spencer's door. When Ms. Spencer opened the door, Brenda found herself standing in front of an emotionally distraught woman. Ms. Spencer was crying uncontrollably, and her body was quivering with rage. She attempted to speak, but her incoherent protestations were indecipherable. As Brenda tried to calm her down, she couldn't help noticing that the children had taken over her classroom and had even gotten into her personal belongings. Ms. Spencer should never have turned her back to the children, but this was clearly not the time to reproach her. Instead, Brenda consoled her and tried to help her regain her composure.

"Just take it easy, Ms. Spencer. What's wrong? Why are you so upset?"

"I can't take this anymore! These children are completely out of control, and they won't listen to a word I say! They ripped up the handouts that I distributed, and just look what they've done to my classroom!"

Brenda looked around the room and observed the chaos. Every single trash can was turned over, and the pink blinds had been ripped off the windows. Although the closet door had a lock, some of the children had jimmied it open and were currently in the process of stealing Ms. Spencer's supplies. Others had snatched her radio and pushed the desks to the side and were in the process of having a dance contest in the middle of the classroom.

"How can the administration expect me to take this kind of abuse? I'm going to pack up my things and leave! Do you hear me, you little assholes? You're all too dumb to learn anyway! You shouldn't be in a classroom! You all belong in a zoo with the rest of the animals!"

As these last words came out of Ms. Spencer's mouth, Brenda saw somebody turn off the radio, and the classroom suddenly became eerily silent. Terror struck Brenda as she wondered what the students would do next. For a moment, everyone remained silent, but Brenda could see that the children were looking at each other. She could sense that they were trying to decide who would speak up and defend the class. Finally, a boy who was well over six feet tall stood up and approached Ms. Spencer.

"Who da fuck you think you talkin' to, bitch?"

Ms. Spencer took one look at the boy and immediately hid behind Brenda, leaving Brenda to face the student all by herself.

What had started out as a Good Samaritan act had suddenly turned into a reenactment of David and Goliath. However, unlike David, Brenda was not in possession of a slingshot and therefore needed to think fast on her feet and find a way to defuse the situation. She tried to recall some of the strategies she had learned in college, but she realized that no college course could ever have prepared a teacher for a situation like this. Therefore, Brenda decided to follow her instincts and attempted to pacify the student with the following words: "I'm sure that Ms. Spencer didn't mean what she said. Why don't you just calm down and go back to your seat?"

For a moment, the student held his ground and glared at Ms. Spencer, but then he finally relented and walked back to his seat. Brenda was both shocked and relieved to see that her approach had actually worked. She then turned away from the children and quietly reprimanded Ms. Spencer.

"What the hell were you thinking insulting these children? Do you want to get yourself killed?"

"I'm going to write my letter of resignation right now, and someone else can deal with these animals!"

"You're not going to write anything. You're going to go to the bathroom and wash your face, and I'll watch the kids until you get back."

After Ms. Spencer left the room, Brenda suddenly realized that she was all alone with the *A* class. It seemed as if they had already forgotten what had happened, as they had reverted back to what they had been doing. Brenda didn't attempt to discipline them or try to get them to do their work. Instead, she just looked

71

at them and wondered what she would do when it was her turn to teach them. She certainly wouldn't follow Ms. Spencer's example of insulting them, but how would she reach out to them? Were they even reachable? Would they listen to her, or would they treat her as they had treated Ms. Spencer? One thing was for certain: she would not allow these children to break her. Come what would, she would hold her ground. After all, she was the adult, which meant she was in charge. No matter what it took, one way or another, these children were going to submit to her authority.

As Brenda pondered this dilemma, Ms. Spencer returned from the bathroom and walked back to her desk. Her face was cleaned up, but she was still visibly upset. Brenda would have liked to have stayed a little longer to help her, but she had her own class to think about. She no longer had any time left to use the restroom, so Brenda went back to her own classroom and waited for the next class to arrive. Her fifth-period class shuffled in, and Brenda waited until they were seated and then took a seat at her own desk. Teachers were expected to be on their feet, circulating and monitoring the class at all times, but Brenda was in dire need of a break. At this point, she didn't care if an administrator walked into her classroom. The children who were presently in front of her were exhibiting the same bad behavior as all the rest, and she had no energy left to fight them. She was both mentally and physically exhausted and felt that it was important to conserve her energy for the biggest fight of all.

At precisely 2:15 p.m., the bell rang, and Brenda braced herself for the *A* class. After being pushed and shoved all day long, she refused to hold the classroom door open any longer, and she assigned one of the children to do it instead. Even though it was her job to watch the hallway, she took a chance and stayed inside the classroom. Not even for a moment could she take her eyes off these children. Almost immediately, fights broke out because there weren't enough seats to go around. As Brenda watched the children fight over the few available seats, she couldn't help but wonder who'd had the bright idea to put thirty-eight children in one classroom. Once the children were finally seated, she took her place at the front of the classroom and introduced herself.

"Good afternoon! My name is Ms. Connor, and I am delighted to have each and every one of you in my class. Why don't we start off by going around the room and introducing ourselves?"

"Why don't you go fuck yo'self instead?" screamed out one of the students.

"Yeah, bitch! This our class!" yelled out another student.

When Brenda heard these comments, her jaw nearly hit the floor. How could these children speak to her this way? Why did they have to behave so belligerently? Brenda could see that the children were watching her, and she knew she had to push her emotions aside. The last thing she wanted was for the children to see that they had rattled her. After seeing what had happened in Ms. Spencer's class, Brenda knew that these children didn't censor their language for anyone. The best thing she could do was ignore their obscenities and find a way to get down to their level. Therefore, she took a deep breath and tried to reach out to them a second time.

"I understand that some of you may feel angry and frustrated to be back in a classroom. However, I need you to understand that I'm here for you. More than anything, I want to see all of you succeed. What would you like me to do to help you achieve your goals?"

"Why don't you get on yo' knees and suck my dick, bitch?" yelled out one of the students.

Brenda frowned as the children laughed at her. She looked at the clock and saw that she still had forty minutes left until dismissal. As far as Brenda was concerned, those forty minutes might as well have been an eternity. It seemed to her that the hands on the clock weren't moving at all. She could feel herself losing control and decided it was time to try one of the interventions on the disciplinary matrix.

"Young man, you are never to speak to me like that again! This is my classroom, and if you don't show the proper respect, I'll call your parents!"

"Go 'head! My mama a ho, and my daddy in jail!" retorted the student.

Brenda sighed in disgust. Threats were clearly not going to work. These kids were not afraid of her, and they certainly weren't afraid of any of the interventions on the disciplinary matrix. If anything, the interventions paled in comparison to the challenges they faced in their day-to-day lives. During her morning and evening commutes, Brenda would see groups of children on the streets, roaming together in packs, and wonder why they were so reluctant to go home. Brenda soon discovered that these packs served as adoptive families. Children who were neglected and abused could find solace with other children who were also neglected and abused. These children lived by their own code of conduct and defied any authority that was not their own. Some of these kids had already been in jail, and others were well on their way. To them, school was merely a place where they could receive two free meals and temporary sanctuary from the streets a few hours each day. To some extent, Brenda felt sorry for these children and wanted to help them. However, instinctively, she felt that getting involved was a bad idea. Brenda had heard stories of kindhearted teachers who had gone out of their way to drive kids home or give them money for food. Quite often, these acts of kindness were misconstrued, and teachers were punished rather than rewarded for their generosity. However sorry she felt for the children, Brenda had to think of herself first. Her job description specifically stated that her duty was to teach math, and that was all she intended to do. And because Brenda took her teaching responsibilities seriously, she made one last attempt to reach out to the children.

"You know, when I was in school, I also struggled in math. As a matter of fact, most people around the world find math to be one of the most difficult subjects to learn. Even Albert Einstein struggled with math when he was a child."

"Who dat?" asked a girl in the front row.

Brenda recoiled as she heard the words come out of the little girl's mouth. If these children weren't using profanity, then they were using some form of slang. Every time a child opened his or her mouth, Brenda felt as if her ears were being violated. Sometimes she couldn't even understand what they were saying. Why did these children speak so poorly? Their command of the English language, or lack thereof, troubled Brenda deeply. In good conscience, she had to correct these children. She wasn't the reading or language arts teacher, but wasn't it every teacher's responsibility to correct a student when he or she made a grammatical mistake? If these children were going to succeed in school and in life, they would have to learn to read, write, and speak the English language properly.

Just as Brenda was about to answer the little girl's question, the bell suddenly rang, and the children got up for dismissal. Protocol demanded that Brenda walk her students to the bus loop; however, she remained behind and watched in silent horror as the children trashed her classroom. She hadn't expected them to walk out in a polite and orderly manner, but she hadn't expected them to vandalize her classroom either. Just as they had done in Ms. Spencer's room, the kids threw trash cans against the walls, ripped the blinds off the windows, and, for good measure, turned over every desk and ripped every poster off the wall as they exited the room.

When the last student finally left, Brenda broke down and began to cry. She had managed to not cry in front of the children, but now she could no longer hold back her tears. She should have been standing at her post at the bus loop, but she chose to stay behind and weep silently at her desk instead. This nightmare was not what she had signed up for when she had accepted this job. She had wholeheartedly believed that she could teach any child, but who could teach children such as these? What would happen when it came time to teach the curriculum? How was she ever going to get them to do the work? After everything she had experienced, she didn't even want to come back. She wanted to follow Ms. Spencer's impulsive lead and submit her resignation. However, the temptation to walk out and never look back was not a realistic solution. She had financial responsibilities to consider and felt ashamed at the thought of facing her family as a failure. So what was she going to do? How would she endure this misery for nine more months? As far as she could see, her only option was to grit her teeth and withstand the torture for as long as she could.

CHAPTER 5

The curriculum map provided only two days for teachers to become fully acquainted with their students before they had to start teaching the curriculum. Within this period of time, Brenda needed to finish reviewing the rules, consequences, and rewards, as well as distribute the textbooks. To track the number of textbooks issued, the administration required the students to fill out book slips. Students received free textbooks for every subject area, and some of the textbooks were quite costly. The Glencoe textbook from which Brenda was required to teach cost approximately eighty dollars to replace. Therefore, in an effort to help with loss prevention, every teacher was required to have one set of textbooks in the classroom, and every child was instructed to leave the issued textbooks at home. Therefore, Brenda gave each student two book slips along with explicit directions on how to fill them out. She would keep one of these slips for her records, and the children would glue the other one inside the covers of their books.

Brenda had specifically asked her students to purchase glue sticks as one of the required supplies, but not surprisingly, most of the children came unprepared. Brenda had anticipated this, so she had bought the supplies herself. She hated spending her own money, but what other choice did she have? The children refused to accommodate her requests, and the funding allocated to the school was clearly not intended for purchasing school supplies. Therefore, Brenda made the onetime investment for a class set of scissors, glue sticks, rulers, and protractors. Unfortunately, certain items needed to be purchased on a regular basis. Pencils and paper were two things the children never seemed to have but constantly needed. Therefore, in an attempt to save money, Brenda frequented the local dollar stores and stocked up on supplies whenever she could find a sale.

As Brenda handed out the glue sticks, she repeatedly reminded the children to use them sparingly. A few listened, but as usual, the vast majority disregarded her instructions. Once the glue sticks were in their hands, they instantly became toys. The students smeared glue not only on the book slips but also on themselves. They lathered their hands with glue and then touched desks, chairs, backpacks, and anything else within their reach. Brenda sighed with disgust. Why couldn't these children follow simple instructions? Why had she been punished with children who were not only low academically but also lacking in common sense?

"Ms. Connor, I need another glue stick!" yelled out one of the children.

"What happened to the glue stick that I gave you?"

"It broke when I wuz usin' it!" responded the child.

"Did you press too hard?"

"No! It ain't my fault! The glue stick wuz bad!" cried out the child defensively.

Brenda reluctantly gave the child a new glue stick and showed him how to use it properly. As she helped the child, she suddenly realized that these children would need her help to do just about everything. Even the most miniscule task would require her assistance. Had Brenda known that gluing the book slips would turn out to be such a hassle, she would have just done it herself. But then again, how would the children ever learn? If she did everything for them, they would never learn to do anything for themselves.

"Ms. Connor, I need a glue stick too!" yelled out a second child.

"Did your glue stick also break?"

"No, I ate mine."

"Why did you eat it?"

"Cuz I wuz hungry."

"Well, glue is not food. I'm going to need you to promise me that you won't eat any more of your school supplies. Do you think that you can do that?"

"I dunno," responded the student.

This was not the type of conversation that Brenda had ever expected to have with a sixth-grade child, but these children were full of surprises. In the future, she would have to be more careful to take nothing for granted. There was no telling what the students were capable of doing. She had to watch them constantly and repeat her instructions incessantly. Were they not listening, or were they simply incapable of comprehending? Brenda could not say. All she knew for sure was that she couldn't trust them. Not even for a split second could she take her eyes off of them. Gluing the book slips took well over twenty minutes and would have taken much longer if Brenda hadn't rushed them along. Once everybody was finished, she collected the glue sticks and then gave the following instructions: "These textbooks are for you to keep at home. You don't need to bring them back to class until the end of the school year. Now, I want you to take the textbooks and put them away in your backpacks."

"I ain't got no backpack, cuz my mom says it make me crippled!" yelled out one of the children.

"Well then, where will you put your book?"

"Right in here!" responded the child.

Brenda watched as the little boy pointed to a bag with wheels. This child was pushing his books around in a piece of luggage! What an ingenious idea! Brenda was sorry that she hadn't thought of this when she was a student. She had been forced to carry her heavy textbooks in a denim backpack that frequently tore due to the excessive weight. Her parents could only afford to buy her one bag per year, so she was constantly sewing up the gaping holes. When sewing no longer worked, she resorted to stapling, until finally, the whole thing came apart. She had never become crippled from carrying heavy textbooks, but it would have been far more convenient and far less backbreaking if she had owned a bag that she could have pushed rather than carried.

"After you've put your books away, I want you to take the book that is under your chair and place it on top of your desk."

As Brenda gave these directions, she once again walked up and down the aisles, checking that each child placed the correct book in his or her bag. Her lack of trust was not unfounded, as she soon discovered that seven children had accidentally reversed the books. It was truly exhausting to have to constantly repeat and recheck everything that she asked the children to do. She recalled that when she was in the sixth grade, her teacher had taught from her desk. She had remained seated most of the time and had stood up only on rare occasions to jot things down on the board. She'd never had to circulate the classroom the way Brenda did. When she'd issued instructions, she could depend on the class to follow them to the letter. Unfortunately, Brenda could never sit at her desk while a class was in session. Besides the fact that the administration frowned upon teachers sitting, Brenda discovered that as soon as she sat down, the class would become rambunctious. The longer she stayed seated, the more the bad behavior escalated. She was forced to position herself in the middle of the class at all times. She had found an old stool that she occasionally leaned upon, but she had not yet dared to sit on it. Her legs were constantly tired and aching from standing throughout the day, and she found herself thankful that she had listened to her mother and grandmother and had invested in a pair of sensible and comfortable shoes.

Once every child had the correct textbook on top of his or her desk, Brenda set upon the task of giving each child a handout.

"The paper that I'm giving out is a scavenger hunt that will help you become more familiar with your textbook. Every answer can be found inside your textbook, and you will have fifteen minutes to complete the activity. When I call time, I want you to put your pencils down, and we'll go over the activity together."

Brenda smiled as the children opened their books and diligently searched for the answers. For the first time since she had started teaching, the class was actually quiet. Their silence was a clear indication that they were enjoying the activity. Activities like this one were essentially what separated the good teachers from the bad teachers. Every teacher knew his or her subject area, but not every teacher knew how to present it. As a student, Brenda had suffered for years with teachers who lacked the ability to teach. Ironically, math had been her worst subject. Time and time again, she had encountered teachers who would transform simple concepts into complex, unsolvable problems. Brenda had dreaded asking for help, for fear of how her teachers would react. During high school, her frustration had peaked, and she had completely shut down. She had stopped relying on the help of others and had eventually resorted to just teaching herself. She'd checked out self-help books from the library and created study groups with other students in the same predicament. It had been one of the most difficult and challenging times in her life, but in the end, her perseverance had paid off in the form of good grades and, eventually, a full scholarship to college.

Unfortunately, Brenda's students lacked this magnitude of motivation and were far more inclined to yield to failure rather than strive for success. Therefore, she channeled her creative side to develop various games in an attempt to spark their interest and create a love for learning. Brenda was compassionate toward the struggles of her students and understood firsthand what it felt like to be in a constant state of confusion and fall further and further behind with each passing year. Yet she often wondered if her students appreciated the painstaking efforts she took to develop these gamelike lessons. Just as math was difficult to learn, it was equally, if not more, difficult to teach. It was not like other subjects that required only rote memorization. Math was a subject area that demanded respect and tolerated nothing less than absolute perfection. How would these children, who had no inclination toward learning, ever master the material and utilize the knowledge to successfully solve the problems on the FCAT?

Laziness and lack of interest on the part of the children were not Brenda's only challenges. The fact that she had so many English Language Learners (ELL) only added to her problems. Many people thought mathematics was a universal language devoid of language barriers; however, mathematics was by no means language neutral. Children learning English as a second language needed to master vocabulary in every subject area, including math. Therefore, a solution was needed to help facilitate the process. During the planning week, Brenda's NESS coach had recommended that she use some of her display boards as a word wall. The purpose of a word wall was to help the children master vocabulary. Every time a teacher introduced a new word, he or she wrote it on a piece of paper and posted it on the display board. The words were within constant view of the children, and a teacher could revisit them periodically throughout the course of the school year. The teacher could develop countless games and activities in conjunction with the word wall, and over time, the words would become so numerous that they would eventually cover not only the display board but also every wall in the classroom.

Besides the word wall, the textbook was another excellent aid in helping to master vocabulary. Brenda had had the good fortune of acquiring her class's textbook soon after she was hired. She had thoroughly familiarized herself with its layout and had created the scavenger hunt to show the children the versatility of the book. She was completely impressed with how the book was structured. There were fourteen chapters that covered areas such as algebra, geometry, and statistics. The individual chapters focused on teaching only one concept at a time and were never longer than two or three pages. Every chapter highlighted relevant vocabulary words and provided step-by-step examples of how to solve the problems.

The textbook was user friendly not only for the child but also for the teacher. Lesson planning was not difficult, because there were only three pages to review. A teacher didn't even have to come up with practice problems for homework. There were always plenty of problems at the end of each chapter. Best of all, a teacher didn't need to create his or her own exams. The teacher's textbook came with workbooks for every chapter. Within these workbooks were quizzes, tests, and FCAT-level activities. One special workbook provided activities that focused on projects involving the use of construction paper. Brenda loved this workbook above all the others because she knew that the children would enjoy cutting and folding the brightly colored paper into different shapes, all the while learning about different mathematical concepts.

Even though Brenda had an arsenal of educational tools and strategies at her disposal, the threat of failure still gnawed away at her nerves. As she watched her students struggle over a simple ten-question scavenger hunt, she was struck with a sudden realization: many of these children were going to fail regardless of her efforts, and she alone would be at fault. She could try to cover herself by placing the blame on the children, the parents, or even the system itself, but in the end, she alone would be held accountable. Brenda now finally understood why so many of the teachers were disgruntled. Once again, she recalled her conversation with Mrs. Clifford and felt herself burn crimson with shame at the things she had said. Like so many others who had never worked in the public school system, Brenda had been quick to place the blame on the teachers. Initially, she had come in as a defender and protector of children, but she had quickly discovered that they were already protected. If anything, they were overly protected. They fearlessly ran the school with their violence, obscenities, and blatant disrespect for authority, knowing full well that at the very worst, they would receive only a slap on the wrist. If anything, the teachers were the ones in need of protection. The school was like a war zone where a teacher's only weapon was a useless and nonthreatening disciplinary matrix. Brenda constantly feared for her safety. At times, she would stare at the children and wonder if they were capable of hurting her. She knew one thing for sure: these children wouldn't hesitate to get in her face if pushed too far.

This had been confirmed by the display of hostility she had witnessed in Ms. Spencer's classroom. Many of the children she was forced to teach had volatile tempers and were prone to sudden acts of violence. She had seen their violent streak the first day of school during the walk to the cafeteria, but would they ever physically attack her? She wanted to give these kids the benefit of the doubt but knew instinctively that many of them would be unable to control their animalistic tendencies. In order to protect herself, she would have to tread carefully. She would be careful not to provoke them and would simply have to back down if they refused to learn.

Fear was only one of the many emotions Brenda battled with since beginning this job. Sometimes anger would replace fear, and try as she might to control it, she would become so enraged that she would become physically sick. She had been healthy her whole life, but extreme duress was causing her body to gradually break down. She would have headaches, body aches, and sore throats from constantly yelling at the children. She was barely twenty-one years old but felt as if she were trapped in the body of an eighty-year-old woman. However, as bad as she felt, she couldn't help noticing that others around her felt far worse. She heard the other teachers complaining about high cholesterol, heart disease, and, of course, the all-too-popular topic of high blood pressure. Yet the medical issues were only half of the conversation. Following a person's full medical history were the recommendations for medications. The school system provided fairly decent health insurance, and Brenda's coworkers took full advantage. For many, the slightest ache or pain demanded immediate medical attention. Yet contrary to her coworkers, Brenda felt a strong aversion to doctors. Many in the medical profession favored dispensing over diagnosing, and Brenda refused to be medicated for the rest of her life. Instead of popping pills, she would simply have to find an alternative method to manage her stress.

During her deepest and darkest moments of despair, Brenda would turn to her friend and fellow math teacher, Mr. Fisher. They had met at the first departmental meeting and had been inseparable ever since. Mr. Fisher was sympathetic to her struggles because he was in exactly the same situation. His job was identical to hers, and he was dealing with all of the same problems. They had exactly the same schedule and discussed all of their concerns during breaks and in between class changes. Brenda was grateful to have found someone who was willing to listen and provide guidance. As it turned out, Mr. Fisher had a significant amount of experience helping those in distress. Before embarking upon a career in education, he had been a man of God, working as a pastor in a church. This was a wonderful coincidence since Brenda was also a Christian. It was wonderful to find someone she had so much in common with. Not only could she discuss work-related issues, she now had someone to talk to when she had questions concerning God and the Bible.

Talking to Mr. Fisher about her problems relieved much of Brenda's stress, and the encouragement and advice that he provided proved more therapeutic than any prescription written by a doctor. However, Brenda accrued other benefits from this friendship—benefits of a more substantial nature. For one thing, she could always depend on him whenever she needed help with the children. For example, if a child was out of control, a teacher could call security. Unfortunately, the teachers could not always count on the security guards to come. Therefore, Mr. Fisher and Brenda helped each other by sending their bad children to each other's classrooms. This turned out to be an excellent solution since children normally did not behave as badly in another teacher's class as they did in their own.

Mr. Fisher was also a lifesaver when she needed to go to the bathroom. As hard as she tried, Brenda couldn't train her body to use the restroom during the designated times. She cut down on liquids and ate a bland diet, but still, her body refused to cooperate. Every day, like clockwork, her stomach would begin to cramp during third period, exactly thirty minutes after she had eaten her lunch. She attempted to call security, but quite often, they never showed up. When Brenda couldn't hold it in any longer, she would line the kids up and take them to the library. The library had a restroom, and the librarian could watch the children while Brenda relieved herself. However, Brenda hated to do this. She dreaded the interrogation she received from the children after she finished her business in the bathroom. They instinctively knew why she was taking them to the library and heightened her embarrassment by demanding to discuss her delicate situation in full detail.

"Ms. Connor, we goin' to the library cuz you need to shit?"

"What you eat for lunch, Ms. Connor? You eat those tacos? My dookie huge after I be eatin' tacos!"

"Ms. Connor didn't eat no tacos! I bet she be eatin' the hot dogs! When I be eatin' hot dogs, my turds be huge! How long yo' turds, Ms. Connor?"

Although Brenda ignored these inquiries and never dignified such inappropriate questions with a response, she still felt humiliated inside. She knew that the children weren't purposely trying to embarrass her. They simply enjoyed discussing a subject that they themselves could easily relate to. However, once she and Mr. Fisher devised a plan, she never had to take the children to the library again. Together, they masterminded a plan where they would select two students to hold each of their classroom doors wide open. While the children were holding the doors, the teacher who needed to go to the bathroom could go, and the teacher who stayed behind watched both of the classes simultaneously until the other teacher returned. They would never have to call security, and the teacher who needed to go to the bathroom could leave discreetly without ever arousing the attention of the children.

Besides time-outs and bathroom breaks, Brenda and Mr. Fisher also supported one another in the classroom. Teaching was one major component of a teacher's job description, and paperwork was the other. Even though her day ended at 3:30 p.m., Brenda could never leave with the children. After the last bus left, she would return to her classroom and begin phase two of her day, which consisted of cleaning the classroom and catching up on paperwork. It was her preference to stay after school, but teachers could do their paperwork before school started or complete it at home. One could easily identify the teachers who took their paperwork home. After school, they would pull miniature carts loaded with files down the hallway and through the parking lot. Brenda absolutely refused to take paperwork home. She knew herself well enough to know that once she got home, nothing was going to get done.

During the planning week, Brenda had felt as if she were drowning under a tsunami of paperwork, but in time, she found her rhythm and got herself into a manageable routine. She always worked on her lesson plans first. In her mind, there was no need for lesson plans since the curriculum map laid out the lessons for each day. However, lesson plans went into far greater detail than the curriculum map by requiring teachers to list strategies by using codes. Coding strategies was the most time consuming part of creating a lesson plan and, in short, was a complete pain in the ass. Brenda had absolutely no patience for something that she felt was a complete and utter waste of time. And because of her impatience, she eventually threw caution to the wind and randomly selected codes. She was taking a huge risk, but who would ever know? Administrators sporadically checked lesson plans to make sure they were current, but no one had the time or the desire to carefully inspect them. There were only two reasons that this document even needed to exist. First, it needed to be readily available when a substitute was called in to cover a class. Second, and more importantly, lesson plans were considered legal documents. On the last day of school, teachers were required to submit their plans to their administrator, and the administrator had to sign off, saying that the plans had been received. The lesson plans were then placed in an official box that was sent downtown to a storage facility. All lesson plans were saved indefinitely in case someone ever threatened to sue the school. It was not uncommon for someone to show up years later claiming that a teacher had failed to teach a particular topic. If someone ever attempted to do this, the school district covered themselves by retrieving the lesson plans and presenting them as proof that the teacher in question had indeed done his or her job.

Another time-consuming activity involved setting up the lesson. In Brenda's day, teachers rarely put much effort into designing lessons with bells and whistles. Most teachers followed the basic recipe of lecturing and then allowing time for seatwork. For years, this method had been an acceptable and effective formula for successful learning, but now things were different. In college, Brenda had often heard her professors use the quote "Don't be a sage on the stage but a guide on the side." The adage was a way of reminding teachers to not infuse class time with incessant talking. Instead, children needed to make discoveries on their own with only a minimal amount of instruction from the teacher.

One would have thought that stepping aside and allowing children to learn on their own would make the teacher's job easier; however, this method of teaching actually quadrupled the teacher's workload. To create an inspiring lesson that would actively engage a low-level child was extremely difficult, especially in the area of math. For example, the powers that be strongly endorsed the use of workstations, but this system was an absolute nightmare to implement. A teacher would have to set up four separate activities in four different locations of the classroom and place the children in teams. The children would work together to complete the activity and then move on to the next station when the teacher called time. While the children worked on the activity, the teacher would be in continuous rotation but would intervene only if a child was in need of help.

Brenda would have gladly endorsed this method of teaching if she had thought it was effective, but she knew her children well enough to know that they lacked the maturity to do any kind of group work. The fact of the matter was that this strategy worked only if a child had an interest in learning. Furthermore, the administration failed to understand that motivating low—level children was nearly impossible. Putting them in groups only increased the probability of bad behavior, and constant movement around the classroom increased the likelihood that a fight would break out. Keeping the children seated and sequestered from one another eliminated both of these problems. Brenda knew that the administration would disagree with her theory. They had already gone so far as to criticize the setup of her classroom. According to them, the arrangement of her classroom failed to encourage cooperative learning. They scrutinized her rows of desks and strongly suggested that she rearrange the desks into groups of four. Were these people out of their fucking minds? Why were they trying to make her job more difficult? She listened politely to all of their suggestions and took into account what they had to say, but in the end, she held her ground and kept the arrangement of her classroom exactly as it was.

Besides work stations, the higher-ups also wanted to see teachers use manipulatives in every lesson. A manipulative was any item that aided a child in learning the material. The scavenger hunt Brenda had created was an excellent example of a manipulative. Also, the supplies she had bought could also be considered manipulatives. Brenda was all for using anything that helped children learn, but her lack of trust made her hesitant to use manipulatives in the classroom. She could deal with the kids eating or breaking her supplies, but what if they used her supplies to hurt another person? It was uncanny just how easily everyday items could be turned into dangerous weapons. For example, Brenda had noticed that her students stole the plastic forks from the cafeteria and used them to stab each another. Most of the time, the forks would break before any real damage was done, but on some rare occasions, enough pressure was applied to draw a few drops of blood. Another act of violence that the children seemed to favor involved the use of rulers. Much to Brenda's surprise, rulers were the one school supply that her students actually brought to school. Even more fascinating, not one single child had purchased a plastic ruler. Everybody seemed to have a preference for the wooden rulers. This seemed like an odd coincidence, but at first, Brenda didn't give it much thought. She was just grateful her students took an interest in measurement. Unfortunately, measuring was not the intended purpose of these rulers. The children removed the rulers' metal piece and used it to whip their classmates. By applying just the right amount of pressure and using just enough speed, a child could cause the formation of a painful welt that would leave somebody in pain for days.

Though the paperwork was excessive, Brenda and Mr. Fisher found a way to manage it without losing their sanity. Since they both taught the same grade and dealt with the same level of children, it was perfectly acceptable for their paperwork to be identical. Therefore, after some discussion, they divided the paperwork between them and, in the process, cut their workload in half. This was a major breakthrough for Brenda. To date, this job had been filled with nothing but trials and tribulations, but things were finally starting to take a turn for the better. Educating the children was still a major concern, but at least she was slowly becoming desensitized to their nastiness. Furthermore, the weekend was right around the corner, and Brenda waited with eager anticipation for the opportunity to have two fun-filled child-free days to do all of her favorite activities.

CHAPTER 6

On Saturday morning, Brenda awoke feeling refreshed and rejuvenated. Waking up early was still not agreeing with her, and she cherished every single day that she could sleep in late. When she wasn't forced to wake up early for work, she lingered for hours in her bed. She would drift in and out of languor until at last, she would shake off the somnolence and begin her day. However, even after she was awake, she still remained in bed. Besides using her bed for sleep, she ate, read, and even navigated the Internet in her bed. Her mother frowned upon this habit, but Brenda could never understand why. In college, she had lived in cramped dormitories where each student was issued one desk and a single-mattress bed. She had shunned the hard wooden desks and gravitated toward the bed, which was spacious and considerably more comfortable. Although Brenda had long since graduated and now rented an apartment of her own, she was still a college student at heart. She was not one to readily accept change; instead, she held on to her old habits and continued to engage in student-like behavior.

Furthermore, even if Brenda had wanted to sit at a table or recline on a couch, she could not do so, because she didn't own any furniture. Her family and friends had raised enough money to help her rent an apartment, but furnishing it was entirely her responsibility. At present, her newly acquired apartment had few pretensions. It was meagerly furnished with a mattress and a twelve-inch television that currently resided on top of a crate. Unfortunately, as a new employee, Brenda had to wait a full month before she received her first paycheck. Until then, she had to make do with what little savings she had. Since she was strapped for cash, food and bills took precedence over furniture. However, the one thing that Brenda could not go without was the Sunday newspaper. It was the one thing she looked forward to reading every single week. She'd search through the classifieds, looking for items that she could purchase to furnish her apartment. People possessed the most peculiar things, and the elderly owned the antique furniture that Brenda loved most of all. If Brenda didn't find anything appealing in the classifieds, she moved right along to the obituaries. Living in Florida guaranteed a lengthy obituary section, which Brenda studied meticulously from cover to cover. The children of the deceased were always in a hurry to sell off their parents' belongings and would quite often sell them for pennies on the dollar. Brenda often wondered why the children didn't keep some of the memorabilia for themselves. Wasn't there anything that held any sentimental value at all? Sadly, most children all but bypassed the grieving process and set their sights upon the financial payout. Anything that had any value was put up for sale, including the home itself. As soon as Brenda had some money, she would purchase some of the items and furnish her new home. The way she saw it, the dead were no longer in need of materialistic things, and it was better for their belongings to be purchased and enjoyed rather than thoughtlessly discarded in the back of some Dumpster.

As Brenda read the paper with her morning coffee, she occasionally looked up and imagined what her apartment would look like fully furnished. At present, it was almost completely bare, but quite truthfully, she really didn't care. It was exciting to finally be living on her own. Getting a professional job was her first milestone, and renting her first apartment was the second. At first, she had been skeptical about living by herself. She had lived the majority of her life at home and then moved on to college, where she had lived with a string of roommates. Up until now, she had never really known what it felt like to be independent. Her first night in the apartment had been a frightening experience, and the silence had seemed almost deafening. However, over time, Brenda's entire perspective had gradually begun to change. She crossed over to the other side of the spectrum and embraced her newfound solitude. This was not altogether unusual since her life outside of the apartment was constantly filled with noise. Her days consisted of screaming children, complaining parents, and an administration that never missed an opportunity to criticize. Who wouldn't appreciate a few hours of silence each day? As soon as Brenda walked through the front door, the problems of the day magically melted away. Over time, she had not only accepted the silence but also grown to crave it. She hated the telemarketers who disrupted her peace late at night and rarely interacted with friends and family during the week. She was not isolating herself on purpose but was merely conserving much-needed energy to help her get through the next day.

Brenda truly treasured these moments alone, because she knew that this arrangement would not last forever. Her fiancé, Joseph, had recently proposed to her, and they were now in the process of saving for a wedding. What should have been a happy time in her life had turned out to be a complete and utter nightmare. Neither she nor Joseph had any significant savings, and their salaries barely covered their day-to-day expenses. Because they couldn't rely upon their parents for help, they opened a joint bank account and set every dollar aside that they could spare. After numerous calculations and recalculations, they came to the conclusion that they couldn't afford to have the wedding of their dreams. To Brenda, the obvious solution was to reduce the number of people who were invited. However, her viewpoint conflicted with Joseph and his exceedingly large family. To Joseph's mother especially, the thought of a small wedding was like an affliction. Brenda had tried to rationalize with her by showing her the spreadsheets of calculations, but she was unresponsive to either logic or rationalization. Instead of doing the right thing and offering a financial contribution, her recommendation was to charge the wedding expenses to a credit card. If they needed more money, Joseph's mother said, they could always take out a loan. After all, why should her son go without, when money was readily available and there for the taking?

Brenda couldn't believe the audacity of this woman! Who the hell was she to force Brenda into debt? As it was, both

Brenda and Joseph were already crippled financially. Besides their student loans, they both had car payments and staggering credit card debt. Her loans and car payment had been a necessity, but Brenda sorely regretted the day she had signed up for a credit card. In college, the credit card companies had flocked to her campus and bedazzled the students with huge credit lines and an easy application process. Brenda hadn't needed anyone to cosign the paperwork, and the reps hadn't even bothered to do a background check. The entire process had taken all of fifteen minutes, and she had even walked away with a free gift. Within two weeks, her new credit card had arrived in the mail, and it hadn't been long before she went on her first shopping spree.

Brenda couldn't understand how she had gotten herself into such a financial mess. She was only beginning her adult life, and she was beginning it with a huge deficit. However, she wasn't the only one who had accrued a massive amount of debt. Her future betrothed was even far worse off than she. Whereas she had only one credit card to her name, Joseph had several, all of which were maxed out to the limit. Just as Brenda loved antiquing for furniture, Joseph loved antiquing for cars. He had a particular fondness for going to auctions and buying vintage cars that the police had repossessed. The cars themselves were not all that expensive, but renovating them nearly broke the bank. Joseph was handy and saved money by fixing the cars himself, but purchasing the parts proved to be quite costly. Once the cars were fixed, the plan was to flip them and pocket the profit. However, Joseph never sold a single car. When Brenda confronted him for an explanation, he openly admitted that he hadn't even tried. He had become attached and couldn't bear to let any of his precious vehicles go. So at the present time, Joseph owned six newly remodeled cars but still lived at home with his mother.

Brenda could have been judgmental about Joseph's spending habits. After all, a person had only one body and therefore needed only one car. However, Joseph could have thrown this same reasoning right back in her face. When she wasn't antiquing, she was spending money on designer shoes, and why did she need so many pairs of shoes when she had only one pair of feet? They were both guilty of excessive spending, and they both needed to make better choices in the future. Brenda was doing her part by trying to cut costs with the wedding. Why couldn't Joseph do the same? Why did he insist on inviting so many people, when they could have a small ceremony instead? Sometimes she could see that he was leaning in her favor, but she knew he lacked the backbone to stand up to his mother. However, unlike Joseph, Brenda wasn't afraid of this woman, and she wasn't afraid to speak her mind. So the two of them would go at it, hour after hour, like two boxers in a ring. Both were strong-willed women and were reluctant to back down, but Brenda, being younger and more ferocious, almost always won the fight in the end.

However, Brenda gained no satisfaction from these altercations. She did enough fighting in her job and hated when the belligerency spilled over into her personal life. Yet what she hated most of all was the person she was starting to become. Over the course of only a few short weeks, she had somehow transformed into a miserable and combative woman. Brenda couldn't pinpoint exactly when the change in her disposition had occurred, but she knew that she was no longer her pleasant and outgoing self. The process of her transformation was gradual but was continuously evolving for the worse. Brenda would think back and try to recall when she had last been happy with her life. There had been brief moments of happiness at her job, but these rare occurrences were like firecrackers that would flare up momentarily and then quickly fizzle out. And now, on top of everything else, she had to contend with problems in her personal life. Remarkably, she and Joseph had dated all through college and never had a single fight. These days, however, all they ever did was fight, and every single fight they had was about money.

As Brenda reminisced about her college years and tried to recall happier times, she came to the realization that the last time she had been truly happy with her life was on her graduation day. From start to finish, the entire day had gone off without a hitch. All of her friends and family had been present for her special day, and not one single drop of rain had fallen from the sky. The food had been delicious and plentiful, and the day had been filled with celebration and revelry. Brenda smiled as she played back the events of that day, but then she suddenly recalled a single moment when things had gone awry. She had completely forgotten about her aunt Margery! She had forgotten how her aunt had nearly ruined her big day with her negativity and cynicism. She hadn't wanted to speak to her aunt at the time, but now she suddenly had a change of heart. On the outside, it seemed that her aunt had a rough and tough exterior, but who was the woman underneath? Had she always been this hostile, or had the events of her life made her this way? Like Brenda, she worked in the public school system, and she no doubt faced the same challenges Brenda did. Did the pressures of her job have something to do with her demeanor? Was she also fed up with the workings of the educational system? At present, Brenda could not say, but she was going to make it her priority to find out.

Someday in the near future, she would pick up the phone and call her aunt, but not today. This was one day she could not afford to have ruined. Today held special meaning for Brenda because it would be the first time since she had started college that she would go back to her old neighborhood roller-skating rink. Before she had left for college, skating had been her entire life. The rink was open five days a week, and Brenda had made sure she was in attendance each and every day. Her mother had introduced her to—or, rather, forced her into—the sport. When Brenda was only twelve years old, her father had accepted a job that required him to work the graveyard shift. He had been able to sleep uninterrupted Monday through Friday, but the weekends had posed a problem. Since there was no school, Brenda's mother had had to find an activity to get her and her sisters out of the house so that their father could rest during the day. Besides being nearby, the rink was cheap and full of children Brenda's age. Up until that point, Brenda had never laced up a pair of skates; however, after her introduction to the sport, it hadn't taken long for her to realize that she was not a natural-born skater.

Brenda could still vividly remember how badly she had behaved the first time she went to the rink. Her first complaint had involved having to wear the ugly brown rental skates with the frayed laces and worn-out wheels. Besides that, Brenda hadn't liked the idea of having to wear secondhand skates that had been worn by countless other people. However, the appearance of the skates had been the least of her problems. Once the skates were on, Brenda hadn't had the faintest idea of what to do. Her mother had gotten her started by holding her hand and walking her across the carpet, but once on the floor, she had been left to fend for herself. She still remembered how she had hesitated when surveying the rink for the first time. The smooth floor had been in excellent condition, coated with some type of varnish that brought forth a beautiful shine. However, neither the quality nor the coating on the floor had been of any help to her. She had first needed to learn the ABCs of skating—agility, balance, and control—before she could successfully master the sport. The rink itself was massive and home to skaters of varying levels of expertise. She had noticed other skaters who, like herself, were terrified, but she had seen many others who flew effortlessly around the exterior or danced gracefully in the interior. Most of the people skating had actually looked as if they were having fun. After a few minutes of careful observation, Brenda had decided it was time to take a chance and venture out on her own. After all, if everyone else could do it, then why couldn't she?

Unfortunately, as soon as her feet touched the wood, Brenda had lost control, fallen backward, and instantaneously hit the floor. She had barely taken two steps, and already she had fallen flat on her ass. Going down was apparently the easy part. Picking oneself up required substantially more skill. Her mother had seen her fall and run to her rescue but hadn't let her quit. She had coaxed her into trying it again and reassured her that it would get easier with each attempt. Brenda had been skeptical, but she'd heeded her mother's advice and given it another go. Thank goodness there had been a wall nearby for Brenda to hold on to. She had taken full advantage of it and held on for dear life as she walked slowly and carefully around the rink. However, her dependence on the wall had skewed her posture severely and hindered her from skating properly. Unfortunately, letting go had been completely out of the question. Brenda had relied upon the wall the same way a cripple relied upon a crutch. She had looked like an old lady bent over with age, walking around with an imaginary walker, but she hadn't cared. All she'd cared about was not falling down. As Brenda had struggled to stay on her feet, she had noticed the people who flew past her. How in the world did they maintain their balance? Weren't they afraid of falling down and getting hurt? Signs plastered all over the building had cautioned people to skate at their own risk. Brenda, who didn't like taking unnecessary risks, had promptly decided that once she completed the first lap, she would inform her mother that skating wasn't for her and that she was ready to go home.

It had taken Brenda nearly half an hour to make it once around the rink, and she had fallen several times before exiting the floor. She had stumbled over to the snack bar and found her mother sitting in the far corner, crocheting a scarf. She had flung herself onto a bench across from where her mother was sitting and begun unlacing her skates.

"What do you think you're doing?"

"I'm done! I hate skating, and I want to go home!"

"What do you mean you want to go home? You barely even gave it a chance!"

"There's no way I'm ever going to be able to do this! Didn't you see me out there? I couldn't even let go of the wall! I fell twelve times, and everyone's pointing and laughing at me!"

"Look, I know this is your first time and you're having some difficulty, but I'm afraid that you're just going to have to keep at it. You know that your father needs his rest, and you kids need to be out of the house. Your sisters seem to be getting the hang of it. Why don't you ask them for help?"

"I don't want their help! I want to go home, and I want to go now!"

After this last outburst, her mother had said nothing, and Brenda had assumed that she had won the fight. Just as she'd bent over to take off the first skate, her mother had stood up, forcefully grabbed her by the ear, and led her back onto the floor. Before she had released her ear, she had left Brenda with one final warning: "Now, you listen to me! Your ass can take a beating from me, or it can take a beating from the floor! The choice is yours."

Brenda had been flabbergasted! How could her mother be so cruel? Didn't she see how she struggled? Why wouldn't she just let her quit? It wasn't fair! However, although she had been fuming with frustration, she had shut her mouth and kept her feelings to herself. It was unwise to cross her mother a second time, so she had resumed skating and continued to slip and fall as she made her way around the rink. The session had been six hours long, and by the third hour, Brenda had practically been in tears. Her entire body had ached, and she had all but lost feeling in her feet. She had desperately wanted to skate as the people around her did, but her body had simply refused to cooperate. From time to time, the deejay had played a song that she liked, but she hadn't been able to keep up with the kids who had formed a train and shuffled to the beat. As Brenda had labored to make it through the session, she'd begun to think of what her mother had said. Was she actually going to force her to skate every weekend? Brenda had shuddered at the thought and wondered if there was a way to convince her mother to change her mind. Maybe she could implore her sisters to unite with her, or perhaps her father could find a new job. Regardless, Brenda had been determined to get her way and give up skating forever.

As it turned out, Brenda's sisters had never sided with her, and her father had never changed jobs. The only thing that had ended up changing was Brenda's attitude. At her mother's insistence, she had kept at the sport, and after a few weeks, she had begun to show improvement. Walking had gradually turned into rolling, and eventually, she had gained enough confidence to let go of the wall altogether. After a few months, she had found her rhythm and begun to incorporate a few dance moves into her routine. Before she knew it, she had found herself joining in on all of the group skates and had learned the various sequences to each of the shuffles. She had never had the advantage of taking lessons from a professional, but there had been no shortage of talented skaters at the rink. During breaks, she had watched these people and tried to mimic their various movements and techniques. Surprisingly, once she had found her balance, everything else had just naturally fallen into place. When she'd no longer had anything new left to learn, she had choreographed her own dances and had felt a sense of accomplishment when she became the envy of the rink.

Looking back, Brenda was grateful that her mother had never let her give up. Over time, skating had become her outlet whenever she had problems in her life. High school especially had been a wretched time full of teenage angst and confusion. Excessive acne, braces, and a series of bad perms had barred Brenda from all of the popular cliques and made her a virtual outcast among her peers. However, all things considered, her lack of popularity had bothered her little. The skating rink had been where she shined, and she'd relished all of the attention she received. There had been no shortage of admirers of the opposite sex, many of whom Brenda had dated and discarded on a weekly basis. At her peak, she had been skating twenty to thirty hours a week, and over time, the exercise had begun to show. Her once-flabby frame had become taut, and the last of her baby fat had finally melted away. During those years, she'd never had to watch her weight and had been able to eat whatever she wanted. Unfortunately, all that had changed once she went away to college. Eating had replaced skating, her high metabolism had slowed down, and the pounds had begun to pile on. But now things were about to change! She was settled in her new apartment and felt secure in her new job. Now was the time to focus on herself. She hated the way she looked, and she was resolved to do something about it. And what better way to do it than by reentering the sport she had once so loved?

Although Brenda had stopped skating, she had never discarded her skates. Her mother had kept them for her while she was in college and had given them back to her on her graduation day. Brenda suddenly felt a twinge of nervousness as she opened the closet door. Four years was a long time. Would her body remember, or would she have to relearn the sport all over again? The fact that she was severely out of shape only worsened the situation. She took her skates out of the closet and carefully inspected them. She recalled how she had saved for months and managed to buy them just shy of her fifteenth birthday. She had worked endless hours washing dishes at her part-time job in a pizzeria for minimum wage before she had been able to afford to buy the skates of her choice. She could have opted for the cheaper skates, but in her mind, quality was nonnegotiable. The skates she had selected were top of the line and had cost her a small fortune. However, Brenda was glad now that she had made the investment. Upon closer inspection, she was pleased to discover that with the exception of a few scratches, her skates were in excellent condition and could still take any and all manner of abuse.

It was no accident that her skates were still like new. She had waited a long time to buy them, and once she had them, she had been methodical with their maintenance. She knew that a decent pair of skates could last a person a lifetime if properly maintained. To Brenda, this meant regularly polishing the boots and lubricating the bearings. Not surprisingly, skaters tended to replace the wheels more than anything else. Since her particular set of wheels had cost well over two hundred dollars, she had taken great pains to preserve them. To maintain their integrity, she had never skated outside on the concrete and had assiduously cleaned them after each use. After some experimentation, Brenda had discovered that a soft cloth doused with rubbing alcohol proved to be the most effective and least abrasive way to clean the grime off of her wheels. Her friends from the rink had teased her about her compulsion for cleanliness, but how many of those people today could boast that they still had their original set of wheels?

Brenda had created not only a cleaning ritual for her skates but also a preparation ritual for herself. Skating was not just about exercising; it was also about socializing. Brenda might not have been popular in high school, but she had been at the top of the pecking order at the rink. And in order to maintain her elite status, she'd had to maintain her appearance. However, achieving absolute perfection required considerable time and planning. Not surprisingly, her coiffure had consumed the majority of her time. She had felt that her hair needed to be not only stylish but also arranged in such a way that it would not interfere with her skating. Back in the day, she had sported a perm and worked with a diffuser for well over an hour to achieve the perfect curls. These days, however, she saved a significant amount of time by tying her hair into a knot and adding a hair attachment to create the illusion of longer and fuller hair. Then there was the task of selecting the perfect outfit. During her teenage years, Brenda had had a preference for Daisy Duke shorts and halter tops, but sadly, she was a teenager no more. Because of her new, fuller figure, she was forced to dress more conservatively. Fortunately for her, the majority of her weight was concentrated in her lower body. Because she was a pear-shaped woman, she decided it was best to accentuate the top half of her body by wearing brightly colored tops and deaccentuate the bottom half of her body by wearing only black.

It was almost time to leave for the rink, and Brenda was just about ready to go. She needed only to add the finishing touches, which included her makeup and perfume. As a kid, she had avoided makeup altogether because it smeared when she sweated. However, Brenda wasn't sure how much sweating she would be doing tonight. Tonight was just about becoming reacclimated to the sport. Her game plan was to start out slowly by skating on the carpet and then maybe attempt to skate on the floor. She had the urge to jump right back in and pick up where she had left off, but Brenda knew that this type of rashness would only lead to an accident. When people took unnecessary risks, they ended up hurting themselves and, quite often, hurting the people around them. Skating was a dangerous sport, and at some point, even the most skilled skaters eventually got hurt. Even Brenda was not exempt from this rule. Over the years, she had had her share of broken ribs and busted knees and had sprained both wrists more times than she cared to remember. As a kid, she had never allowed herself to indulge in the pain. Her answer to every injury had been either an ice pack or, if the injury was more severe, soaking in a tub of hot water mixed with Epsom salts. She'd had only one accident that required medical attention. She had once attempted a spin that had spiraled horribly out of control and had resulted in a broken arm. This one careless mishap had put her in a cast for nearly two months. Yet even this setback hadn't been enough to put her out of commission. She had taught herself to skate with the cast and had eventually mastered the spin that had broken her arm.

However, Brenda was no longer that same fearless skater. She had a job now and could not afford to miss work because of an injury. To ensure her safety, she decided to wear a pair of wrist guards and kneepads. In truth, Brenda hated to wear this protective gear. She was essentially advertising to everyone that she didn't know how to skate. She would never have been caught dead wearing any of this when she was a teenager. As a matter of fact, she didn't know anyone who wore any sort of safeguarding, with the exception of one boy. Brenda didn't know his name, but he had attended her high school and had skated at the Friday night session. He was a homely fellow who'd had all the attributes of a nerd. He'd worn braces, glasses, and a hearing aid, all of which had made him an excellent target for bullies. As if all this weren't bad enough, he had also padded every part of his body and had even worn a bicycle helmet to protect his head. This kid had been just begging to get ridiculed, and that was exactly what had happened. Everybody at the rink had mocked him, including Brenda, who'd stationed herself at the forefront of the abuse. The Friday night session was designed for experienced skaters. If this boy was so afraid of getting hurt, Brenda had wondered, then why didn't he attend the children's session on Saturday morning and leave the night sessions to experienced skaters, such as Brenda? Looking back, Brenda felt ashamed at how badly she had treated this boy. She felt especially bad about the time she had stolen his helmet and worn it on her head as he chased her around the rink while all of her friends laughed and cheered her on. Now, as a young adult, she couldn't believe that she had ever been so cruel. After all, there had been a time when she too had been a beginner skater. However, once she'd begun to excel, all of her past struggles had become a distant memory. As her abilities had grown, so had her ego. She had never missed an opportunity to flaunt her skills, even if it meant doing it at the expense of someone else's feelings.

As Brenda caught a glimpse of the flashing florescent lights illuminating the outside of the rink, she began to wonder who she might see. Would some of her friends still be there? Would the people she had bullied in the past recognize her? All these thoughts raced through her mind as she did a loop around the parking lot. Once she found a spot and turned off the ignition, she couldn't bring herself to get out of the car. The more she thought about it, the more this seemed like a really bad idea. What was she thinking? She couldn't go inside and face all of these people! What would they say when they saw her? Would they politely ignore the fact that she had gotten fat, or would they make light of it? And what about her inability to skate? What would people think when they saw her falling and flailing all over the place? This was definitely a bad idea. The more she thought about it, the more she realized that there was no way this was going to turn out well. But then Brenda remembered how much fun she used to have and the remorse she had felt when she'd been forced to give up skating. The bottom line was that she had to start somewhere. It would be difficult in the beginning, but she had mastered the sport once, and perhaps she could master it again.

As Brenda entered the rink, she was pleasantly surprised to discover that little had changed since she had left. The carpet was different, and the building had been repainted, but as far as she could see, everything else was exactly the same. She couldn't resist going into the pro shop and checking out the latest style of skates. She was shocked to discover that skates similar to her own were now going for double what she had paid seven years prior. Brenda was glad she had had the good sense to preserve her skates. With all of her financial woes, there was no way she could afford to buy a new pair now. After she finished window shopping, she decided it was time to get down to business. She sat down and slowly started to put on her skates. They slid on easily, and Brenda was relieved to see that they still fit perfectly. So far, everything was going smoothly. She started to feel optimistic and decided it was time to get up and try to roll on the carpet. She started slowly at first and then went a little faster. She skated to one end of the building and then turned around and skated back to the other end. She did this about ten times and never fell down once. Brenda couldn't believe it! It was actually starting to come back to her. This wasn't so difficult!

Why had she been so afraid? It was time to stop doubting herself and get out on the floor!

Unfortunately, as soon as she stepped onto the wood, she immediately fell down. It was like déjà vu, with the exception that her mother wasn't there to rescue her this time. Brenda lay there, agitated, and lingered a moment before she picked herself back up. She should have known better. The floor was nothing like the carpet, and she should have proceeded with caution. However, she would not allow herself to become frustrated. She was no longer a whiny twelve-year-old brat who quit at the first sign of difficulty. She was a grown woman who could draw from her previous experience to relearn the sport. Therefore, she picked herself up and tried again. She knew that the first thing she needed to do was steady herself and find her balance. She took one lap around the rink and then decided it was time to take a leap of faith and leave the security of the wall. As she ventured out to the center of the floor, she couldn't help noticing that the sensation of rolling felt strange and familiar at the same time. Since the wall was no longer within her reach, all she could do was believe in herself and trust that her body would instinctively remember what to do. As she skated, she felt like a small child learning how to walk for the first time. She tripped and stumbled along the way, but she managed to not fall down a second time. As she skated, she began to look more closely at the people who passed by her. So far, she didn't see a single person she recognized. Where were all of her old friends? Who were all these new people? Brenda had not expected this, and as she labored to not fall, she began to wonder where everyone had gone.

Four years didn't seem like a long time to Brenda, but apparently it was long enough for people to change and move on to bigger and better things. She really couldn't blame her friends for quitting the sport. She herself had abandoned it when she went off to college. Since the majority of her friends were within her age range, she suspected that like her, they had also left for college or had moved away to pursue careers. Although her friends were no longer in attendance, the rink was by no means empty. A new crop of skaters had emerged, and Brenda was astonished by their advanced skills. She had never seen skating like this before! She had always prided herself on being one of the best, but she was now quickly humbled by what she saw. This new generation of skaters shunned the basic shuffle that had helped solidify her popularity, considering it to be antiquated. It had been replaced with more elaborate routines that placed a huge amount of emphasis on footwork. In Brenda's day, only a select few were skilled enough to dance in the center of the floor. Now it appeared to be the status quo. Everywhere, people paired up and created complicated combinations that included multiple steps and intricate movements. If she was going to compete with this crowd, she would have to seriously step up her game. Brenda was so mesmerized by what she saw that she neglected to pay attention to where she was going. She ended up rolling in the wrong direction, and before she could stop, she collided into a young man, and they both ended up falling on the floor.

Brenda felt bad about falling, but she felt even worse that she had taken somebody down with her. The guilt quickly lifted once she saw that the young man wasn't hurt and was already up on his feet. Unfortunately, she had a little more difficulty getting up. The wall was well out of her reach, and there was nothing else around to hold on to. As Brenda struggled to stand up, the young man approached her and suddenly extended his hand.

"Do you need some help getting up?"

"Yes, I think I do. I was so impressed with the skaters who were dancing in the center that I didn't even notice where I was going."

"I guess they're all right, but I remember the way you used to skate. There's nobody here that could match your style or technique."

Brenda was dumbfounded. Who was this kind stranger? She examined him from top to bottom, but still, there was no recognition. Was he one of her old boyfriends? Was he one of her skating partners from back in the day? Why couldn't she remember? She prided herself on having a fairly good memory, but try as she might, she could not place his face.

"You don't remember me, do you?"

"I'm so sorry, but I just don't recognize you."

"Why don't you imagine me with a bicycle helmet on my head? Do you remember me now?"

Brenda's stomach dropped. It suddenly dawned on her that she was standing face-to-face with the boy she had tortured all through high school. Out of all the people for her to run into, why did she have to run into him? As she stared at him, she found herself at a complete loss for words. What could she say? Should she do the right thing and apologize for years of merciless bullying, or should she take the coward's way out and make a run for it? Unfortunately, try as she might, she couldn't run away. She couldn't believe it was actually him. He looked nothing like his former self. Where were the glasses? Where were the braces? The hearing aid was all that remained and was the only reminder of the person he used to be. How incredibly different he looked! Whereas Brenda's beauty had wilted over the years, this young man's beauty had blossomed. She was so enamored by his good looks that she couldn't even speak. All she could do was hang her head in shame and brace herself for the verbal beating that was sure to come.

"I recognize you now. I'm so sorry that I was so cruel to you. I should never have picked on you. I know that I don't deserve your forgiveness, but I still hope that you can accept my apology."

"Of course I accept your apology! Despite all of the mean things that you did to me, I always admired you. I even had a crush on you in high school."

"Now I feel really bad. Why can't you just tell me how fat and unattractive I've become, and then we'll be even."

"I can't do that! You're still the same beautiful girl to me."

"Well, as you can see, I certainly can't skate like I used to. Are you sure you don't want to tease me about that?"

"No, I don't like to make people feel bad about themselves. However, I might be able to help you out. If you want, you can borrow my old bicycle helmet to protect your head while you skate. I remember how much you loved to wear it."

At this, Brenda couldn't help bursting into laughter. He not only was kind but also had a sense of humor. Brenda really wished that she had gotten to know him better when they were kids. Why had she allowed herself to submit to peer pressure? Why couldn't she have set herself apart from the crowd and helped him then the way he was helping her now? It grieved her that she could not erase the sins of her past. In front of her stood a special man who exhibited a kindness that Brenda rarely encountered. If she could not change the past, then she would set her concentration on the future. She was determined to make amends and decided that now was as good a time as any to offer her hand in friendship. She had many questions but wondered if he would grace her with the answers. She decided to test the waters with an invitation: "I was just about ready to take a break. Would you like to join me for a soda?"

"I could go for a soda. Let's go find a seat."

"You know, I don't even remember your name."

"My name is Michael."

"May I ask you a personal question?"

"I bet I know what you're going to ask me. You want to know why I wore the helmet."

"The thought did cross my mind."

"Believe it or not, I actually had to wear it."

"No you didn't. From what I can remember, you were a relatively good skater."

"You don't understand. When I was ten years old, the doctors found a tumor on my brain. Fortunately, it wasn't cancerous, but it still had to be removed. Once the surgery was complete, the doctor advised that I abstain from all dangerous sports. However, I loved skating so much that I begged my mom not to make me quit. The only way she'd let me skate was if I wore the helmet. My poor mother was terrified that even the slightest injury would kill me, so she padded me from head to toe."

"I wish I would have known. You should have told me."

"Would it have made a difference? Would you have been any nicer to me?"

"Probably not. But I assure you, I'm a different person now. I'm really glad that I ran into you, and I'd like to get to know you better."

"Well, I'm here every Saturday night, and I'll be glad to help you any way that I can."

"You would really take the time to help me after everything I've done to you?"

"Absolutely! I finally get to spend time with the girl of my dreams, and you'll have all the help that you need."

"I honestly don't know why you're being so nice to me. I don't feel like I deserve your forgiveness."

"Life is too short to hold grudges. When the doctors first found the tumor on my brain, I thought I was going to die. All I could do was pray that it wasn't cancerous. When the biopsy came back cancer free, I thanked the Lord for answering my prayers. The healing process was a long and painful journey, but deep down, I always believed that I would make a full recovery. The difficulties that I faced as an adolescent paled in comparison to the challenges that I faced with my health. Even though I hated getting picked on, I was just so grateful to be alive. If the Lord could give me a second chance, then the least I can do is give you a second chance too."

Brenda spent the remainder of the session sipping soda with Michael and reminiscing about the past. Listening to Michael speak about his experiences touched Brenda deeply and helped her put her own problems into perspective. Maybe things were not as bad as they seemed. Her present reality was daunting and often quite unbearable, but it was not hopeless. She could create her own destiny and dictate the terms upon which she would live her life. If she wasn't happy, then she needed to do something about it. She had many more years ahead of her, and she had no intention of living them out in misery. For the time being, she would work within the constrictions of her life. She wasn't ready to give up on Joseph yet, nor was she ready to throw in the towel and abandon her career. If she could persevere a little bit longer, perhaps things would get better and change. However, if they did not, then she herself would have to change. If the time came where she could no longer bear it, she would simply cut her losses and move on to the next phase of her life.

CHAPTER 7

Over time, a person could adjust to nearly anything, but try as she might, Brenda could not adjust to the bad behavior of her students. It was her responsibility to prepare the children for the math FCAT, but because of their reluctance to comply with the rules, teaching had become virtually impossible. Had the administration given her free reign, she would have suspended all of the troublemakers in her class. However, as it was, the school district mandated that she first enforce other interventions and write a referral only as a last resort. Since approximately 90 percent of her students had behavioral issues, Brenda was forced to stay late every night, documenting the various episodes of bad behavior displayed by the students in her class. Essentially, recording these incidents became like a part-time job for which she was neither appreciated nor compensated. Unfortunately, there was no way around this procedure. Before an administrator accepted a referral, the teacher was required to submit extensive documentation that included dates, interventions taken, and the outcomes of the interventions. Had only a handful of students misbehaved, the process would have been far more manageable. However, in Brenda's case, the majority, not the minority, were constantly in trouble.

Accurately maintaining this amount of paperwork required a high level of organization. To keep the files organized, Brenda housed her paperwork in a binder and constantly revisited it whenever she needed to update her notes. Teaching frequently came to a complete standstill so that Brenda could document bad behavior as it was occurring in real time. Every free moment was an opportunity to fine-tune her notes and further elaborate on each of the incidents. Over time, the binder became an appendage, an extension of her body that followed her to the most unusual of destinations. She took it with her to meetings, the teachers' lounge, and, on more than one occasion, the bathroom. If she suddenly remembered a particular detail, she would rush to jot it down. It was of the utmost importance that she be meticulous with her documentation. Without it, she could never justify writing so many referrals. Her grand plan was to have every troublemaker removed from her classroom and punished with suspension or, better yet, expelled from the school. Once these children were removed, harmony would be restored, and the remaining children would finally be able to learn. The creation of such a glorious utopia was a tantalizing thought but, in reality, an unattainable fantasy. One Friday afternoon, Brenda happened to mention her plan to Mr. Brown, who was one of the veteran teachers on the Gulls team, and much to her dismay, he neither praised nor commended her for her efforts. Instead, he rewarded her diligence with scathing sarcasm and a lengthy lecture that included a harsh reality check.

"That's a terrible plan! The last thing that you want to do is write too many referrals."

"But I've documented everything! How can an administrator refuse to process a referral if a teacher has extensive documentation?"

"How can you expect an administrator to process over one hundred referrals in a single month? Who has that kind of time?"

"If I can stay late every single night compiling the documentation, then my administrator can stay late processing the referrals."

"How do you think it looks to an administrator when a teacher spends the majority of his or her time dealing with discipline? I'm going to tell you right now what your administrator is going to say. She's going to want to know why you can't manage your students. If she sees how much time you've been spending documenting behavior, she'll naturally assume that teaching has fallen by the wayside."

"But you know what kind of children I'm forced to deal with! Everybody knows! How can I teach children who don't want to learn? Within a forty-five-minute period, I average about eight minutes of actual teaching. It's not even eight consecutive minutes! It's a minute here or a minute there when, by the grace of God, the class happens to quiet down. My entire class period is spent yelling and breaking up fights. Who can teach under conditions such as these? I need to get rid of the troublemakers so that I can teach the few who actually want to learn."

"You can do whatever you want, but I've been in your shoes before, and I can tell you right now that you're playing with fire.

The administrators will support you to an extent, but they'll cover their own asses first before they cover yours."

"What the hell is that supposed to mean?"

"It means that just as writing too many referrals reflects poorly on you, processing too many referrals reflects poorly on them."

"What difference does it make how many referrals they process?"

"Just as you have to answer to an administrator, the administrators have to answer to the principal, and the principal has to answer to the district. Since all referrals are processed electronically, the district is immediately notified when a referral is written. If too many referrals are coming out of a school, it raises a red flag that the school has lost control of their student population. Lack of control suggests a decline in student learning, which in turn will result in the plummeting of FCAT scores. No principal wants a surprise visit from the district because of excessive referral writing. Therefore, the principal sets a quota, and the administrators are forbidden to exceed it."

"I can't believe this! If I can't write referrals, then I can't suspend students. And if I can't suspend students, then all my time will be spent dealing with behavior. Nobody's going to learn anything! Everyone is going to end up failing my class!"

"Actually, that's another bad idea. I strongly advise that no matter how poorly they do, you don't fail any of your students."

"What! You expect me to pass students who disrespect me on a daily basis, never come prepared, never do their work, and spend the entire class period misbehaving?"

"That's exactly what I'm saying. Make no mistake—punitive measures will be taken against you if you fail your students."

"What! Why do I get penalized for their refusal to do the work?"

"Aren't the majority of your students on an IEP?"

"On a what?"

"On an Individual Educational Plan."

"What's that?"

"It's a plan tailored to meet the needs of the individual child. For example, if a child is struggling in the area of math, the plan will list strategies that will help the child meet his or her educational goals. Also, the plan discusses behavioral issues and any handicaps that the child may have. However, an IEP not only strives to improve a child academically but also safeguards him or her against failure."

"So let me get this straight. If one of my students has an IEP but chronically misbehaves and refuses to do the work, I still have to pass him or her and promote him or her to the next grade?"

"That's exactly what you have to do."

"I can't believe what I'm hearing! Not only can I not punish a student with a referral, but now I have to go against my ethics and pass a student regardless of his or her performance? What's happened to the educational system in this country? It's a complete joke! Now I understand why their behavior is so out of control. These children are untouchable! We're completely at their mercy, and they know it! Why are teachers held accountable for everything? Why is there no accountability on the part of the children or their parents?"

"I understand your frustration, but you must remember that the laws in this country are created by nonteaching people who think that they know how to educate students better than the teachers. Ever since the 1983 *Nation at Risk* report was published, government involvement has metastasized, and their mission has been to find a way to improve education in this country."

"I vaguely remember learning about this report in college, but I'm ashamed to admit that I never actually read it. What exactly did it say?"

"In short, the report concluded that the United States was once an unchallenged preeminence in the areas of commerce, industry, science, and technological innovation but has since been overtaken by competitors around the world. By now, I'm sure that you've noticed how much the curriculum design has changed since we were in school. The new set of skills that students will need for the future goes well beyond the curriculum that was taught in the last century. Students need a deeper knowledge of trends in science and technology in order to be globally competitive. To achieve this, the United States has created its own educational response to globalization with a curriculum that involves critical thinking and expectations that include making a hundred percent proficiency in the areas of math, science, and reading by the year 2014."

"Is that even possible? Do you really think that every single student in this country will meet the requirements by 2014?"

"Of course not! After teaching for over two decades, I've come to the conclusion that there are four components necessary to a child's success. If even one of these components is missing, it's unlikely that the child will succeed."

"Four components? I can only think of three components necessary to a child's success. First and foremost, the child needs to want it. If the child is unwilling to work hard and strive for success, failure is inevitable. Then there's the support of the parents and, lastly, the performance of the teacher."

"What about community support?"

"Why do we need community support?"

"Take a look around you. Look at where your children come from. Where can they go if they need help? Now imagine for a moment that you work in a wealthy neighborhood. Imagine that you teach in a school by the Intercostal Waterway, where the majority of people live in mansions and have a yacht floating in front of their homes. Children from affluent neighborhoods have access to the best schools, libraries, and museums. Furthermore, if a child from a wealthy family struggles, parents are able to pay for a tutor. Who helps your students if they struggle? Their parents can't afford tutors! Everything is against the children of the poor, and statistics have shown that the vast majority won't even graduate from high school."

"So what do you propose that I do? The children are against me, the administration is against me, and now you're telling me that the government is against me. Should I just sit idly by and allow my students to become a statistic, or is there some sort of a loophole in the system?"

"You can't change the system, but you can implement other methods to meet the criteria set by the NCLB. Didn't you mention earlier that a few of your students have a desire to learn?"

"I have a handful in every class who try their very best each and every day. They come to school prepared, and they always want to sit at the front of the class. They never give me any problems, and they even help out by trying to encourage the bad children to settle down."

"Here's a thought. Why don't you create an after-school study group for those children who want to learn? They'll have the benefit of one-on-one instruction with a teacher, and you'll increase the likelihood of making gains on the FCAT."

"I honestly don't have the energy to stay after school to help these children. As it is, I have to stay late every night just to stay afloat with my paperwork. If I tutor after school, I'll fall behind with everything else. There just aren't enough hours in the day to get everything done."

"Well, that was one idea. If you're unwilling to tutor after school, then you'll need to find a way to get their behavior under control."

"How can I do that if I can't write a referral?"

"You need to start being more creative with your disciplinary methods. There are ways to minimize bad behavior without writing a referral. Just be careful that you don't do anything that borders on child abuse."

"I would never physically assault a child!"

"Physical assault is only one type of abuse."

"What other kinds of abuse are there?"

"I can remember a situation not too far back where a science teacher had an unruly student who refused to settle down. Like you, the teacher carefully documented the bad behavior and implemented all of the interventions. Nothing the teacher did could control the child's behavior, and one day, the teacher just snapped. He removed the child from his classroom and left him next door in the science storage area all by himself."

"What's abusive about that?"

"Well, he did more than just leave him alone in the room. He found an old animal cage and locked the child inside for the duration of the period. Surprisingly, he almost got away with it. Apparently, the child liked being locked in the cage and never complained to his parents. The only reason that the teacher got caught was because of his own negligence. One Friday afternoon, he forgot to let the child out of the cage after class was over, and the child's parents called the school when the child didn't come home. The child was eventually found later that evening by the janitor, who promptly reported the incident to the principal."

"What happened to the science teacher?"

"What do you think happened? He was fired on the spot!"

"I certainly don't condone what the teacher did, but I can understand what drove him to do it. These children will push you to the edge, and at some point, you just reach a breaking point."

"You're not allowed to have a breaking point in this profession. It only takes one mistake to destroy your entire career. The teacher who locked the child in the cage has permanently stained his record and will never be able to teach again."

"I don't deny the severity of the situation, but it just seems to me that the punishment was very one-sided. The teacher tried to work within the constraints of the educational system, and the system failed him. His methods were certainly deplorable, but why wasn't the child's behavior ever addressed by the administration? Doesn't it seem strange that the child enjoyed being locked in a cage for hours at a time? I'm not a doctor, but it seems to me that there was something mentally wrong with the child. Maybe he couldn't handle the stress of sitting in a classroom. Maybe he was happiest when he was in a solitary state."

"So what you're saying is that the teacher should have been rewarded rather than punished for his actions?"

"Don't twist my words around! You know that's not what I'm saying! What I'm saying is that the child may have had some psychological issues. Was he ever tested for mental illness? Were his parents ever made aware of his phobia of other children?"

"I don't know, but I'm sure that the child had an IEP. The teacher knew what he was dealing with and should have handled this particular child with care. What he did was inexcusable and completely unacceptable."

"Again with the IEP! It's like a get-out-of-jail-free card for a child! So long as they're on an IEP, nothing can touch them! If this child had mental issues, he should never have been mainstreamed! He should have been placed in a special classroom that was more conducive to his needs. Don't you see that the administration was setting the teacher up for failure?"

"We can continue to argue, or you can wake up and face the cold, hard facts. Like it or not, this is the way things are. You have two choices: you can either adapt or leave the profession. Who do you think you are anyway? Do you think that you can just walk in here and change things? Do you think that you can succeed where all others have failed? You're just a first-year teacher who knows absolutely nothing about the inner workings of the educational system! Let me guess—you selected this school because you thought that you could make a difference. Am I right? Did I hit the nail on the head? Well, rip the halo off your head and chop the wings off your back! Nobody appreciates a goddamn thing you do, least of all the children! You're here to do a job, and that job is to churn out numbers. Don't you understand that children are not looked upon as human beings? They're nothing more than walking test scores who either make or break a school's reputation. Many first-year teachers are terminated because they refuse to fall in line and teach to the test. Working conditions have become so unbearable that most teachers burn out and quit before they even reach their fifth year of teaching. If you're going to have any kind of longevity in this profession, you better smarten up and get with the program!"

CHAPTER 8

Brenda felt completely derailed after her conversation with Mr. Brown. Just when she thought she had come up with a brilliant plan, she hit yet another bump in the road. Now what was she going to do? She would have to revamp her entire strategy and find some alternative method to deal with her disciplinary issues. She would still write some referrals but not as many as originally intended. She would have to be more selective and write referrals for only her most badly behaved children. But what would she do about the rest? She could follow Mr. Brown's advice and start thinking outside of the box. There were bound to be other ways to discipline children that bordered on neither the abusive nor the illegal. However, deviating from the disciplinary matrix could result in serious consequences. At the very least, following the matrix safeguarded Brenda from any backlash. So long as she adhered to the matrix's guidelines, the administration was compelled to back her up. If she pursued nonprescribed methods of discipline, would the administration still back her up? The more she thought about it, the more reluctant she was to deviate from the administration's methods. After debating the issue from every angle, Brenda decided to stick to her original plan. She was unwilling to take the risk of suffering the administration's wrath and decided that the best thing to do was to revisit the matrix.

Brenda took the matrix out of her binder and began to thumb through it. She had examined it countless times before, but this time, she would concentrate on the intricacies of the plan. Perhaps she had overlooked something critical. The disciplinary matrix was a long-winded legal document and, therefore, was tedious to read. However, Brenda read it. She read all of it, and for good measure, she read it in full a second time. Yet even after combing over it twice, she was none the wiser. She had reverted back to it so many times that she had practically memorized it. At the beginning of the school year, Brenda had mocked the matrix and had scoffed at the idea of ever having to use it. However, within the course of only a few short weeks, she had completely changed her tune. She had become a fervent believer in it and had implemented every iota of information faithfully. The matrix was a bible for behavior, and in it were the ten interventions—otherwise known as the ten commandments—of discipline. Brenda had religiously incorporated the laws of this document into her everyday life and was reluctant to become blasphemous by following the advice of Mr. Brown. Out of the ten interventions, there had to be at least one that would have some significant impact on student behavior. As she looked over the document for what seemed like the hundredth time, Brenda concluded that calling parents would probably prove most effective in helping to improve behavior in her classroom.

Although somewhat effective, calling parents was Brenda's least favorite intervention. As a matter of fact, she hated this intervention more than all of the other interventions combined. For one thing, most parents couldn't be reached before five o'clock. If she called before then, she stood the chance of reaching a child who would almost always slam the phone down in her ear. Secondly, most of the phone numbers were disconnected. By now, Brenda had a better understanding of the population of people she was working with and understood that the reason phone numbers didn't work was because people didn't pay their phone bills. Most of her students' parents were living below poverty level and either worked minimum-wage jobs or simply didn't work at all. Just as Brenda's students received a free breakfast and lunch, their parents received a free handout from the government. Although the government provided sustenance in the form of food stamps and welfare checks, it failed to provide the most important thing of all: education about how to manage money. Brenda's students were not the only ones lacking in mathematical skills. Their parents were even less versed in basic computation and, as a result, lacked the ability to live on a budget. Although the money they received was but a pittance, it was sufficient to cover smaller necessities, such as the phone bill. They were spending money that was intended for living expenses elsewhere, and it didn't take long for Brenda to solve the mystery as to where the money was going. In fact, she needed only to look as far as her students. All Twin Palms Middle School students were required to wear the mandated navy-blue shirt with khaki pants, but accessorizing was left up to the individual child. Brenda noticed that the boys often wore expensive brand-name sneakers, and the girls wore elaborate weaves and carried couture bags filled with expensive cosmetics. Also, every one of her students owned a cell phone—not an outdated phone like hers, but a phone equipped with the latest technologies. If they could afford luxuries such as these, then why couldn't they afford to buy pencils and notebooks for school? Why was it her responsibility to buy their school supplies while their parents spent money on frivolous things?

It enraged Brenda to see her students so bedizened when she herself was forced to go without. She worked for a living but still scrimped to make ends meet. She couldn't afford to waste money on her appearance even though her graying hair was in desperate need of coloring and her chipped nails were in dire need of a manicure. She would have liked nothing more than to pamper herself with a day of beauty but simply could not justify spending the money. She had expenses to think of— namely her wedding, which was looming just over the horizon. Her conscience would not allow her to squander a single cent, save for her one cherished night of roller-skating. Her lesson had come late in life, but she had finally learned to live frugally. Unfortunately, most people were not like her. Most people never learned to economize and continued to spend well beyond their means. All around her, people were sinking deeper and deeper into debt, living only for today and never giving any thought to tomorrow.

From time to time, Brenda did manage to get through and speak to a child's parent or guardian. On those rare occasions when someone actually picked up the phone, she never knew what to expect. It wasn't easy to call a parent to complain about his or her child's behavior. After all, she was essentially blaming the parent for being a derelict and not fulfilling his or her parental responsibilities. Therefore, she was careful to handle the matter delicately. To avoid confrontation, Brenda developed a technique to discuss behavioral issues without implying that the parent was at fault. It was a sandwich technique where Brenda began the conversation by stating one of the child's strengths, continued the conversation by addressing the problem, and ended the conversation on a positive note by stating another one of the child's strengths. Brenda hated to do this little song and dance, but she had to say something nice if she was going to get the parents on her side. If she acknowledged the good as well as the bad, then maybe the parents would support her and discipline their children at home.

The technique worked most of the time, but there were occasions when it seriously backfired in her face. Some parents were closed-minded and didn't want to hear anything negative about their children. They refused to take responsibility and often became defensive when accused of parental neglect. How could Brenda say such terrible things about their children? They never misbehaved at home! Why would their little darlings act up at school? Surely, Brenda had somehow perpetrated the bad behavior. Such naïveté on the part of the parents always astonished Brenda, but she remained polite nevertheless. She calmly listened to their ranting and raving, but in the end, she always held her ground. After all, she spent more time with their children than they did. Unlike many of the parents, she took the time to get to know these kids on a personal level. The people Brenda spoke with on the phone might have had biological ties to their children, but few had actually earned the right to be called parents. If anything, Brenda and the other teachers who taught their children were closer to being their parents than the people who were actually related to them by blood.

Yet a small percentage of parents did take an interest in their children's education and were not ashamed to admit that they had lost control. These were the conversations that made Brenda grateful she was only the teacher and not the parent of a particular child. No matter how badly a child behaved, Brenda was obligated to deal with the bad behavior for only one hour a day five days a week. Parents, on the other hand, had no such luck. Theirs was an ongoing struggle, one that occurred on a daily basis and only intensified with each passing year. Some fought the good fight up until the child turned eighteen and left home, but many others conceded to the bad behavior and allowed their children to do whatever they pleased without restraint. Brenda couldn't help but feel sorry for these parents. She believed them when they said they had done the best they could. Raising children in this day and age was no easy feat. A parent could do everything by the book, but outside influences could still cause a child to turn out badly. Brenda felt moved when parents cried to her over the phone and beseeched her for help. She felt especially sympathetic toward parents who openly confessed to being afraid of their own children. Like teachers, parents needed to handle their children with care. Children knew their rights and knew how to pick up the phone and call the police. Illegal immigrants were especially careful to not push their children too far. The last thing they needed was for their children to report them to the INS, leading them to be deported back to their own country.

Brenda could certainly relate to the fear felt by the parents of her students. She herself had learned early on to not antagonize these children and was ever fearful for her own safety. This paranoia followed her into the classroom and even subtly crept into her teaching methods. For one thing, Brenda refused to write on the board. It took only a split second for all hell to break loose, and she could not risk turning her back and taking her eyes off of her students for even a single moment. Instead, she favored using an overhead projector, which allowed her to face forward and keep one eye on the class while keeping the other eye on the machine. Even turning her back to answer the classroom telephone could lead to catastrophic consequences. When the phone rang, she elected to walk backward rather than forward, all the while blindly tapping around her desk until she felt the familiar form of the phone. Unfortunately, there were a few unavoidable instances when she couldn't help but turn her back to her students. But even then, she was still watching. She had learned to grow eyes in the back of her head and could sense when a student was about to misbehave. Yet for all her alertness, some students still managed to get under her radar. The tiny spitballs that Brenda spent many a planning period picking out of her hair provided evidence of this.

A child's continued bad behavior was somewhat condonable if a parent tried his or her best and failed, but it was completely unacceptable if a parent didn't try at all. The way that some parents spoke about their children struck Brenda as completely heartless. She knew better than anyone how difficult a child could be, but it never occurred to her to give up on any of her students. As much as they pushed her—and God knew that they pushed—she never belittled or berated any of them. Despite everything, she still believed that every child had the potential to succeed. At times, even her worst students surprised her with a correct answer or an intuitive question. These sudden sparks of intelligence validated what Brenda had known all along: these children were not intellectually barren; they were just in need of love and were lashing out for lack of attention. They needed an outlet for their pain, and speaking to her was one of the many ways that they would unburden their souls. Brenda would listen in silence and offer the occasional tissue, but rarely did she ever offer advice. It was presumptuous to think that she had the answers to their problems. Besides, she suspected that advice was not what they were searching for. They were just looking for someone who cared and who was willing to take the time to listen.

However, not all children were willing to disclose the intimate details of their home lives. Brenda would occasionally get tidbits from her students, but she didn't really see the full picture until she spoke to the parents. It sickened her to hear how some parents spoke about their own children. It was as if they were completely destitute of all maternal and paternal feelings. Whenever Brenda complained about behavior, parents often resorted to calling their children losers or idiots. Calling home rarely provided the parental support that she yearned for, but at least it gave her a glimpse into the home lives of her students. Communicating with both students and parents helped Brenda gain a better understanding of why children behaved the way they did. As much as she disliked making these calls, she couldn't deny being fascinated by the things that she heard. She was astonished at the way people lived their lives and how little they cared for their own children. Brenda, having been raised in a loving and supportive environment, could not relate. Her parents had nurtured her from the day she was born and had made it their priority to be involved in every aspect of her life. Sadly, many of her students lacked this level of stability. Most of her students came from extended families where new branches were always sprouting out of the family tree, and much to her horror, old branches would occasionally overlap. Children who came from these families were nothing more than an encumbrance to the adults who habitually walked in and out of their lives. Yet no matter how dismal the circumstances, Brenda refused to give up. She had to keep calling until she found somebody who cared.

Late one Tuesday afternoon, Brenda set her focus on a child from one of these families. She had called the little boy's mother numerous times only to be told that her son was Brenda's problem during school hours and would eventually become the government's problem once he turned eighteen. However, Brenda did not discourage easily and decided to pursue another avenue and talk directly to the child instead.

"John, I'm very disappointed with your performance in my class. I think that we need to have a discussion about your behavior."

"Man, yo' trippin'!"

"Well, let's take a look at the facts. You refuse to do the work, and you're constantly out of your seat. And although I've repeatedly reminded you, I haven't seen any improvement in your behavior. I've called your mother, but she seems unwilling to cooperate. I think that it's time we gave your father a call."

"Which father?"

"What do you mean which father?"

"Well, my real daddy in da pen for murder. I ain't got his digits, but I gots Bob's digits."

"Who's Bob?"

"Bob da man dat my mama livin' wit now. Bob's da bomb 'cause he don't beat me like Jim use to!"

"Who's Jim?"

"Jim wuz Mama's ole boyfriend. They hook up at da club and got shitfaced. Mama brought him to da crib, and he dug dat hole out. After dat, he ain't wanna bounce. He ain't got no job and be chillin' on da couch. When I gets home, I gotta be quiet or Jim get angry and beat da shit out of me."

"Your mother actually let this man beat you? Why didn't she call the police and have him arrested?"

"She call the po-po, but they ain't tryin' to hear dat shit. We got to steppin' and move in with Tom. Tom ain't a chump like Jim. He be ballin'!"

"All right, that's enough. I don't want to hear anymore. None of the men that you just described qualifies as a suitable father figure."

"True dat! They all a bunch o' cocksuckers!"

"I think we need to end this conversation right now. I'll see you tomorrow in class."

"Okay. Holla at yo' lata, shawty!"

Since the conversation had taken place during Brenda's planning period, she had a few minutes to reflect on what had just happened. She couldn't get over how this boy had taken inventory of his mother's lovers with such dull indifference. To him, there was nothing abnormal or indecent about her behavior. Although he clearly disliked some of the men, he had never mentioned feeling neglected or unloved. His entire life had been lived in the shadow of his mother's sexual escapades, and over time, her lewd and licentious behavior had become a commonplace occurrence in his life. Because he had never known anything else, it had never occurred to him to question the fairness of his fate. Brenda slumped into her chair and wondered what she should do. Speaking with this child was the one thing that she shouldn't have done. She should have stuck to the matrix and just called the parents instead. The last thing she wanted to do was get involved with the personal lives of her students. She just couldn't emotionally stomach the things she heard. Try as she might, she could never fully detach herself from the suffering of these children. Their misfortunes penetrated her soul and left her feeling depressed and drained at the end of every school day. For the sake of her emotional well-being, she had to pull away. She needed to build a barrier between her and her students or else she wouldn't be able to do her job.

So Brenda hardened herself and continued to make the necessary calls. She tried to keep the conversations professional and discouraged parents and children from becoming too personal. After a while, it dawned on her that she could make her calls during class time rather than wait until the end of the day. If by chance she was able to reach a parent, the child would be readily available to explain his actions over the phone while his fellow classmates looked on. The more she thought about it, the more she realized that this was the answer to all of her problems. Her students hated talking to their parents on the phone. Brenda would watch with guiltless delight as children took the phone and made pitiful attempts to defend their position to their parents. She grinned as the children squirmed and stuttered while their parents screamed at them over the phone. Knowing full well that their classmates were watching, some of the children tried to hide their distress by turning their backs to the class or attempting to conceal their emotions by covering their faces with their hands. Sometimes a conversation would become so overheated that a child would suddenly begin to cry. In Brenda's opinion, this was by far the best thing that could possibly happen. Crying was unacceptable at the middle-school level, and children were teased mercilessly if they broke down in tears. This tactic might have been cruel, but it was also extremely effective. The child in question usually learned his or her lesson, and the rest of the class learned it too. Instinctively, Brenda knew that what she was doing was probably wrong, but she was willing to take the risk. She had finally hit upon something that worked, and she was going to continue to do it until somebody told her not to.

However, this strategy was not foolproof and had unforeseen consequences. One Monday afternoon, as Brenda was teaching algebra to her third-period class, she had to stop multiple times to correct the behavior of one little boy. The student's name was Austin, and he was by far one of Brenda's most challenging students. Since her conversation with Mr. Brown, Brenda had decided to study all of her students' IEPs. Most of the IEPs were two, maybe three pages long; however, Austin's IEP resembled a miniature packet and had the thickness of a small book. This child had every problem imaginable and was severely below grade level in both reading and math. It would take nothing short of a miracle for Austin to make gains on the FCAT, but still, Brenda refused to give up. She tried everything she could think of to pacify him, but nothing seemed to work. If she nagged him about his behavior, he would scream and bang his head against the wall. If she tried to threaten him with an intervention, he would counterattack by threatening her life.

Brenda was at her wit's end with Austin and decided enough was enough. She stopped teaching midlesson, took out her phone log, and dialed his father's number. Much to her surprise, the number actually worked, and Austin's father picked up the phone.

"This is Ms. Connor, calling from Twin Palms Middle School. I have your son Austin sitting in my class right now behaving very badly and disrupting my lesson. I've asked him to settle down numerous times, but he refuses to listen. When I threatened him with an intervention, he threatened to kill me. I could really use your help in this matter. I would really appreciate it if you could punish him when he gets home."

"Oh, I can do better than that!"

This was the only thing Austin's father had to say and then he hung up the phone. Brenda, on the other hand, still had much more to say and wished that he had stayed on the line long enough to talk to his son. Still, it seemed that he disapproved of his son's behavior and would take steps to ameliorate the situation at home. Since the conversation was over, Brenda didn't think any more about it and resumed teaching her class. After she finished teaching the lesson, she had her students begin the classwork activity. She maneuvered her way up and down the aisles, looking over students' shoulders and stopping occasionally to correct papers and answer questions. She was so engrossed with helping her students that she didn't notice when a stranger walked into her room. It wasn't until a child started screaming that Brenda turned around to see what was going on. As soon as she turned around, she realized that Austin was the one making all of the commotion. The stranger had taken him by the collar and lifted him into the air and was in the process of shaking him frantically.

"Who are you, and what in God's name are you doing to that child?"

"Don't you remember? You just called me a few minutes ago, complaining about my son's behavior."

"You're Austin's father?"

"That's right! I'm here to make sure that Austin never acts up in your class again."

"I appreciate your support, but you can't just barge in and interrupt my class. You need to discipline Austin at home."

"I think that it would be far more effective if I disciplined him right here in full view of his classmates."

Before Brenda could intervene, Austin's father grabbed her yardstick from the board and began beating his son brutally in front of the entire class. The man was powerful, and she could hear her yardstick crack every time it hit the boy's behind. He beat his son vehemently and would not desist even when Austin cried out for mercy. Brenda knew that she had to do something. She needed to call security or, better yet, call the police. However, she could not bring herself to pick up the phone. Watching Austin get beaten gave her a sinister satisfaction. This beating was retribution for the countless times he had misbehaved in her class. It might have been vicious and perhaps even excessive, but it was also long overdue. An entire class of students had missed out on an education because one boy refused to follow the rules. Brenda had tried to work within the behavioral guidelines of the educational system, but the system had gotten her nowhere. However, Austin's father appeared to have a system of his own. His system did not involve the implementation of multiple interventions and hours of endless documentation. His was a more concise, less complicated, more effective system. At one point, Brenda heard Austin cry out to her for help. The pain in his voice tugged at her heart, and for a brief moment, she felt compelled to help him. However, at the last minute, she reconsidered. If she stopped this punishment now, Austin would just revert back to his old ways and continue misbehaving in her class. For the first time, real progress was taking place, and she would not interrupt the beating, no matter how difficult it was to watch. Therefore, she turned her back to him and tried to focus her attention on the rest of the class. She looked at her students and saw that they were watching the scene. They saw what could happen when a child disrespected a teacher and, hopefully, would think twice before making the same mistake.

The beating came to an abrupt end when Brenda's yardstick snapped in half. Austin's father apologized for breaking the ruler and even offered to reimburse her for the damage. However, Brenda wouldn't hear of it. The loss of one yardstick was a small price to pay for a year's worth of good behavior. After the beating was over, she instructed Austin to take his seat and thanked his father for handling the situation.

"It was my pleasure. I don't think that you'll have any more problems with Austin, but if you do, please feel free to call me anytime."

After Austin's father left, Austin, still shaken with fear, returned to his desk and whimpered in his seat. The other students, stricken with shock, took to murmuring among themselves. At that moment, regret began to kick in. Brenda realized that news of this beating would most likely spread throughout the entire school. Although she herself had not been a participant, she would nevertheless be found guilty of standing idly by while a child had been physically assaulted. There was a good chance that this momentary lapse in judgment would result in a meeting with her administrator. But was she really at fault? Who was she to tell a parent how to discipline his or her child? She hadn't asked the father to come to the school. He had come of his own accord and had handled the situation as he had seen fit. The way she saw it, the beating had been a parental decision in which she'd had no right to intervene. If she got in trouble, this argument would be her alibi. If this excuse didn't fly, then she would play dumb and feign ignorance. Whatever happened, Brenda wasn't going to waste her time worrying about it. For now, she was going to revel in the moment and celebrate her victory.

CHAPTER 9

Even though teaching in and of itself was a miserable and ungratifying job, Brenda had to admit that the profession had some excellent perks. During her training week, she had received a folder full of important handouts, one of which was a schedule for the school year. This page listed the calendars for the months of August through June and used a coloring system to highlight days of special importance. Yellow represented days off, orange represented planning days, and blue represented half days. Schools also shut down for extended periods of time during holidays, such as Thanksgiving, Christmas, and Easter, and teachers enjoyed a paid summer vacation that lasted approximately eight weeks. When the time off was added together, a teacher worked approximately nine months of the year or, to be exact, 196 calendar days.

No other profession could compare to teaching when it came to time off. In addition to the school-mandated holidays, teachers were also able to accrue sick and personal time. Teachers earned four days of sick leave on their first day of employment and continued to accrue sick leave throughout the school year, amounting to one day each month. Teachers were also granted six personal days to use whenever and however they wished.

Brenda couldn't believe the number of days that she had off! She was still in contact with many of her friends from college, and nobody had it as good as she did. Most of her friends worked at jobs that observed only six holidays a year and offered only two weeks of vacation. In comparison, she was far better off. She worked fewer days and still received her full salary. She was even paid for summer vacation. How wonderful was that? While everyone else had to work through the summer, she would get paid to sleep in late and lounge by the pool. No matter how you sliced it or diced it, this was an ideal work situation. It made the job slightly more bearable and gave teachers the necessary downtime to recuperate and recharge.

However, the one drawback was that a shortage of days made it that much more difficult to keep up with the curriculum map. As it was, the schedule was already aggressive, and whoever had designed it had neglected to take unexpected circumstances into consideration. The map dictated that Brenda should teach a new topic every day, test students twice a week, and reserve certain days for projects and computer time. The rigidity of the schedule made it impossible for anyone to keep up. After a while, even the most efficient teachers fell behind. The schedule was highly unrealistic because it failed to block out time for unexpected events and neglected to take into account that class time would occasionally be needed for assemblies, book fairs, and field trips. And what about the weather? This was Florida, and hurricanes could knock out the power and shut a school down for days. And what if someone got sick? If teachers missed a few days of school, the administration instructed them to spiral back and teach the material when they had the spare time. But who had time to spare? Class time always passed by quickly, and it flew by when a teacher had to deal with issues of discipline. Brenda loved having so much time off but would have gladly sacrificed a few of her precious days in exchange for a chance to keep current with the curriculum.

According to the school calendar, the first of these color-coded days was a planning day. It was technically a working day, but to Brenda, it was exactly the same as having a day off. She still had to come to work and put in her time, but she would be able to do so in a child-free environment. Brenda was ecstatic when her first planning day rolled around. It came on a Friday, which was an excellent way to end the week. On that Friday morning, she treated herself to a few extra minutes of sleep and an extra long shower. She picked out a navy suit to wear but then quickly came to her senses and placed it back in her closet. Who was she getting dressed up for? Nobody was coming to her class today! For once, she could wear whatever she wanted. She decided to fish out a pair of skating pants from the dryer and wear them with her old college sweatshirt. As she looked at herself in the mirror, it occurred to her that this was the first time she had ever dressed down for work. Some teachers made a habit of dressing down every day, but Brenda felt that dressing casually set a poor example for the children. In order to be regarded with respect, a teacher needed to dress the part. Still, it felt good to be out of her ill-fitting clothes. It felt liberating to wear whatever she wanted without fretting over how disheveled she looked.

The drive to work was also surprisingly pleasant. Brenda usually dreaded the morning commute, but not that day. She wasn't particularly upset when an accident blocked two of the three lanes on the highway, nor was she peeved at how long it took the tow truck to move the cars out of the way. While others around her cursed and shook their fists, she sat patiently in her car and listened to one of her books on tape. Usually a situation like this would have stressed her out, but not that day. It didn't matter if she was a few minutes late to work. There were no meetings scheduled for 8:00 a.m. and no students arriving at 8:45 a.m. She still had to make her presence known by signing in at the front desk of the main office, but it was unlikely that anyone would notice her walking in a few minutes late. Brenda felt so confident she wouldn't get caught that she even decided to stop at one of the local fast-food restaurants for breakfast. She wasn't so bold as to eat in, but she was willing to risk a few minutes to go through the drive-through and order her favorite value meal, complete with a large, hot coffee drenched with extra cream.

When Brenda arrived at work, she was shocked to discover that the entire parking lot was empty. She laughed at herself for feeling guilty about sleeping in late and stopping to buy breakfast. It was obvious to her that nobody was going to be on time that day. As she scanned the empty parking lot, she regretted not sleeping in longer. She thought it absolutely scandalous to arrive thirty minutes late to work, but it seemed that her coworkers were willing to push the envelope even further. Brenda wondered just how far people were willing to go. Would they dare come to work an hour or even two hours late? If other people were willing to throw caution to the wind, then more power to them, but she was willing to go only so far. There were cameras everywhere, and they were strategically placed in every hallway of the school. The administration took great pains to know what everybody was doing every minute of the day, and the security guards kept their eyes glued closely to the surveillance footage. Micromanagement was the name of the game, and she was careful to not fall victim to the administration's traps.

Brenda quickly got over her regret once she realized that she had her choice of parking spaces. She usually parked in the most remote location to prevent her car from getting vandalized by the children, but today there were no children. She had absolutely nothing to fear and parked in the space closest to the main entrance. How wonderful it felt to not have to walk through the grass and all the way around the building! It felt even more wonderful to walk blissfully in peace. On regular school days, walking through the faculty parking lot was a lot like walking through a battlefield. Every morning, an array of lewd hand gestures—or sometimes just a single finger—greeted Brenda. She would keep her head down and walk quickly, but she still couldn't dodge the filth flying out of her students' mouths. Even when she tried to be inconspicuous, she would still get pelted by a string of obscenities. What a treat it was to finally be able to walk at a casual pace, unabashed by students, and with her head proudly held high!

When Brenda walked into her classroom, she felt surprisingly calm. On most days, she felt frazzled, never quite knowing what to do first. However, today she could take her time and carefully plan out her agenda. She turned on the lights and took a moment to look at her unsullied classroom. Everything was in order, and for once, it would stay that way. She wouldn't have to clean the class during her planning period and again at the end of the school day. There would be no books to pick up off the floor or boards to erase. She wouldn't have to sweep up sunflower seeds and paper balls, nor would she have to scrape gum and candy off the walls and desks. For once, her classroom would remain in immaculate condition for the duration of the day.

Brenda walked over to her desk but faltered momentarily before she sat down. She first had to perform her daily ritual of checking for thumbtacks and other sharp objects that students might have left on her chair. Her students were mischievous and were always on the hunt for new and creative ways to spook her. The first time they had gotten her was with a whoopee cushion. They had placed it on her chair while she was at the door, watching the hallway during the class change. When she sat down to take the attendance, the whoopee cushion deflated with a comical agony, and the entire class broke out into laughter. Brenda wasn't especially angry over this prank. After all, she hadn't been an angel either as a child. She had been notorious for her skills with a rubber band and had shot many a teacher in the back of the head when they least expected it. Unfortunately, her students were always pulling pranks on her. Brenda found signs of their handiwork all around her work area. They wrapped her pencils and pens in worms and rearranged the papers on her desk. Sometimes they filled her drawers with roaches and geckos and slimed the handles with glue. What disturbed Brenda the most was their tendency toward teamwork. Her students were surprisingly organized and worked together to pull off many of these stunts. One time, she forgot to hide her coffee, and one of her students snatched it when she turned her back. The child placed the coffee in his bag, quietly waited for dismissal, and then took the coffee to the bathroom, where he proceeded to urinate in it. He then handed the coffee off to a child who was in the class right after his. At the start of the next period, the second child walked over to her desk and returned the coffee to its original location. As soon as Brenda picked up the cup, the children giggled in unison. Their failure to resist laughter allowed her to thwart a nearly disastrous situation, and she hastily disposed of the tainted coffee and was cautious to hide all things edible thereafter.

However, today there would be no need for her to hide her coffee. She would be able to place it on top of her desk instead of hiding it away in her bottom drawer. It was a rare treat to be able to sit at her desk at this hour of the day and enjoy a cup of coffee. Brenda was never able to sit at her desk when she had a classroom full of children. Even when her students were testing, she still had to keep a watchful eye. When she was a child, teachers had handed out the exam, and the students had dutifully completed it. However, this was not the case with her students. Because so many of the children refused to do homework or study for exams, most came unprepared on testing days and expected Brenda to take their tests for them. They would cleave to her and refuse to let go until she helped them solve the problems. If she refused to help, they would throw a fit and blatantly refuse to take the test. Some of her students even went so far as to spit on the test, crumple it into a paper ball, and throw it back in her face.

However, the students were not the only ones who suffered on testing days. Brenda also paid dearly for their lack of preparation. After all, she was the one who had to grade their papers, and because there were no multiple-choice questions on the tests, students needed to work the problems out and show the steps that they used to find the solution. She encouraged her students to show their work so that she could at least issue partial credit if their answer was incorrect. However, most of her students rarely ever made the effort. They would randomly make things up and turn a thirty-minute testing period into a complete waste of time. As if this weren't bad enough, she was also required to test for higher-order skills. Certain questions required students to write a short narrative explaining how they had arrived at their answers. Brenda dreaded reading these short responses, because she could not understand their writing. She was amazed to discover that her students wrote exactly as they spoke. Their responses were barely legible and were littered with slang and incorrectly spelled words. Still, she tried desperately to not fail them. Mr. Brown had warned her to pass all of her students regardless of their performance in her class. However, Brenda could not bring herself to just give out good grades to students who didn't deserve them. She wanted her students to take pride in their work. She wanted them to earn their grades and not walk around with a sense of entitlement. She helped them in every possible way, including giving them twenty points of extra credit on every exam. She purposely made the extra-credit questions easy in order to boost their self-esteem. Yet for all her efforts, failure was usually the final outcome.

Brenda peeked into her maroon workbag and cringed at how many packets of exams she had to grade. She was aghast at how far she had fallen behind with her paperwork. It was not like her to procrastinate, but at the moment, her personal life required her immediate attention. Her impending wedding was causing her great duress, and although she did everything she could to cut corners, she couldn't manage to stay within a budget. It also didn't help that her fiancé wanted the best of everything. She loved Joseph dearly but had never hated him more than at this particular junction of her life. She couldn't believe the things that he was asking for! He wanted ice sculptures, fancy linens, and a honeymoon that was equivalent to three months' salary. At some point, they had reversed roles; he had become the demanding bride, and she had become the parsimonious groom. They fought constantly over the most trivial details and rarely ever reached an agreement. At times, the fighting became so ugly that they would separate for days at a time. Their latest blowout had been over the guest list. The majority of the guests were relatives from his side of the family, and Brenda had attended enough family weddings to know that many of these people would not leave an appropriate gift. She had begged him to trim the list, but he had outright refused. His refusal had resulted in an outburst in which she'd accused his family of being a bunch of freeloaders and stated that nobody was going to get a free ride on her dime. She had made these remarks in the heat of the moment, but the damage had been done. The fight had taken place three weeks ago, but he still hadn't forgiven her. No matter how often she called, he refused to pick up the phone and left her wondering if they were still even engaged.

As Brenda sat at her desk, inhaling the aroma of her coffee, she recalled her argument with Joseph and began to cry. Her emotions overwhelmed her at the most inopportune times, and once the waterworks started, there was no way she could stop crying. Thank goodness she was all alone! Just to be on the safe side, she closed the blinds and turned off the lights. She didn't want people to see her in such a fragile state, and she certainly didn't want anyone asking questions. Brenda might have been young and somewhat naive, but the one thing she understood was human nature. By now, she had made a few enemies and knew they could use the details of her private life as ammunition to destroy her career. There was little loyalty or decency, only discord and dissension, among the employees. However hard it might be, she needed to find a way to keep it together. People would likely mistake her pain for weakness, and this was not an environment in which she could afford to show vulnerability.

After wiping away the last of her tears, Brenda picked up the first packet and took out a red marker. Without the interruption of her students, it was likely that she would be able to finish grading the exams and input all of the grades before the end of the day. Mr. Brown's words echoed once again in Brenda's mind, and she was careful to use her red marker sparingly. To avoid failing her students, she had to be extremely lenient with her grading. If a child wrote something that even remotely resembled the right answer, she gave full credit. However, it wasn't always easy for her to overlook their mistakes. Many of her students were careless and sloppy with their work. They placed decimal points incorrectly, left off percentage signs, and rarely reduced fractions. Yet despite these oversights, she inflated every grade and passed every single student. It sickened her to do this, but what other choice did she have? Teachers everywhere had to accept the corrupt politics of the educational system and participate in this mockery if they wanted to keep their jobs.

Gifted and Montessori students, however, were the exceptions to the rule. These children's parents—otherwise known as helicopter parents—closely inspected every graded assignment and immediately picked up on the minutest of mistakes. Whereas the parents of Brenda's students cared too little, the parents of Montessori and Gifted children cared too much. They nitpicked over every detail and were involved in every aspect of their children's education. These were the parents who volunteered their time to help in their child's classroom and who aided with supervision in the cafeteria. They attended all of the sporting events and chaperoned every field trip. Many of these parents were part of the upper echelon of society, and Brenda often saw fashionably dressed mothers picking up their children from the bus loop in Jaguars and Porsches. Their appearance and mode of transportation led her to believe that many of these mothers probably didn't work for a living. They had all the free time in the world, and they chose to spend it by aggravating the people who taught their children. Yet for all their intrusiveness, teachers had to tolerate their behavior. After all, the children of these parents kept the school afloat by making gains on the FCAT.

There were challenges that came along with working with every level of child, and every teacher was forced to pick his or her poison. Traditional teachers, such as Brenda, were plagued with bad behavior and low grades but unobtrusive parents. Montessori and Gifted teachers basked in high scores and good behavior but dreaded parental involvement. As hard as she had it with her students, Brenda felt that she had the better end of the deal. Low-level children who were at the bottom of the barrel would most likely go up. They were far more likely to make gains than their higher-scoring counterparts. If a child was already at the top, how much higher could he or she possibly go? If anything, it was more likely that child would drop. Brenda taught one advanced class, and this was the class that stressed her out the most. Would her high-level students be able to make the necessary gains, or would their scores plummet? Brenda also worried about the natural drop that occurred in FCAT scores when students entered middle school. It was a well-known fact that the FCAT grading system in middle school differed significantly from the FCAT grading system in elementary school. In elementary school, the grading system was far more lenient and, as a result, inflated student test scores. In middle school, the system was more demanding, which in turn caused many students to experience an automatic drop once they entered the sixth grade. Therefore, students had to work harder and be more knowledgeable just to maintain their scores from the previous year.

Not all of the tests Brenda graded were ones she'd created. Some were assessment tests that the district had developed. Children were periodically tested throughout the course of the year on specific areas, otherwise known as strands. In math, students were tested on five strands: number sense, geometry, algebra, measurement, and probability. These exams were always multiple choice and were graded with a scanning machine. Once a paper was graded, the machine registered the grade and electronically sent it to a database that anyone with clearance could access. Assessment exams provided valuable information to both teachers and administrators. They showed children's strengths and weaknesses and revealed trends in overall student understanding. However, assessment exams were not always accurate—at least not with Brenda's students. She noticed that since the exams were multiple choice, the children didn't make much of an effort to work out the problems. They treated assessment exams exactly the same way they treated her exams: they barely read the questions and used little, if any, logic to work out the solutions. Although assessment exams were not counted as part of a child's grade, they still needed to be taken seriously. Brenda constantly stressed the importance of assessment exams and begged her students to do their best, but as usual, they didn't give a damn. Instead of working out the problems or at least attempting to make educational guesses, most of her students used the bubbles to make pictures. They strategically shaded bubbles to create boats, animals, and various other things. Brenda had heard teachers lamenting over the way students "Christmas treed" assessment tests, but she hadn't actually believed this to be true until she saw it happen in her own class. And when she saw it, a horrific thought entered her mind: if they made pictures out of their assessment exams, then it was likely they would also make pictures out of their FCAT exams.

Once Brenda had entered all of her grades, she needed to go to the copy room to make copies for her administrator. Copies of grades needed to be on file in case a parent ever came back at a later time to complain. This was more of a necessity for the Gifted and Montessori teachers, but school policy dictated that all teachers observe the procedure. Since every teacher was required to do this and today was the last day to get grades in, the line at the copy machine wound in a serpentine fashion around the corridor and went halfway around the building. Brenda sighed with disgust as she saw the long line of people standing in front of her and was infuriated that the school had only one copy machine. Actually, there was one other copy machine in the school; however, it was reserved for the Montessori and Gifted teachers only. Brenda couldn't understand why the second machine wasn't made accessible to all of the teachers. Why were Traditional teachers looked upon as being so lowly? She pondered the unfairness of the situation and suddenly realized that segregation existed not only among the teachers but also among the students. It was a well-known fact that the school considered Traditional students inferior to the Montessori and Gifted students. And because they were considered inferior, the school separated them in every possible way. They weren't permitted to intermingle with Brenda's students in the 900 hallway but were instead cloistered away in a better section of the school. A noticeable separation existed even in the cafeteria. Brenda's students were forced to eat their lunches indoors in subzero temperatures while their Montessori and Gifted counterparts enjoyed their lunches outside on the warm patio. Even the higher-level children's educational materials were superior. They didn't need to make do with broken computers and a shortage of textbooks. Everything was at their disposal, and the Traditional teachers quickly took notice of these unfair advantages. Interestingly, the administration took no initiative to conceal the blatant discrimination that took place at the school. It was simply the way things were done. High-scoring students received preferential treatment and were looked upon as an investment that needed nurturing in order to yield high FCAT scores. Brenda's students, on the other hand, were viewed as a crippling loss. They were the excess refuse who contributed little and, in return, received almost nothing. They had to accede to whatever substandard resources were offered to them and had no choice but to willingly accept their second-rate status.

After waiting for what seemed like hours, Brenda finally got her turn at the copy machine. She quickly made her copies and then returned to her classroom to check her grades one last time. Once teachers finalized their grades, there was no going back. Brenda went into the grading software and began to scroll slowly through her grades. She made sure every student had a minimum of eighteen grades and double-checked each student's final grade. As she did this, she accidentally hit a combination of keys that caused the computer to freeze up. Brenda gasped out loud when she saw the screen turn blank. What was she going to do now? It had taken her over three hours to enter these grades! Would she have to start all over again? Was there any way to retrieve the grades? Where could she go to fix her computer?

At this moment, she remembered Mr. Gold. He had left an excellent impression on her during the planning week with his detailed handouts and easy-to-follow trainings. He was currently the school's IT specialist but had originally started out as a teacher. Although he was no longer a teacher, the spirit of teaching had never left him. He had a way of explaining complicated computer language so that even a layman could understand. Brenda was never afraid to ask Mr. Gold for help. She knew that he would never ridicule her, no matter how stupid the question. He was a patient and kind man who didn't mind explaining things multiple times. Brenda had approached him in the past with various computer-related issues, and he had fixed the problem every time. Her current situation was worse than anything she had ever dealt with before, but perhaps he could come to her rescue again. Maybe it wasn't too late to breathe life back into her computer and resurrect her missing grades.

Brenda nestled her computer in her arms as if it were a sick child and ran toward Mr. Gold's office. It was nearly five o'clock, and people were beginning to leave. Her heart was palpitating with the fear that he wouldn't be there; however, when she arrived at his office, she was relieved to discover that he had not yet left for the day. He greeted her with his usual Cheshire-like smile and gently pried the computer out of her arms. He had seen her in a state of panic before and took a moment to reassure her that everything would be okay. As he began diagnosing her computer, Brenda took a seat in the corner and watched with awe as he worked his magic. He placed her computer on what she affectionately called his "operating table" and plugged various wires in her computer. She had absolutely no idea what he was doing, but she enjoyed watching him work nevertheless. It was truly a gift and a rare privilege to be allowed admittance into the genius of this man's mind. After merely ten minutes, Mr. Gold stepped aside and proudly proclaimed that he had successfully corrected the problem. Brenda, who had run into his office holding her breath with anticipation, let out a sigh of relief when her computer turned back on. Words could not express the relief she felt when she saw her grades suddenly reappear on the screen. She not only thanked but also hugged Mr. Gold for a job well done. Her reaction might have seemed overly dramatic, but she didn't care. Her computer was fixed, and now she could finalize her grades and go home.

Chapter 10

Brenda had few things to look forward to during the course of her day, but one thing that never failed to brighten her spirits was her planning period. She was fortunate to have a planning period that fell right in the middle of the day. Other teachers were not so lucky. For instance, the elective teachers had their planning during first period, and the eighth-grade teachers had to wait until the last period. Teaching classes back-to-back was exhausting work, and Brenda was grateful to have been assigned a schedule that spaced her breaks evenly throughout the day. She cherished her forty-five minutes of uninterrupted time and hung on anxiously each day until it arrived. For one period a day, children became a mere afterthought and administrators desisted from their dictatorial control and retired quietly to their offices. Brenda whimsically wished that every period could be a planning period. However, reality dictated that it could not be so; therefore, Brenda made do with what little she was afforded and savored every free moment she had.

Without a shadow of a doubt, Brenda wholeheartedly believed that no one could take this time away from her. According to the union rules, the planning period was one of two protected periods of the day when a teacher could use the allotted time for class preparation or, instead, as a period of relief. At times like this, Brenda was thankful to be a member of the union. She was grateful for their existence and for the principles upon which they were based. It was difficult for her to see the fifty-dollar deduction for union dues in her biweekly paycheck, but she felt that membership was well worth the expense. It gave her peace of mind to know that the union would be there to defend her rights during the turbulent times and safeguard her job should her relationship with the administration ever become calamitous.

Brenda was astonished when she was called in for a meeting one Wednesday afternoon during her planning period. Actually, she wasn't the only teacher required to attend. A general announcement was made over the intercom, requesting the attendance of all the Gull and Mockingbird teachers. As Brenda exited her classroom, she happened to run into Mr. Morrison, who was in the process of locking his door.

"Mr. Morrison, why have we all been summoned to the administration office?"

"Probably because we're in some kind of trouble."

"Really? What kind of trouble?"

"I don't know. I imagine that it has something to do with the behavior of the children."

"But student behavior has always been a problem. Why is the administration making a point of addressing it now?"

"Ms. Connor, try not to get yourself overly worked up. It was only a guess. I have no idea what this meeting is in reference to."

"Well, what I don't understand is how they can call a meeting during our planning period. I thought that our planning and lunch were duty-free periods. I thought that the union handbook specifically stated that these periods were to be used at our own discretion and were not to be infringed upon by the administration."

"You're absolutely right, Ms. Connor. The administration is most certainly in violation of the union contract. Why don't you go ahead and file a grievance?"

"That sounds like an excellent idea! What will happen after I file a grievance?"

"Absolutely nothing."

"What do you mean that nothing will happen? Wouldn't the union follow through with an investigation or, at the very least, issue a consequence?"

"Sure they will. Then when they're finished, they'll promote you to a higher position and double your salary."

"You don't need to be so cynical, Mr. Morrison. I'm just saying that the administration is in the wrong and should be dealt with accordingly. Shouldn't someone inform the union of this outrage? Wouldn't they want to take action against this offense?"

"Ms. Connor, allow me to explain to you how things work. Once you file a grievance, the union will notify the party that's at fault and will then issue a warning. Once the offending party is notified, the union's job is done."

"That's it? All they get is a verbal warning? What's to stop them from doing it again?"

"Absolutely nothing. Don't you understand? This is not a democracy but a dictatorship where the administration ultimately has the final say. If you file a grievance, you will only bring negative attention upon yourself. You will be labeled as a complainer and be targeted as a troublemaker. Do you really want to get on the administration's bad side? If I were you, I'd just keep my mouth shut, slap a smile on my face, and put on the pretense of a team player."

"How can you stand there and be so dismissive? As employees, we have rights, and we should be protected when those rights have been violated. Your rights have been violated too! We should file a grievance together! Better yet, all of the teachers should come together as a united front and file a grievance as a group! Then the union will be forced to take action!"

"Ms. Connor, you need to learn to pick your battles. The union is extremely limited in their capacity to protect the employees. The entire county has only eight union representatives who oversee a total of three hundred schools. Our union representative alone has to manage thirty-six schools all by himself. Do you really think that he has the time to give your case any serious consideration? You better think again! If you're lucky, he might drop by and visit the school. Once or twice a year, he makes a pilgrimage to each of the schools in his jurisdiction and sets up shop for the day in the teachers' lounge. He comes peddling his union paraphernalia and tries to convince nonmembers to join. Perhaps you could confront him then with all of your concerns. It's unlikely that you'll be granted an audience, but at the very least, you'll walk away with a free calendar and some nifty new pens."

"I can't believe what I'm hearing! What's the point of joining the union if their only concern is to collect dues? What the hell am I paying for? They deduct one hundred dollars every single month from my paycheck! If they're as useless as you say, I should discontinue my membership and pocket the extra money!"

"I wouldn't do that if I were you, Ms. Connor. As useless as the union may seem, they still provide a certain level of protection. Just remember, you're employed in a right-to-work state. You could be fired at a moment's notice and would have no legal rights in the eyes of the law. And because you're a new employee, you face the greatest risk of all of losing your job. According to the union handbook, a new employee has to go through various probationary periods before he or she can become a tenured teacher. First, you have to complete the ninety-seven-day probationary period. Once you've completed that, termination becomes slightly more difficult because detailed documentation must first be recorded and assistance must first be provided. At the end of each year, you'll be given an evaluation by your administrator that will judge you on eleven different performance areas. You must earn a 'Satisfactory' rating in every one of these areas in order to successfully pass your evaluation. If you earn a 'Needs Improvement' or 'Unsatisfactory' rating in even one of these areas, you'll automatically be terminated. If you receive satisfactory evaluations for three years in a row, then you'll be awarded a professional services contract."

"So what you're saying is that I need to hang on for three years before I can expect any kind of job security. If I receive satisfactory evaluations during my first three years of employment, then I'll become tenured, and the union will guarantee that my job will be protected for the remainder of my career."

"Theoretically, that's how it's supposed to work, but unfortunately, the times have changed. Because of standardized testing, a teacher's job is no longer secure. If your students score below the required expectations, you can be sure that the administration will find a way to circumvent the union contract and go after your job. And it's not just the administration who's going after teachers' jobs. The government has also started targeting teachers. Our state representatives want to eliminate tenure altogether and place teachers on a year-to-year contract. This means that if you have even one bad year where your students score poorly on the FCAT, you could be terminated on the spot. If all this isn't bad enough, teacher salaries have also been attacked. We used to follow a step salary schedule that guaranteed minimal raises each year and significant raises on certain key years. However, as of recently, teachers' salaries have been frozen. No teacher has received a raise of any kind for the last three years! To make matters worse, the state wants to eliminate the step salary schedule altogether and base compensation purely on test scores. This means that teachers who fail to meet the expectations not only will be denied raises but also could very well see deductions in their overall salary."

"How can the union allow this to happen? They're not doing anything to protect the employees! The teachers should take matters into their own hands and strike! Every single teacher in the state should stand up and fight for their rights!"

"That's a novel idea, but you seem to have forgotten where you work. This is Florida, and it's not an employee-friendly state. Have you read the union handbook lately? Read it and you'll see that teachers who unite together with the intention of striking are immediately terminated."

As Mr. Morrison continued to complain about the union and gripe about the misfortunes of being a Floridian, Brenda found herself passing by Ms. Spencer's class. The voice over the intercom had specifically requested the presence of all Gull and Mockingbird teachers, but the reading teachers were exempt from attending the meeting. They were required to teach during their planning period and could not leave their rooms unless coverage was provided. It suddenly occurred to Brenda that the reading teachers never enjoyed a duty-free planning period. Here she was complaining about the loss of one planning period, not realizing that the reading teachers lost their planning period every single day. She glimpsed into Ms. Spencer's room and saw her huddled in her usual corner, stricken with fear while the *A* class took control over her classroom. Brenda's heart went out to Ms. Spencer. It was sheer misery to teach this class for just one period a day. How could anyone survive this hell for two periods in a row? Yet the teachers who were forced to forgo their planning periods never protested. They too were members of the union and well within their rights to complain, but they never uttered a single word. For fear of losing their jobs, they chose to remain silent. No one dared to rise up and fight against the administration. Not one single person was willing to set the example and speak up. Brenda would have gladly spoken up, but she couldn't afford to lose her job either. If anything, she needed to be on her best behavior. She had successfully completed the first phase of her probationary period, but she wasn't out of the woods yet. She still had her year-end evaluation to worry about and then two more years after that.

Mr. Morrison and Brenda were the last to arrive and joined the other teachers in the lobby of the administration office. The voice over the intercom hadn't specified where they were supposed to go, so they waited patiently for someone to come get them. After about ten minutes, the head security guard, Mr. Davenport, appeared and motioned for the teachers to follow him. Brenda wondered where Mr. Davenport was taking them. She always dreaded coming into this building and wished that she could return to the safety of her classroom. However, she followed the other teachers and found it strange when Mr. Davenport led them toward the copy room. Was this meeting about paperwork? Were they here to make copies? Perhaps Brenda had been too quick to expect the worst. Maybe everything was going to be all right after all.

Unfortunately, Mr. Davenport bypassed the copy room and turned instead into a side room. Brenda had passed this room countless times before and had assumed it was a closet used to house janitorial supplies. However, when Mr. Davenport unlocked the door, she was amazed to discover that the room served an entirely different purpose. Apparently, this was the surveillance room, and twenty-four monitors were turned on, each showing live footage of various sections of the school. Since the room was so small, the teachers had to squeeze together in order for everyone to fit inside. Since Brenda was one of the shortest teachers, she got a spot in the front row. From where she was standing, she had an excellent view and used the opportunity to examine each of the monitors individually.

Brenda carefully viewed the monitors one by one, taking note of the places being filmed. She had worked at the school long enough to know where all of the cameras where located but had always wondered if there were a few strategically hidden. It was a well-known fact that employees forfeited their rights to privacy the moment they stepped foot on school property. However, cameras were only one way to violate a teacher's privacy. The administration could also go through a teacher's classroom as well as his or her personal belongings. This was a practice that Brenda could personally attest to. Not long ago, she had stayed late one night to reorganize her classroom closet. Since the lights in her room had been shut off and the door had been locked, it had appeared as if she'd left for the day. Although she had been in the closet with the door shut behind her, she had still been able to hear people entering the room. She had heard their laughter, and despite the barrier that existed between them, their voices had been audible enough for her to easily follow their entire conversation.

"It looks like she left for the day. Let's take a look around and see what we can find."

"Take a look at this! The whole drawer is full of candy! Isn't her ass fat enough already? I think I'll leave her the phone number for Weight Watchers before I leave."

"Oh my God! Look at what's in this other drawer! Is that a dead lizard? Are these dead roaches? Oh shit! Some of them are still alive! How can somebody be this disgusting?"

"Look at the bottom drawer! She has two coffee cups down here. Somebody needs to tell her that this isn't a trash can!"

"Check this out! The dumb bitch forgot to take her purse and workbag home. Why don't we take a look inside?"

Brenda had been confined to that dark closet for almost an hour, sitting on the cold floor and praying in earnest that nobody would find her hiding inside. She had listened helplessly as her assistant principal, a security guard, and the school principal had mercilessly mocked her character and brazenly invaded her privacy. She had never felt so violated in her life. To her face, they had always behaved politely, but now, not realizing that she was there, they had let down their guard and shown their true colors. Everything that they had said and done was offensive and extremely hurtful. Brenda had wanted nothing more than to jump out of the closet and catch them in the act. She had wanted to see the looks on their faces and gloat as they stammered and stuttered their apologies. However, she had never left her spot. She had never even flinched, for fear that someone would hear her. Nothing would have been gained by making her presence known. Besides, there had been another benefit to remaining silent. It had given her an opportunity to hear how they really felt about her. Judging by their comments, Brenda had realized that these people thought very little of her. This realization struck fear into her heart. She needed these people to like her or, at the very least, respect her. She needed their help and support with the children, but more importantly, she needed them to give her a satisfactory evaluation so that she could pass her probation. If she'd sprung out of the closet and accused them of misconduct, there was no doubt in her mind that she would have gotten fired on the spot.

After the infringement upon her classroom, Brenda had taken inventory of all her personal belongings. She had made up her mind that everything that was not necessary for student learning needed to go and had packed up her makeup, her perfume, and even her hair clips. She had also packed up the few personal items sitting on top of her desk. She had one small plant, a picture of her family, and a few knickknacks that she had bought at the beginning of the school year. After cleaning out her desk, she had moved on to her workbag and purse. Her workbag was devoid of any personal items, but her purse was an entirely different matter. She had money, credit cards, and over-the-counter medications. Brenda had shaken her head as she debated what to keep and what to discard. In the end, she'd decided to not throw anything away. The solution had been obvious: she would stop bringing her purse into the classroom and instead keep it locked safely away in the trunk of her car.

Brenda had felt relieved after removing everything from her classroom. There was no telling when the administrators would make another late-night appearance, but at least now she would be ready. There was nothing incriminating left in her classroom. She had packed up and taken home everything that was questionable. However, Brenda knew that the administrators had other ways of catching the employees, and one of those ways was the surveillance footage. But now she had the upper hand. She had been given a personal invitation to enter the surveillance room and had been offered a front-row seat to examine what was being taped. She wasn't especially interested in the monitors that showed the hallways or parking lot. She wanted to see if cameras had been placed in certain sections of the school. Had they set up cameras in the classrooms? Were there cameras in the teachers' lounge or in the faculty bathrooms? To Brenda's relief, none of the monitors showed footage in those areas. It seemed that most of the focus was on the entrances and exits of the building. Brenda also couldn't help noticing that none of the monitors provided sound. This was a godsend since she sometimes forgot about the cameras and gossiped with other teachers in the hallway. After surveying the footage, Brenda still couldn't figure out why she and the other teachers had been brought into this room. However, if they were indeed in some kind of trouble, she logically deduced that it was because of something that had been seen and not because of something that had been heard.

As Brenda studied the monitors, Mr. Davenport slid a videotape into a VCR. After hitting the rewind button, he turned around and proceeded to explain the purpose of the meeting.

"As you all know, we have had an ongoing problem with student behavior. We have an especially difficult group of sixth graders this year, and the administration has been overwhelmed with issues of discipline. The administrators and I have done everything in our power to support you, but it's ultimately your responsibility to keep the students in line. As you will soon see, most of you have fallen short in the area of behavioral management. As teachers, you need to enforce the rules and issue the appropriate consequences when those rules have been broken. You're here today to view surveillance footage taken from the sixth-grade hallways. The tape that you're about to watch shows your students walking from the cafeteria back to their classrooms."

So that was why a meeting had been called—to admonish and berate them for something that was completely out of their control. Brenda looked at her fellow colleagues and noted their sudden discomfort. Some fidgeted nervously, while others tried to move away from the monitors and make their way toward the back of the room. Two of the teachers refused to be shamed in front of their peers and left the room without even asking for permission. However, Brenda had an entirely different take on the situation and couldn't wait to see the footage. After all, she had the privilege of walking the *E* class to and from the cafeteria every day. Walking that class was nothing less than a pleasure. Her students always walked quietly and obediently in a single-file line. She could hardly wait for Mr. Davenport to play the tape. Let everyone see how well her students behaved! Let them marvel at her superior behavioral-management skills and praise her for a job well done!

The only things missing from the meeting were the popcorn and stadium seating. Brenda felt as if she were at the theater, impatiently waiting for the movie to begin. Just when she felt she could no longer wait, Mr. Davenport finally pressed Play on the VCR. The first teacher to appear on the tape was Mr. Morrison, who was escorting the *A* class down the 900 hallway. Brenda saw Mr. Morrison's face drop when Mr. Davenport pointed out the boisterous behavior and commented on his lack of control. Directly following Mr. Morrison was Mr. Fisher, and although his class behaved slightly better, he still received a rancorous review. Mr. Davenport continued on, ridiculing each teacher individually, solely focusing on everybody's faults. As Brenda watched the monitor, she suddenly detected a noticeable pattern in the footage. Whenever the classes walked through the cafeteria, they did so in an orderly manner because the security guards were standing nearby to assist with dismissal. However, as soon as the classes exited the cafeteria, the teachers were left on their own to handle the children. And since everybody was dismissed at exactly the same time, lines mixed together, and teachers struggled to keep their students apart. In Brenda's mind, the lack of student control was not the teachers' fault but the administration's. If the administration would stagger the dismissal by letting only one class out at a time, teachers could concentrate on their own students and avoid interference from the other classes.

Another problem that Brenda quickly detected was the lack of security in the hallways. It wasn't necessary to post the security guards in the cafeteria. Every perimeter of the cafeteria was already secured with ample coverage. Three administrators and three office employees were stationed inside and were more than capable of controlling the children. All of the security guards should have been posted outside, evenly dispersed from the cafeteria to the 900 hallway. As far as Brenda was concerned, Mr. Davenport had no right to blame the teachers. What exactly did he expect them to do? Ten teachers were left all alone to manage nearly three hundred children, most of whom were poorly behaved and unresponsive to discipline. The last thing that the teachers cared about was the appearance of their lines. All they cared about was getting the students safely back into their classrooms and avoiding the possibility of a fight breaking out.

As Brenda watched the footage, Mr. Davenport suddenly paused the VCR and addressed the teachers with the following question: "Can anyone tell me what the children are doing right here?"

As Mr. Davenport stepped aside, everybody in the room leaned in to see the image that was frozen on the screen. Even though Brenda was right up front, she couldn't quite make out what was going on. To her, it seemed as if the children were playing some kind of a game. It almost appeared as if they were playing leapfrog. This was a game that she herself had played as a child. It was an innocent game in which one child sat in a squatted position while another child jumped over the squatted child like a frog. However, the children on the video were not doing any type of jumping. Since Brenda and the other teachers appeared to be confused, Mr. Davenport hit the Play button so that everybody could see exactly what was going on.

Once the tape began to play, Brenda quickly realized that the children were not playing leap frog at all. They were mimicking a sexual activity known as tea bagging. One child would either squat or lie flat on his back with a wide-open mouth while another child hovered over and dangled his private parts in the first child's mouth. Brenda couldn't believe what she was seeing! Were her eyes deceiving her, or were these sixth graders actually engaging in a sexual activity practiced by adults? As far as Brenda could see, they were only going through the motions. At the very least, it was a relief to see that pants remained zipped and body parts remained concealed. However, the footage was still disturbing. Why were these children doing this, and where had they learned it? Brenda understood that children of this age were going through puberty, and she realized that their bodies were changing, but this was still unacceptable behavior. And the fact that they did it out in the open, in full view of anyone who passed by, made it that much more reprehensible. However, this was not the most disturbing part of the footage. Even more disturbing was the complete and utter disregard from the teachers. Nobody made an effort to stop the children. A few teachers took notice but satisfied their curiosity with a cursory glance and then just walked on by. Brenda didn't see herself on the tape, nor did she recall the incident. Had she personally witnessed the situation, she would definitely have interceded and put a stop to such unscrupulous behavior.

But could she have stopped it even if she had seen it? Would the children have listened to her, or would they have ignored her and continued with their carnal behavior? The surveillance footage was certainly shocking, but it wasn't the first time Brenda had seen her students behave immorally. Lewd and lascivious behavior was an everyday occurrence in her classroom. Not a single day went by when she didn't confiscate notes from her students that went into great detail about their sexual escapades. Some children didn't even bother writing notes. Many spoke openly about their experiences right in front of her and didn't even care that she was listening. Brenda didn't need to see the surveillance footage to know that many of her students were sexually active. She had personally witnessed conversations about their sexual conquests on several occasions. As a matter of fact, a conversation of a graphic nature had taken place on that same day between two girls in her second-period class.

"I been fuckin' my boyfriend three months, but I keep catchin' him lookin' at other bitches."

"Dat 'cause you pussy ain't tight! You gotta let him fuck yo' up the ass!"

"Ain't dat gonna hurt?"

"Hell yeah! It gonna hurt like a mothafucker! But it only gonna hurt the first time. After dat, it gonna feel good! You got lubricant?"

Brenda had been mortified when she'd heard this conversation take place between two of her sixth-grade students.

It was absolutely appalling to hear prepubescent girls speak this frankly about sex. They spoke about anal sex much the same way other people spoke about the weather. What bothered Brenda most of all was the candidness of their conversation. Hadn't they seen her standing right behind them? Why hadn't they at least made an effort to hide what they were saying? They could have concealed their conversation by whispering or at least waited until the class was over. But no! They had shamelessly carried on, debating which techniques were most effective when it came to pleasuring teenage boys. It had been absolutely stupefying to hear young children speak so maturely about sex. As a matter of fact, they knew more about sex than she did! Brenda had listened in awe as the girls listed the pros and cons of various sexual positions and deliberated over the effectiveness of various types of birth control. She had attempted to rebuke the girls, but they had only laughed in her face. As far as they were concerned, she was the abnormal one. To them, she was a relic with antiquated beliefs who was unwilling to fast-forward to the present and let go of the past.

It bothered Brenda tremendously to see such an influx of sexual behavior at the middle-school level. It seemed to her that keeping children pure in this day and age was damn near impossible. Children had access to all forms of technology and were constantly being exposed to images intended for the eyes of adults only. It also didn't help that parents weren't home to monitor what their children were watching. Brenda's students often went home to empty houses and occupied their time by watching television or surfing the Internet. Unfortunately, they also had access to the Internet at school. Brenda dreaded Tuesdays more than any other day of the week because that was the day she was issued the laptop cart. Computers were meant to be used as educational aids but were instead used to surf prohibited sites. The school tried to set up blocks, but the children always managed to find a way to bypass the barriers. Whenever Brenda saw a student on an inappropriate site, she would immediately confiscate the computer. However, since she could not be everywhere at once, some students managed to get under her radar. To compound the problem, the administration was always watching what the children were viewing. If a child was on a pornographic site, Brenda was sure to get a call from her administrator, followed by a harsh warning advising her to be more conscientious of student activity on the computers. After receiving these threatening calls three weeks in a row, Brenda had decided to discontinue laptop usage altogether. Quite frankly, it wasn't worth the aggravation. Her students clearly had no interest in using the laptops for learning. They didn't care that she was the one who got in trouble each time they accessed a forbidden site. Until they learned how to follow the rules, Brenda had decided it was best to revoke their laptop privileges for the remainder of the school year.

Over time, Brenda had become desensitized to the things she saw, and collecting illicit notes and suppressing inappropriate conversations eventually had become a part of her everyday routine. Like it or not, children were going to engage in sexual behavior, and with so many children sexually active already, it was virtually impossible to contain the situation. The children in the surveillance video had gotten caught only because they were out in the open and their actions had been captured on tape. However, most children were not so careless. Like Brenda, the children were cognizant of the cameras and knew exactly which areas were being taped. And the one place where they knew they could hide was in a student bathroom. Children had five minutes in between classes and often congregated in the bathrooms until the last possible minute. The administrators always remembered to check the bathrooms but rarely remembered to check underneath the stalls.

On one particular day, Brenda decided to use the student bathroom during her planning period. Upon entering, she heard a child moaning in one of the stalls. She peeked underneath the door and saw a little girl on her knees, bent over the toilet. *Must have been something she ate,* thought Brenda to herself. The lunch that day had been a lethal combination of boneless ribs and a lump of macaroni plastered together with processed cheese. Brenda suspected that the meal had not agreed with the girl and that she was in the painful process of regurgitating the food. When Brenda heard the little girl gag, she recoiled in disgust. She could tolerate most bodily functions, but she had a serious aversion to vomit. Just the sound of someone retching would make her break out into a cold sweat. And if she saw or smelled vomit, then she would surely begin vomiting herself.

Brenda could have fled the scene and used another bathroom, but she decided to stay and comfort the suffering child through her ordeal. Therefore, she gently knocked on the bathroom door and offered her assistance.

"Are you all right in there? Is there anything I can do to help?"

Instead of receiving an answer, Brenda heard somebody suddenly jump onto the floor. *That's strange,* thought Brenda to herself. The little girl was still on her knees and couldn't have possibly made that sound. Was there somebody else in the stall with her? Brenda knocked on the bathroom door again, this time more aggressively, demanding an explanation. When nobody answered, she got on her knees and looked underneath the door a second time. Her suspicion was immediately confirmed: there were two children in the stall.

"Open the door now, or I'll call security!"

After about ten seconds, the door swung open, and a girl and boy stood before Brenda, dressed only in their undergarments. The little girl was stripped down to her bra, and the boy had his pants wrapped around his ankles, with his penis protruding out of his underwear. Brenda suddenly felt like a fool. The little girl was not sick at all! The moaning, gagging, and kneeling had had nothing to do with vomiting. She had been giving this boy a blowjob! Brenda had not seen the boy initially because he had positioned himself above the girl by standing on top of the toilet. How in the world was she supposed to handle this? What kind of consequence was a teacher supposed to issue for oral sex? Brenda didn't recognize the boy, but the little girl was one of her students from the *E* class. After giving the matter some thought, Brenda decided to handle the situation discreetly. She sent the boy away and took the girl back to her classroom to discuss what had just happened.

"Claudia, I can't believe what I just saw! You're one of my smartest students, and you're always so well behaved. Why would you do something like this?"

"Cuz boys like it when I give 'em head and let 'em cum in my mouth."

"You mean that this isn't your first time?"

"I ain't even gonna front! I been doin' dis since I wuz nine."

"But why? Are you looking for attention? Do you think that this will help you become popular?"

"I already popular, Ms. Connor. I suck dick to get paid!"

"What do you mean that you get paid? Are you accepting money in exchange for sexual favors?"

"Hell yeah! Do ya think I do dis shit fo' free? On da real! I gots to get mines!"

"Well, how much do you charge for your services?"

"Depends on what I gots to do. The meter be runnin' when I gets on my knees."

"Well, how much did you charge that little boy in the bathroom?"

"Five dollars."

"Five dollars!"

"You think I shoulda charge more?"

Brenda had absolutely no idea how to handle this mess. She was reluctant to call home, because Claudia was one of her favorite students. She knew that teachers weren't supposed to show favoritism, but how could she not? Claudia exemplified the perfect student, and children like her were the reason Brenda had gone into the teaching profession. Here was a child who was not only intelligent but also hardworking and respectful. She was insightful and was always quick to challenge Brenda's mind with thought-provoking questions. This was the type of child teachers yearned for—a child who was not only a pleasure to teach but also sure to make gains on the FCAT. Where had things gone wrong in Claudia's life? Were her parents even aware of what she was doing? Did they know that their daughter was prostituting herself for money? Brenda couldn't comprehend how a straight-A student who thought so much of her grades could think so little of herself. She knew that she should contact Claudia's parents, but she couldn't bring herself to do it. She had a fondness for this child and did not want to betray her trust by exposing her shame. Brenda had few students who brought such happiness into her life. Children like Claudia offered a glimmer of hope in a dismal environment that did nothing but propagate despair. Despite the severity of the situation, Brenda decided to keep their conversation confidential. As it was, she had enough misfits to contend with. She couldn't afford to have yet another child misbehaving and falling behind in her class.

In the end, Brenda decided not only to keep the matter private but also to refrain from scolding Claudia. What was the point? There was absolutely nothing she could say or do to change the mind-set of this child. Brenda had seen many disturbing things in the course of her employment, but to date, none had impacted her as much as this one incident involving Claudia. At this point in her career, she was no longer easy to shock, but still, she couldn't help feeling saddened by the way some of her students behaved. She wanted desperately to go back to a time when young people still had values and took great pains to hold on to their virtues. Yet no matter how fervently she hoped, time would continue to move forward and things were never going to change back to the way they once were.

CHAPTER 11

When Mr. Davenport's meeting was over, the teachers filed out of the surveillance room one by one and listlessly returned to their classrooms. The teachers had no time to recover from the ambush; they were forced to choke down their humiliation and go back to work. Brenda checked her watch and realized that the bell was about to ring. The meeting had left her feeling drained and utterly exhausted. Yet as bad as she felt, she could not allow herself to fall apart. She needed to tap into her reserves and find the energy to push through the last two periods of the day. The next class would soon be arriving, and Brenda would be expected to stand in front of her students and teach with her usual vigor. She needed to gather her bearings and find a way to conceal her melancholy from her students. Children were naturally inquisitive and could easily detect the slightest change in a teacher's mood. They could sense when a teacher wasn't feeling up to par, and they would ruthlessly use that moment as an opportunity to strike. A teacher who felt downtrodden never received sympathy from the students. Instead, just the opposite would occur. A teacher with a weakened constitution would have to fight that much harder just to maintain control. Children relentlessly attacked a depressed teacher much the same way a disease attacked a body with a compromised immune system. Continuous attacks of this sort could eventually break a teacher down and ultimately cause a shift in power. Brenda refused to allow this to happen to her. If she forfeited control now, she would end up just like Ms. Spencer—cowering in a corner while her students took dominion over her classroom.

As the teachers walked out of the surveillance room, Brenda made every possible effort to make sure she wasn't the last person out of the room. She wanted to stay close to the other teachers until she was safely out of the building. Although the meeting was over, that did not necessarily mean the scrutinizing was over. Because there was no shortcut or back door, all of the teachers were forced to walk past the offices of the administrators in order to exit the building. Brenda knew that most of the administrators would be sitting in their offices with their doors wide open. The last thing she wanted was for an administrator to notice her and subject her to yet another period of humiliation. Therefore, she needed to find a way to hide herself. She gave this dilemma some thought and decided on a strategy that was used by animals in the wild. She burrowed her way through the crowd of teachers until she found herself directly in the center. By positioning herself this way, she would be more difficult to spot and less likely to be singled out. Her small stature would come in handy yet again, as she would be able to hide behind the taller teachers in case an administrator walked by. Brenda felt that this was a brilliant maneuver on her part. She watched enough Animal Planet to know that predators snatched their prey based on their location in the pack. Animals on the outside were always the first to be picked off. Brenda was confident that as long as she kept up with the group and kept herself concealed, she would make it safely out of the building.

Unfortunately, Brenda was not the only one who watched Animal Planet. The other teachers also felt as if they were prey for the administration and proceeded to walk quickly, all the while pushing their way into the center of the group. Brenda tried to hold her ground, but it was no use. She was no match for the larger and stronger teachers. She fought as hard as she could to hold her place but was eventually thrown out and left open for attack. She tried to catch up to the others but suddenly realized that she was all alone, standing directly outside her administrator's office. She should have made a run for it but couldn't refuse the temptation to look inside. As Brenda surveyed the scene, she made eye contact with her administrator, and much to her dismay, Mrs. Harrison presented her with an invitation to step inside.

"Hello, Ms. Connor! Come on in, and pull up a chair."

"I can't right now. The bell is about to ring, and I have to get back to my classroom."

"This will only take a moment. Come inside, and shut the door behind you."

Brenda hesitated momentarily before she entered Mrs. Harrison's office. Entering this office was analogous to plunging into a frozen lake. She had to first take a deep breath and brace herself before she could enter the room. As she walked inside, she took a minute to study the surroundings. The first thing that caught her eye was the paperwork scattered throughout the room. Next to the principal's office, Mrs. Harrison's office was the largest room in the building. It was so huge that it held not one but two large desks. However, despite the generous furnishings and spaciousness of the room, the majority of Mrs. Harrison's paperwork had spilled onto the floor. Before Brenda sat down, she couldn't help noticing one pile in particular that had been thrown carelessly into a corner of the room. She caught sight of her name and realized that this pile contained all of the referrals she had written since the beginning of the school year. Brenda couldn't help but feel outraged. She had worked so hard to follow the disciplinary matrix and had dutifully implemented all of the interventions. She had spent countless hours editing the notes in her binder so that she could provide the most accurate documentation. She had often wondered why none of her referrals had been processed. Now she had her answer: Mrs. Harrison had never even taken the time to look at them. When Brenda had first placed them in her mailbox, they had been in mint condition. Now they were just a pile of trash. The referrals that she had worked so hard to create were completely ruined. And as far as Brenda could see, her referrals had never even been taken off the floor. Because she couldn't stomach seeing her paperwork strewn all over the floor, she picked up the pile and attempted to place it neatly upon Mrs. Harrison's desk. However, lack of concern and excessive abuse caused the papers to disintegrate in her hands. Countless footprints had left the sheets in tatters, and as a result, the documents were virtually illegible. Upon seeing this, Brenda had a change of heart and decided to just throw the referrals away. It pained her to do this, but what was the point in keeping them? Her assistant principal clearly didn't give a damn, and Brenda couldn't bear to see her precious paperwork rotting away in a corner of Mrs. Harrison's office.

Keeping current with paperwork was a hardship for anyone who worked in the educational field. Even Brenda was guilty of occasionally falling behind. However, she had never in her life witnessed procrastination like this. Mrs. Harrison was in a leadership position and was therefore responsible for setting an example for her staff. How could somebody in such a high position be so slovenly? Why wasn't she held accountable for the piles of unprocessed paperwork currently residing on her floor? Why weren't there consequences for her actions? Why wasn't anyone pulling her into an office and dissecting her shortcomings? Brenda demanded retribution for this neglect! She wanted to take her case to a higher power and file a formal complaint. She wanted to fetch the principal and watch with glee as Mrs. Harrison shrunk under the weight of his interrogation. However, Brenda knew that this would never happen. The principal was probably well aware of the situation and had simply chosen to not acknowledge it. Besides, going over Mrs. Harrison's head was ill advisable. Like it or not, this woman was her direct supervisor. When it came to the hierarchy of the school, Mrs. Harrison was at the top of the food chain, while Brenda lingered somewhere below. The entire situation was incredibly unfair, but what could she do? Mrs. Harrison was unfettered in her power to either make or break Brenda's career, and in order to secure her place at this school, Brenda would have to put her feelings of hatred aside and find a way to gain favor with this woman.

Since her office was in such disarray, it took Mrs. Harrison many minutes to locate the notes she needed to conduct the meeting. In the meantime, Brenda had a few moments to look closely at the woman who, within a few short minutes, would surely tear her apart. Initially, Mrs. Harrison had left a positive impression on Brenda. She had drawn Brenda in with her alluring facade, and Brenda had bought into the belief that Mrs. Harrison's number-one priority was to support her staff. However, her image of this woman had been completely shattered once the people around her had begun to talk. According to the rumor mill, Mrs. Harrison had been a teacher for only three years before receiving a promotion to the position of assistant principal. Now, anyone who worked in the school system knew that competition was fierce for the higher-level positions. Only the most experienced and most educated individuals were selected for these coveted spots. How had Mrs. Harrison secured her job with such minimal qualifications? Had she been selected on merit alone? Had she perhaps been in the right place at the right time? According to the gossip, although she lacked many of the necessary qualifications, she still had a competitive edge. She possessed credentials that no other applicant had, and those credentials had ultimately helped her to land the job.

Brenda had learned early on that privacy was a foreign concept in the public school system, and she was wary to trust anybody in the workplace. The cameras were a constant reminder that she was being watched, and her classroom was fair game for anyone who might walk in. She conversed little with her colleagues and was cautious to speak only about school-related topics. However, Brenda soon discovered that the loss of privacy extended to not only the teachers but also the higher-ups. Whether the administrators liked it or not, their private lives were open for discussion—and the teachers talked! When it came to gossiping about the supervisors, everybody was a willing participant. Whenever Brenda saw a cluster of people whispering, she knew there was gossip in the air. If the people talking were teachers she trusted, she would actively participate and interrupt to ask questions. However, if the gossip came from teachers she distrusted, she would stand by diffidently on the edge of the circle, anxiously trying to hear what they were saying. Either way, she always got the scoop. And it was through the grapevine that Brenda discovered the manner by which Mrs. Harrison had procured her position. She had apparently created quite the scandal at her last school. It seemed that she had engaged in a sexual relationship with the principal and had threatened to expose the affair to his wife. In exchange for her silence, the principal had contacted his friends at the district and requested that she be given preference as soon as an assistant principal position became available. As luck would have it, the first available opening was at Twin Palms Middle School. The situation had worked out perfectly for both parties involved. The principal had been able to save his marriage, and Mrs. Harrison had received a promotion with a significant raise in pay.

And the scandal didn't end there. As Brenda sat across from Mrs. Harrison, she could see that this woman was pregnant. Over the months, her swelling belly had become more difficult to hide, and her protruding shame was out there for the whole world to see. Nobody knew who the father was, but it was common knowledge that her marriage was on the rocks. Although she was well educated and fiercely ambitious, she had made one fatal flaw: marrying a man who was nowhere near her equivalent. Why had she married such a loser? It was an enigma that nobody could explain. This man pulled her down in every imaginable way. It was rumored that he refused to work and had a gambling addiction besides. And as if this weren't bad enough, he was against the use of birth control. They had five children already and were barely able to make ends meet. Her new position brought with it an increase in salary, but the income still wasn't enough to comfortably support a family of seven. And with an eighth person on the way, they would have to pull the purse strings that much tighter.

Mrs. Harrison's relationship struggles got Brenda thinking about the personal problems in her own life. On the plus side, she and Joseph were once again on speaking terms, but they had made little headway with regard to their finances. If anything, their financial situation was worse than ever. They were both still heavily in debt, but Brenda was the only one willing to cut back and make sacrifices. She had finally learned how to manage her money and had even taken a part-time job to expedite the process of paying off her debt. Joseph, on the other hand, had chosen the opposite direction. Within a few short months, he had doubled his debt and had been reduced to borrowing money from family and friends just to stay afloat. Since their engagement, Brenda had gone through a gamut of emotions. At the beginning, she had tried to reason with Joseph. When reasoning didn't work, she had attempted to move him with her tears. When crying didn't work, she had resorted to yelling and screaming. She had done everything short of getting on her knees and begging. In the end, nothing made a difference. Brenda had to accept the harsh reality that nothing would ever curtail this man's spending. She was at the end of her tether and needed to decide whether she wanted to follow through with the marriage or sever the relationship and move on.

Because of her problems with Joseph, Brenda was compelled to feel compassion toward others who struggled with their relationships. Under different circumstances, she would have felt sympathetic toward the discord that existed in Mrs. Harrison's marriage. Yet as she looked upon this woman, all she could feel was contempt. The neglect involving the referrals had been offensive in and of itself, but Mrs. Harrison had committed a crime far more heinous than this. Brenda had not forgotten and could not yet forgive her involvement in the violation of her classroom. She remembered that evening—Mrs. Harrison was the one who had gone through her purse and workbag. The principal and security guard had been content with just looking through her desk, but this woman had taken things a step further. She had crossed the line by going through Brenda's personal things. Could this be the reason Mrs. Harrison had called Brenda into the office? Was Mrs. Harrison going to question her about something she had found in Brenda's classroom that night?

Brenda sat across from Mrs. Harrison, sick with anxiety, waiting with anticipation to hear what this vile woman had to say. All of a sudden, she felt herself become nauseated. This was the first time she had ever been called into an office. She'd had numerous part-time jobs throughout high school and college and had never once gotten into trouble. What could she have possibly done wrong? Was it something serious? Was she going to lose her job? Would today be her last day of work? Just as Brenda was about to start hyperventilating, Mrs. Harrison found her notes and began the meeting.

"How are you doing today, Ms. Connor?"

"Fine."

"I've wanted to talk to you for a long time, but I've been so busy trying to catch up with my paperwork. What did you think of Mr. Davenport's meeting?"

"I thought it was informative."

"Did you have an opportunity to see your class on the footage?"

"No. There wasn't enough time to watch the entire tape."

"Well, Ms. Connor, I saw the tape, and I must say that I'm very concerned with your inability to manage your students."

Inability to manage her students? What the hell was she talking about? Brenda never had a problem managing the *E* class. Although she was ever watchful, the children in that class never misbehaved. She was more concerned about the children from the other classes. Like clockwork, a fight would break out every day right after lunch. Brenda would do her best to keep her students moving, but the children always wanted to stop and watch. And since all of the administrators and security guards were posted inside the cafeteria, the teachers were left on their own to break up the fights. Some of the teachers would try to intervene by throwing themselves in between the quarreling students, but Brenda always kept walking. She was concerned only about the safety of her class, and she took pride in the fact that none of her students had ever gotten hurt.

"I don't understand why you're so concerned. I've never had a problem managing the *E* class. The children always follow my instructions, and to my recollection, a fight has never broken out in that class."

"Well, Ms. Connor, I viewed the tape, and I personally found the footage to be very disturbing."

"I think maybe you've mistaken me for another teacher. I can assure you that my students have never been anything but well behaved. Why don't we view the tape together, and you'll see that there's no reason for you to be concerned."

"Ms. Connor, I know what I saw on the tape, and furthermore, I find your tone highly offensive. I don't appreciate a subordinate questioning my authority. I'm your direct supervisor, and I suggest that you remember your place."

"Please forgive me if I stepped out of line. I'm only trying to understand why you're so concerned. Would you please just tell me what you saw on the tape?"

"I'd really like to continue our discussion, but I'm afraid we've run out of time. The bell is about to ring. You need to get back to your classroom, and I need to get to my post. However, I'd like to continue this conversation at a later time. I have other concerns that need to be addressed."

"How many other concerns do you have?"

"Frankly, Ms. Connor, I have quite a few. I'll need a full period to address all of them adequately, and unfortunately, I don't have the time to do it this week. We'll have to wait until after the Christmas holidays to have a meeting."

"You're going to make me wait an entire month? Why can't we just have the meeting today after school?"

"How can you be so selfish, Ms. Connor? Don't you see all of the paperwork on my desk? Just look at all of the referrals that I need to process!"

Mrs. Harrison was still talking as Brenda stormed out of the room. Perhaps it was rude to leave so abruptly, but emotionally, she could endure no more. Brenda felt Mrs. Harrison was a termagant woman who was contemptuous and incapable of engaging in rational discourse. She could no longer bear to look at her, much less carry on a conversation with her. Brenda fumed with rage as she walked back to her classroom. How could this woman have sat across from her and blatantly lied to her face? The lying wasn't even the worst of it. The manner in which Mrs. Harrison had conducted the meeting sent shivers down Brenda's back. Mrs. Harrison's cordial behavior and smiling face were confirmation that this woman was evil through and through. For some reason unbeknownst to Brenda, Mrs. Harrison was set upon destroying her. What egregious sin had she committed that she be so maligned? Brenda suddenly broke into a cold sweat.

This wasn't over. If anything, it was just beginning. The wheels had been set in motion, and the worst was yet to come. What was she going to do now? She knew that the union was useless, but was there somebody else she could talk to? Was there anyone she could go to for help? Brenda could think of only one person she could trust. Unfortunately, she still had two periods left to teach. Brenda could hardly compose herself after what had just happened; however, she had to hold on. She had to find a way to pull herself together and make it to the end of the day.

CHAPTER 12

As Brenda walked back to her classroom, she mustered what little strength she had left to hold back her tears. How was she expected to teach after being so viciously chastised by Mrs. Harrison? Not knowing what else to do, she decided to pray for help, and just as she finished praying, she looked up and saw her teammate Mrs. Kane walking toward her.

"Ms. Connor, I saw you in Mrs. Harrison's office. Are you all right?"

"Actually, I'm not all right. You wouldn't believe the accusations that bitch made against me! And when I attempted to defend myself, she became offended. I think that there's a real possibility that I may lose my job."

"Don't say that! Nobody's going to fire you! As a first-year teacher, you're entitled to make some mistakes. Don't pay any attention to that vindictive whore! Just go back to your classroom and concentrate on teaching your students."

"The meeting left me so disoriented that I can't concentrate on anything. Maybe I should've just asked for the rest of the day off."

"That's the worst thing that you could've done! Don't ever let them think that they can get to you. When I was a first-year

204

teacher, they tried to pull the same shit on me. Nothing I did was ever good enough. By midyear, I got fed up with playing their game and decided that it was time to change the rules. I stood up for myself and started running the show my way! The moment I asserted myself was the moment that they left me alone."

"I'll try to stand up for myself in the future, but I still don't know how I'm going to get through the rest of the day."

"Maybe I can be of some help. I'll give you the laptop cart, and that way you won't have to teach."

"But it's your day to use the laptops!"

"Don't worry about it. I'll just show a movie instead. You just concentrate on using the remainder of the day to recuperate."

"How can I possibly recuperate with the administrators lurking the hallways? What if somebody walks into my classroom?"

"Don't worry about that. The location of my classroom provides an excellent view of the hallway. If I see somebody coming, I'll call you immediately."

"I don't know what to say. How can I ever repay you for your kindness?"

"You don't need to repay me. Just take care of yourself and try not to take everything that they say to heart."

Brenda thanked Mrs. Kane and wheeled the laptop cart to her classroom. As she pushed the cart down the hallway, she lost control and started to cry. The tears that gushed forth came not from sorrow but from an overwhelming sense of gratitude. In her despair, Brenda had prayed for help, and in accordance with her prayers, help had been miraculously granted. However, she knew that many challenges still lay ahead. Mrs. Harrison was only beginning her reign of terror. She was out for blood, and Brenda needed to prepare herself. She couldn't afford to break down every time this woman attacked her. Praying brought her some relief, but what she really needed to do was toughen up. She needed to shake off her sensitivity and take the necessary steps to fortify herself against future attacks.

Once the computer cart was inside, Brenda ran to her door and greeted her students one by one as they entered her class. As she stood by the door and watched the children walk inside, she noticed that something was different. For one thing, every child who entered her classroom did so in an orderly manner. Nobody was stepping on her feet or shoving her up against the door. Brenda made a mental note of the children who entered her room and quickly noticed a pattern. Not one single troublemaker had shown up to her class! Her worst children appeared to be absent. And Brenda's good fortune didn't end there. The children who were present were actually following her instructions. Brenda watched in utter amazement as her students quietly left their seats and claimed their assigned laptops. It shocked her to the core to see them working on the school-mandated websites rather than listening to music or looking at porn. For once, her classroom phone remained silent. Not one person from the front office called to complain about a child navigating a prohibited site. Brenda had dreamed of this day, and now it had finally come! As was her regular habit, she looked up at the clock to check the time. Most days, she prayed for the hands to move swiftly, but today, she prayed for the hands to slow down or, better yet, not move at all.

Still, Brenda couldn't help wondering where the rest of her class was. When she took attendance, she discovered that more than half of her students were missing. Was this a mere coincidence, or was there some rational explanation? Brenda had to find out what was going on, so she decided to ask the children.

"I'm sorry to interrupt you while you're working, but can somebody tell me why so many children are missing?"

"They in trouble, Ms. Connor."

"What do you mean that they're in trouble? Did something happen in gym class?"

"You didn't hear what happen?"

Of course she hadn't heard what had happened! How could she have? She had been too busy getting her ass chewed out by Mrs. Harrison. Now that she thought about it, she noticed that none of the administrators had been at their posts during the last class change. While talking to Mrs. Kane, Brenda had heard the intercom instruct all security, administrators, and office personnel to report to the gym. Not just security and the administrators, but all office personnel! Why the need for so much backup? It didn't take long for Brenda to piece this puzzle together. During gym class, her students had somehow taken over control and were presently running the show. Brenda couldn't help but laugh at the irony of the situation. Less than an hour ago, she had been accused of being unable to manage her students, and now the administration had lost control.

Brenda reveled in the thought of her students running amok. She knew that once the kids got riled up, it was nearly impossible to get them under control. And secretly, Brenda was rooting for the children. Now that they were unleashed, there was no limit to their destruction. Brenda smiled at the thought of the mayhem they would cause. Brenda hoped for the worst so that the administrators could experience firsthand what she and every other teacher at Twin Palms Middle School were forced to experience every single day.

Brenda knew the children missing from her class were in some type of trouble, but she had yet to discover their crime. What could they have possibly done? It pained her to disrupt the class a second time, but the gossip inside of her just needed to know. Therefore, she opened up the floor for discussion and asked the children to elaborate on what had happened.

"Actually, I haven't heard anything. Can somebody tell me what happened?"

"You shoulda saw it, Ms. Connor! All da teachers wuz locked in da equipment room!"

"How did all three gym teachers get locked inside the equipment room?"

"They wuz tricked, Ms. Connor!"

"How were they tricked?"

"One kid fake a seizure, and they come runnin'! Then some kids lock da doors, and they wuz all stuck inside!"

"Then what happened?"

"They be rippin' off da basketball nets, and then they be breakin' da tennis rackets! Then they all take off! We see them in da parking lot! They be jumpin' on da cars and runnin' cross da street!"

"Weren't there any other adults around?"

"Da janitor walk in, but it wuz too late. He be yellin', but ain't nobody be tryin' to hear what he sayin'. Dis they school, and they be callin' da shots!"

So that was why so many of her students were missing! After completing their rampage, they had taken off and run away. No wonder the administrators had requested backup. They needed every available adult to retrieve the missing children and escort them back onto school grounds. The situation was worse than Brenda had originally thought. The safety of the children was at stake. If even one child got hurt, the school would be held liable, and the administrators would be charged with negligence. Brenda didn't want to see any of her students get hurt, but she would have loved to have seen the principal get fired. As it was, Mr. Jenkin was already treading on thin ice. His reputation was marred with rumors of sexual harassment and mismanagement of school funds. A blunder of this magnitude would not only warrant punishment from the district but also earn the school a spot on the evening news. No principal wanted to see his or her school on TV. This type of notoriety could end a person's career and bar that individual from ever working with children again.

Although the thought of Mr. Jenkin losing his job lifted Brenda's spirits, she couldn't stop thinking about her meeting with Mrs. Harrison. She needed someone to talk to and decided that after school, she would pay a visit to Mr. Fisher. After she finished up at the bus loop, she walked over to his classroom and was relieved to see that he had not yet left for the day.

"Hi, Mr. Fisher. Can you spare a few minutes to talk?"

"Sure I can! What's on your mind?"

"You can't believe the day that I just had!"

"I had an unusual day too. My last two classes were virtually empty! I was told by my students that some of the kids escaped from the gym and fled the campus."

"That's what I heard! How do you think the administration will handle it?"

"Well, I heard that all of the missing children were recovered and were punished with three days of suspension."

"That's it? Just three days? My kids told me that some of the gym equipment was destroyed! Who's going to reimburse the school for the damages?"

"Probably no one. The school will simply have to eat the loss, and the children will just have to do without."

"You know, it seems to me that the children run this school. They run wild, destroying everything in their path, without the slightest regard for authority. And what's their punishment? A couple of days of suspension! And how are they going to spend it? Watching television and playing games on the computer! Do you know who I really feel sorry for?"

"Who?"

"The gym teachers."

"Because they were locked in the closet?"

"Because they're going to get blamed!"

"I've never seen you this upset before, Ms. Connor. Is it because of Mr. Davenport's meeting? I don't think that you have anything to worry about. I don't even recall seeing your class on the footage."

"It's not Mr. Davenport's meeting that's bothering me. It's the meeting that I had with Mrs. Harrison afterward that's stressing me out."

"Mrs. Harrison pulled you into her office? What did she have to say?"

"Nothing good! She said that she saw my students on the tape and felt concerned about my classroom management skills."

"What was her concern?"

"She wouldn't tell me! And when I asked to see the tape, she became defensive and extremely hostile. She told me that I was out of line for questioning her judgment."

"Really? Then what happened?"

"Well, she had to cut the meeting short because the bell was about to ring. However, just before I left, she said that she wanted to continue the meeting at a later date. Apparently, she has a whole list of concerns and requires an entire class period to discuss them."

"That sounds terrible! When will the next meeting take place?"

"She wants to wait until after the Christmas holidays to have the meeting! I begged her to have it this week, but no! The fucking bitch is going to make me wait an entire month! How am I supposed to enjoy the holidays with this hanging over my head?"

"I bet that she could have found the time to schedule the meeting before the holidays. She just wanted to ruin your vacation and stress you out for the next couple of weeks."

"Well, mission accomplished! I feel absolutely miserable. I have a pounding headache, and my body aches all over. And don't even get me started about how I felt when I was sitting in her office! The nausea was so bad that I almost threw up in her trash can!"

"I know how you feel, Ms. Connor. I felt just as bad when she called me into her office."

"What! You got in trouble too? What for?"

"She said that I failed too many of my students on the first report card."

"How many did you fail?"

"I failed over seventy percent of my students."

When Brenda heard this, she felt a surge of guilt shoot through her body. She had followed Mr. Brown's advice but had failed to pass it along to Mr. Fisher. She should have warned him on the last planning day to not fail any of his students. Unfortunately, the issue had completely slipped her mind. The whole day had been one big frenzy of entering grades and making copies. She hadn't budgeted enough time to stand in line at the copy machine, nor had she anticipated the crashing of her laptop. However, despite these unexpected obstacles, she had still managed to get her grades in on time. Once everything was finished, she should never have rushed home. She should have lingered a little while longer and advised Mr. Fisher to change his grades.

"I can't believe that we both got in trouble! Doesn't that bitch have anything better to do with her time than torment the math teachers?"

"Actually, we're not the only teachers that she's going after. I've heard that Ms. Spencer and Mr. Morrison have also been called into her office."

It now became clear to Brenda why none of her referrals had been processed. Mrs. Harrison was not sloppy, nor was she lazy. She was using every available moment to document her staff. During the past few weeks, she had come into Brenda's classroom on several occasions to observe her teaching. She always sat in the back of the room, silently watching and jotting down notes. Although she stayed only a few minutes, Brenda couldn't help but feel concerned. She voiced her concerns to one of the veteran teachers, who told her not to worry. Teachers were observed sporadically throughout the school year, and the best thing to do was ignore the intrusion and continue teaching the class. The administrators had a checklist they were required to complete after each observation. The checklist—or instrument, as it was called—checked for various competencies and was formatted into two columns. If a teacher satisfied a certain criteria, the administrator would check off the right column. However, if the teacher failed to meet the criteria, the administrator would check off the left side. Once the list was complete, the administrator tallied the check marks from both columns and then used them to review overall staff performance. Teachers were told that the data was used only for statistical purposes; however, Brenda knew better. She knew the real reason behind the documentation: Mrs. Harrison was going to use the information not only for statistical purposes but also to build a case against the teachers.

But why had Mrs. Harrison targeted so many teachers? Wasn't it enough to make an example out of just one? Every teacher she was targeting had passed the first phase of the probationary period, which meant that termination could occur only with ample documentation. The infliction of this amount of paperwork on oneself seemed ludicrous to Brenda. Was the end result really worth this much aggravation? Rationally, it just didn't make any sense. There was something else going on, and Brenda was determined to find out exactly what it was.

"Why is Mrs. Harrison going after so many teachers? Why didn't she just pick one?"

"Ms. Connor, you're not looking at the bigger picture. You have to understand the reasoning behind what she's doing."

"You don't have to tell me the reason! Anyone with a pair of eyes can see that she's an evil bitch."

"I'm afraid that there's a little more to it than that. Mrs. Harrison is a newcomer to this school and, like us, has to prove herself to her superiors. If she fails to meet the expectations set by the principal, she could very well find herself out of a job."

"What expectations does she need to meet?"

"Well, do you remember the staff meeting that we had a few weeks ago?"

"The meeting that focused on the assessment scores?"

"That's the one! Do you remember what was discussed at the meeting?"

"Of course I remember! The principal prattled on endlessly about how poorly the sixth-grade students performed on the reading and math portions of the exam. Then he had the audacity to blame the teachers for not properly preparing the students. How can we possibly be expected to prepare the students for an assessment exam that is administered so early in the school year? Besides, is he aware that the children don't take the exam seriously? I don't know about you, but my students make pictures out of their assessment exams."

"My students do exactly the same thing. But you should know by now that nobody cares about our struggles. All anybody cares about are high test scores. And since so many of the sixth graders performed poorly on the assessment exam, the principal probably accused Mrs. Harrison of not adequately supervising her teachers."

"So what you're saying is that if she documents and micromanages us, student scores will go up?"

"I think that we both know that no amount of documentation will ever bring up student scores. And since student scores will never go up, Mrs. Harrison needs to find an alternative way to protect her job. And the best way that she can do that is by passing the buck and shifting the blame onto the teachers."

"It's all beginning to make sense now! You and I are math teachers, and Ms. Spencer is a reading teacher. Who better to blame than the teachers who teach in the FCAT-tested areas? But wait a minute! What about Mr. Morrison? He's a social studies teacher. Why is Mrs. Harrison going after him?"

"It seems that Mr. Morrison has recently gotten himself into some trouble. He's far too outspoken, and his recent outbursts have caught the attention of the administrators."

"What did he say?"

"He dared to speak out against the administration's golden boy."

The golden boy Mr. Fisher was referring to was Mr. Richard—or, as Brenda liked to call him, Richard the Rat. She had been warned early on to avoid this man at all costs, and she heeded this invaluable advice by doing everything humanly possible to keep her distance. However, staying away from him proved to be somewhat difficult since Mr. Richard was a teacher on her team. Like it or not, she had to communicate with him during team meetings and parent/teacher conferences. But thankfully, for the most part, she was able to avoid him. All the rumors about him proved to be true, and Brenda was careful to not cross him. He was highly favored by the administration, and they never denied him anything he requested. In his defense, the favor was rightfully deserved. He went above and beyond the call of duty by doing tasks that no one else wanted to do. He spent his free time answering phones at the reception desk, assisting with hallway duty, and participating in after-school activities. However, it wasn't the ass kissing that was of greatest concern to Brenda. What teachers did during their free time was their own business. What worried her the most was the amount of time he spent in the administration office. While on her way to the copy room, she often saw him conversing with Mrs. Harrison, and sometimes she even found him sitting in the principal's office.

Everyone always left his or her door wide open, and Brenda would occasionally overhear what they were saying. Mr. Richard was a talebearer and was quite adept at captivating his listeners with stories that were severely exaggerated or completely untrue. There were no bounds to his treachery, and the administrators proved to be attentive audience members who themselves were culpable for not discouraging his backstabbing ways. Mr. Richard's Judas-like behavior, although despicable, curried favor with the administration and entitled him to job security for the rest of his career. He was untouchable, and he knew it. Brenda was shocked at what he was able to get away with. From her classroom, she had an excellent view of the courtyard, and she often saw him engage the children in physical activities, such as football and soccer. While she struggled to get the children to learn, he passed the hours by playing games. As a result of his reluctance to teach, Brenda was the one who ultimately suffered. The children protested against her lengthy assignments and demanded to know why they couldn't play games in her classroom. As it was, the kids already hated her, and this only made things worse. Brenda would have liked nothing more than to file a grievance, but she never called the union. Not once had she complained, and now she was grateful that she had kept her temper in check and her mouth sealed shut. Had she loosened her tongue and spoken against Mr. Richard, she might have found herself in exactly the same predicament as Mr. Morrison.

"I didn't know that Mr. Morrison was in trouble. What did he say against Mr. Richard?"

"Apparently, he criticized him for not standing at his door during the class change."

"That's it? That's all he did?"

"Well, he did a little more than that. During the class change, Mr. Richard had taken his usual place with the administrators by the water fountain rather than standing at his door. Since he wasn't at his door, he couldn't control his students, and the kids ended up running into Mr. Morrison's class. When Mr. Morrison discovered that Mr. Richard was bullshitting with the administrators rather than standing at his door, he became enraged. He ran across the grass to where the administrators were standing, bellowing every step of the way and attracting the attention of every teacher that stood nearby. Once he was face-to-face with Mr. Richard, he sarcastically reminded him that he was not an administrator and needed to stand at his door like everyone else. It was an ugly spectacle that was gossiped over for weeks. Don't you remember the incident, Ms. Connor?"

"Of course I remember! I was cheering for him the entire time! It's about time that somebody put that rat in his place!"

"Maybe so, but he behaved unprofessionally, and in the end, Mr. Richard had his revenge. I heard that he filed a grievance with the union and that Mrs. Harrison documented the incident and reprimanded Mr. Morrison with a verbal warning."

"And what about Mr. Richard? Shouldn't he have been punished too? After all, Mr. Morrison was right. He should have been standing at his door during the class change."

"What kind of stupid question is that? Of course he wasn't punished! His standing at this school is solidified, and so long as he has the support of the administration, no one will ever be able to bring him down!"

"Well, at least it wasn't a serious offense. In a few weeks, it'll all be forgotten, and then perhaps they'll leave Mr. Morrison alone."

"I'm afraid that Mr. Morrison isn't out of the woods just yet. He stands accused for another more serious crime. I saw Mrs. Harrison personally deliver a letter to his classroom last week and watched as the blood drained from his face as he read it. During the planning period, I tried to console him, but we both knew that no amount of reassurance was going to erase the accusations listed in the letter."

"What did the letter say?"

"Apparently, Mrs. Harrison accused him of conducting himself inappropriately with a student."

"He did something to one of the students?"

"Mrs. Harrison accused him of touching a little girl."

"I don't believe it! Not Mr. Morrison! He would never do anything like that!"

"That's what I said! Mr. Morrison and I are good friends, and I don't believe for a minute that he'd ever touch a child. After I finished reading the letter, I asked him to tell me his side of the story and explain what happened."

"What did he say?"

"During one of the class changes, he instructed his students to line up for dismissal. One little girl refused to get out of her seat, so Mr. Morrison walked over to her desk, took her by the hand, and escorted her over to the door."

"Did the girl file a complaint against Mr. Morrison?"

"No. The child never said anything. Unfortunately, Mrs. Harrison saw Mr. Morrison holding the girl's hand and automatically assumed the worst."

Brenda knew that Mr. Morrison could never hurt a child. His only real fault was that he was a man working in a profession dominated by women. Had a woman done exactly the same thing, nobody would have ever complained. It was an unfortunate fact that men were treated differently than woman in the teaching profession. Simply by virtue of their sex, they faced condemnation for the most harmless of physical gestures. Brenda knew many male teachers who took every precaution to avoid physical contact with their students. At best, all they could do was offer a handshake or a pat on the back. This was a shame since some children at the middle-school level were still in need of nurturing. Students approached Brenda every day with outstretched arms, anxiously waiting to be hugged. Try as she might, she could never deny a child who needed to be consoled. If anything, she looked forward to these tender moments and saw them as opportunities to strengthen the bond between teacher and child.

"I can't believe that Mrs. Harrison would go to these lengths to attack a teacher. Doesn't she realize what this could do to Mr. Morrison's career?"

"The only career that she cares about is her own. She'd fire each and every one of us if it would save her job."

"Most of the kids like Mr. Morrison. I think that it's highly unlikely that the little girl will speak against him. Besides, I think that out of the four of us, Ms. Spencer is the administration's primary target. If somebody's going to lose their job, it's going to be her."

"What makes you think she'd lose her job first?"

"Let's just say that I have a feeling."

Brenda didn't just have a feeling; she knew for certain that Ms. Spencer's days were numbered. Anyone with a pair of eyes could see that this woman was visibly falling apart. Brenda helped her whenever she could, but despite her best efforts, the children were slowly but surely chiseling away at her sanity. Whenever Brenda entered her room, she found Ms. Spencer either huddling in a corner or crying at her desk. She had given up teaching altogether and instead paced back and forth in a frantic manner, stopping every two to three minutes to check the time. The children were killing her inch by inch and, nobody gave a damn. The administrators and security guards occasionally peeked through her window but then quickly walked on by. Why didn't anyone ever stop to help her? Didn't anyone care that this woman was on the verge of a mental breakdown? After giving the matter some thought, Brenda came to the realization that Mrs. Harrison wanted Ms. Spencer to collapse. If the children could successfully break her, Mrs. Harrison would have one less teacher to document and would then be able to set her focus firmly upon the remaining three.

Outwardly, Brenda appeared to be a supportive teammate, but her motive for helping Ms. Spencer wasn't entirely altruistic.

There was another reason that she wanted to save this woman's job: Ms. Spencer acted as buffer between Brenda and Mrs. Harrison, and as long as she stayed employed, she was sure to get the brunt of the abuse. Whereas Brenda and Mr. Fisher had been called into the office only once, Ms. Spencer was a frequent flyer who visited Mrs. Harrison's office no fewer than three times a week. Brenda was learning quickly and now understood how the system worked. Because of all the paperwork involved, Mrs. Harrison could only terminate, at most, two teachers per year. Brenda had read the union handbook and discovered that before a teacher could lose his or her job, a professional development plan had to be put into place. This plan was a monstrosity to maintain and required endless hours of documentation and observation on the part of the administrator. If Ms. Spencer were to be placed on this plan, the heat would most likely be taken off of Brenda. Mrs. Harrison's attention would be diverted, and Brenda would then be able to finish out the rest of the year in peace.

However, Brenda was concerned that Ms. Spencer wouldn't last long enough to be placed on a professional development plan. More than once, she had walked into Ms. Spencer's classroom only to find her packing up her belongings and typing a letter of resignation. Thus far, she had convinced her to stay, but the day would eventually come when Brenda wouldn't be able to stop her. She knew that she was helping Ms. Spencer for the wrong reasons, and the guilt she felt lay heavily upon her soul. However, her survival was at stake. She had managed to make it halfway through the school year, and after winter break, she would only have to hold on for five more months. If she could successfully finish out the year, she could then request a transfer to another school. But until then, she needed to find a way to take the attention off of herself. And if the only way to do it was by stabbing somebody else in the back, then so be it.

CHAPTER 13

Just when Brenda thought she couldn't last another day, relief came in the form of Christmas vacation. She couldn't believe that she had two whole weeks to do whatever she wanted. No other profession offered this much time off—but no other profession dealt with this level of stress. Everyone was excited to go on break, and as the time grew nearer, people throughout the school discussed their vacation plans. Some were flying home to visit family members, while others were planning luxurious trips to far-off destinations. Unfortunately, Brenda could afford neither. However, this did not bother her in the least. During the last few weeks, work had overtaken her life and had left little time for much else. These fourteen consecutive days off would finally allow her to shift her concentration from work to home. It had been six months since she had moved into her apartment, and boxes were still piled high, waiting to be unpacked. Recently purchased paintings decorated the floors rather than the walls, and antique vases collected dust rather than flowers. Brenda was ecstatic to have so much time off from work. She would now have the opportunity to complete all of her household projects and turn her apartment into a real home.

However, her enthusiasm quickly waned after her meeting with Mrs. Harrison. This unfortunate encounter killed any and all desire to be productive. No matter how hard she tried, she could not forget the things that Mrs. Harrison had said. The incident had spiraled her into a deep depression, and as a result, she spent the greater part of her first day off in bed. All she felt like doing was pulling the covers over her head and hiding herself away from the world. Her bed was a safe haven that provided temporary refuge to a traumatized girl who was in constant fear of losing her job. Every so often, she would peek out from underneath the blankets and look at her clock. She cringed every time a minute passed by, knowing full well that she was that much closer to having to return to work. As Brenda watched the minutes fly by, a sudden thought struck her: she didn't have to go back to Twin Palms Middle School! She could do whatever she wanted! If she wasn't happy, then she would simply quit and find another job. Instead of decorating her home, she would get on her laptop. She would spend every waking hour filling out applications and sending out résumés until she landed the job of her dreams.

For a brief moment, Brenda blithely lost herself in this fantasy until common sense kicked in and plunged her back into reality. Fourteen days was nowhere near enough time to find another job, especially a job within the teaching profession. It had taken her nearly six months to find this job. Besides, teaching positions were not readily available year-round. Finding a job midyear was virtually impossible. Positions were already filled and would most likely stay that way unless somebody gave birth, quit, retired, or died. Needless to say, it was improbable that Brenda would find employment anytime soon. And if she broke her contract now, she would never be hired in the county again. Besides, quitting her job was completely out of the question, especially now that she was finally getting her life back on track. With only six months of employment behind her, she had already managed to pay off one of her credit cards and some of her student loan debt. At this rate, she would be able to pay everything off in less than five years. The thought of living debt free had always been a distant dream but now appeared to be an attainable reality. However, in order for her to meet these lofty goals, she would have to find a way to hold on to her job.

Brenda was proud of her accomplishments and wanted to share her good news with Joseph, but once again, they weren't speaking. They hadn't spoken in weeks, and Brenda was uncertain as to whether or not she should continue with the wedding preparations. Until she knew how Joseph felt, everything would have to come to a halt. She had already put down deposits for the reception hall, the photographer, and even the honeymoon. If the wedding was cancelled, she would lose all the deposits. Since Brenda couldn't afford to waste any more money, she decided it was time for her and Joseph to have a conversation about their future. Since they couldn't communicate amicably, Brenda had no other choice but to enlist the help of a third party. As a county employee, she received many benefits, one of which was access to the Employee Assistance Program, a program created to offer support to people who were struggling in their personal and professional lives. A person in crisis could receive help over the phone or attend one-on-one counseling. Brenda hated the thought of sharing her problems with a complete stranger, but in a desperate attempt to salvage their relationship, she swallowed her pride and called one of the counselors listed in the network.

Her only dilemma was convincing Joseph to go with her to see the counselor. After all, it was pointless for her to go alone. If they were going to work things out, they would have to attend the sessions together. Unfortunately, Joseph was not the talkative type. Brenda could already foresee that he would have difficulty articulating his feelings. Only one person in his life was privy to his innermost thoughts: his mother. Over the last few months, Brenda had grown to despise this woman. As far as Joseph's mother was concerned, her son could do no wrong. Her excessive coddling got on Brenda's nerves, and her reluctance to cut the umbilical cord only added additional stress to an already-rocky relationship. Brenda hated the influence this woman had over her son. Even though he was a grown man, she still treated him as if he were a child. She doted on him by cooking his meals, cleaning his room, and doing his laundry. Whereas Brenda hadn't been able to wait to move out, Joseph was quite content to live at home. And who could blame him? He was pampered by a woman who acted as both mother and maid and whose sole purpose in life was to pander to her son.

Needless to say, Joseph's relationship with his mother was a major concern to Brenda. For one thing, Brenda was nothing like his mother. She had no intention of mimicking this woman's behavior once she was married to her son. She was a career woman who expected a man to pitch in and do his share. Unlike Joseph's mother, she would never have the luxury of staying home while her husband went out to work. Joseph's meager salary would never be enough to support her or a family. Brenda would always have to remain gainfully employed in order for them to make ends meet. Therefore, it seemed only fair that they should share the household responsibilities. But Brenda wondered if Joseph would agree to this arrangement. Would he be willing to help out, or would he expect Brenda to fill his mother's shoes? These were the types of issues they needed to discuss with the counselor. They needed to clarify and establish the expectations they had for one another before a marriage could take place.

Sometimes it seemed as if the problems she had with Joseph were endless. The trouble had stemmed first from his excessive spending and now from his refusal to leave the nest. A terrible thought entered Brenda's mind: if she married this man, she would also be marrying his mother. There was no à la carte option here. Joseph and his mother were a package deal. Someday his mother would die, but until that glorious day came, this woman would forever be a thorn in Brenda's side. She would continue to control her son and compete with Brenda for his affection. Anybody could see that Joseph and his mother had a special bond—one that had developed over the course of two decades and had only grown stronger with each passing year. Brenda hated to admit that she was jealous of their relationship. She yearned for Joseph to love her the way that he loved his mother, but how could he when all they ever did was fight? And when they fought, the person he always ran to was his mother. The pattern was always the same. After a fight, Joseph would cowardly flee the scene and run right into her arms. The old bitch would always be ready and waiting to console her poor battered son. Joseph would then divulge all of the intimate details of their fight, and like clockwork, Brenda would promptly receive a threatening phone call. Whenever Brenda attacked Joseph, his mother would respond in kind with venomous retaliation against her. Needless to say, it wasn't an ideal situation, and Brenda was unsure whether or not she was prepared for a lifetime of feuding with both mother and son.

Brenda was at her wit's end, and counseling was her last hope. But what if counseling didn't work? What would she do then? She had invested four long years in this relationship, and if she broke up with Joseph now, she would have to start all over again. She would have to reenter the dating scene and repeat the process of weeding out the riffraff until she met Mr. Right. This process could take years, and Brenda wasn't getting any younger. Besides, she was comfortable in her relationship with Joseph. When his mother wasn't interfering, they always had a good time. They connected on every possible level and had numerous things in common. Unfortunately, these precious moments had become few and far between. As the wedding grew nearer, Joseph's mother started to monopolize more and more of her son's time. Whenever he and Brenda went out, she would call on the hour, every hour. She needed to know exactly where her son was every minute of the day and constantly asked when he was coming home. Brenda hated it when Joseph picked up the phone. Why couldn't he just ignore her calls? When they were out together, why couldn't his concentration just be on her?

On the surface, it seemed that Joseph's mother had complete control; however, there was one crucial and necessary need that she could not fulfill—and the area in which she fell short was precisely the area in which Brenda excelled. As a young man in his sexual prime, Joseph had needs, and Brenda saw to it that she satisfied those needs. Even after four years together, their sexual chemistry was still going strong. She knew exactly what turned him on, and her sexual prowess kept him coming back for more. Her thirst for revenge and quest for control propelled her to indulge even his most bizarre fantasies. When he was locked in her embrace, all else was forgotten. Clothes were not the only things that came off during their moments of intimacy. When aroused, the cell phone that had seemingly become an extension of his body was turned off and carelessly tossed aside. There was never any fighting, nor was there any conversation about his mother. When he was in a climactic state, his mother became a mere afterthought, and Brenda was his only focus.

Brenda knew that she had a valuable weapon at her disposal, and she wielded her power mercilessly. She had no inhibitions when it came to sex and kept their relationship stoked with toys and an assortment of pornography. She was willing to try anything as long as it kept Joseph away from his mother. However, her desire to keep Joseph all to herself eventually backfired when one day, he asked her to dress up like a dominatrix. After so many years together, it seemed as if conventional sex no longer satisfied his lust. It appeared he had a masochistic side and wanted Brenda to bring him to submission through abusive language and physical degradation. Brenda wasn't sure if she felt comfortable descending into this realm of depravity, but what other choice did she have? She had made her bed, and now she had to lie in it.

The first step in the process involved dressing the part, and the outfit Joseph picked out for her included a black leather bodysuit, fishnet stockings, and boots with six-inch heels. Even with his help, it took Brenda over half an hour to get dressed. When she was finished, she looked at herself in the full-length mirror and discovered that she was pleasantly surprised at how she looked. Black was naturally slimming, and the constrictive nature of the corset smoothed out her muffin top and gave her a beautiful silhouette. Although quite flattering, the outfit was by no means comfortable. The corset cut off Brenda's circulation and made it nearly impossible for her to breathe. Although Brenda liked what she saw, she didn't like the way she felt. Her only consolation was that the discomfort would be temporary. Once their role playing was over, the suit was coming off.

At least Brenda wasn't alone in her suffering. Joseph had also purchased a leather outfit for himself, which turned out to be two sizes too small. The pants only went up to his knees, and he could button the vest only halfway. He should have tried the clothing on first, but dressing rooms weren't always available in specialty stores that sold such clothing. After they were both dressed, Joseph went to the other end of the room and took a box out from underneath the bed. Brenda watched him closely and wondered what was in the box. As it turned out, the box contained the instruments of pain that Brenda would use to help fulfill Joseph's deepest and darkest fantasies. Brenda didn't like any of this, but it was too late to back out now. He had carefully organized everything down to the last detail, and all she could do was wait patiently for him to tell her what to do next.

"So what do you want me to do now?"

"I want you to pretend that I'm one of your students and that I've misbehaved. I'm a bad boy, and I need to be punished!"

"How do you want me to punish you?"

"How would you punish one of your students?"

"Well, it's unlikely that I would dress up like a dominatrix. I'd probably write a referral and call it a day."

"Are you going to take this seriously or not? I went to a lot of trouble to put this together, and all you're doing is making jokes. Why can't you at least make an effort to make this work?"

"All right, I'll try harder. What should I use to punish you?"

"I have an idea! Why don't you whip me with your yardstick?"

Not this again! Brenda's yardstick had been used as a weapon once before and had failed to withstand the abuse. How many more rulers was she going to have to replace? Couldn't they just use the items that were in the box? The yardstick belonged to her, and the last thing that she wanted was for her personal belongings to be incorporated into their sex play.

"I don't think so. My yardstick is used for measuring, not for whipping."

"That's it! If you're not going to cooperate, then let's just forget the whole thing! Besides, I'm starting to get hungry.

I think that Mom's making a lasagna tonight. If I leave right now, she and I will be able to finish some last-minute Christmas shopping."

That did it! Those words were just the push Brenda needed to help get her into character. She went into the other room and rummaged through her school supplies until she found her yardstick. On the way back, she picked up the box that Joseph had taken out from underneath the bed and examined each item individually. For a split second, she was taken aback by the things that she saw, but she quickly got over it. This was no time to be squeamish. She had already come this far, and she intended to finish what Joseph had started.

"You're not going anywhere until I give you permission to leave!"

"What are you doing?"

"How dare you question me? Your job is to do as you're told! Now get on your hands and knees, and lick my boots, you mama's boy!"

Much to Brenda's surprise, Joseph actually got down on all fours and began licking her boots, and even more surprising, she liked it. She felt invigorated with a sense of power that she had never felt before. She could demand whatever she wanted without fear of refusal. No matter how distasteful the request, Joseph would be obligated to do it, and Brenda intended to make the experience absolutely degrading. This was her chance to repay him for everything he had put her through, and she intended to use every toy in the box to maximize the humiliation.

"Crawl on your hands and knees, and pick something out of the box!"

Joseph did exactly as he was told and slowly made his way toward the other end of the room. As he attempted to reach out his hand, Brenda immediately slapped it away and scolded him. "Who said that you could use your hands? If you're going to walk like a dog, then you can reach like a dog! Pick it up with your mouth, and bring it back to me!"

Brenda was curious to see what Joseph had picked out. She loved seeing him humiliated and was anxious to start inflicting some pain. When he crawled back, she was pleased to discover that he had selected a leather collar. She yanked the collar out of his mouth and fastened it tightly around his neck. She then grabbed a leather belt from the closet, looped the belt through the collar, and fashioned a makeshift dog leash. From there, she continued to taunt him.

"How does it feel to be treated like a dog? Do you want me to tighten the collar around your neck?"

"Oh God, yes!"

"Dogs don't talk! They bark!"

"Woof!"

Brenda did as he asked and then, without warning, kicked him so forcefully that he fell face first onto the floor. For a brief moment, she worried that she might have taken things too far, but all of a sudden, she heard Joseph moan in delight. She wiped the sweat from her brow and exhaled with relief. Joseph was all right, and it was safe to continue.

"What else have we got in this box? Is this a leather harness? Why don't you strap it on so that I can have some fun?"

Once again, Joseph did as he was told and strapped himself into the harness. Once it was on, Brenda jumped onto his back and started riding him like a horse. To aggrandize the humiliation, she yanked on the leash whenever she wanted to change directions and used her yardstick to beat him whenever he made a mistake.

"That's enough! Now get on the bed and lie flat on your back with your arms spread wide open!"

Once Joseph was on the bed, Brenda placed a spandex hood over his head and a rubber ring around his penis. Brenda then used the final items from the box—the wrist restraints—to handcuff him to the bed. Once restrained, she took her yardstick and moved it gently across his body. As she caressed him with the wood, she remembered all the times he had made her cry. She recalled the endless fights, the tension with his mother, and now this humiliation of being forced to dress up as a dominatrix. As these thoughts raced through her mind, her touch gradually became more forceful. She began to whip various sections of his body and did so without the slightest bit of remorse. Essentially, she viewed this act as payback for all of the pain he had inflicted upon her. And because her pain ran deep, she scourged him that much harder. By the time she was finished, Joseph's back was covered with bruises and welts. In truth, it hadn't been her intention to beat him so severely, but once she got started, she didn't know how to stop. She had repressed her frustration for far too long, and today it had finally all come out. Brenda couldn't remember the last time she had felt this good. Beating the shit out of Joseph was far more therapeutic than talking to any counselor. And the best part of all was that it had all been Joseph's idea. If she had indeed gone too far, he had only himself to blame.

CHAPTER 14

Going back to work after so many days off proved to be a melancholy experience. Brenda tossed and turned most of Sunday night and woke up Monday morning with a splitting headache. She had spent most of the night worrying about what would happen once she went back to work. Would Mrs. Harrison pull her into the office on her first day back, or would she let her sweat it out for a couple of days? Brenda feared it could be weeks before this woman scheduled her for an appointment, and she was damned if she was going to wait that long. It was better to just get the whole ordeal over with as quickly as possible. Rather than allowing Mrs. Harrison to blindside her, Brenda decided she would take command of the situation and initiate the conversation. As soon as she got to work, she would bypass her own classroom and march herself directly into Mrs. Harrison's office. From there, she would demand that Mrs. Harrison prioritize her above all else and schedule the meeting for that very morning.

However, as usual, things did not work out as planned. As Brenda made her way toward the administration building, she heard the intercom direct all teachers to the media center for a faculty meeting. Brenda sighed as she abruptly stopped in her tracks and changed directions. Not a single day went by that Brenda wasn't required to attend one meeting or another. Unlike the planning and lunch periods, the first hour of a teacher's day was not a duty-free period. Tuesdays and Thursdays were reserved for parent/teacher conferences, and Mondays, Wednesdays, and Fridays were reserved for various other meetings. On Mondays, teachers were required to attend a faculty meeting where they were forced to listen to the principal prattle on endlessly about policies, procedures, and particulars related to the FCAT. Wednesdays were the grade-level meetings, which were the meetings Brenda dreaded most of all. Since she was the only sixth-grade teacher with a SMART classroom, all the teachers piled into her room once a week to hear Mrs. Harrison get on her pulpit and preach about the importance of maintaining student control. Since Mrs. Harrison was unacquainted with the technology in a SMART classroom, it was Brenda's job to operate the equipment while she conducted her meeting. And when Friday rolled around, teachers were expected to sit through Best Practices, which was the biggest bullshit meeting of all. Best Practices brought teachers together who taught within the same subject area. The teachers would be herded into groups according to their grade level and would then be instructed to discuss strategies that had proven effective within their classrooms. Unfortunately, the intended purpose of this meeting was rarely ever achieved. Most of the teachers shared Brenda's lack of enthusiasm and spent the hour staring lethargically at one another or passed the time by catching up on gossip. To outside observers, it would have appeared as if the teachers had a bad attitude and were unwilling to share. However, this was not the case at all. The greatest obstacle to a teacher's success was lack of motivation, and no strategy would ever prove effective if a child was unwilling to learn. Brenda knew this. Every teacher at Twin Palms Middle School knew this. Only the administration remained in a state of denial, and until they opened their eyes and acknowledged this unfortunate truth, the teachers would forever be forced to waste their time and attend these pointless meetings.

Fortunately, today was not Friday but Monday, and Brenda was anxious to see her colleagues and hear how they had spent their Christmas vacations. However, when Brenda entered the media center, an uncomfortable silence welcomed her. Instead of conversing about the holidays, everybody was sitting in his or her seat, frozen with fear. Brenda immediately sensed that something was wrong and scanned the room for the principal, but he was nowhere to be found. Not wanting to attract unnecessary attention to herself, she took her seat with the others and watched uneasily as Mrs. Harrison walked up to the podium and commenced the meeting.

"Thank you for showing up promptly to today's faculty meeting. I hope that everyone is rested and ready to return to work. As you well know, the FCAT is just over the horizon, and we need each and every teacher at Twin Palms Middle School to shift into high gear and give one hundred and ten percent to all of our students. Be forewarned that from here on out, all the administrators will be visiting classrooms on a more frequent basis. We want to make sure that only FCAT-related material is being taught in the classrooms. The FCAT practice and sample test workbooks have just arrived and must be distributed to the students first thing this morning. We expect all math and reading teachers to center their curriculums on these workbooks and drill students on only FCAT-related concepts."

Brenda tilted her head back and groaned loudly when she heard these words come out of Mrs. Harrison's mouth. This standardized exam was a perpetual misery in her life. It was a specter that had followed and haunted her since the beginning of the school year. It weighed heavily upon her mind during the day and tortured her with insomnia at night. And now it would continue to antagonize her for the next three months. With the administrators visiting more often, Brenda would have to abandon the curriculum map altogether and focus solely on teaching to the test. To further add to her anxiety, she had already looked through the practice booklet. It was available online, and Brenda had printed a copy for herself over the holidays. On a day when she'd had no distraction, she had permitted herself the allotted time of an hour and a half and had embarked upon the task of completing the exam. Even though she was a math teacher and considered highly qualified by the state of Florida in her subject area, she had needed the full hour and a half to complete the exam. Each question was constructed as a miniature story and was at least one paragraph long. To complicate things further, the questions were exceedingly difficult and required numerous steps to solve. Her students would never take the time to be methodical with their problem solving. Instead, they would randomly fill in the bubbles and complete the exam within a matter of minutes. Even her higher-level students were doomed to failure. The questions were not the only craftily constructed items on the test. The answers were carefully thought out as well. Whoever had developed this exam had taken the time to look at the questions from a child's point of view. Children were inclined to forget certain steps, and the developers of the exam had foreseen these mistakes and listed every conceivable wrong answer a child might come up with. As a math teacher, Brenda couldn't help but be impressed with the design of the FCAT. She liked the situational questions and the overall structure of the exam. Unfortunately, she wasn't the one who had to take it—her students would have to take the exam and would be expected to make the necessary gains.

Brenda quickly grew bored with Mrs. Harrison's speech and started daydreaming about other things. Although she had just come back from Christmas break, she was already thinking about her next vacation. As Brenda counted down the days until spring break, her attention was suddenly drawn back to Mrs. Harrison. Discussion about the FCAT appeared to be over, and another woman had joined her at the podium. Brenda's eyes widened with fear as the woman took Mr. Jenkin's seat, and her ears perked up as soon as Mrs. Harrison began to talk.

"Now on a somber note, I'm sorry to report that Mr. Jenkin will no longer be our acting principal. It appears that he has been brought up on charges of sexual harassment and is currently under investigation by the school board of Dade County. We don't know when he'll return, and we request that all teachers behave discreetly and refrain from asking questions pertaining to his dismissal. This is an unfortunate time to have lost our principal, but fortunately, the district has appointed someone else to fill his position. Let's all take a moment now to give a hearty Twin Palms Middle School welcome to our new interim principal, Mrs. Bonner."

Brenda wasn't the least bit surprised to hear that Mr. Jenkin had been brought up on sexual harassment charges. As far as she was concerned, he was an arrogant, lustful little man who lacked the leadership skills necessary to run a school. *Good riddance to him and his insatiable appetite for sex!* Yet although Brenda was happy to see him go, she couldn't help but worry about the person who would be taking his place. Mr. Jenkin might have been a sexual pervert, but he had never been a threat to her. She had never been one of his sexual targets, and he had never taken an interest in her teaching. As a matter of fact, Brenda was fairly certain that after these many months, he still didn't know her name. In fact, he had scarcely seemed conscious of her presence at all. Would she be lucky and have this kind of anonymity with the new principal, or would she have to deal with another Mrs. Harrison? It was bad enough being micromanaged by one overbearing bitch. What would it feel like being micromanaged by two?

Brenda hated to be pessimistic, but a new principal meant a new set of problems. Furthermore, it didn't help that Mrs. Bonner was a woman. Brenda was all for equality and women's rights, but she dreaded the prospect of having to work for yet another woman. This viewpoint might have seemed hypocritical to some, but every woman she had ever worked for had turned out to be a backstabbing, two-faced bitch. Case in point: Mrs. Harrison, a first-year administrator who had failed miserably in every aspect of her job. The sixth graders were completely out of control and were credited with being the lowest-scoring students in the entire school. On top of that, Mrs. Harrison was pregnant. At some point, she would have to go on maternity leave and force the remaining administrators to pick up the slack. There was no budget to fill her position, nor would compensation be provided to those who would have to assume her responsibilities. All of these things were strikes against her character and jeopardized her future as an assistant principal. Therefore, she needed to do everything in her power to cover her ass, and the way she did it was by shifting the blame onto those who had the misfortune of working for her.

Brenda was tired of always having to play the blame game. When FCAT scores were low, the district blamed the principal, the principal blamed the administrators, the administrators blamed the teachers, and the teachers blamed the students. Why was it so important for the children to do well on this exam anyway? Why didn't the people who made these laws understand that not all children were capable of excelling in the areas of math, reading, and science? Why were all children forced into this cookie-cutter system? Typically, children who struggled in these areas were gifted in other areas. Many of Brenda's lowest-performing students were artistically, physically, or musically inclined. However, the educational system didn't nurture or foster any of those skills. In fact, it did just the opposite. Whenever the school made budgetary cuts, those programs were first to go. To save money, schools always eliminated physical education, art, and music. And what did they replace those programs with? They followed Mr. Jenkin's example and doubled up in one of the FCAT-tested areas.

Brenda had barely worked six months and was already fed up with how the system worked. She was fed up with the politics, and she was fed up with the management. However, if she was going to have any longevity, she needed to seriously adjust her attitude. She needed to stop being so negative and start looking at the glass as half full rather than half empty. So what if Mrs. Bonner was a woman? Was it fair to condemn someone without even giving her a chance? No, it was not. Brenda rethought her position on the situation and decided to give this woman the benefit of the doubt. She would hear what Mrs. Bonner had to say and would then form her opinion accordingly.

"My name is Bernadette Bonner, and the district has appointed me to be the interim principal for the remainder of the school year. The most important thing that you need to know about me is that I'm in the business of education. My job is to run this school and ensure that all of our students make the highest possible gains. And in order for our students to be successful, each and every one of you must step up to the challenge and do everything in your power to make this happen. Just as I'm in the business of education, you must be in the business of teaching. Your top priority is to raise FCAT scores and elevate Twin Palms Middle School to an *A* school. As far as I'm concerned, failure is not an option. Every child has the potential to succeed if only given the proper guidance. We have approximately three months until the FCAT and cannot afford to waste class time on frivolous games or activities. As Mrs. Harrison mentioned earlier, the administrators will be doing more classroom walk-throughs and observations over the coming weeks. It will be their business to monitor what teachers are teaching in their classrooms. Teachers who fail to adhere to these expectations will be severely reprimanded and may be placed on a professional development plan."

There were times when Brenda hated being right, and this was one of those times. Mrs. Bonner's monologue confirmed Brenda's worst fears. As she had accurately predicted, this woman was going to be another Mrs. Harrison. She was going to pose yet another threat to Brenda's already-rocky career. There was absolutely nothing in this woman's speech that had been uplifting or encouraging. At least Mr. Jenkin had tried to bond with the staff. His initial interaction with the employees had involved introductions and a speech full of hope and promise. This woman was the exact opposite. She took a more authoritative approach when it came to management. With her, there was no going around the room and getting acquainted with the staff. She only cared about the bottom line, and the bottom line was raising FCAT scores. All in all, this woman left a poor impression on Brenda. Using threats was no way to motivate people to do their jobs. It only lowered morale and made people that much more reluctant to go the extra mile. And what was all that business talk about? The only thing Brenda was in the business of was staying employed until the end of the year and then transferring to another school the first chance she got.

As she looked around the room and studied the expression on everyone's face, she suspected that many of her colleagues felt the same way she did.

After the meeting was over, the teachers quickly dispersed and returned to their classrooms. Brenda checked her watch and realized that she had roughly one minute to grab her belongings and sprint across the courtyard. Why did the administrators always have to yammer on until the last minute? God forbid they gave the teachers a few extra moments to gather their bearings and ease comfortably into their day. Unfortunately, the teachers at Twin Palms Middle School were afforded few leisurely moments. Teachers taught bell to bell, breaking only for a thirty-minute lunch and a forty-five-minute planning period. It was a relentless schedule that exhausted even the most energetic of teachers. Brenda especially was not physically ready for the challenges that lay ahead. Even after having fourteen days off, she wasn't ready to resume fighting with the administration, the parents, and, most of all, the children.

Just as Brenda was about to leave, she heard somebody call her name. It was Mrs. Harrison, beckoning her to come over. Brenda checked her watch once more and realized that if she didn't leave now, she would be late for her first class. She hesitated momentarily but then made her way over to Mrs. Harrison.

"Good morning, Mrs. Harrison. Did you want to see me?"

"Good morning, Ms. Connor. I need you to report to my office in five minutes. Our last meeting was cut short, and I would like to continue where we left off. I have several concerns regarding your performance in the classroom and feel that they need to be addressed immediately."

"What about my first-period class? Who's going to teach my students?"

"No need to worry about that, dear. One of the security guards has been assigned to cover your class. I need to go to my post now, but I'll see you in a few minutes."

As Mrs. Harrison walked away, Brenda suddenly felt afraid. She wasn't especially disturbed by what Mrs. Harrison had said but by how she had said it. This woman was notorious for being exceedingly polite. She never yelled, and she rarely lost her temper. She lulled her victims into a false sense of security and attacked them when they least expected it. A person could easily gauge the seriousness of his or her situation just by the sweetness of her tone. Brenda had anticipated the phony smile but had not been prepared for what had come next. Mrs. Harrison had never called her "dear" before, nor had she ever offered to provide coverage for her class. These were both telltale signs that she was in serious trouble. Her only real consolation was that the misery would soon be over. All that was left to do now was man up and brace herself for the impending interrogation that was sure to come.

Brenda reluctantly walked over to Mrs. Harrison's office and found that Mrs. Harrison was already there. She took a deep breath and then walked inside. Before she could even open her mouth, Mrs. Harrison held up her hand as if to silence her and then used the same hand to motion for her to sit down. Apparently, she wasn't interested in hearing anything Brenda had to say. It was clear she didn't want to waste any time listening to Brenda's side of the story. All she wanted to do was dive right in and commence with her accusations and finger pointing.

"Thank you for coming, Ms. Connor. I'd first like to start off by saying that I've noticed that you've had considerable trouble in the area of behavioral management. On more than one occasion, I've witnessed your students engage in rambunctious behavior. Why haven't you taken the necessary steps to get your students under control?"

"But I have taken the necessary steps! I have a binder full of documentation that shows the interventions that I've implemented and copies of all of the referrals that I've written!"

"Oh yes! I'm aware of all your documentation, but how do you expect me to process such a large number of referrals?"

"Because that's your job! You have no right to place all of the blame on me! I did my part, but did you do yours? When have you ever helped me with student behavior? Did you ever process any of my referrals? Show me what you've done to help remedy this problem!"

Brenda knew that she had stepped over the line, but she didn't care. She was sick and tired of taking this bitch's abuse. She detested playing a game that she knew she was ultimately destined to lose. If she was going to go down, she would do it kicking and screaming every step of the way. Let the bitch fire her! No job was worth this amount of stress.

"May I remind you that I'm your direct supervisor? I'm going to have to ask you to adjust your tone and conduct yourself in a professional manner. Now then, where did I leave off? Oh yes!

It's been brought to my attention that you've been making phone calls during class time."

"I never make calls during class time!"

"Are you sure, Ms. Connor?"

"Of course I'm sure! The students always have my undivided attention."

"That's not what I've heard. According to my sources, you've been calling parents during class time. Is this true, Ms. Connor?"

It was true, but how had she found out? No doubt her students had ratted her out. Brenda was speechless and twisted and writhed in her seat as Mrs. Harrison looked on with an evil smile.

"I don't appreciate being lied to, Ms. Connor. You should know by now that I'm aware of everything that takes place at this school. It's futile to try to hide anything from me. I know that you've been making calls during class time, and I also know that one of the parents you called came into your classroom to physically discipline his child. How could you have allowed this to happen?"

"It wasn't my intention for the child to get beaten. The child refused to follow my instructions, and I only called the father as a last resort. I never thought that he'd come to the school. He showed up unannounced, and before I could say a word, he grabbed my yardstick and started beating his son."

"Why didn't you intercede and stop the beating?"

"I didn't feel that it was appropriate to tell a parent how to discipline his child."

"Why didn't you call security?"

"It all happened so quickly! I didn't have time to call security."

"How could you just stand there and allow a child to get beaten? I don't care who's doing the beating! You handled the situation very poorly, and I'm afraid that I'll have to write you up for the incident. Furthermore, I'll be keeping a close eye on you for the remainder of the school year. As per Mrs. Bonner's instructions, I'll make it my business to visit your classroom as frequently as I can."

Upon hearing this, Brenda felt herself become nauseated. The all-too-familiar sickness in the pit of her stomach that she had grown to dread had suddenly returned. She couldn't believe it! Mrs. Harrison was writing her up! Now her personnel file would be forever tainted because of this one mistake. Who did this bitch think she was? She wasn't stuck in a classroom day after day, fighting with unruly children! The only contact she had with the children was during the five minutes between each class change. As Brenda felt herself boiling over, she couldn't help noticing the smirk that was slowly spreading across Mrs. Harrison's face. This meeting wasn't about behavioral management at all! Mrs. Harrison just wanted to exert her control and see how far she could push Brenda. There was no way Brenda was going to let this woman push her over the edge, so she pulled herself together and thought about how she could beat this woman at her own game. Like a bolt of lightning, the answer came to her: instead of reacting belligerently, she would humble herself. She would throw Mrs. Harrison for a loop by taking responsibility for her mistakes and asking for her help.

"You're absolutely right, Mrs. Harrison. I shouldn't have been calling parents during class time, and I should've shown better judgment. However, you must believe me when I say that I'm doing the best that I can. You have to understand that the interventions on the disciplinary matrix don't work with my students. Calling home during class time may have been inappropriate, but it was the only strategy that worked. It was never my intention for anyone to get hurt. I was simply trying to live up to your expectations by finding an alternative way to maintain classroom control. I would greatly appreciate any advice that you could offer to help me improve myself as a teacher."

The smirk that had seemed permanently imprinted on Mrs. Harrison's face suddenly began to fade away. As she stuttered to find a suitable response, Brenda reveled in her victory. It might have been only a minor victory, but it was a victory nonetheless. Few people were able to stump Mrs. Harrison, but Brenda had found a way. However, Mrs. Harrison quickly recovered and retaliated.

"My advice to you is to gain the respect of your students. What you don't seem to understand is that in order to gain respect, you must first show respect."

"I've always respected my students!"

"No, you haven't. You've never connected with your students on a personal level. As far as I can see, you don't take an interest in who they are or where they come from."

"I've tried to bond with my students, but most of them are unwilling to open up to me. What else can I possibly do?"

"Why don't you speak to Mr. Simon? He's worked at this school for over thirty years and understands our diverse population of students. The kids adore him and have always thrived under his instruction. I recommend that you observe him in action during one of your planning periods. Pay special attention to how he interacts with the students and how well they behave in his class. He won't mind if you observe him, and he won't turn you away if you ask for his help. Just remember, being knowledgeable in your subject area isn't enough. You need to go the extra mile and find a way to connect with your students."

CHAPTER 15

Brenda felt fairly shaken after her meeting with Mrs. Harrison and decided not to rush back to her classroom. Coverage had been provided for the duration of the period, and Brenda had fifteen minutes until she had to go back to work. She headed for the parking lot and unlocked her car door. She then put the seat all the way back, lay down, and looked up at the sky. It was a beautiful Florida day, and Brenda could hear all kinds of noises in the distance. As she listened to the sounds around her, it suddenly occurred to her that there was a world outside of Twin Palms Middle School. There were people who were employed at jobs they loved and who were living lives full of happiness. Would Brenda ever know such happiness? She desired to be happy, but a single decision at a job fair had radically altered her life. She played back that fateful day when the recruiter had sold her on the idea of accepting this job. What a fool she had been to think that she could actually make a difference! Why hadn't she listened to her aunt Margery and done her research before accepting the job? Her circumstances could have been considerably better had she selected a better school. What was she going to do now? She already had one strike against her, and failure to show improvement would only lead to more strikes and, inevitably, termination. Brenda shifted in her seat and set her mind upon the task of finding a solution to her impossible dilemma. The only way to pacify Mrs. Harrison was to improve student behavior. And the only way she could improve the children's behavior was by gaining their favor. But how could she do that when so many of the kids hated her? Strict discipline and an abundance of work had caused her to become the most hated teacher on her team. Personally, she didn't care what her students thought of her, but for the sake of her job, she needed to start caring. Getting the children to like her would now have to become every bit as important as raising FCAT scores.

Amid the accusations, Mrs. Harrison had actually provided Brenda with some invaluable advice. Mr. Simon was renowned for his ability to raise FCAT scores with the lowest-level children, and Brenda decided she could profit from his help. She had long since given up on her NESS coach, and she decided to pay Mr. Simon a visit during her break. Brenda was reluctant to sacrifice her planning period, but this was an investment in her career. She could grade papers and plan lessons some other time. Her job was on the line, and she needed to take action if she was going to make it to the end of the school year.

That afternoon, Brenda dismissed her third-period class, locked her door, and walked across the campus to Mr. Simon's classroom. Because she took a detour to the bathroom, she arrived a few minutes late and was unable to get inside. She could see through the window that his class had already started, and she didn't want to be disruptive by knocking on the door. Fortunately for her, he saw her gazing through the glass and let her inside. Since the class was jam-packed, Brenda made her way to the back of the room and leaned up against a wall. Once she found a comfortable position, she looked around the room and suddenly felt ashamed. Her largest class was half this size and nowhere near as well behaved. All the children had pencils in their hands and had their workbooks open to the correct page. What the hell was this? Brenda had to work a second job to pay for her students' supplies, but in Mr. Simon's class, everybody came prepared. How in the world had he managed to pull this off? And why wasn't anyone screaming or fighting? It took Brenda at least fifteen minutes to quiet her students down and begin her class. Why didn't the kids act up in Mr. Simon's class? Why did children willingly and obediently follow his directions and not hers?

Brenda had barely spent five minutes in Mr. Simon's class and was already thoroughly impressed with what she saw. The rumors had all been true. This man was indeed a gifted teacher. He was the kind of teacher Brenda had strived for months to become, only to fail miserably with each attempt. What was his secret? What was this hold that he had over the children? Perhaps it had something to do with the way he conducted his class. As Brenda puzzled over this conundrum, she noticed that Mr. Simon had wheeled out a television and was in the process of hooking it up to a VCR. It had to be a hassle connecting and disconnecting the equipment numerous times a day. Brenda was grateful she was in a SMART classroom, but she suddenly felt undeserving of the privilege. She watched as Mr. Simon inserted a tape, and she waited eagerly for him to begin his class.

"Who in this class likes to watch football?"

"I do!" screamed the entire class.

"Well then, let's watch some football!"

Mr. Simon hit a button, and the tape began to play. Within a matter of minutes, the class was in an uproar, and everyone was jumping out of his or her seat.

"Look! There's Mr. Simon!"

When Brenda heard this, she moved closer to the television, and sure enough, Mr. Simon was standing on the sidelines. She would never have recognized him had the children not pointed him out. Apparently, the footage had been taken in the seventies, when Mr. Simon was a choreographer for a cheerleading squad of a popular football team. Brenda couldn't help but let out a chuckle when she saw Mr. Simon on the tape. He was sporting the style of the day, which included platform shoes and bell-bottom pants. Her chuckle soon turned into roaring laughter as she saw Mr. Simon line up with the cheerleaders and assist them with their routine. He didn't hesitate to throw himself into the mix by joining the ladies in doing kicks, splits, and cartwheels. Brenda had never seen anything so ridiculous in her entire life and continued to laugh even after Mr. Simon had paused the tape. When she finally calmed down and regained her composure, she couldn't help but notice that the children were laughing too. Some were pointing their fingers at the television, and others had toppled out of their seats. And while everyone was having a good time, Mr. Simon stood nearby and laughed right along with the class.

"So? What did you think of the tape?"

"You a trip, Mr. Simon!"

"Did everyone have a good laugh?"

"Hell yeah!"

After this brief dialogue, Mr. Simon passed out a worksheet and grouped the students into pairs. Brenda took a copy for herself and listened as Mr. Simon provided the instructions.

"Today's handout is from the sports section of last Sunday's newspaper. I want you to study the football scores and then answer the questions that are on the front board. If you have any problems, ask your partner for help. You have thirty minutes to complete the activity, and then we'll go over the answers together."

As the children worked studiously on the activity, Brenda decided it was time to leave the safety of her corner and make her acquaintance with the famous Mr. Simon. She felt nervous at first but quickly overcame her fear when Mr. Simon motioned for her to come over.

"So what brings you to my classroom, Ms. Connor?"

"I've been having some trouble with student behavior, and Mrs. Harrison suggested that I observe your class."

"Did you find it helpful?"

"I found it remarkable!"

"Well, I've been teaching for a long time, and after a while, you're bound to find a formula that works."

"But how do you get them to sit so quietly and behave? And how did you manage to get them to come prepared with their supplies? Why does everything fall into place so easily for you and not for me?"

"You certainly have a lot of questions, Ms. Connor. I'd love to sit down and talk to you, but as you can see, I have a class in session. However, I'll be available after school if you'd like to continue this conversation."

"I'd love to continue this conversation! I'll definitely stop by your office after school."

As Brenda left Mr. Simon's classroom, she looked at her watch and realized that the bell was about to ring. She'd have to stay late to catch up on her paperwork, but she didn't care. Watching Mr. Simon in action had been worth the loss of her planning period. Everything Mrs. Harrison had said about this man had turned out to be true. He not only knew his subject area but also had found a way to connect with the children. Behavioral management was clearly not an issue in Mr. Simon's class. Not once had she seen him reprimand a child or stop class to call a parent. It was doubtful that he even owned a copy of the disciplinary matrix. Discipline was entirely unnecessary when children willingly took the initiative to learn. Seeing Mr. Simon's interaction with his students greatly improved Brenda's spirit and reignited her passion for teaching. He was living proof that low-level children were teachable and capable of learning. Thank goodness there was a teacher like Mr. Simon at Twin Palms Middle School! She was grateful that he was not only approachable but also agreeable in helping her with her own students. She couldn't wait until the day was over! As soon as the kids left, she would go over to Mr. Simon's office and learn from the master himself.

As promised, Mr. Simon was sitting in his office when she arrived. Without knocking first, Brenda opened the door and collapsed into the nearest chair.

"Bad day, Ms. Connor?"

"Is there any other kind of day at Twin Palms Middle School?"

"I'm sorry to hear that you're so unhappy."

"Will it ever get better, or are things only going to get worse?"

"Well now, that's up to you. What are you willing to do to improve the situation?"

"All I want is for the children to like me the same way that they like you."

"Well, what have you done to earn their respect?"

"Not very much, I suppose. All I really care about is raising FCAT scores."

"Well now, there's your problem. If you want to connect with your students, you're going to have to learn to get down to their level. Have you ever talked to them?"

"I've tried to talk to them, but they don't want to open up to me."

"You can't just give up! Maybe they feel intimidated speaking to you on school grounds. Perhaps you should speak to them on their own turf."

"What are you saying? Should I visit them at home?"

"Why not? I do home visits every week. As a matter of fact, I have two visits scheduled for this very afternoon."

"Really? Would you mind if I tagged along?"

"Not at all! Grab your things, and meet me in the parking lot in five minutes."

Brenda bolted out of Mr. Simon's office and rushed back to her classroom. She sidestepped the mounds of paperwork sitting on her desk and grabbed her workbag and keys. She stopped momentarily to look around but then quickly exited the room. As usual, her classroom was in shambles, but Brenda didn't care. She had been offered a rare opportunity to look into the lives of her students. Working late into the night to catch up on her work was a small price to pay for what she was about to see. However, as she reached the faculty parking lot, her enthusiasm suddenly waned. Was this really a good idea? Was it safe to venture into the ghettos of Miami with nightfall only a few hours away? Mr. Simon would be with her, but could he guarantee her safety? And what about the families? Would they show her hospitality, or would they kick her out of their homes?

Brenda reached the parking lot and found Mr. Simon already sitting in his car. She took her place in the passenger seat and stared cogitatively at the scenery while he set his concentration upon the road. She knew little of this neighborhood even though she drove through it every single day. In the mornings, she rushed to get to work on time, and in the afternoons, she rushed to beat the evening traffic. She never actually took the time to examine what the neighborhood had to offer. As Mr. Simon drove down the residential streets, Brenda saw some of her students walking on the sidewalks, and others were sitting on the bus benches. She was pleasantly surprised to discover that the neighborhood had some pleasing attributes.

Perhaps she had misjudged the surroundings. Maybe this wasn't a poverty-stricken, crime-ridden neighborhood. Maybe the homes from which her students came were not so bad after all. As Mr. Simon pulled into the driveway of the first house, he turned to Brenda and started to speak.

"Before we go inside, let me offer you some advice. Be careful that you don't get too close to the cages."

"What? Why do these people have cages? What's inside the cages?"

"Don't worry about it. Everything's going to be all right. Now come and help me with the bags."

Brenda followed Mr. Simon to the back of his car and proceeded to help him unload the trunk. Much to her surprise, the trunk was loaded with garbage bags full of clothes and shopping bags full of food. As Brenda studied the items in the bags, she finally realized the true purpose of this visit. Mr. Simon wasn't here to address student behavior, nor was he here to discuss academic achievement. His only purpose was to check on his students and provide for their basic everyday needs. As Brenda helped carry in the bags, she decided that no matter what she saw, she would stay quiet. No matter how distasteful the situation, she would make every effort to keep her opinions to herself.

However, it took everything she had to hold her tongue after walking up five flights of stairs in a building that had no air-conditioning. There was no elevator, and Brenda had to stop multiple times to rest and catch her breath. Once she made it to the top, she dropped the bags on the floor and leaned up against the nearest wall. There was no ventilation of any kind, and Brenda felt as if she were suffocating as she labored to catch her breath. Beads of sweat ran down her body and soaked through her work clothes. Her perfectly tailored suit had absorbed every single droplet and now draped her body in an unflattering way. She could feel her feet throbbing inside of her sensible shoes and sorely regretted not packing her sneakers. As they waited for someone to answer the door, Brenda made use of the time by taking off her shoes and rubbing the arches of her feet. It felt so good to take her shoes off that Brenda contemplated whether or not she should just keep them off. However, when the door opened and the rooms of the apartment were in full view, Brenda reconsidered and quickly slipped her shoes back on.

As soon as the door opened, Brenda's senses instantly went into a state of shock. Her sense of smell was assaulted first and made her reluctant to go inside. Where was the smell coming from? The lack of air and pungency of the odor made Brenda dizzy and caused her to nearly pass out. When she finally managed to work up the courage to go inside, her vision was attacked next. As she followed Mr. Simon into the apartment, she suddenly felt her eyes well up with tears. She was assailed by an overpowering stench that caused her to involuntarily cry. As she wiped the tears from her eyes, she scoured the house and immediately found the source of her agitation. From top to bottom, the apartment was stockpiled with cages filled with animals. At first, Brenda heeded Mr. Simon's advice and kept a safe distance away from the cages, but she then reconsidered and slowly edged her way over to get a closer look. She placed a handkerchief over her mouth but continued to gasp for air as she examined each of the cages individually. Was this some kind of a pet store? Were these animals a source of income for this family? Brenda soon came to the sad conclusion that these poor creatures were not for sale. Upon closer inspection, she could see that most of the animals were sickly or were on the verge of dying. As Brenda looked upon the suffering that surrounded her, her tears began to flow more heavily. She no longer cried from the putridity but from pity for these poor, unfortunate creatures. Never in her life had she seen animals treated so badly. The cages covered every inch of the home, leaving only a small pathway to get from room to room. The cages were undersized and overfilled, leaving the animals with no room to stand. The weaker ones were forced to the bottom and were then trampled on by the stronger ones. The cages were caked with filth, and the animals were severely malnourished. Many were eating their own feces and the flesh of those that had died around them. Brenda had to turn away as one little rabbit attempted to chew off his own leg to stave off starvation. How could anyone be so inhumane? Brenda's anguish suddenly turned into anger as she looked around the apartment for the people responsible for this atrocity. She had tried to keep quiet, but if she didn't speak up, all of these animals were surely going to die.

However, being the nonconfrontational person she was, she decided it was best to call the police. Why should she get involved in this mess? She would let the police handle the situation according to the letter of the law. She opened her bag and started searching for her phone. Had she remembered to pack it, or had she left it at home? Brenda was sometimes forgetful, but today she was in luck! Her phone was nestled under some files and a snack she had forgotten to eaten during lunch. However, before Brenda could dial those three important digits, Mr. Simon intercepted the call by snatching the phone out of her hands.

"What do you think you're doing?"

"What does it look like I'm doing? I'm calling the police! Look at all of these poor animals! These people don't deserve your help! What they need is to be prosecuted to the fullest extent of the law!"

"Don't be so hasty, Ms. Connor. I know that this looks bad, but you don't understand. You don't see the full picture."

"What's there to understand? Just take a look around! How can you possibly condone this? How can you just stand idly by and do nothing?"

"Look, I understand how you feel, but the children are my main priority. The police have already been notified and are in the process of removing the animals from the premises. In the meantime, I'm doing what I can to make sure that the family has food on the table and clothes on their backs. I'm sorry that you had to see this, but you're going to have to find a way to keep your emotions under control. You need to remember that most of our students don't come from stable families. Most of these kids come from broken homes and have been severely neglected. More often than not, the home lives of these children will not be up to your standards. However, the last thing that you want to do is come into these homes with a judgmental attitude. You need to find a way to detach yourself from the things that you see and set your focus on meeting the needs of the children."

Mr. Simon might have had a valid point, but Brenda couldn't bear to stay in the apartment a minute longer. While he was still talking, she sprinted down the hallway and out the front door. She descended the five flights of stairs with lightning speed and took a deep, cleansing breath as soon as she got outside. She was about to get into Mr. Simon's car, when she caught sight of her reflection in the passenger window. The extreme humidity in the apartment had caused her hair to become limp and lifeless. Her clothes had fared no better, as they were now two sizes too big and thoroughly drenched with sweat. Worst of all was the way she smelled. The rancidity of the apartment had permeated her skin, and the smell lingered in her hair. Without a doubt, it would take a few showers and vigorous exercise to fully expel the stench that had overtaken her body.

Brenda paced restlessly as she waited for Mr. Simon to come back to the car. She didn't want to go on any more home visits, but what could she do? She had committed herself to this expedition, and now it was her responsibility to see it through. Maybe the next home visit wouldn't be so bad. How could it be? How could anything possibly top this? As Brenda tried to reassure herself, she saw Mr. Simon come out the door and walk toward the car. He had already scolded her once, but judging by the frown on his face, she sensed that it would be prudent to brace herself for round two. As Mr. Simon neared the car, Brenda lowered her eyes and shamefully looked at the ground. She couldn't bear to look him directly in the eyes. She felt guilty and wanted to apologize, but the words wouldn't come out of her mouth. When Mr. Simon got in the car, she slipped in quietly beside him and anxiously waited to hear what he had to say next.

"All right, Ms. Connor, before we go to the next house, I need you to promise me that you won't make another scene. I'm going to warn you right now that you're not going to like what you see. I need your word that you'll be on your best behavior."

"I promise that I'll behave. Are these people animal hoarders too?"

"Not exactly. But allow me to offer you some advice. Whatever you do, don't sit down! Stay in an upright position at all times, and if you decide to bring your bag inside, whatever you do, don't put it on the floor!"

Oh God! Not more advice! What was she going to see now? What ghastly spectacle would she be forced to witness this time? Brenda had come to dread Mr. Simon's advice and wished that he wasn't so vague with his warnings. Why had he cautioned her against sitting down? Did these people not own chairs? Perhaps they were in the process of redecorating. Maybe all their furniture was in storage and the floors were being redone. Brenda tried to rationalize the situation as best as she could, but deep down, she knew it was all wishful thinking. Instinctively, she knew she was going to see something disturbing. She had promised Mr. Simon that she would be on her best behavior, but fear of the unknown made her uneasy. She watched anxiously as Mr. Simon made one turn after another, fearing the moment when there would be no more turns left to take. Why had she ever agreed to do this? Even more importantly, why hadn't Mr.

Simon warned her in advance? Had he been forthright, Brenda would never have agreed to accompany him. Now it was too late, and there was nothing she could do. As Mr. Simon made the final turn and parked in the driveway, Brenda wondered if perhaps he would let her stay in the car. He didn't really need her help, and he certainly didn't need to deal with her paranoia. Truly, she felt it would be best for both of them if she just waited outside.

"Let's go, Ms. Connor! Get out of the car, and help me with these bags!"

"Why don't you just go without me? I'll wait here until you come back."

"What? You come to me for help, whining that the kids don't like you, and now you want to back out? I went out of my way to help you because I thought you were serious about improving yourself as a teacher. Obviously, I was mistaken. Quite frankly, I don't appreciate you wasting my time, Ms. Connor."

"I'm sorry, Mr. Simon. I am serious about improving myself as a teacher. I just had a momentary lapse of weakness. Here, let me help you get the bags out of the trunk."

For the second time that day, Brenda helped Mr. Simon unload the trunk and followed him to the front door. She was relieved to discover that at least this time, there were no steps to climb. This was not an apartment building but a ranch-style home with only one floor. As Mr. Simon rang the bell, Brenda started to feel optimistic. This time, she wasn't winded from walking up flights of stairs, nor did she feel claustrophobic or lightheaded for lack of oxygen. It was now early evening, and a balmy breeze had replaced the scorching heat. The surrounding palm trees were swaying back and forth, and Brenda couldn't help but be captivated by the pink and purple hues that decorated the sky. Her feet no longer ached, and her clothes were finally beginning to dry. Brenda was still skeptical about what she was going to see, but at least things were off to a good start. Best of all, this was the last visit of the day. She and Mr. Simon would go inside and deliver the goods, and then she would finally be free to go home.

As Brenda tried to look at the bright side of things, it suddenly occurred to her that nobody was coming to the door. What was this? Was it possible that nobody was home? Maybe the family had forgotten about the appointment. Maybe they were ashamed of their home and were hiding in the dark. Whatever the reason, Brenda didn't care. She was more than happy to reload the trunk and call it a day. Unfortunately, Mr. Simon proved to be more persistent and continued to ring the bell. However, after the tenth ring, he gave up and turned to Brenda.

"I don't think that anybody's home. They must have forgotten that I was coming. I'll have to call them tomorrow to reschedule for another time. Let's just head back to the school."

"Sounds good to me! Let me help you with the bags."

As Brenda bent over to pick up the first bag, she suddenly stopped dead in her tracks. She heard the faint sound of someone shuffling around inside the house and feared that Mr. Simon had heard it too. She looked over in his direction and saw that he was still occupied with the bags. He hadn't heard anything, which meant there was still a chance they could get in the car and drive away. Brenda looked up and saw the silhouette of a person walking through the house and realized that someone had heard the bell. What was she going to do now? She had to act quickly or else be forced to go through with the visit.

"Let me help you with those bags, Mr. Simon."

"Why, thank you, Ms. Connor! Wait a minute. Did you hear something?"

"Nope! Let's get going before it gets dark."

"No, I think I definitely heard something. Let me just ring the bell one more time."

Just as Mr. Simon stretched out his hand, the door suddenly swung open, and an old woman in her seventies greeted them and invited them to walk inside. Brenda was sorry she had failed in her attempt to escape but was relieved to discover that unlike the last home, this one did not emit any noxious smells. Once again, she felt herself begin to perspire underneath her multiple layers of clothing, but this didn't bother her in the least since her clothes were already ruined. What did bother her, however, was the lack of lighting. There wasn't a single light turned on in the entire house. Why were these people living in the dark? Couldn't they at least turn on one light so that she and Mr. Simon could see where they were going? Brenda soon grew frustrated with stumbling into tables and knocking over chairs and decided to take matters into her own hands. She ran her hand along the wall and, in less than a minute, felt the familiar form of a light switch. It took all of two seconds for her to turn it on, and before she knew it, she had illuminated the entire room.

"Oh my God! Who turned on the lights? Hurry! Shut the lights off before it's too late!"

Upon hearing this, Brenda turned off the lights, but it was already too late. Hundreds of cockroaches had come out of hiding and were presently racing up and down the hallway. Brenda jumped out of their way and up onto a nearby coffee table, but there were roaches there too! They were living in between the pages of magazines and perched on the sides of coffee cups. Some were closing in on Brenda and trying to climb onto her shoes. As far as she could see, roaches were everywhere. The home was alive with vermin. She stood amid a full-blown infestation and watched, aghast, as they took control over the entire house. She knew that she would eventually have to leave the safety of the table, but where would she go? Where could she go in a house that was overrun with roaches?

Brenda now understood the meaning of Mr. Simon's warning. It was imperative that she remain standing at all times or risk a roach harboring a ride in her bag or on her person. Why in the world had she ever brought her bag into the house anyway? Why hadn't she just left it in the car? Well, there was nothing she could do about it now. All she could do was be vigilant while inside the house and sanitize her clothes and workbag when she got home. As Brenda debated what to do next, she suddenly noticed that Mr. Simon was staring at her. He was none too pleased with her reaction, and although he said nothing, the look in his eyes struck fear in her heart and prompted her to get off the table. She stepped down slowly, taking great pains to not step on any of the roaches, and then joined Mr. Simon in the living room. Even though she was extremely exhausted, she was careful to not sit down. She cradled her bag in her arms and was careful to not lean up against the wall. As Mr. Simon spoke with the family, Brenda kept her full concentration on the roaches. Although she found them repugnant, she couldn't help but marvel at their resilience. The initial shock had finally worn off, and she ventured off on her own to study them more carefully. Brenda had never seen versatility like this! They were quite the acrobats, hanging upside down from the ceiling and dangling from the chandelier. After completing her tour of the living room, she turned a corner and found herself in one of the bathrooms. By accident, she brushed up against a wall, and hit another light switch, and lo and behold, the roaches came out of hiding and took off once again! This time, however, they scurried to get out of the sink and the bathtub. Brenda leaned in for a closer look and made a fascinating discovery. The roaches appeared to be coming into the home through the plumbing. They were adept little climbers that could squeeze their way through the narrowest of pipes. Just then, Brenda remembered that she had a small flashlight attached to her keychain. She turned the flashlight on and pointed it directly down the drain. With the aid of her flashlight, she could see hundreds of cockroaches huddled together, hanging on for dear life. What would happen if she turned on the faucet? Maybe the water pressure would flush them out and kill them once and for all. However, Brenda soon discovered that roaches didn't drown easily, for when she lifted the toilet seat, she was startled to discover a family of roaches buoyant inside the toilet, looking directly up at her.

Brenda shuddered when she saw the roaches swimming in a toilet full of human excrement and decided once and for all that she had seen enough. She could only stomach so much and hoped that Mr. Simon was finished conversing with the family so that they could finally leave and go back to the school. However, just as she was leaving the bathroom, she heard the familiar voice of one of her students call out her name.

"Hi, Ms. Connor! Whatya doin' here?"

"Mr. Simon and I came to drop off some food and clothes for your family. How are you doing?"

"I'm doin' great! I'm goin' to the kitchen and gettin' a snack. Wanna come?"

"I'm not sure if that's such a good idea. I should probably find Mr. Simon and help him with the bags."

"Oh, come on, Ms. Connor! I'll make you a snack too!"

Before Brenda could refuse, the child grabbed her by the hand and proceeded to take her into the kitchen. She followed willingly at first but then had to be dragged over the threshold. The sight that unfolded before her eyes was like a nightmare she could not awaken from. There were so many roaches that the white walls appeared to be black. The outbreak in this room was of biblical proportions, and one had to wonder if God was punishing the people who lived in this house. It was no mystery why the roaches preferred this room above all the others: they had easy access to the food and didn't hesitate to help themselves. When the child opened the cabinet door, Brenda looked inside and could see that the roaches had gnawed their way through the bags and boxes and had found their way into the food. When she opened the freezer, she was shocked to see roaches in there too. Was there any place they could not live? Wasn't there any way to kill them? Little did Brenda know, her questions would soon be answered.

"Come here, Ms. Connor! You gotta see this. It's so cool!"

Brenda walked over to where the child was standing and watched him open the microwave door. Once the door was open, the light automatically went on and startled the roaches inside. Brenda watched in horror as the child placed his sandwich on top of the roaches and then shut the door.

"Watch this, Ms. Connor!"

Brenda watched with empathy as the trapped roaches frantically ran from one end of the microwave to the other with no feasible way out. She knew that they were being electrocuted, and she jumped back when their small bodies exploded from the intense heat. Despite her aversion to roaches, it hurt her to see any living creature in such agonizing pain. Unfortunately, her student did not share her remorse. Still laughing, he opened the door and pointed to their singed remains. He then took out his roach-encrusted sandwich and put it on a plate.

"Wait! Don't eat that! It's covered with roaches!"

"It ain't no thang. All you gotta do is flick 'em off. Ya want half?"

"Get that sandwich away from me! Where's Mr. Simon? I have to get out of here!"

After running frantically through the house, Brenda found Mr. Simon waiting for her by the front door and realized that it was finally time to go. As she followed him back to the car, she felt a sudden sense of relief. The events of the day had left her feeling haggard, but at least the day was finally over. Her meeting with Mrs. Harrison was but a distant memory, and the home visits were ordeals she would never repeat. She looked over at Mr. Simon and could see that he was tired too. He was driving well below the speed limit and was struggling to stay awake. It had been a long day for Brenda, but every day was a long day for Mr. Simon. It took a special person to be this devoted to his students. For all of his sternness and endless lecturing, Brenda still respected him and held him in the highest regard. She couldn't help but admire his unfaltering dedication to not only the children but also their families. She might have called herself a Christian, but Mr. Simon was the embodiment of Christlike behavior. Brenda now realized what she had to do to gain the favor of her students. But was she willing to do it? Was she willing to follow in Mr. Simon's footsteps and make the necessary sacrifices? Brenda needed some time to think it over. This job already forced her to sacrifice her energy and patience. Was she willing to go the extra mile and sacrifice her time and money too? Brenda didn't know. Deep down, she sympathized and wanted to help, but quite honestly, she wasn't sure if she had anything left to give.

CHAPTER 16

It was now exactly two weeks before the FCAT, and everybody was bustling to get ready. Meetings were scheduled every day of the week—sometimes two per day. The administrators were always making fresh demands upon the teachers, and they in turn did their best to acquiesce. Many of the requests were irrational and illogical, but all practicality went out the window when desperation set in. Not even Brenda's administrator was immune to the pressure. Her usual calm and collected demeanor had vanished, replaced with anxiousness and a temperament similar to that of a hyena. Throughout the year, the sixth graders had consistently scored poorly on the assessment exams, which was a clear indication that they would also score poorly on the FCAT. As far as Brenda was concerned, there was nothing more she could do and the few days that remained were not enough to make any significant impact on student scores. Unfortunately, Mrs. Harrison did not share her cynicism. She still had faith that the children would somehow pull through. She impressed these delusional beliefs upon her staff and grappled over how to best utilize the last few days. Brenda halfheartedly checked her e-mails each morning and winced as she read over the latest musings from the mind of Mrs. Harrison. Needless to say, this was the most trying time in Brenda's career. It took everything she had to control her temper and, more importantly, her mouth. Her one saving grace was the knowledge that one day soon, this misery would be over. She hoped that once testing was finished, the tension would dissipate and things would go back to normal.

However, until that blessed day came, Brenda and the other sixth-grade teachers were forced to humor Mrs. Harrison and submit to each and every one of her ridiculous requests. Her administrator had conceived a number of ludicrous ideas over the course of the school year, but Brenda's jaw literally dropped when Mrs. Harrison called an emergency meeting a week before the FCAT and insisted that the teachers use the last few days to conduct student data chats. These so-called data chats were one-on-one conferences that teachers held with their students during class time. Brenda had been required to do these chats once before at the beginning of the school year. It had been a horrendous experience—one that she did not care to repeat. She recalled the grueling ordeal of analyzing the assessment data for over one hundred students and deciphering the infinite stream of numbers to pinpoint each child's weakest area. Once she completed the research component of the process, she then had to sit with students individually, discuss the breakdown of their scores, and ask them to state their future goals. In theory, the strategy was intended to rally student enthusiasm and encourage self-improvement. However, in reality, all it did was take time away from instruction and compromise behavior in the classroom. In order to conduct the data chats, Brenda had to remove herself from the center of the class and sit down at her desk. Without her stature hovering over them, the children felt less intimidated and were far more likely to get off task and begin talking. Once seated, her full attention was directed toward the student sitting opposite her, and because her concentration was diverted, the bad behavior would escalate until finally a fight inevitably broke out. No activity could keep her students fully occupied while she conducted her data chats. Without her constant presence and persistent urging, she was sure to lose control.

Why did Mrs. Harrison have to do this right before the FCAT? Brenda didn't need to conduct data chats to know her students' weaknesses. She had spent enough time and had given enough exams to know that across the board, their weakest area was measurement. And knowing this, she had developed a week's worth of lesson plans centered on that topic. Now those lesson plans were as good as garbage. Because of Mrs. Harrison's idiocy, Brenda would have to spend the last days before the FCAT engaging her students in idle conversation rather than optimizing the time by enhancing their test-taking skills. As Mrs. Harrison discussed the nuts and bolts of conducting a proper data chat, Brenda took a moment to scan the room. By the look on everyone's face, she could see that nobody was on board with this idea. She detected a subtle look of disgust in everybody's eyes, but nobody had the courage to speak up. Maybe she should be the one to speak up, she thought. If no one took a stand, this bitch would get her way, and the teachers would lose the last few precious days they had left before the FCAT. But then again, maybe it was best to stay quiet. Wasn't she in enough trouble already? Did she really want to pay another visit to Mrs. Harrison's office? No, she did not. She would hold her tongue and pray to God that somebody else in the room had the mettle to stand up to Mrs. Harrison.

"Mrs. Harrison, I think I speak for all of the teachers when I say that conducting data chats so close to the FCAT is a poor idea. We should use every single minute of class time for instruction and worry about the data chats later."

"Is that right, Mr. Morrison? Well, let me tell you something. I make the decisions around here, and I say that it's time for another round of data chats. Furthermore, I don't give a damn what you or anyone else thinks! Nothing I say is ever up for negotiation, nor is it open for discussion! And if anyone else in this room ever feels the desire to challenge me again, I suggest that you start looking for another job!"

Yikes! What the hell was all that about? Those words were harsh even for Mrs. Harrison. What could have sparked an outburst like this? Maybe it was the pregnancy hormones, or perhaps the overwhelming stress had finally caught up with her. Whatever the reason, Brenda was glad she had fought the urge to be impulsive. She felt bad for Mr. Morrison, but to be completely honest, he no longer had anything left to lose. He had been on Mrs. Harrison's shit list from day one and was, at that moment, circling the toilet and going down the drain. For her part, Brenda had played the unwilling spectator who watched in utter dismay as her beloved friend and colleague faced systematic torture at the hands of the administration. Just as the teachers relied upon a matrix to discipline their students, the administrators had their own matrix to discipline the staff. Brenda had supported Mr. Morrison through every phase of this heart-wrenching odyssey only to see him sink deeper and deeper into despair. What had started out as occasional documentation had later evolved into aggressive micromanagement and had now concluded with a professional development plan. There were days when Brenda secretly wished Mr. Morrison would go elsewhere for support, but he always came to her. Why couldn't he keep his problems to himself or share them with someone else? However, despite her overwhelming discomfort with everything that was going on, Brenda never turned Mr. Morrison away. Hard as it was, she forced herself to watch and seized every opportunity to ask questions, for there was no telling when her own time might come—that fateful day when she herself would be placed on a professional development plan. It was certainly within the realm of possibility. It was no secret that Mrs. Harrison hated her and wanted her gone. Was it possible that she was witnessing a preview of her own future? If Mr. Morrison lost his job, would she be Mrs. Harrison's next target? And if she were placed on a professional development plan, would she be forced to go through the same grueling process? These questions constantly circled in Brenda's mind, tormenting her endlessly, making her that much more determined to make it to the end of the year and transfer to another school.

As far as Brenda was concerned, Mr. Morrison was innocent of any wrongdoing. Like Brenda, he did the job to the best of his ability and had persevered through numerous bouts of bad behavior and lack of parental involvement. All year long, she had watched him battle the children and parents, never believing for a moment that the day would come when he would have to do battle against his own administrator. The person who had been put in place to help him had now turned against him. For his part, Mr. Morrison fought back gallantly and denied every accusation against him. Brenda had always admired Mr. Morrison in the past, but she had never admired him more than she did now. Being placed on a professional development plan was no mere slap on the wrist. It meant constant interrogation and relentless harassment on the part of the administration. It was a modern-day torture mechanism specifically intended to create a barbaric work environment, and it put a person's endurance to the test. How someone could work under such conditions, Brenda did not know. Every day, from her classroom window, she saw people walking in and out of Mr. Morrison's classroom with their clipboards and tape recorders in hand. She estimated that Mr. Morrison was receiving an average of four visits per day. It went without saying that the one person who never failed to visit was Mrs. Harrison. Her preference was to come during the last period of the day, when the children were naturally at their rowdiest. Other visitors included district personnel, the school's union representative, the behavioral specialist, and, occasionally, the interim principal. Everyone who entered Mr. Morrison's classroom did so with the false pretense of providing assistance, but in truth, all they really wanted to do was catch him in the act of violating school policy.

However, catching him in a violation was no easy feat, as Mr. Morrison was not the type of person who crumbled easily under pressure. If anything, everyone's incessant badgering only fueled his ambition and made him that much more determined to pass the professional development plan. Mr. Morrison took special care to dot his i's and cross his t's during this tumultuous time of his career. He surpassed everyone's expectations and passed all of his observations with flying colors. However, despite his best efforts, Brenda knew that Mrs. Harrison would eventually find a way to get him fired. If she couldn't take him down legally with a professional development plan, then she'd resort to dishonest or illegal measures to get her way.

And that was exactly what she did. On one beautiful Friday afternoon, after everyone else had gone home, Brenda decided to stay late and call parents. After making half a dozen calls, she took a break and went to the bathroom. While she was washing her hands, she saw Mrs. Harrison turn the corner and make a beeline down the 900 hallway. Brenda immediately felt her heart seize in her chest. Was Mrs. Harrison looking for her? Was she in some kind of trouble? Her heart resumed beating when she saw Mrs. Harrison bypass her classroom and stop in front of Mr. Morrison's door. Brenda knew for a fact that Mr. Morrison had already gone home for the day. His door was locked, and the lights were off. Anyone passing by could clearly see that Mr. Morrison was not there. However, Mrs. Harrison refused to budge and remained standing in front of his door. She lingered momentarily and then placed her hands against the glass and looked inside. Brenda slowly stepped away from the bathroom sink and walked out to the courtyard. What was this bitch up to now? Because Brenda didn't have a clear view, she walked quietly across the grass and hid behind a tree. From her hiding place, she could see that Mrs. Harrison was carrying a large bag and had an oversized keychain in her hand. She took one of the keys off the keychain and proceeded to unlock the door. At that moment, Brenda knew what she was going to do. She had purposely waited for Mr. Morrison to leave so that she could search his room. Administrators had keys to all of the classrooms and could freely walk in and out at their leisure. As Brenda had discovered just a few months before, it was perfectly acceptable to violate a person's privacy and go through his or her personal belongings. Brenda fidgeted anxiously behind the tree and wondered what she should do. Should she call Mr. Morrison and warn him about what was going on? No! She needed to stay out of this. There was nothing to gain by becoming involved. As much as she liked and respected Mr. Morrison, she couldn't afford to be a martyr and risk losing her job.

It took Mrs. Harrison many minutes, but eventually, she got inside. Once the door shut behind her, Brenda moved away from the tree and inched her way toward Mr. Morrison's classroom. She knew that she should just stay away, but she couldn't resist spying on Mrs. Harrison. If she got caught, Brenda shuddered to think what Mrs. Harrison would do. However, despite the overwhelming risk, she moved forward and continued her surveillance. What she found most curious of all was the bag Mrs. Harrison was carrying in her hand. Even from a distance, Brenda could see that it was bulging to the point of bursting. What was in the bag, and why was she taking it into Mr. Morrison's classroom? Brenda maneuvered her way carefully down the hallway, tilted her head ever so slightly, and shot a quick glance into Mr. Morrison's room. Fortunately for her, Mrs. Harrison had her back turned to the window. She had kept the lights off purposely and was standing next to Mr. Morrison's desk. Brenda moved in for a closer look and could now clearly see what Mrs. Harrison was doing. She had removed the bag from her shoulder and had emptied its contents onto a nearby chair. Despite the darkness, Brenda could make out the familiar forms of medicine bottles. As she watched Mrs. Harrison strategically place the bottles in each of the desk drawers, she suddenly felt herself become faint. The realization of what Mrs. Harrison was doing had finally dawned upon her. She was planting the medications in Mr. Morrison's desk on a Friday afternoon and would conduct a random search of his classroom first thing Monday morning. School policy dictated that teachers were not to bring prescription or nonprescription medications onto school grounds. Even commonly used items taken for granted by most people were not permitted in the classroom. Brenda had learned this lesson on the first day of school. She had been found guilty of plugging in an air freshener, which Mrs. Harrison had confiscated before the day was over. Mrs. Harrison had not written her up for so minor an offense but had left her with a stern warning and threats of serious repercussions should the incident happen again.

Since Brenda could no longer bear to watch the scene that unfolded before her eyes, she carefully slinked past Mr. Morrison's window and made her way back to her own classroom. She slumped into her chair and sighed sadly to herself. Come Monday morning, a guiltless man would be called into the office and would have to stand trial for a crime that he hadn't even committed. Fortunately, all hope was not yet lost. There was still a minute chance that he could redeem his innocence. Like Brenda, Mr. Morrison was a member of the union and was therefore entitled to union representation. But then again, what difference did that make? To Brenda, the word *union* was synonymous with the word *useless*. During the course of her first year at Twin Palms Middle School, she had witnessed more atrocities and scandals than she cared to admit. And where was the union when all this was happening? Anyone and everyone associated with that sham of an organization always appeared to be conveniently unavailable whenever somebody needed help. The representative assigned to Brenda's school was always out in the field or preoccupied with other appointments. No one could ever reach him by phone, and the secretary at the union building was reluctant to take messages. Indeed, it was quite likely that Mr. Morrison would have to stand trial alone or, even worse, exhaust his personal funds to pay for legal representation.

The only glimmer of hope in this tunnel of darkness was that Mr. Morrison was an established teacher. He had passed all of the probationary periods and had earned satisfactory ratings on every one of his evaluations. As a result, he had been awarded a professional services contract. It was certainly a notable milestone, one that Brenda hoped to someday personally achieve, but what actual benefit existed in having such a contract? Was this contract the ticket to a lifetime of job security, or was it merely a flashy yet worthless title that held no real meaning? Brenda had posed this question to her fellow colleagues on numerous occasions only to get mixed responses. Because she couldn't get a straight answer, she referred to the union handbook and, in doing so, discovered that the one benefit to obtaining such a contract involved the issue of placement. In the event that a school downsized, a contracted teacher wouldn't be terminated but would instead be placed wherever there was availability. On the one hand, a teacher would be grateful just to have a job, but on the other hand, a teacher had no control over where he or she would be sent. Brenda had heard of surplused teachers driving upward of one hundred miles each day to get to and from their jobs. A long commute was one thing, but there was the more serious threat of clashing with the new administration. Most principals preferred to handpick their own employees and frowned upon the prospect of inheriting some other school's sloppy seconds. Any teacher caught up in the whirlwind of a surplus was entirely at the mercy of his or her new principal. Although some schools welcomed the teachers with open arms, the vast majority treated them like new teachers, plunging them to the bottom of the professional ladder and forcing them to claw their way back to the top.

Placement in the event of a surplus was all fine and good, but Brenda was more interested in the union's position on tenure. After going over the handbook with a fine-tooth comb, she came to the conclusion that the union had no position on tenure. In no place did the handbook even use the word *tenure*. There might have been a time when a teacher could become tenured, but that time was no more. With the advent of No Child Left Behind, teachers were no longer entitled to any type of job security. One year of low FCAT scores was all it took for a teacher to be yanked out of the classroom and thrust into the unemployment line. However, Mr. Morrison's particular situation had nothing to do with test scores. Because he was a social studies teacher, he was not subjected to the accountability requirements and was therefore spared the anguish felt by the reading and math teachers. And what about all those stellar reviews? How could anyone fire a teacher who had consistently received satisfactory evaluations? To give him a poor evaluation now was completely out of the question. It would be a glaring contradiction to his past performance and would show a lack of consistency on the part of the administration. On paper, Mr. Morrison appeared to be the ideal teacher. With such an impeccable record, they'd never be able to get rid of him. The administration needed to abandon the professional development plan altogether and devise a plan more conducive to their goals. They needed to do something that would not only tarnish his reputation but also accelerate his demise and ensure his dismissal. And what better way to accomplish this goal than by strategically placing a few medicine bottles in his desk drawers?

After examining the issue from every angle, Brenda came to the sad conclusion that Mr. Morrison was going to lose his job. Despite his seniority at the school and his membership in the union, the overriding factor was that Florida was not an employee-friendly state. There were many benefits to living in Florida, but employment was not one of them. In this particular state, employers could hire and fire at will. It was unlikely that any lawyer would take Mr. Morrison's case and come to his defense. How could anyone prove that he hadn't brought the medications to school? It would be his word against theirs, and as it was, everyone who was in a high position was against him. The only silver lining in this sorry saga was that he hadn't been fired on the spot. The ninety-day professional development plan had bought him some time and had allowed him to pocket a few extra paychecks. Furthermore, Mr. Morrison was not a man without skills. Teaching was only one of his many talents. As soon as Mrs. Harrison had gotten on his case, he had immediately updated his résumé and aggressively started looking for a new job. Brenda was fascinated to discover that he had both an appraisal and real-estate license as well as a master's degree in construction management. He didn't need to chain himself to this profession. He was free to cast off the shackles and go somewhere where he would be appreciated.

Unfortunately, the loss of one person's job wasn't enough to satiate Mrs. Harrison's appetite for destruction. She wouldn't be appeased until she destroyed everyone who crossed her path. Unfortunately for her, there wasn't enough time to put another person on a professional development plan. Right now, everyone's top priority was preparing for the FCAT. However, even though Mrs. Harrison could not put another professional development plan in place, there was still a strong likelihood that she was going to fire someone else on Brenda's team, and the person next in line was Ms. Spencer. Even though she was the most experienced teacher on Brenda's team, she lacked the fortitude and finesse necessary to do the job. Brenda vividly remembered the first day of school, when she had intervened on Ms. Spencer's behalf. Since then, not a day had gone by when Brenda didn't sacrifice some portion of her planning period to help Ms. Spencer manage her students. Interestingly, none of the other teachers on the team ever offered to help. Instead, they did just the opposite. They treated Ms. Spencer like an outcast and shunned her as she walked by. Coincidentally, Mr. Morrison had experienced similar treatment shortly after Mrs. Harrison had written him up. How could people be so heartless? To Brenda, Mr. Morrison and Ms. Spencer seemed reminiscent of the lepers from biblical times. These two teachers were confined to their classrooms and alienated from the rest of the school. It seemed that nobody wanted to be associated with someone who was going to lose his or her job. Should anyone dare to get too close, the same fate could befall that person.

Brenda knew that Mr. Morrison would eventually land on his feet, but what about Ms. Spencer? Unlike Mr. Morrison, Ms. Spencer had an excitable temperament and showed numerous signs of emotional instability. She was prone to fits of aimless weeping and spent the majority of her time cowering under her desk. Why didn't anyone ever come to her rescue? Why did everyone ignore her cries for help? Even though Brenda was new to the profession, she was learning quickly how things worked. There was no room for compassion or pity in the workplace. She worked in a cutthroat environment where everyone was only out for him or herself. Even the security guards no longer came to help. Brenda would see them during her planning period, congregated around a bench, smoking their cigarettes and laughing behind Ms. Spencer's back. It almost seemed as if everyone wanted her to fail. There was no need to place this woman on a professional development plan; she was visibly falling to pieces, and it would only be a matter of time before she completely and totally collapsed.

And that was exactly what happened. One day, Brenda saw Mr. Davenport and two other security guards escort Ms. Spencer out of her classroom. From her window, Brenda watched as they dragged her down the hallway while she cried hysterically and spoke incoherently. All the teachers came out of their classrooms to view the spectacle, watching in awe as the guards took Ms. Spencer away. Once the excitement was over, everyone but Brenda went back inside. She followed from a safe distance and watched as the security guards led her toward the administration building. Once there, they marched her into Mrs. Harrison's office and remained there for approximately five minutes. Brenda hid herself behind a cubicle at the other end of the hallway and waited for the security guards to come out. As soon as they were gone, she emerged from behind the cubicle and walked quietly down the hallway. Dying to hear what was being said, she leaned up against the wall and placed her ear against the door. Fortunately for her, the doors in the building were paper thin and posed no obstacle to hearing the conversation within. Brenda listened carefully but could only hear Ms. Spencer's frantic weeping. She leaned in a little closer, and then *smash*! It sounded as if some large object had been thrown against the wall. What could have happened? Had somebody gotten hurt?

Just as Brenda began to back away from the door, she saw the same two security guards running back down the hallway. They were coming right at her and had no doubt realized that she was eavesdropping at the door. *Oh God!* What had she gotten herself into? Why hadn't she just gone back into her classroom like everyone else?

However, much to Brenda's relief, the security guards zoomed past her and bolted into Mrs. Harrison's office. Because of all the excitement, they forgot to shut the door. This time, Brenda had full view of what was going on and was stunned by what she saw. Shards of glass were everywhere, and Mrs. Harrison was lying on the floor, cushioned by mounds of unprocessed paperwork, with Ms. Spencer straddled on top of her. Ms. Spencer had grabbed her by the hair and was in the process of banging her head against the tile floor. Brenda couldn't believe what she was seeing! Blood was everywhere, and Mrs. Harrison was screaming for help. Brenda watched with delight as one of the security guards attempted to restrain Ms. Spencer only to be punched in the face. Seeing that his partner was incapacitated, the other security guard got on the phone and called the police. Brenda smiled to herself as she listened to the guard request backup. The police department was clear across town, and it was rush hour besides. There was no way that anyone was going to get to the school anytime soon.

Unfortunately, Brenda was completely mistaken in her assumption. A nearby officer responded to the call and was at the school in less than five minutes. As the officer entered the room, Brenda frowned with disappointment. *Why did he have to come so quickly?* She would have liked nothing more than to see Ms. Spencer get in a few more shots. Directly behind the police were the paramedics. Brenda moved out of the way and watched as they placed Mrs. Harrison on a gurney and wheeled her out of the room. Ms. Spencer followed right behind with her hands handcuffed together and her eyes full of shame. Brenda followed this sad procession all the way to the parking lot and watched as the paramedics loaded Mrs. Harrison into the ambulance. She had been beaten so savagely that she was presently going in and out of consciousness. Brenda watched stolidly as the paramedics attended to her wounds and monitored her vitals. Judging by her condition, it was unlikely she would come back to work anytime soon. And while she was laid up in the hospital, her staff would continue on without her, celebrating their newfound freedom and reveling in her absence.

But what was to become of Ms. Spencer? Brenda shifted her glance away from the ambulance and turned her attention toward the police car. Ms. Spencer was in the backseat, waiting to be taken away. Her head still hung low, but for one brief moment, she looked up and caught Brenda's eye. Sorrow and an undeniable look of regret were written all over her face. Her eyes begged for help, but there was nothing Brenda could do. This time, Ms. Spencer would have to fend for herself. Brenda watched as the officer got into the car and started the ignition. Where was he taking her? Was she going to go to jail, or would she just lose her job? Either way, it was doubtful she would ever teach again. Brenda sighed as the police car drove away. None of this should have ever happened. Things should never have gotten this out of control. Excessive abuse and lack of support had finally caused this poor woman to crack. Did she even deserve to be punished? No, she did not. As far as Brenda was concerned, the situation should have been reversed. Ms. Spencer should have been placed in the ambulance, while Mrs. Harrison should have been taken away in the police car. In a perfect world, Mrs. Harrison would have been the criminal and would have been charged with neglect and abuse of a subordinate. Unfortunately, Brenda did not live in a perfect world, nor did she have the perfect job. Within this profession, everyone was dispensable, and one wrong step could destroy a person's entire career. As Brenda walked back to her classroom, she began to wonder about her own future. How many more years would she be able to withstand the abuse before she had a mental breakdown? She prided herself on being tolerant, but everybody had a limit. How far could she be pushed before she finally reached her breaking point?

CHAPTER 17

On the night before the FCAT, Brenda set her alarm extra early for the next day. Under no circumstances could she be late on the most important of all days. When her alarm went off the next morning, she didn't dawdle but jumped out of bed and started to get ready for work. She looked out her bedroom window and saw that it was still dark outside. Brenda hated driving in the dark, but today, she had no choice. On this day, her commute needed to be seamless. The usual morning traffic could not deter her from getting to work on time. This was the one day of the year that she couldn't afford to be late. There would be no time to stop for coffee, nor would she be able to cruise leisurely through the back roads of the neighborhood and take in the sights. Today, she would have to stick to the major highways and put the pedal to the metal.

Once Brenda drove through the school gate, her natural inclination was to park in her usual spot by the side of the building, on top of the grass. However, today she decided to make an exception and adjust her routine. She would risk the safety of her vehicle and park in the faculty parking lot instead. She still had plenty of time to spare but instinctively sensed that it wouldn't hurt to be early. On a day such as this, being on time wasn't good enough. The importance of the day demanded that the teachers rise above their usual mediocrity and go the extra mile. As Brenda walked to her classroom, she couldn't help noticing that the school was eerily quiet. Where was everybody? How peculiar that not one single teacher could be found! Remembering what day it was, Brenda suddenly realized that everyone was at the administration building, picking up the testing materials. Not wanting to be late, she took a quick detour and arrived at the office in less than two minutes. However, there was no need for her to have rushed. Things were moving along at a snail's pace, and Brenda sighed with disgust as she took her place at the end of the line. There were at least twenty people in front of her, all anxiously waiting for their turn. What was the holdup? Why hadn't the administrators coordinated the distribution of materials more efficiently? There was no excuse for this standstill! The higher-ups had had months to prepare for this day and had a superfluity of staff assisting them through every phase of the process. So what was the problem? Why couldn't these people get their shit together? Enraged by what she saw, Brenda began to tap her foot irately against the pavement. Was this what she had gotten up early for? She could have just as easily slept in late, and nobody would have been the wiser. Just as Brenda was about to explode, somebody finally called out her name. After waiting in line for forty-five minutes, it was finally her turn to pick up her FCAT testing materials.

As Brenda entered the room, she took a moment to look around. The conference room, which was generally used for parent/teacher conferences, had been temporarily transformed into the FCAT storage room. The chairs that belonged in this room had been wheeled out into the hallway and replaced with large boxes that were piled high to the ceiling. In the center of the room was a rectangular table that was currently camouflaged with pencils, papers, calculators, and other testing-related materials. The guidance counselors had been pulled out of their offices and drafted into helping with the retrieval of the boxes. Brenda watched as the counselors climbed up and down the ladders, and she wondered how long it would take them to find her box. Once she had her box, the first thing she did was open the lid and look inside. She had already checked her box the night before, but protocol required that she check it one more time. She counted the test booklets as well as the test sheets and made sure she had enough pencils. It wasn't necessary to count the calculators, since only the eighth-grade students were permitted to use them. After counting the materials, each teacher was instructed to report to his or her administrator for one final inspection. The seventh—and eighth-grade administrators were standing nearby, but Mrs. Harrison was nowhere to be found. No doubt she was still in the hospital, recovering from her injuries. Thanks to Ms. Spencer's bang-up job, there was no telling how long Mrs. Harrison would be out. It looked as if she was going to be absent during testing and, with any luck, the remainder of the school year.

After an administrator signed off on her box, Brenda was finally free to return to her classroom. Once there, she had less than fifteen minutes to prepare before the arrival of her first class. Thank goodness she had done the bulk of her preparations the night before! She sat down at her desk and reviewed the FCAT checklist one last time. The first item on the list pertained to the setup of the classroom. The desks were to be spaced out at least two feet apart, and the boards had to be wiped clean. As for the classroom walls, all educational posters that could aid a student during the exam needed to be removed. Some of the teachers chose to cover their posters rather than remove them, but what was the point of that? Why spend hours covering them over when it took only a few minutes to rip them down? Besides, Brenda had no intention of putting them back up. With only two months left to go, she needed to start packing things away. Directly behind the FCAT checklist was a second, lengthier checklist regarding the end-of-the-year procedures. Even though it was still relatively early, teachers needed to start packing things away. To Brenda, such a massive undertaking hardly seemed feasible. Taking down posters was the easy part. What about her classroom and the adjoining closet? She would have to box up everything she had accumulated over the course of the year and place it in storage. Where in the world would she find the time to get everything done before the last day of school?

Once Brenda had completed every requirement on the checklist, she lifted the lid off the box and took a peek inside. The booklets, all neatly stacked in a pile, were sealed shut with some sort of adhesive tape. Brenda randomly selected a booklet and tried to read its contents but could not do so without breaking the tape. This obstacle greatly frustrated her, and she angrily flung the booklet back into the box. She couldn't take the suspense any longer! What kind of questions were on this exam?

Did her students even have a remote chance of passing? Brenda began to pace nervously back and forth across the room liked a caged animal. Everything was riding on this standardized test. Her job at the school as well as her entire career depended on this one exam. What if her students didn't make the necessary gains? How would their low test scores impact her future at the school? Would the administration show leniency toward a first-year teacher, or would they go for the jugular and terminate her at the end of the school year?

At promptly 9:00 a.m., Brenda's first-period class shuffled into her classroom. According to the checklist, the children were not permitted access to their backpacks during the exam. Therefore, Brenda had the children place their bags against the back wall and then instructed them to return to their assigned seats. Looks of fear radiated from their eyes as they did what they were told. There was some small comfort in knowing that she wasn't the only one terrorized by this test. However, the greater comfort was in knowing that her students had some semblance of concern. Their trepidation was a clear indication that regardless of the outcome, they wanted to do well on the exam. Brenda had never seen fear in the eyes of her students before, and seeing their uncertainty struck pity into her heart. Despite their refusal to learn and their relentless resistance to discipline, she still cared for her students. She often hated their behavior, but she never hated them. And although it was her job to play the part of a strict disciplinarian, Brenda was not entirely devoid of compassion. Good or bad, she had grown to love these children, and more than anything, she wanted to see them succeed.

As soon as everyone was seated, Brenda took out her FCAT script and read the directions verbatim to the class. The first set of instructions involved the test sheets. Every sheet had a sticker listing the child's name and social security number, but certain sections still needed to be bubbled in. As the children frantically bubbled away, Brenda walked across the room and opened the box. This was it! This was the moment she had been waiting for! She took out the booklets and placed one on top of each student's desk. Then she stepped back and watched eagerly as her students used their pencils to break the seals. However, once the booklets were open and the questions were revealed, Brenda was hesitant to leave her desk. Was it really wise for her to walk over to the students and lean over their shoulders while they were taking the exam? If she got too close, someone might ask for help. Was it a good idea to place herself in such a compromising position? Brenda needed to think this scenario through before she made any rash decisions. Would she be able to deny a child who looked longingly up to her for help? Was she capable of being that heartless? Brenda felt completely torn. Instinctively, she knew it was best to keep her distance, but she really wanted to see the questions on the exam. Brenda sat down at her desk and thumbed through her paperwork. The best course of action was to keep herself busy while her students took the exam. Unfortunately, it was no use. Nothing she did could hold her attention for longer than a few minutes. In the end, Brenda decided to go against her better judgment. What was the harm in walking over and lingering just long enough to catch a glimpse of the questions? Her students were so engrossed with solving the problems that they probably wouldn't even notice she was there. And if anyone confronted her, she would simply turn her back and walk away.

With great apprehension, Brenda walked over to the student closest in proximity to her desk. At first, the little boy didn't even notice she was there. Many minutes passed before he even acknowledged her presence. However, once the boy made eye contact with her, Brenda immediately regretted her decision and wished that she had never walked over. Thirty minutes had passed by, and the boy had not filled in one single answer. The child in question was clearly struggling and was teetering on the brink of failure. To complicate things further, the little boy latched onto her hand and refused to let go. Brenda quickly averted her eyes and escaped the child's grasp, but this only made matters worse. Tears of frustration began to fill his eyes, and before she knew it, the child began to bawl. No amount of cajoling could calm him down, and despite her best efforts, the little boy refused to be comforted. Brenda couldn't believe how quickly things had gotten out of control. Her worst fears were being realized, and she didn't know what to do. Why hadn't she just stayed at her desk? Why did she always have to go looking for trouble? Brenda looked around the room and saw that she needed to act quickly. The entire class had taken notice of their hysterical classmate and had abandoned taking the test. It was imperative that she quell the child's crying, or else everyone was going to fail the FCAT.

"Please don't cry, Justin. Just take a deep breath and do the best you can."

"I don't get this, Ms. Connor! Ya gotta help me!"

"You know that I can't do that! I could get into serious trouble if I gave you the answers to the test."

"I ain't gonna tell on ya, Ms. Connor."

"Me neither!"

"Yeah! We ain't gonna tell! Nobody ain't gonna say nothing, Ms. Connor!"

Brenda watched in horror as her students ganged up on her and solemnly swore to remain silent if she divulged the answers to the exam. The obvious thing to do was refuse their request, but the words wouldn't come out of her mouth. Instead, she looked at her students and pondered the proposition they had placed before her. Ethically, she knew that what she was contemplating was wrong. Even if her students honored their end of the bargain, would she be able to carry this violation on her conscience? And what if somebody accidentally said something? With more than thirty students sitting in her class, somebody was bound to squeal. And what if she got caught? The administration wouldn't waste their time with documentation and disciplinary plans. They would take swift action and terminate her on the spot. But then again, what if she didn't give them the answers? What would happen to her then? Brenda could tell by all the moaning and groaning that most of her students were probably going to fail. Why not just give them the answers? At this point, what did she have to lose? Brenda felt trapped and didn't know what to do. No matter how she rationalized it, one way or the other, she was going to get screwed. However, be that as it may, she still needed to make a decision. Every child in the room was staring up at her, anxiously awaiting her response. She struggled over this quandary for many minutes but then finally made up her mind.

"I'm sorry, but I can't give you the answers. Try to think back to the strategies that we discussed, and if you're completely stumped, then use the process of elimination to make an educated guess."

"But we promise!"

"I said no! Now get back to work!"

With this, Brenda returned to her desk, and her students resumed taking the test. She knew that she had made the right decision, but if she had known for certain that every child would have stayed true to his or her word, she would have gladly given them the answers to the exam. A year ago, she would never have considered doing something like this. In the beginning, she had come into the profession with the best of intentions. She had believed in the school's mission statement and had strived to uphold its principles. Now she no longer cared about anything but herself. She had been beaten and battered for so long that she no longer gave a damn about integrity or honesty. She had tried to work within the constraints of the educational system, but time and time again, the system had betrayed her. Brenda thought back to the endless hours she had spent documenting students and all the nights she had stayed late to call parents. Had anyone ever rewarded or even acknowledged her for all of her hard work? Of course not! Her referrals had ended up in the trash, and she had ended up sitting in Mrs. Harrison's office. Brenda looked at the binder sitting on her desk and felt tempted to trash it right then and there. Why was she still holding on to it? She had long since given up on documenting students, and she rarely ever called students' homes. It had been weeks since she had updated the binder, and it no longer accompanied her wherever she went. The old Brenda would have frowned upon such negligence, but the new Brenda felt no remorse at all. Her entire morale had changed for the worse, and it was unlikely she would ever feel enthusiastic about her job again.

After exactly an hour and a half, Brenda called time, and the children lined up to go to the cafeteria. However, before they could leave, all of the testing materials needed to be returned to the box and locked in the closet. This requirement was emphasized in bold print on the checklist, and Brenda was cautious to adhere, lest some administrator or security guard randomly decided to inspect her classroom. Once she had safely locked away the materials, Brenda took a moment to reread the checklist. The last section focused on student conduct and reminded all Twin Palms Middle School employees that managing student behavior during FCAT testing was a collaborative effort. Teachers were expected to monitor behavior within the classroom, but everybody's cooperation was required in the hallways. Brenda glanced out her classroom window and could see the security guards posted along every corridor of the building. She could see by the looks on their faces that they were none too pleased about having to assist with the students. She watched them grudgingly put out their cigarettes as the students began to make their way down the hallway. Since the seventh—and eighth-grade students were still testing, it was of the utmost importance that the noise level be kept under control. To help maintain order, the administrators and interim principal were also present for the sixth-grade procession to the cafeteria. Their piercing stares were ever watchful for bad behavior, and the aggressiveness of their body language insinuated that they were ready to pounce at the slightest hint of trouble. Seeing that she was being watched, Brenda carefully maneuvered her students through the hallway, shushing them every step of the way. However, she temporarily lost her momentum when she passed by Ms. Spencer's and Mr. Morrison's classrooms. A wave of sadness suddenly washed over her when she saw substitute teachers sitting at their desks. At the beginning of the school year, she had started out on a team of five, and now only three remained. She choked down her sadness and refocused her concentration on her students. Ms. Spencer and Mr. Morrison were gone, but she was still there. It was time to think of herself now and put this foolish nostalgia behind her. Her survival was paramount, and making it through the last few weeks was the only thing that mattered.

Once Brenda reached the cafeteria, she was surprised to discover that even in there, communication was to be kept to a bare minimum. The children were expected to eat their lunches in complete silence and had to raise their hand or whisper quietly to attract the attention of an adult. It seemed cruel to impose such harsh restrictions on young children, but no discussions were permitted during FCAT testing. The administration took every precaution to prevent the students from disclosing the answers to the exam. For the moment, things seemed to be under control, but there was no telling how long the peace would last. As far as Brenda could see, the children resented having to remain quiet during their lunch break. Most were irritable, and a number of them were fidgeting in their seats. How long could they sit quietly before they blew up and released all their pent-up energy? A behavioral backlash was brewing, but Brenda didn't care. After all, this wasn't her problem. This was her duty-free break, and it was hers to spend however she pleased. She could have forgone her lunch period to help with the children, but why would she do that? When had the administration ever gone out of their way to help her? Needless to say, she didn't feel the least bit guilty about dumping the kids on the administrators and retreating to the teachers' lounge. She was in dire need of a break and desperately needed the half hour to recoup her energy. The day had been long and stressful, and it wasn't even half over. For the sake of her own sanity, she needed to turn her back and walk away.

Apparently, Brenda wasn't the only one who felt overwhelmed by the challenges of the day. Upon entering the lounge, she could see that the sentiment prevailed upon everybody in the room. Some of the teachers stared into the distance, while others fought the urge to doze off and fall asleep. Few, if any, had any appetite. However, everyone suddenly perked up when Mr. Richard entered the room. He was carrying a large basket filled with meats and cheeses, all immaculately arranged and tied together with a beautiful red bow. Everyone followed him with his or her eyes, but nobody dared to utter a word. Once he was gone, Brenda was the first to break the silence and speak up.

"Who do you think that's for?"

"Isn't it obvious, Ms. Connor? It's a present for Mrs. Harrison."

"What? Why would Mr. Richard waste his money on that nasty bitch?"

"Because he knows how to play the game."

"What's that supposed to mean?"

"Don't you see, Ms. Connor? Mr. Richard takes every opportunity to shine in front of the administration. Haven't you seen him volunteering in the office and helping out in the hallways? Haven't you seen him around after school? Did you know that he stays late almost every day to play football with the kids?"

"I know! That rat bastard makes everybody look bad!"

"Actually, I think we could all learn a thing or two from Mr. Richard. Maybe we should all pitch in a few dollars for a gift certificate and a nice card."

"I'm not pitching in for anything! She can rot in that hospital for all I care!"

"From your mouth to God's ears, Ms. Connor. However, we need to acknowledge the possibility that she might come back. Then what are you going to do?"

"I'll just do what I've always done. I'll go about my business and do my job to the best of my ability."

"Oh Ms. Connor, when are you going to learn? Doing your job is simply not enough. The higher-ups favor those who take initiative. You need to follow Mr. Richard's example and start volunteering your spare time. For starters, you could use your planning period to help in the office, or you could stay after school and start a club."

"What! You expect me to work for free? I get paid for a forty-hour week, and forty hours is all that I intend to work!"

"With an attitude like that, you won't last two years in this profession. Take my advice and find a way to get into Mrs. Harrison's good graces, or else you won't have a job. Look at Mr. Richard. He's been here for ten years and will probably be here for ten more. Do you think that he's lasted this long because he's such an exceptional teacher? I don't think so! He's outlasted all of us because he has his fingers firmly lodged in all of the proper assholes and can be relied upon to do what others will not. And look at how it's paid off! No matter what happens, he knows that he'll never lose his job."

Try as she might, Brenda couldn't argue with this last point. Although she found Mr. Richard's alacrity to be annoying, his can-do attitude had definitely paid off. He seemed to be the only teacher on her team who was immune to the stress and illness that naturally came along with the job. As a matter of fact, Brenda had heard that he hadn't taken a sick day in over five years. How could this be? She was surrounded by teachers who were plagued with everything from the common cold to conditions that required ongoing medication. And even though Brenda herself was still young and in the prime of her life, the stress of the job had taken a serious toll on her health. Her compromised immunity lacked the ability to ward off sickness, and her body was deteriorating before her eyes. She caught everything that the kids had and then some. Although she compulsively washed her hands multiple times a day, her throat was always sore, and her nose was always running. As of late, she was battling some kind of stomach bug that was wreaking havoc on her digestive system. As hard as she tried, she couldn't hold anything down. Everything she ate made her want to vomit. Even more problematic was when she threw up. The all-too-familiar queasiness always set in during the earlier part of the day. Now more than ever, Brenda wished that she had an office job. How nice it would be to have the freedom to just get up and walk over to the bathroom! People in other professions had no idea how good they had it. To be able to use the bathroom without first asking for permission was a luxury unknown to those who worked in the teaching profession. Legally, she couldn't leave the kids unattended, so what was she supposed to do? Her only other option was to throw up in her trash can or, if time permitted, run outside and puke in the bushes. When her agony intensified and was more than she could bear, Mr. Fisher ultimately came to her rescue. He covered both of their classes so that she could escape for a few minutes from the watchful eyes of her students and lean over an actual toilet to empty out the contents of her stomach.

Brenda had many friends, but few were as special as Mr. Fisher. Without his help, she would have surely fallen apart. Nobody else helped her, and she had no vacation time to see a doctor. She tried various herbal remedies, but nothing she took was ever strong enough to eradicate the bug that had seemingly taken over her body. With no relief in sight, Brenda began to worry. Her condition was worsening with each passing day, and she didn't know what to do. What was wrong with her? She'd always been healthy in the past. Why couldn't she get better? The only good thing that came out of this misery was that Brenda began to eat less. Because food aggravated her condition, she effortlessly reduced her caloric intake. This was not the way that she wanted to lose weight, but at least the pounds would finally come off. As bad as she felt, Brenda couldn't help feeling ecstatic over all of the weight she was going to lose. For the first time in her life, she couldn't wait to hop onto a scale. At this rate, she was going to lose all of her excess weight in no time at all! By the end of the year, she'd be able to throw out all of her fat clothes and finally take her skinny clothes out of storage.

However, after a month of subsisting on only liquids and the occasional banana, Brenda saw no difference at all. Nothing felt looser, and some of her pants actually felt tighter. How could this be? Brenda decided it was time to get on a scale and see what was going on. When the number came up, she was startled to discover that instead of losing weight, she had actually gained weight. How could this have happened? How could she have gained weight when she hardly ate anything at all? Suddenly, a thought struck her like a flash of lightning: When was the last time she had gotten her period? She realized that two whole months had passed since her last menstruation. Was she pregnant? It would certainly explain her nausea and lack of appetite. But how could this be? She and Joseph were always so careful. They almost always used protection, and when they didn't, he always pulled out. She didn't like having unprotected sex, but she trusted him nevertheless, and now this had happened. Brenda began to hyperventilate and collapsed into a nearby chair. What was she going to do now? How could she support a child when she could hardly support herself? Should she tell Joseph? Should she seek advice from her mother? No! For the time being, she would keep this to herself until she received confirmation that she was indeed pregnant.

After FCAT testing was over, the children were released from their worries and were free to enjoy the rest of the school year. However, Brenda knew no such freedom. Although the FCAT was a burden no more, she had a new set of problems to contend with. Over the next two weeks, she took over fifteen home pregnancy tests, all of which tested positive. She could no longer deny that she was pregnant. Now what was she going to do? Although she wanted to have a child eventually, she didn't want to have one right now. How could she raise a child when everything in her life was in such disarray? And how would Joseph react to the news? Their relationship was already hanging by a thread. News like this would surely send him running for the hills, and then what would she do? Could she raise this baby on her own? She would have her family's support, but she would also have the stigma that came along with being a single mother. But what other option did she have? Could she carry this child to term and then give it up for adoption? No, she could not. She could never part with her baby once she saw it and held it in her arms. The only other option left to consider was abortion. Brenda knew lots of girls in college who had had abortions. She had heard the stories and knew that it was a quick procedure with minimal downtime. She could have it done on a Saturday and be back to work first thing Monday morning. Abortion was the only solution she could think of that would solve all of her problems. But could she do it? Could she kill the tiny mite of life that was growing inside her body? Brenda didn't know. Unfortunately, she needed to make her decision quickly. Within a few weeks, she would begin to show, and her shame would be exposed to the entire world. If she was going to have an abortion, she would have to do it now or else go through with the pregnancy.

CHAPTER 18

Without the menacing presence of Mrs. Harrison in her life, Brenda passed the remaining months with relative tranquility and eased gracefully into the last week of school. She gleefully crossed off the days on her calendar and ripped the paper from the wall with childlike enthusiasm whenever a month finally reached completion. Next to her calendar hung the end-of-the-year procedures. During the FCAT, Brenda had carelessly cast this list aside, but now this document commanded her full attention. Brenda had so much to do before the last day of school that she hardly knew where to begin. The list was only one page long, but it was jam-packed with relevant information. It seemed that everybody in every facet of the school had his or her demands. Administrators needed copies of grades and lesson plans, department heads required book counts, the computer specialist needed teachers to return the laptops, and the security guards were in charge of inspecting classrooms and collecting keys. And then there was the issue of the classroom itself. Apparently, breaking down a classroom was every bit as difficult as setting one up. Brenda had begun the process weeks in advance, but she still found herself racing against the clock. She had begun gradually at first but when struck with the realization that she was running out of time had grown anxious and quickly picked up the pace. Now here she was, in the last week of school, relieved that the bulk of the work was finally done. The only thing left to do was tie up the loose ends and congratulate herself on a job well done.

However, Brenda could not in good faith take full credit for her success. The children had made the greatest contribution to this cause and had ultimately helped her meet many of the deadlines on the checklist. With the end only days away, everyone was in high spirits, and even Brenda's worst students were willing to offer a helping hand. Just as she enjoyed ripping the pages off of her calendar, her students enjoyed ripping her classroom to shreds. Brenda had never seen enthusiasm like this before! No one shied away from the physicality of the work, and the children actually fought each other for the coveted role of teacher's helper. For the first time ever, Brenda relinquished all control and allowed her students to take over the management of her classroom. She watched with sheer fascination as one group of students gingerly wrapped her belongings in bubble paper and packed them carefully into the cardboard boxes. At the opposite end of the room, Brenda observed how a second group of students meticulously took inventory of the textbooks and then placed them in neat piles up against the wall. Most astonishing of all were the students who volunteered to tackle her closet. Cleaning out the closet was a mammoth task, one that Brenda had put off until the end of the school year. The clutter inside the room was a full year's worth of accumulation. From top to bottom, stuff was everywhere, and what did not fit on the shelves was scattered haphazardly around the floor. Perhaps she could have avoided this predicament if the school had built bigger closets. Or maybe Brenda needed to be more selective and learn how to throw things away. Either way, this monstrosity needed to be cleaned out, and it needed to be done soon. Had Brenda waited much longer, the closet would surely have burst, and everything inside would have oozed out from underneath the cracks and onto her classroom floor.

Clearly, the final days of school were happy days where fun could be found in even the most unpleasant of tasks. Seeing that everything was under control and her presence was no longer needed, Brenda sat down at her desk and treated herself to a long-overdue and well-deserved repose. As she rested, she looked upon the children who, within a few short days, would no longer be her students. After having spent a full year with them, she thought that she knew everything about them. She was well acquainted with their many flaws, but who would have ever thought that they had an industrious side? Why couldn't they have shown this level of enthusiasm with their studies? Why did they embrace physical labor yet shun the opportunity to advance their minds? Brenda could not say, nor was it any longer her concern. All she cared about now were the eight child-free weeks of vacation ahead of her. She yearned to taste and savor the idleness of summer and could hardly wait for the last period on the last day of school, when she would walk her students to the bus loop for the last time and wave good-bye to them as the buses pulled out of the depot.

However, until that day arrived, Brenda needed to remain ever watchful and alert to the fact that Mrs. Harrison might come back. Even though the end was near, Brenda wasn't out of the woods just yet. Although Mrs. Harrison had been physically assaulted by Ms. Spencer and had recently given birth to a baby girl, there was still a miniscule chance that she might show up before the last day of school. It went without saying that Brenda dreaded the prospect of her return. She had grown accustomed to working unsupervised and couldn't go back to being micromanaged. She had become lax in her ways and, over time, had completely abandoned her vigilant behavior. There was no more peeking through the blinds of her classroom window, nor was there any fear of being called into the office. The overwhelming stress that had taken such a toll on her health had gradually dissipated, as she no longer had to look over her shoulder or worry about impromptu visits from her administrator. Rationally, it didn't make sense for Mrs. Harrison to come back so close to the end of the school year. Her body had experienced severe trauma and needed an extended period of time to heal. Besides, what was the point in coming back to work now? What kind of difference could she possibly make in these last few days?

Obviously, the rational thing to do was to stay home and get better—but Mrs. Harrison was not a rational woman. On the contrary, she was a highly irrational woman who was prone to acts of stupidity and erratic behavior. And because this was the case, Brenda gradually reverted back to her old habits of watching her back. Involuntarily, her body would tense up whenever the phone rang or when someone walked into her classroom. However, the greatest threat to her peace of mind was the computer sitting on her desk. She compulsively checked her e-mails multiple times a day, always searching for anything from Mrs. Harrison. E-mail was Mrs. Harrison's preferred method of correspondence and was the way she contacted the teachers to notify them of impending meetings. However, no matter how many times she checked, Brenda always came up empty. What was this? Maybe Mrs. Harrison wasn't going to come back after all. Maybe this one and only time, Brenda had misjudged her. She had let her paranoia get the best of her and had worked herself up for nothing. Why did she do this to herself? Why did she always have to jump to conclusions and assume the worst? In truth, her paranoia wasn't her fault. After being so badly brutalized, Brenda found it impossible to believe that she could make it to the end of the year unscathed. She needed to take a deep breath and calm down. None of the other teachers seemed overly concerned. Why couldn't she stop with all of her needless worrying and just sit back and enjoy the last few days of the school year?

However, just as she was about to let her guard down and give Mrs. Harrison the benefit of the doubt, an e-mail showed up late one Wednesday afternoon. Brenda felt the floor drop from underneath her feet when she saw the subject line "!!!URGENT MEETING!!!" staring back at her with capital letters and an excessive use of exclamation points. Her worst fears had been confirmed. Mrs. Harrison was coming back, and she wanted to have a meeting with the sixth-grade teachers. But what was the meeting about? Brenda thought about the e-mail on the ride home and concluded that it probably had something to do with the children. She had trouble sleeping that night, as she did every night when she knew she had an impending meeting with Mrs. Harrison. However, she managed to salvage a few precious hours and sleep soundly with the knowledge that at least this time, Mrs. Harrison hadn't singled her out. Whatever the crime, the entire sixth-grade team was at fault and would be scrutinized as a whole.

On the last day of school, when everyone else was walking on air, Brenda was walking on eggshells. By midmorning, she had chewed off all of her fingernails and had nearly gnawed off her fingers, waiting in anticipation for the meeting to begin. Not surprisingly, the other teachers also shared her concern. All morning long, her classroom phone rang off the hook with anxious-ridden teachers making inquiries as to what the meeting might be about. Yet Brenda, always ready with the latest gossip, had no information to provide. She and the other teachers would simply have to wait until their planning period for Mrs. Harrison to disclose the details. Waiting was difficult enough, but walking to the administration building was outright agonizing. Why did Mrs. Harrison have to do this today? Why did she have to be a bitch to the end? Brenda shook her head and sighed deeply with disgust when the bell rang and fourth period finally rolled around. After dismissing the children, she headed toward Mrs. Harrison's office, terrorized at the thought of what she was going to hear. However, when she arrived, she was surprised to discover that Mrs. Harrison was not there. Instead, a note was posted, instructing the teachers to meet her in the conference room.

Mrs. Harrison, with her usual cotton-candy-like sweetness, was ready and waiting outside the door to greet the teachers. She held a stack of folders that she proceeded to distribute once everyone had entered the room. When Brenda received her folder, she opened it and saw that it contained the final grades for all of her students. She had handed in these printouts a week ago. Why were they being handed back to her now? Upon closer inspection, she noticed that certain names were highlighted in yellow marker. Upon even closer inspection, she realized that the highlighted names were the students she had failed. Brenda's mind suddenly drifted back to the beginning of the school year. She recalled Mr. Brown's advice, which she had carefully heeded by never giving any grade lower than a D. Up until now, she had played the game perfectly. All year long, she had fabricated grades and had passed failing students. She had acted like a puppet, looking the other way while her administrator worked the strings. But now she couldn't bring herself to do it. She was tired of playing games and decided it was time to take a stand. IEP or no IEP, certain students didn't deserve to be promoted to the next grade. If her decision to fail students was going to get her in trouble, then so be it! What else could Mrs. Harrison possibly do to her? Perhaps she'd get called into the office. Or maybe this time, she'd get fired. Either way, she no longer cared. It was time that somebody stood up to Mrs. Harrison. Somebody needed to speak up and put an end to this charade once and for all!

Brenda looked around the conference room and saw that like her, everyone had been handed a printout. It seemed that Brenda was not the only one who had failed students. Every single teacher sitting in the room had names highlighted in yellow. It finally became clear why they were all there: Mrs. Harrison was going to ask the sixth-grade teachers to change their grades. Brenda leaned back in her chair and reconsidered her position. Was it really wise to speak her mind, or was it better to conform to school policy? In all honesty, she didn't know what to do. She was frustrated and fed up with everything even remotely related to the field of education. Time and time again, she had tried to adjust to the politics, but no matter how hard she tried, she never managed to acquire a taste for the corruption that surrounded her. Instead, she had been an unwilling participant, always doing what she was told, ever fearful of losing her job. And now here she was, once again forced to go against her ethics. Like it or not, this was the way things were done. Year after year, schools pushed children through the educational system regardless of whether they met the requirements or not. What impact could Brenda possibly make if she chose to speak up now? Would her protests bring about change, or would she just further infuriate Mrs. Harrison? After giving the matter considerable thought, Brenda realized what she needed to do. If she wanted to keep her job, she would have to shut her mouth. She would have to submit to the will of her administrator, change her grades, and promote her students to the next grade.

"I apologize for calling this meeting at the last minute, but we need to have a discussion about the report cards. I was very disappointed when I saw these printouts. How many times have I told you not to fail your students? I've discussed this matter with you countless times before, but you still insist on defying me. As soon as this meeting is over, I expect all of you to go back to your classrooms and change these grades!"

On hearing this, Brenda couldn't contain herself and suddenly exploded. "Why should we change our grades? Why should children on IEPs get special treatment? Why should they be allowed to coast by when everyone else has to make an effort and put in the work? I don't know what kind of bullshit system we're working for here, but I'm sick and tired of these children getting preferential treatment! All year long, I've done nothing but deal with bad behavior and uncooperative parents! And now you have the audacity to sit there and tell me to change my grades? What was the point of giving all those exams and grading all those papers? Why did I spend hour upon hour putting together lesson plans and teaching classes? Everything I did was just a colossal waste of time. Here's a thought: Why don't we just do away with testing and teaching altogether? Why don't we just give every single child at Twin Palms Middle School an A regardless of his or her performance? Then everyone will be happy!"

Although it felt absolutely invigorating to speak her mind, the thrill of the moment quickly wore off, and regret instantly set in once Brenda realized what she had done. How could she have been so outspoken? She had tried to stay quiet, but the words had somehow escaped from her lips. It was too late to take it back now, but maybe there was still a slim chance that she could fix this. Brenda scanned the room, hoping somebody would back her up, but nobody said a word. Some of her colleagues stared at her in utter astonishment, while others kept their eyes glued to the floor. Brenda looked behind her and saw Mrs. Harrison glaring back at her with daggers in her eyes. Seeing her obvious rage, Brenda quickly turned back around and hunched her body over in a penitent manner. There was no doubt in her mind that she was going to pay dearly for this outburst. This time, she had overstepped her boundaries and had gone too far. Brenda suddenly felt herself become sick. Her body broke out into a cold sweat, and her hands began to tremble. Her stomach fared no better, as wave after wave of nausea pulsated through her body. She tried to calm down for the sake of her unborn child but could not find a way to suppress her stress. What was Mrs. Harrison going to do to her? What terrible punishment would she inflict on her this time? Brenda fidgeted nervously in her seat, waiting anxiously for Mrs. Harrison to make her next move.

"This meeting is now adjourned. Take these printouts back to your classrooms, and make the necessary changes before you leave for the day. You're all dismissed—except for you, Ms. Connor. You and I need to have a talk."

Brenda remained behind and watched sorrowfully as her colleagues left the room one by one, leaving her all alone with Mrs. Harrison. One would have thought she would be used to these extemporaneous meetings by now, but even after all this time, speaking with her administrator still made her physically sick. She had a sensitive soul and took even the mildest of criticisms to heart. Others around her could shake things off—why couldn't she? Why did she have to take chastisement so personally? Deep down, she knew that she was a good teacher. Why did she always let her administrator's negativity get her down? As the last of the teachers left the room, Brenda straightened herself out and sat upright in her seat. No matter what Mrs. Harrison said, she would maintain her composure and hold her ground. She braced herself as Mrs. Harrison shut the door and sat down on the opposite side of the desk. She watched as her administrator opened her bag and took out a binder. She flipped through it ever so slowly, licking her forefinger as she turned each page. Brenda could see that she wasn't going to be leaving anytime soon. Mrs. Harrison was going to take her sweet-ass time and savor every second of the hunt before she made her kill. As she turned the pages one by one, Mrs. Harrison looked up every so often and smiled in Brenda's direction. She was clearly enjoying herself and was relishing the opportunity to rip her apart. But what was she looking for? She already had the printouts sitting in front of her. Was there some other concern she wanted to address?

As Brenda sat in her seat, feeling perplexed, Mrs. Harrison pulled out two folders from the binder and placed each of them in front of her.

"Do you know what's in these folders, Ms. Connor?"

"No."

"Would you like to know what's in the folders?"

"Not really."

"The first folder contains your students' FCAT scores. Would you like to know how your students did?"

"I don't think so."

"Well, I'm going to tell you anyway. The vast majority of your students did not meet the required expectations. As you can see, most of your students dropped one or more levels."

Brenda took the folder from Mrs. Harrison's hand and studied the scores carefully. It was true! Only a handful of her students had made gains. How could this have happened? She had worked so hard to prepare the children for the test. Where had she gone wrong? It had been an uphill battle from day one, but how could they have done this poorly? Was this all that she had to show for all of her hard work? What could she have possibly done differently? Was it her fault that the students didn't do the work? Was she actually going to get blamed for these low scores?

"Cat got your tongue, Ms. Connor? You were so opinionated during the meeting, and now you're suddenly so quiet. Haven't you got anything to say for yourself?"

"I don't know what to say. I did the best that I could with what little support I had. I don't know what more I could've done."

"So what you're saying is that you're incapable of doing your job without assistance?"

"I'm more than capable of doing my job, but I'm not a miracle worker. How am I supposed to teach children who don't want to learn?"

"The children are not the problem, Ms. Connor—you are. Personally, I don't believe that you have what it takes to be a teacher. You don't have the training or the personality to work with our diverse population of students. Now, I could fire you right here and right now just based on these low FCAT scores, but I'm going to give you an opportunity to redeem yourself."

"You're going to let me keep my job?"

"Open up the second folder, and take a look inside."

Brenda reached for the other folder and saw that it contained her evaluation. Much to her surprise, Mrs. Harrison had given her satisfactory scores in every category. She had successfully passed her one-year probation and had even been offered a teaching position for the following school year. Why was Mrs. Harrison being so kind to her? Why hadn't she fired her when she had the chance? Instead of being appreciative, Brenda suddenly felt afraid. This was too good to be true. Instinctively, she knew that she was in grave danger. She knew that Mrs. Harrison had an agenda, but what was it? What vile thing would this woman do to her now?

"You claim that my performance is substandard, yet you still give me a satisfactory evaluation? What's the catch?"

"Well, Ms. Connor, after giving it some thought, I realized that I'm partially responsible for your shortcomings. As you just said, I wasn't here to provide you with support. Between my maternity leave and the incident with Ms. Spencer, I was out for almost half of the school year. I wasn't here to provide you with the assistance that you so desperately needed."

"Assistance?"

"That's right. But make no mistake—next year, I'm not going anywhere. I'll be in your classroom every day, observing your teaching and critiquing your performance. And when I can't make it to your class, I'll send the math coach in my place. I'll see to it that you have all the support that you need to manage your classes and increase your test scores. I'll also make sure to pencil in time to meet with you and discuss your progress on a weekly basis. If I don't see improvement within the first three months, I'll then move on to the next phase and put you on a professional development plan."

After Mrs. Harrison finished laying out the details that would lead to Brenda's eventual demise, she leaned back with an air of arrogance and waited patiently for a reply. Unfortunately, Brenda didn't have anything to say. What could she say? Instead of firing her, this woman had strategically found a way to prolong her pain. How could Brenda possibly endure another year of this misery? Dealing with the children was bad enough. Now she would have to deal with her administrator too. Would she be able to stand the constant presence of Mrs. Harrison in her classroom? And how would she endure the weekly meetings? Brenda recalled how the administration had placed Mr. Morrison under a microscope and dissected him during his professional development plan. Was this the same fate that awaited her? Was she also being set up for failure? It was suicide to accept Mrs. Harrison's job offer under these conditions, but what other choice did she have? Where else could she possibly go? Unlike Mr. Morrison, she had no other prospects and lacked the qualifications to work in another field. As Brenda mulled over what to do, she could feel Mrs. Harrison's stare piercing her soul. She would have liked to counterattack with some witty comeback, but sadly, Brenda had nothing clever left to say. Instead, she felt drained and defeated and would have liked nothing more than to crawl into a corner and die. She could feel her eyes begin to water and had to fight hard to hold back the tears. Her lower lip quivered uncontrollably as she quickly grabbed her belongings and dashed out of the room.

She ran toward her car but stopped abruptly midway. She felt a sharp pain in her side and leaned against a wall to catch her breath. What was this? Was something wrong with her unborn child? After a few moments, she straightened herself up and tried to run again. This time, she made it as far as the bathroom and staggered into the nearest stall. The tears that she had tried so hard to hold back in Mrs. Harrison's office now flowed freely as she began to push through the pain. In between pushes, Brenda looked down and nearly fainted when she saw blood in the toilet. She felt as if she were in labor and gripped the handrails each time she had a contraction. It felt as if someone were stabbing her lower spine and ripping her uterus open. She realized that she was hemorrhaging and needed to go to a hospital, but she couldn't get off the toilet. She felt dizzy every time she tried to stand up and would immediately fall back down. Even if she could get to a hospital, there was nothing anybody could do. She was having a miscarriage and could do nothing to save her unborn child. Copious amounts of blood had spilled into the toilet, and after an hour of excruciating pain, she lost the baby.

Once the pain subsided, Brenda stood up slowly and began the process of cleaning herself up. She wiped the blood off her legs and washed her face in the sink. Once she finished, she looked at herself in the mirror and saw that her eyes were sunken and her hair was still wet with her agony. She felt strong enough to walk to her car and drive herself home, but she was reluctant to leave. She wanted to take one last look at her baby and say her good-byes; however, at the last moment, she changed her mind. Because she couldn't bring herself to look upon the remains of her dead child, she said a little prayer and just walked away. From beginning to end, her entire day had been filled with nothing but sorrow, but it was finally over. Now she could go home, collapse in her bed, and immerse herself in her grief.

CHAPTER 19

Summertime was a glorious time in Florida and was by far Brenda's favorite season of the year. Tourists—otherwise known as snowbirds—would leave in droves during the early spring and wouldn't return until the following fall. Huge trucks lined up outside the various condo communities, waiting to transport cars and other personal items back to the north. Within a matter of a few short weeks, Brenda's condo community transformed from a bustling minimetropolis to a virtual ghost town. The mass exodus of tourists cleared out not only Brenda's community but also much of South Florida, and when the tourists left, the aggravation left with them. The number of car accidents on the roads significantly decreased, parking spots were easier to find, and the lines outside of restaurants and other popular venues all but disappeared. Brenda loved all of these benefits, but more than anything, she loved the quiet that blanketed her community once everybody left. She was more than happy to brave the scorching heat and torrential rains in exchange for some peace and quiet. During the peak months of the tourist season, her building was at full capacity, and somebody was always making noise. Her handyman neighbor who lived above her would wake her up in the mornings with his banging, and her half-deaf neighbors who lived next door would blast their televisions late into the night. But now everybody was gone, and Brenda was finally left alone to enjoy the solitude that surrounded her.

All year long, Brenda had waited eagerly for this moment to come, and now it was finally here. She had two full months to spend however she pleased, and she was intent on making the most of every single day. There was so much that she wanted to do, so much that she had put off during the school year. Now she finally had the time. She had originally planned on spending the summer decorating her home, catching up with friends from college, and throwing herself into her skating, but now everything had changed. Mrs. Harrison had dashed her hopes for the summer, and now her new plan was to find a job. There would be no sleeping in late or lounging by the pool. She would have to spend every waking moment searching through the classifieds and applying for everything she was even remotely qualified for. However, before she could start applying, she needed to revisit her résumé. This document, which would distinguish her from every other applicant, was in dire need of revision, and she needed to update it to match her current qualifications. Without a strong résumé, Brenda knew she would never get a job and would therefore be forced to return to Twin Palms Middle School and face the wrath of Mrs. Harrison.

Brenda had attempted to find a job once before during the Christmas holidays, yet she had made little headway and had given up the search once she'd returned to work. This time, however, giving up was not an option. The words from her last meeting with Mrs. Harrison still echoed in her mind, and the fear of future meetings and other altercations fueled Brenda to get serious about seeking alternative employment. Unfortunately, the process was far more difficult than she anticipated. The economy was still in a recession, and the unemployment rate was higher than ever. Although Brenda adhered to a strict schedule and diligently applied for jobs every day, she never got any leads. Why wasn't anyone calling her for an interview? If she wasn't the most qualified candidate, then why didn't employers send her a rejection letter or at least leave a message on her voice mail? After a while, Brenda began to wonder if some of the jobs she was applying for were even real jobs. Were these employers really hiring, or were they just placing the ads to gauge the employment market? Brenda hated wasting her time on jobs that didn't exist, but what other choice did she have? She had no way of distinguishing between a real job and a phantom job, so she applied for everything, anxiously waiting by the phone yet never receiving any calls.

Despite her overwhelming frustration, Brenda relentlessly pushed on with the job search and continued to apply each and every day. However, halfway through her summer vacation, when she still hadn't found a job, she realized that she needed a new plan of action. Fortunately, she remembered something she had read in the employee handbook regarding hardship transfers. She retrieved the handbook from her workbag and discovered that there was indeed something written to that effect. If a person had to drive more than twenty miles to get to work, he or she automatically qualified for a transfer to a school closer to his or her home. This was it! This was the answer to all of her problems! She would still be able to teach within the Miami-Dade system, just not at her particular school. She would have a fresh start with a new administration and would finally be able to put all the ugliness of Twin Palms Middle School behind her. Nobody could stop her from transferring, not even Mrs. Harrison. Brenda smiled at the thought of Mrs. Harrison's reaction when she didn't show up on the first day of school. Who would she target next? Which poor unsuspecting newcomer would she set upon destroying if Brenda was no longer at the school?

As Brenda sat down to fill out the necessary forms, she felt like a fool for not thinking of this before. She had wasted half her summer applying for jobs, not realizing that the answer had been in front of her the entire time. She couldn't get back the time she had lost, but at least she could enjoy what little time remained. She took special care filling out the three-page application, checking and rechecking for any mistakes she might have made. Brenda had filled out many applications during her lifetime but none had been as important as this one. She pored over the pages slowly, reading the questions repeatedly and writing legibly so that there would be no discrepancy over her answers. When she was finished, she drove to the nearest post office and hand delivered the precious document, requesting that it be sent with priority mail. Once the paperwork was mailed, Brenda returned to her car and drove back to her home. Once there, she looked around and decided to spend the remainder of the day ridding her home of the clutter that had accumulated over the last four weeks. Stacks of paperwork were scattered throughout her apartment in various phases of completion. Some applications were partially filled out, while others were finished and ready to be mailed off. Feeling confident that her request for a transfer would be approved, Brenda trashed all of it, sweeping the sheets into a large garbage bag and tying it securely with a rubber band. Then, with the greatest of joy, she flung the bag over her shoulder and skipped all the way to the Dumpster. Once everything was disposed of, Brenda slammed the lid shut and walked away, convinced that within a matter of a few days, she would be assigned to a new school.

With this anxiety behind her, Brenda was now finally free to enjoy the rest of her summer vacation. She was tickled at the thought of all the fun she was going to have and wondered what she should do first. Where did she want to go? Whom did she want to visit? As she considered her options, she suddenly thought of her aunt Margery. Ever since her graduation, she had wanted to contact her but had been afraid of how she might react. Although she still felt fearful, she desperately wanted to put the past behind her and make amends. It was difficult for Brenda to swallow her pride, but she still had many unanswered questions and was anxious to hear what her aunt had to say. Almost exactly one year ago to the day, her aunt had tried to warn her about the public school system, but foolishly, she had refused to listen. However, she was ready to listen now. She no longer saw her aunt as a walking repository of complaints but as a valuable source of information. She was now ready to listen and embrace any and all guidance that her aunt had to offer. But would her aunt be willing to help? Brenda thought back to her graduation and grimaced at the thought of how badly she had behaved. Had her aunt forgiven her, or did she still harbor some resentment? There was only one way to find out. Brenda dialed the number and waited nervously for her aunt to pick up the phone.

"Who is it? Who's calling me?"

"Hi, Aunt Margery! It's Brenda. How have you been?"

"How do you think I've been? My arthritis is acting up, and my hemorrhoids are killing me! What do you want? Why are you bothering me?"

"Well, we haven't spoken since my graduation, and I thought that it would be nice to catch up."

"Really? That's the only reason that you're calling me?"

"No. Not exactly. I really need someone to talk to—someone who also works in the public school system. I know that we're not on the best of terms, but would you be willing to meet me sometime for a cup of coffee or maybe get a bite to eat?"

"What's wrong, Brenda? Are you in some kind of trouble?"

"Well, I won't lie to you. I'm having a lot of problems at my job, and I've been cornered by my supervisor on more than one occasion. I think that she wants to fire me, and I don't know what to do."

"All right. I'll be right over."

Brenda couldn't believe it! Her aunt was actually coming over! Just like that, the past was gone and forgotten. Brenda had severely misjudged this woman and regretted that she had waited so long to call her. However, she wished that she had more time to prepare. Her surroundings were hardly hospitable, and her refrigerator and kitchen cabinets were almost completely bare. Maybe the best thing to do was cancel and reschedule for another time. No! She wasn't going to back out now. Her aunt was on her way, and Brenda would simply have to make do with what she had on hand. Therefore, she put on a pot of coffee and scoured the cabinets for any snacks that might be suitable for the occasion. Fortunately, she found a package of unopened crackers in the top cabinet and a wedge of cheese in the back of her refrigerator. She washed the dust off her serving platter and decoratively arranged the snacks in a circular pattern. Once she was finished, she stepped back and examined her work. She wished that she could offer more, but for now, this would have to do.

Just as Brenda was setting out the cream and sugar, she heard the doorbell ring. This was it! Her aunt was here, waiting on the other side of the door. Brenda froze momentarily, not quite knowing what to do. As she made her way over to the other end of the room, she wondered what she would say. After giving it some thought, she decided it was best to remain silent and let her aunt take the lead. She would cordially invite her inside and see where things went from there.

"Hi, Aunt Margery! Welcome to my home! Come inside! May I offer you some coffee? Or perhaps you'd like to have some cheese and crackers?"

"I didn't come here for refreshments, Brenda. I came here because you sounded distressed over the phone. You mentioned something about having problems at your job?"

At this, Brenda broke down and began to cry. "The entire year was a horrendous mess! I did my best, but my best was never good enough. My students scored poorly on the FCAT, and now my administrator is going after my job. Can you believe it? She has the audacity to blame me for their low test scores! How can it be my fault when the kids refuse to do the work? Is this what teaching is about? Is this what I have to look forward to for the next thirty years?"

"Teaching wasn't always like this, Brenda. In my day, teaching was a gratifying and rewarding career. However, since the enactment of the NCLB, everything has changed for the worse. The NCLB has set impossibly high standards and has narrowed curriculums, taking away creativity and forcing teachers to teach only those concepts that are tested on the FCAT."

"I know! I drilled my students mercilessly every day, but no matter how hard I tried, they just couldn't get it! Why can't my administrator understand that the information is beyond their scope of understanding? Some kids simply can't grasp the material. Why can't the test be easier? Why does the NCLB have to set such high standards?"

"I'm sorry to be the one to tell you this, but the test will never get easier. On the contrary, it will only get harder. Although the scores keep getting lower, the stakes keep getting higher. The NCLB will continue to raise the bar, and if schools repeatedly fail to show adequate yearly progress, teachers and administrators alike will face dire consequences."

"I remember you mentioning something about adequate yearly progress at my graduation. What exactly is that?"

"The purpose of adequate yearly progress is to establish clear goals for student learning, measure whether students are reaching these goals, and hold educators accountable for raising student achievement. AYP targets the performance of various subgroups based on race, ethnicity, socioeconomic status, disability, and English proficiency. Every year, states set goals for the percentage of students within each of these subgroups that must perform on grade level in the areas of math and reading in order for a school to make AYP."

"Goals? What kind of goals?"

"Well, every year the NCLB sets proficiency goals. This year, the proficiency goal for math was eighty-three percent. That means that eighty-three percent of your students needed to meet the state's academic achievement standards in order for your school to make AYP."

"Eighty-three percent! How is that even possible? Who could possibly meet such lofty goals?"

"Certainly not me. I've been teaching math for years, and I have yet to meet the proficiency requirements. And every time my students score poorly on the FCAT, I get chewed out by my administrator."

"So you know how I feel! You understand what I'm going through!"

"Of course I understand. I tried to warn you last year, but you refused to listen."

"I know that I should've listened, but in all fairness, you were unbearable at my graduation. You nearly ruined my big day!"

"Perhaps I could've behaved better, but like you, I had work-related problems. Just two days before your graduation, I got called into the office and was forced to answer for my low FCAT scores."

"Unbelievable! Is this how it is everywhere? I wonder how many other teachers in this country are suffering because of the NCLB."

"I don't know, but what I do know is that the suffering has only just begun."

"What do you mean? What more could they possibly do to us?"

"If schools consistently fail to make AYP, they'll be punished with an endless string of penalties."

"Penalties? What kind of penalties?"

"Well, if a school fails to make AYP three years in a row, that school will be identified as needing improvement. Once a school is labeled as such, it will be offered assistance by the district, and students will be given the option to transfer to a higher-performing school. If a school fails to make AYP for four consecutive years, the district will implement certain corrective actions to improve the school, such as replacing the staff or implementing a new curriculum. If by the fifth year the school still hasn't made AYP, the district will initiate plans to restructure the school. The school could be taken over by the state, turned over to a private contractor, reopened as a charter school, or be shut down altogether."

"How can the government do this to the teachers of this nation? Why is this pressure being placed on us?"

"Because the NCLB demands that all students be proficient in math and reading by the year 2014."

"But look at the kids that we have to work with! It's just not realistic! It's completely and totally impossible! There's no way that every single child in this country is going to be proficient in math and reading by 2014. What are the schools going to do? Are they going to fire every teacher who fails to meet the proficiency requirements?"

"No. Not right away. There's a natural progression to these things."

"What do you mean by that?"

"Well, let's take a look at your situation. If your administrator was so dissatisfied with your performance, why didn't she fire you when she had the chance?"

"I don't know."

"The reason that she didn't fire you is because she needs to build a case first. The union demands that certain steps first be taken before a teacher gets terminated. Your administrator has to provide documentation that proves that you're incompetent. Once a paper trail is created and sufficient warning has been given, your administrator then has to provide you with assistance. Have you been given any assistance thus far?"

"No. But at our last meeting, she assured me that she would provide assistance at the beginning of the new school year. Has your administrator provided you with any assistance?"

"I'm afraid that it's gone way beyond that. The district has already stepped in and taken over. Teachers are no longer the only ones that are being targeted. Everyone at every level is in danger of losing his or her job. The district has become a permanent fixture at my school. They visit daily, walk in and out of classrooms, and scrutinize every single thing that everybody does."

"That sounds awful! How can you stand the pressure?"

"I'm counting the days to my retirement. I only need to work for three more years, and then I can get the hell out of this profession and collect my pension."

"Are you going to be able to last for three more years?"

"I don't know. I'm extremely concerned about what's over the horizon. From what I've been hearing, things are only going to get worse."

"Worse? How could things possibly get worse?"

"Starting next year, student scores will factor into teacher evaluations. Scores will go into a statistical equation called a value-added model, which will then issue a grade for teachers that will count for approximately half of their evaluations."

"What are you saying? Half of my evaluation will be based on how my students perform on the FCAT?"

"That's exactly what I'm saying. And that's only part of it. The step salary schedule that has been around ever since I've been a teacher will become a thing of the past."

"So how will they determine our salaries? How will they figure out our raises?"

"How do you think? You'll be compensated based on how your students perform on the FCAT."

"But what if they fail? Does that mean that I won't get a raise?"

"Not only will you not get a raise, but a percentage of your pay may be deducted from your salary."

"What! My salary might actually go down? They can't do that! The teachers won't stand for it! Everyone will unite together and strike!"

"You know very well that that won't happen. This is Florida. If we strike, we lose our jobs."

"Then what are we supposed to do? Are we supposed to sit back and just take this?"

"Well, until somebody speaks up and an uprising takes place, change will never come about. And I hope that somebody speaks up soon, because teaching will become even more unbearable once the FCAT goes away."

"What? The FCAT is going away? That's wonderful news! Why aren't you more excited?"

"Because something worse is coming in its place."

"There's something out there that's even worse than the FCAT?"

"According to what I've read, the FCAT will completely disappear sometime between 2014 and 2015. Although on the surface it may seem like good news, it's actually not. Once the

FCAT disappears, it will be replaced by a more rigorous high-stakes test known as the Common Core State Standards."

"What's that?"

"The standards on this test are designed to be relevant to the real world, reflecting the knowledge and skills that students will need to succeed in college and in their careers. The creators of the Common Core State Standards imported these standards from abroad, borrowing lessons from top-performing countries. The standards are more rigorous, and the lessons are more complex than those of previous standards. Once the FCAT is gone, students will be expected to take end-of-course exams that will be harder than anything that they have ever taken before. No matter how you look at it, the future is bleak. Students will continue to perform poorly, and teachers will continue to take the blame. And when all of the teachers have been fired and all of the schools have been shut down, private contractors will take over, and public education will become a thing of the past."

So there it was. Aunt Margery had laid everything out plainly and had sugarcoated nothing. Had Brenda known all this before, she would never have become a teacher. She would have stayed away from the education field altogether and would have pursued another career. She thought back to her college days and wondered why her professors had concealed this information from her. Why hadn't someone warned her about the obstacles that lay ahead? As Brenda listened to her aunt ramble on, she suddenly realized that she had no one else to blame but herself. Why hadn't she followed her aunt's advice and done her research? How could she have been so gullible, swallowing everything the recruiters had fed her? Now she was stuck and had no idea what to do. An hour ago, she had been ecstatic over the possibility of transferring to another school, but what difference would that make? A new school would give her temporary refuge, but inevitably, she would be targeted again. Brenda was a mathematician and prided herself on being able to solve complex problems, but this was a problem with no solution. Although it was difficult to accept, the situation was completely out of her control. And like it or not, until the laws changed and standardized testing went away, she and teachers all over the country would continue to be persecuted and would forever be at risk of losing their jobs.

CHAPTER 20

One week after her aunt's visit, Brenda received a letter from the school district and was shocked to discover that her request for a transfer had been denied. How could this be? Had she made a mistake filling out the application? Had she unknowingly missed the deadline? Brenda couldn't figure it out. Why had she been rejected? Hadn't she met the qualifications? After reading over the letter carefully, she discovered that she didn't meet the distance requirements. A person had to live at least twenty miles away to qualify for a hardship transfer. Attached to the letter was a map showing that her home was only nineteen miles away from her job. Brenda couldn't believe it! She had been denied because of one lousy mile. Now she had no other choice but to return to Twin Palms Middle School. Her last hope had been extinguished, and come August, she would have to contend once again with Mrs. Harrison.

The remaining weeks of summer flew by quickly, and before Brenda knew it, it was time to go back to work. She didn't relish the idea of going back to her job, but with no other prospects in sight, what other choice did she have? So on the first day of school, she woke up at 6:00 a.m. sharp and grudgingly got ready for work. After showering, she walked over to her closet and bypassed her suits in favor of more comfortable garb. What was the point in getting all dressed up? No one else bothered to get dressed up during the first week of school. After selecting a tank top and stretch pants, she began the grueling process of drying and styling her hair. However, as she ran a comb through her wet locks, Brenda suddenly had a change of heart. Why was she wasting her time? It was much easier to tie her hair into a ponytail and stuff it under a baseball cap. After she finished dressing, she took one last look at herself in the mirror and marveled at how sloppy she looked. She usually took pride in her appearance, but these days, she no longer took pride in anything. She knew that nothing she did would ever please Mrs. Harrison; therefore, she decided to do the bare minimum. And if anyone in the administration had anything to say about her lack of regard, then they could write her up and add their complaints to her ever-growing personnel file.

Once Brenda arrived at work, she walked over to the media center and found most of her colleagues already there. As she looked around the room, she couldn't help noticing that everyone looked just as miserable as she did—everybody but the new teachers. These newcomers were an unfortunate collection of misfits, standing out like sore thumbs, overdressed and overly enthusiastic. And just as Brenda had done the year before, they claimed the seats in the front row, notepads and pencils in hand, eagerly waiting to jot everything down. Brenda laughed out loud at the sight of their zeal and made her way to the back of the room. She took her place with the other veteran teachers and proceeded to check her e-mail; however, before she could turn her computer on, a greeting from a familiar voice unexpectedly interrupted her.

"Hello, Ms. Connor! Got room for one more?"

"Mr. Fisher! How wonderful to see you again! How are you doing?"

"All right, but I'm not ready to come back to work and fight with these kids."

"I know exactly how you feel. At least we won't have the same assholes as we did last year."

"No, we'll just be stuck with a new bunch of assholes."

As Brenda and Mr. Fisher conversed about summer vacation and reminisced about their first year of teaching, the administrators slowly trickled in. Brenda shuddered when she saw Mrs. Harrison and felt a sickness in the pit of her stomach when she smiled in her direction. Walking directly beside her was Mrs. Bonner. As an interim principal, this woman had posed little threat; however, this year, she had been promoted to principal, and she was now free to exert her authority over the staff. Brenda was disheartened to see Mrs. Bonner assume this role. Right off the bat, Mrs. Bonner had rubbed her the wrong way, and she would no doubt continue to be problematic in the future. Yet most disconcerting of all was her relationship with Mrs. Harrison. Over the last few months, the two women had bonded and had developed a friendship that seemed unbreakable. From the first day, Mrs. Harrison had toadied to this woman's every whim and had been obliging in every possible way. She had foreseen Mrs. Bonner's elevation and had secured her own survival by offering herself up as a minion.

Brenda didn't like what she saw, but she was powerless to stop it. Mrs. Harrison knew only too well how to play the game and submitted herself shamelessly to get exactly what she wanted— and more than anything, she wanted to see Brenda lose her job.

After the meeting concluded, the teachers were given the rest of the afternoon to work on their classrooms. Brenda was thrilled to have the rest of the day to herself, but her happiness was curtailed when she saw Mrs. Harrison beckoning her to come over. What did this bitch want now? Why couldn't she just leave her alone? Why did she have to attack her on the very first day of school? Brenda reluctantly walked over and forced herself to smile as she approached Mrs. Harrison.

"Hello, Mrs. Harrison. Did you enjoy your summer vacation?"

"I did, but I'm happy to be back to work. Before you go to your classroom, Mrs. Bonner would like to talk to you. I'm heading over to her office right now. Why don't you come along with me?"

"Right now?"

"Right now."

Brenda reluctantly followed Mrs. Harrison to the principal's office and was surprised to see Mr. Fisher sitting in one of the chairs. She sat down next to him, and they both watched as Mrs. Harrison left the room to make a phone call.

"Mr. Fisher, what are you doing here?"

"Mrs. Harrison pulled me aside and told me that the principal wanted to talk to me. Why are you here?"

"I'm here for the same reason. Do you think that we're in some kind of trouble? Should we be concerned that we're sitting in the principal's office?"

"I don't know, but let's try not to get ourselves worked up. Let's wait and hear what Mrs. Bonner has to say."

Mr. Fisher was right. Brenda needed to take a page from his book and calm herself down. No doubt they were in some kind of trouble, but someone was always in trouble at this school. The year before, it had been Ms. Spencer and Mr. Morrison. Both had lost their jobs, and with the two of them out of the picture, it was now Brenda and Mr. Fisher's turn to place their heads on the chopping block and face execution. Brenda leaned back in her chair and looked around the room. How different it looked now that Mr. Jenkin was no longer there! He had spent an exorbitant amount of money furnishing the office only to have it completely refurnished by the new principal. Brenda gazed with childlike awe at the unbelievable opulence. It was evident that the new principal was not a penny-pincher. Like Mr. Jenkin, Mrs. Bonner had no qualms about mishandling school funds to indulge her lavish tastes. Why she had to replace everything, Brenda did not know. Every piece of furniture that had resided in this room had been less than a year old and in near-perfect condition. Like her predecessor, Mrs. Bonner clearly favored the finer things in life. Thrifty she was not, and little did she think of those around her who had to do without. While the teachers scrimped and saved to buy school supplies, Mrs. Bonner spared no expense. Even in light of the recent financial cutbacks, she showed no restraint. While everyone else was forced to work with broken computers and printers, she surrounded herself with state-of-the-art equipment. Brenda could see evidence of her extravagance throughout the entire room, and she wondered how much more of the taxpayers' money would be wasted before the room was decorated to her satisfaction.

Before Brenda could complete her inspection of the room, Mrs. Harrison returned, accompanied by two other people. Because there were so many people in attendance, it was necessary for everyone to move to the other end of the room and sit at the large, rectangular table. Mrs. Bonner sat at one end of the table, while Mrs. Harrison sat at the other. Brenda and Mr. Fisher sat together in the center, and on the opposite side sat Mrs. Johnson. Brenda was surprised to see that the math coach had been invited to the meeting, and she wondered why Mrs. Johnson was there. Once everybody was seated, Mrs. Bonner took the lead and began the meeting.

"I'd first like to take the time to thank everyone for coming here on such short notice. I understand that the first week of school is a busy time and that administrators and teachers alike need every available moment to prepare for the arrival of their students. With that being said, I'll cut to the point and explain why we're all here. It's been brought to my attention by Mrs. Harrison that the sixth-grade Traditional students scored poorly on last year's math FCAT. As I mentioned when I first arrived at this school, I'm in the business of education. And just as I'm in the business of education, you must be in the business of teaching. Your top priority is to raise FCAT scores, and judging by the printouts given to me by Mrs. Harrison, both of you have failed to meet the required expectations. Therefore, I've come here today with your administrator and the math coach to provide you with assistance. We're here to provide you with support and ensure that this never happens again."

"We don't need assistance!" exclaimed Mr. Fisher.

"Yeah! We don't need assistance!" chimed in Brenda.

"I'm sorry, but I'm afraid that these printouts suggest otherwise. What you need to understand is that we're not here to attack you. Everyone in this room has a common goal, and that goal is to help you improve your performance in the classroom. Both Mrs. Harrison and I want to see you succeed, and we've enlisted Mrs. Johnson to help you meet your goals. She will play an integral part in helping you improve yourselves as teachers by demonstrating strategies that will help increase FCAT scores."

Brenda looked over in Mrs. Johnson's direction and could see that she was none too pleased about being included in this process. Although she was silent, her eyes spoke volumes. It was obvious that she wanted no part of this ridiculousness and had been coerced to participate against her will. She was already overwhelmed with her teaching and departmental responsibilities. How could they possibly expect her to take on this additional workload when she already had so much to do?

"Mrs. Johnson has graciously volunteered to visit each of you twice a week for two periods each day and assist you in your classrooms. She will develop lesson plans, teach your classes, and interact with the students."

"What are we supposed to do in the meantime?" asked Mr. Fisher.

"Yeah! Are we supposed to just sit around and do nothing?" asked Brenda.

"Both of you will be Mrs. Johnson's assistants. You'll be expected to do whatever she requests, and Mrs. Harrison and I will monitor you on a weekly basis by doing observations on the days that Mrs. Johnson is absent from your classrooms. We'll meet again in two months to review your progress and will decide then whether or not we need to take the next step and place you on a professional development plan."

So there it was. The thing that Brenda dreaded the most had finally come to fruition. Mrs. Harrison had allied herself with the new principal and was bent upon destroying her and Mr. Fisher. Throughout the course of this meeting, Brenda tried to put on a brave front; however, try as she might, she could not disguise her distress. She wore a mask of panic and desperation and felt a deep inner hatred for the woman who would ultimately be responsible for her demise. As Brenda looked at Mrs. Harrison, she caught a glimmer in her eye that suggested revenge. Why was this woman so vindictive? What harmful thing had Brenda done to warrant her malice? Had her crime been so great that it necessitated the loss of her job? To Brenda, it seemed that this woman had no modicum of humanity. She was the very definition of evil incarnate, and no exorcism would ever loosen the demon that had latched onto her soul. The smile from earlier that morning was still plastered all over her face, and Brenda felt her stomach churn every time Mrs. Harrison nodded approvingly whenever Mrs. Bonner had something to say. At one point, she looked over and saw that Mr. Fisher was every bit as terror stricken as she was. He concealed his fears far better then she, but he was fearful nevertheless. Like her, he saw the writing on the wall and knew full well that if they were put on a plan, they would surely lose their jobs.

"If there're no further questions, I'd like to conclude this meeting by thanking everyone for coming. I appreciate your cooperation and encourage the both of you to voice any and all concerns that you may have regarding this matter. Both Mrs. Harrison and I have an open-door policy and would be delighted to speak with you should you have any questions."

Brenda could feel the bile rising in her throat and had to fight hard to not throw up on Mrs. Bonner's new furniture. The principal's polite manner made her skin crawl, and she couldn't wait to get out of her office. This woman operated exactly the same way as Mrs. Harrison: luring her prey into a false sense of security and then pouncing on them when they least expected it. Brenda refused to be caught up in her web of lies but knew full well that she had to play her game. She had to concede to all of her demands, no matter how unreasonable or unrealistic. Her first year of teaching had been horrific, to say the least, but the second year would put her endurance to the test. Every day would be like hell on earth, and Brenda wondered if she had the stamina to make it through the next two months.

As soon as the meeting was formally adjourned, Brenda and Mr. Fisher exited the office and headed toward the teachers' lounge. They should have returned to their classrooms, but who could work at a time like this? They both had meetings to attend, books to collect, and classrooms to set up, but none of that seemed important right now. All that mattered presently was what had just taken place. It seemed that all either of them could do was talk about the meeting, so they sat down and contemplated their next move.

"Mr. Fisher, what are we going to do now?"

"Just try to relax, Ms. Connor. They said that we had two months to show improvement. If we do exactly as they say, there's no reason for them to put us on a plan."

"Open your eyes, Mr. Fisher! Mrs. Harrison hasn't come this far just to let us off the hook. Don't you remember what they did to Mr. Morrison? Can't you see that they're setting us up for failure? No matter how hard we try, we're still going to be put on a plan."

"Well, what about Mrs. Johnson? She's always proved supportive in the past. Maybe she'll speak well of us to Mrs. Harrison."

"I sincerely doubt it. Didn't you see the look on her face? She couldn't even look us in the eyes. If she cared about us at all, she would have spoken up and said something when she had the chance. She would've come to our defense rather than just sitting there in complete silence. It pains me to say this, but Mrs. Johnson is not our friend. She's one of them now, and she's going to play a pivotal part in bringing us down."

"Well then, I guess it's out of our hands. The only thing left to do now is place our faith in the Lord and pray that he guides us through this difficult time. We have to be thankful that we at least have each other. Just imagine how hard it would be if you had to go through this all alone."

Leave it to Mr. Fisher to find a bright side to a completely hopeless situation. Throughout this entire ordeal, he had never lost his faith, but Brenda could feel hers dwindling with each passing day. She had prayed, pleaded, and prostrated herself in front of the Lord, but to no avail. She felt like the biblical figure Job, punished ruthlessly even though she had committed no sin. Why the Lord had forsaken her, Brenda did not know. Perhaps this was her penance for some sin she had committed in the past. Or perhaps this was simply the cross she had to bear. But what about Mr. Fisher? Why was Mrs. Harrison going after him? What had he done to incur her wrath? Did she not know who he was? Did she not realize that she was attacking a man of God? What fault could she possibly find in a man who devoted his entire life to the Lord? These questions and countless others circled in Brenda's mind. It was all tragically unfair. It seemed almost criminal to treat someone like this. But still, Mr. Fisher had made a valid point. At least they would always have each other. No matter what happened, neither of them would ever have to go through this situation alone. Come what would, they would face it together and help each other till the very end.

CHAPTER 21

After careful consideration and much deliberation, Brenda and Mr. Fisher decided that the best course of action was to go to the union and meet with their representative. After paying union dues for over a year, it was high time they saw a return on their investment. Therefore, they took a personal day and went together to the union building, which was situated right in the heart of Miami. Brenda had never been to this building before and was astounded by what she saw. In her mind, she had envisioned a grand structure filled to capacity with a workforce devoted to the protection and betterment of the people who worked within the teaching profession. However, in reality, the building was nothing more than a dilapidated, severely run-down warehouse in dire need of repair. As they drove into the parking lot, Brenda was deeply distressed to see only two other cars in the lot. Where was everyone? How could such an organization be so sparsely staffed? With the amount of union dues that teachers were forced to pay, couldn't the union afford to hire a few more people? Brenda was relieved that she had had the good sense to make an appointment rather than just sporadically showing up. Had she not called in advance, she and

Mr. Fisher might have found themselves all alone in the parking lot, locked out with no chance of ever getting inside.

As they entered the main door, they saw a severe old lady wearing glasses and knitting her brow in concentration as she sat hunched over her desk, struggling to solve a crossword puzzle. Without so much as a hello, she pointed her bony finger to a red door and motioned for them to walk down the hallway. Once they arrived at their destination, the pointing continued, as the union representative directed them to sit down while he nonchalantly chatted away on the telephone. Needless to say, Brenda was annoyed by the indifference the people in this building had shown to her and Mr. Fisher. Everyone knew the purpose of their visit. Was it too much to ask for a little compassion? Would it have killed these people to show a little sensitivity? Brenda could feel herself begin to lose patience as the union representative ended one phone call only to make another. Their jobs were hanging by a thread, and this asshole was making personal calls. What kind of bullshit was this? Brenda looked over in Mr. Fisher's direction and could see that he was also vexed, but she knew only too well that he would never speak up. Therefore, Brenda, who was never one to hold anything back, brazenly took it upon herself to kick all subtlety to the curb and make their presence known.

"Excuse me, but would you be so kind as to make your personal calls at a later time? We have a two o'clock appointment and don't like to be kept waiting."

Upon hearing this, the union representative glared his disapproval at her and left the room to finish his conversation.

Once he was gone, Mr. Fisher angrily turned to Brenda and promptly reprimanded her for speaking out.

"What the hell do you think you're doing? We can't make this man angry! Don't you realize that he's the only person who can save our jobs? You need to control your temper and start showing him a little respect!"

"Respect? Why should I show him any respect? Our union dues pay his salary! The way I see it, he should be showing us some respect by getting off of that goddamn phone and doing his job!"

"You know as well as I do that it doesn't work that way, Ms. Connor. Although we're union members and pay our monthly dues, we're still at his mercy. Don't you understand? This is the end of the road. If he can't help us, then nobody can."

As usual, Mr. Fisher was right. Paying union dues entitled them to nothing, save this one meeting with their union representative. Over the last year, they had both paid over a thousand dollars, but no amount of money would ever be enough to save their jobs. It would be their attitude and willingness to cooperate that would ultimately give them a fighting chance. Brenda took a deep breath and tried to compose herself. For her sake as well as Mr. Fisher's, she would have to find a way to massage this man's ego. She needed to borrow a page from Mr. Richard's book and kiss this man's ass until her lips fell off of her face. As much as she hated to do it, she would have to humble herself to the point of groveling if it would save their jobs.

"I'm sorry, Mr. Fisher. You're absolutely right. Attacking this man will get us nowhere. From here on out, why don't you do all of the talking? You're far more collected and more than capable of handling the situation without me."

"All right then. Just stay quiet, and let me deal with this man."

After almost an hour, the union representative returned, looking more perturbed than he had before he'd left. Brenda felt his agitation had something to do with her and the remarks she had made earlier, but she resisted the urge to apologize. After all, she had given her word to Mr. Fisher to remain silent and was determined to keep her promise. Therefore, she leaned back in her chair and waited patiently for Mr. Fisher to initiate the conversation.

"Ms. Connor and I would first like to thank you for meeting with us today. We know that this is short notice and that you're a busy man, but under the circumstances, we had no other choice but to make this emergency appointment. As you well know, our principal has targeted both of us and is threatening to place us on a professional development plan. She's given us exactly two months to show improvement and has enlisted the math coach to provide assistance. We're both at our wit's end and have no idea what to do. Is there anything that you can do to help us?"

"Well, before your principal can place you on a professional development plan, she needs to have a paper trail first. Have either of you been documented over the last year by anyone in your administration?"

"As a matter of fact, we've both been documented by Mrs. Harrison, who's our assistant principal and whom we both answer to directly. We've been called into her office on numerous occasions and have suffered through a number of grueling classroom observations. Because she's always found fault with our teaching and has always falsified her findings, we were careful never to sign any of the documents that were given to us by her. However, the observations were still placed in our personnel files and are now being used as evidence against us."

"It doesn't really matter whether you signed the documents or not. A paper trail has been created, and a case for your dismissal is being built. Providing assistance is the final step before your administrator can legally place you on a professional development plan. If you don't show improvement within the two-month period specified by your principal, you will then be sent a letter informing you to attend a disciplinary meeting. Obviously, the purpose of the meeting will be to place you on a plan. At that time, you may contact me, and I'll come to your school and be present for the meeting."

"Well, I think I speak for Ms. Connor as well as for myself when I say that we don't want to let it get to that point. As our union representative, can't you speak on our behalf? Can't you do something to prevent us from being placed on this plan? Can't you at least go after them for harassment? Don't you understand? We don't deserve to be treated this way! We don't deserve to lose our jobs!"

"I'm going to have to ask you to calm down, Mr. Fisher. I don't think that you fully understand how the process works.

The union is limited in its capacity to help the employees. So long as the administration follows the procedures listed in the union handbook, they're well within their rights to place a person on a professional development plan. The union can't interfere with how a principal chooses to discipline his or her staff. The only time we become involved is when an employee has actually been placed on the plan."

"So what will you do if we're placed on the plan? Will you be able to save our jobs then?"

"Oh, absolutely not! The purpose of the union is not to save jobs. We're simply here to assist with the disciplinary process. Once you've been placed on a professional development plan, you will have exactly ninety days to show improvement and score satisfactory ratings in each of the ten required areas. As your union representative, I will be with you at every meeting to ensure that you're treated fairly and are given the resources and assistance necessary to your success. After that, it's entirely up to you to utilize the resources and make the required improvements. At the end of the ninety days, your principal will ultimately be the one who decides whether or not you'll be terminated."

"What! You mean to tell me that Mrs. Bonner is going to decide whether or not we get to keep our jobs? That's not fair! She's the one who's trying to destroy us! Why can't you be the one to decide? Why can't an impartial judge make the decision? Anybody would be better than Mrs. Bonner!"

"I'm sorry, but that's simply not how it works. The union's only role is to make sure that both parties follow the procedures.

The union doesn't have the authority to make decisions about employment. All the union can do is help mediate and make sure that the employee is treated as fairly as possible."

"So that's it? That's all you can do?"

"I'm sorry that I can't do more, but that's just the way things are. The best thing that you can do is win your assistant principal over and do everything in your power to avoid being placed on the plan."

"We will, but what if it comes to that? What if we're placed on the plan? What are our chances of actually keeping our jobs?"

"Well, as I mentioned earlier, you will be scored in ten different areas. If you don't receive satisfactory scores in every single area, termination will be inevitable."

"What are our chances of earning satisfactory scores in every area?"

"My guess is slim to none. It sounds to me like your principal and assistant principal are out to destroy you."

"Then why won't you help us? How can you call yourself a union when you don't protect the employees?"

"Once again, as I mentioned earlier, the union is limited in its capacity to help the employees. You have to remember that you're working in a right-to-work state. In Florida, the employer has the right to fire an employee at any time without warning. My advice to you is to quit before you're placed on the plan."

"Why would we want to do that?"

"Well, once you're placed on a professional development plan, failure is almost inevitable. So long as your administration follows the procedures and adheres to the rules, you're both doomed to lose your jobs. And if you lose your jobs, you'll never work as teachers in the state of Florida again."

"What! Why not?"

"Once people fail the plan, they're essentially blacklisted from ever working in the education field again. Prospective employers will be alerted once they do a background check, and if they see that you've been placed on a professional development plan, you'll never get hired again. Once you see that you're in danger of being placed on the plan, immediately give two weeks' notice and submit your resignation."

"I can't believe this! Is this all the help that the union can offer? I'm absolutely stunned! What do you think, Ms. Connor? Do you have anything to say?"

Of course she had something to say! Brenda was at the point of bursting but had kept quiet at the insistence of Mr. Fisher. However, now that he had given her permission to talk, she took full advantage and proceeded to give the union representative a piece of her mind.

"As a matter of fact, I do have something to say. First and foremost, I think that what you do here is one big joke, and after this is all over, I will do everything in my power to make people aware of just how weak the union really is. I don't know about Mr. Fisher, but I feel like a complete fool for ever paying a single penny to this sham of an organization. If you had any honor at all, you would pay us back every dollar you took and write a sincere letter of apology to everyone you've failed to help."

"I'm sorry that you feel that way, but as I have repeatedly stated, there's nothing more that I can do. Rather than blaming the union for your shortcomings, maybe you should place the blame on yourselves. I happen to know that your students scored poorly on last year's FCAT, and if your scores are as low as your principal claims, then she's well within her rights to place both of you on a professional development plan."

"How dare you! You have no idea what we went through last year with our students! Have you ever even been in a classroom? Can you even fathom how difficult it is to teach low-level children? I challenge you to try it for a month or even for just a day! I'd bet everything I have that you'd never survive!"

"I'm not going to sit here and fight with the two of you. I've done my job and explained to you the way things work. If you're dissatisfied with what the union has to offer, then you can deal with this mess on your own or seek outside representation. Now then, if there are no other questions, I need to get back to work."

Before Brenda could say anything else, the union representative hustled her and Mr. Fisher out the door and proceeded to make another phone call. Brenda sighed with disgust as she exited the building. She knew that the union was useless, but she had never expected to be treated like this. How could the union representative turn against them? How could he defend the administration and blame them for the children's low test scores? Wasn't he supposed to be on their side? Wasn't it his job to fight for their rights? What kind of a union turned against the very people they were meant to protect? Was this what Mr. Morrison had gone through? Had he too been treated as the criminal rather than the victim? On the car ride home, Mr. Fisher voiced his frustrations, but Brenda barely said anything at all. What could she say? What possible comfort could she offer to a man who was every bit as doomed as she was? The union had been their last hope, and now they were hopelessly alone. The union had failed them, and there was nothing left to do but go back to work and struggle through the remaining days.

CHAPTER 22

The next few weeks were some of the most challenging of Brenda's life. As promised, the math coach visited twice a week and took over instruction while she sat in the back of the room, observing and pretending to take notes. And when the math coach wasn't there, Mrs. Harrison or Mrs. Bonner would randomly show up to her class. Brenda dreaded the sound of these women entering her room. The key rattling, the creak of the door—these were sounds that set her heart racing. She never ceased from teaching, but with her eyes, she took inventory of everything they did. She took notice of where they sat, when they wrote something down, and how long they stayed. And at the end of every week, she dutifully reported to Mrs. Harrison's office, bracing herself for the disparagement to come. To Brenda, Mrs. Harrison sounded like a broken record, always criticizing that there was too much of this or too little of that. No matter how hard she tried, nothing she did was ever good enough, and at the end of each day, when everyone else went home, she and Mr. Fisher would stay late, comparing notes and crying on each other's shoulders. There was no one else now, no one in the entire school who was willing to come to their defense. Like Ms. Spencer and Mr. Morrison before them, they had become pariahs, cast out from their teams and cast out from the school. They had only each other now, and they weathered the storm together as best as they could. But how long could they hold on? How much more could either of them possibly take?

After a few weeks, Brenda grew accustomed to the daily walkthroughs and weekly interrogations, but try as she might, she could not adjust to her new students. She had a new batch of sixth graders and couldn't believe how badly they behaved. Unlike her first year, this year, she had been given nothing but low-level children. She had no advanced class this time, only repeaters and an endless stream of children with IEPs. Children who should have been placed in special classes had been mainstreamed and thrown into her classroom. Both she and Mr. Fisher had back-to-back classes of nothing but troublemakers and students with all manner of behavioral disorders. It was clear that the administration was setting them up for failure. At every other school, students were rotated, and every teacher was expected to take his or her turn. Only at Twin Palms Middle School did a teacher have to teach the same level of children every single year. Why were the Montessori and Gifted teachers exempt from working with the low-level children? Why were they shielded year after year from dealing with the behavioral problems? It wasn't fair, and Brenda was tempted to call the union, but Mr. Fisher urged her not to. If anything, calling the union was the worst thing she could possibly do. Complaining would do nothing more than validate her ineptness as a teacher and confirm that she was unable to do her job. Like it or not, she would have to play the cards she had been dealt and manage her students the best she could.

Because she knew that her days were numbered and that her job was in jeopardy, Brenda eventually gave up altogether on trying to control behavior in her classroom. What was the point? Her students were going to do exactly what they wanted regardless of what she had to say. Attempting to discipline them would only further infuriate them and make it that much more likely that she would get hurt. For some reason, many of the children had serious anger issues, and the last thing she wanted was for them to take their anger out on her. The disciplinary matrix that had played such an important role during her first year of teaching was now nowhere to be found. As far as she was concerned, implementing the interventions listed on the matrix was nothing but a complete waste of time. Why should she stay late every day after school to make telephone calls? Why should she come in early every morning to have parent/ teacher conferences? Most importantly, why should she bother documenting students and writing referrals? Would any of these interventions improve behavior and make a difference in her classroom?

Although Brenda was careful to not provoke the children, fights still broke out because the children provoked one another. Almost every day, she had to call security, who would escort the children out of her classroom. The line outside the nurse's office was constantly filled with kids who had bloody noses and broken appendages. Why these children were so hostile to one another, Brenda did not know. In every class, children took sides, and miniature gangs began to pop up. Bullying became a subject for concern, and even though the principal hosted an assembly discouraging violence, the bullying continued. As Brenda observed the combative nature of her students, she recalled the days of her own childhood and remembered that once upon a time, she herself had also been a bully. She and Michael were friends now, but during her roller-skating days, she had made his life a living hell. However, although Brenda knew that bullying was a part of every child's life, this generation had somehow transformed it into something far uglier and substantially more dangerous. With the advent of new technology, children were now able to do their bullying from a distance. In Brenda's time, children bullied their targets in the schoolyard—or, as in Michael's case, at the skating rink. Now children no longer needed to wait until a specific time, nor did they have to meet at a specific place. They could harass a fellow classmate whenever they wanted just by using their cell phones. Cyberbullying was a new phenomenon and a problem throughout the entire country. Teachers could confiscate the phones, but eventually they had to give them back. And when the teachers returned the phones, children simply resumed where they had left off and continued with their harassment.

It was safe to say that cell phones were a problem throughout the entire school. Besides using them for cyberbullying, children used them to play games, send text messages, and surf the Internet. Worst of all, they used the phones to cheat on exams. It took awhile for Brenda to catch on to what the children were doing, because they concealed the phones in their laps. However, when everyone suddenly got a perfect score on one of her exams, Brenda realized that something was going on. Had they not been so greedy, they would never have aroused her suspicion and would have been more difficult to catch. But being middle-school children—and not very smart children at that—their only concern was immediate gratification, with no thought to the long-term consequences. Once she discovered that the phones were the culprit, she immediately remedied the problem by keeping a closer eye on her students and insisting that they keep their hands on top of their desks at all times.

Brenda wished that she could prevent the children from bringing the phones into her classroom, but unfortunately, they had the right to have the phones in case of emergencies. And because they were given this right, teaching became virtually impossible. As if she didn't have enough to deal with already, now she had to deal with these goddamn phones. Administrators were visiting her three, sometimes four times a day, and everyone who visited her saw her students using the phones. As if all that weren't bad enough, the people from the district were also starting to come into her classroom. Because the school had failed to make adequate yearly progress, district personnel began to trickle in to observe teachers. And because her students had scored poorly the year before, they observed her more than any other teacher on her team. Like Mrs. Harrison and Mrs. Bonner, the people from the district came in without warning with their clipboards and tape recorders in hand. They saw the children playing with their phones and demanded to know why the students weren't on task. And when they finished reprimanding her about the children, they would walk around her classroom, asking, "Why isn't the classroom print rich?" or "Why isn't the word wall more current?" And if they happened to walk in while she was teaching a particular lesson, they would ask, "Why isn't there more rigor?" or "Why can't there be more-differentiated instruction?" During these moments, Brenda often thought back to her summer vacation and the conversation she'd had with her aunt Margery. Was this what her aunt experienced? Were these the same people who came into Aunt Margery's classroom and scrutinized everything she did? It was terrible to have to work under these conditions, but what other choice did Brenda have? Although these people looked as if they hadn't been in a classroom since the Reagan administration, Brenda was forced to submit to each and every one of their demands. They should have retired and been put out to pasture long ago, but instead, they chose to remain, making their rounds at low-performing schools and condemning every single teacher who had the misfortune of crossing their path.

Because many of the district personnel were so old and had been absent from the classroom for so long, they didn't always necessarily know what was best for the children. Brenda wasn't especially offended when they criticized her classroom or even when they criticized her teaching methods. The people in her administration criticized her on a daily basis, and she had, over time, become indifferent to the abuse. She was, however, alarmed whenever she saw someone from the district try to interact with one of her students. After working with low-level children for over a year, she knew exactly how far they could be pushed and how they were likely to react. Certain children simply didn't want to learn and needed to be left alone. However, the people from the district did not always see things her way. Rather than heeding her advice and keeping a safe distance, they often put themselves in unnecessary danger and risked confrontation with a child. Brenda wished that they wouldn't disregard her warnings, but what could she do? These people had an aura of arrogance about them and wouldn't hesitate for a moment to throw their superior skills and years of experience in her face. It didn't matter that their experience was from another time and was no longer relevant in today's classroom. They still believed that they knew what was best, so Brenda had no choice but to take a step back and allow them to make their mistakes.

Approaching the children was risky enough, but some district personnel took things a step further and doled out discipline. Brenda was always nervous whenever someone attempted to correct one of her students. Didn't these people realize that these children were ticking time bombs? Didn't they know that it was only a matter of time before children lost their tempers? Brenda hated to be right about these things, but unfortunately, just as she had predicted, someone eventually got hurt. One Friday afternoon, during her last-period class, three elderly ladies from the district dropped by unexpectedly and visited her classroom. At first, they seemed content to just sit in the back of the room and keep to themselves; however, one of the ladies became fidgety when she heard a student begin to snore. The lady intended her display of uneasiness to be Brenda's cue to walk over to the student, wake her up, and get her back on task.

However, she did no such thing. She ignored the child's snoring and continued to teach her class. Realizing that she was being ignored, the district lady rose from her seat and took Brenda aside.

"Ms. Connor, don't you notice that there's a child sleeping in your class?"

"Of course I noticed, but I let that child sleep whenever she feels tired."

"What do you mean that you let her sleep? Children don't come to school to sleep! They come to school to learn!"

"I'm sorry to be the one to tell you this, but that particular child has no desire to learn. She's a disciplinary problem with a violent streak to boot. It's a blessing to me and to the entire class whenever she falls asleep. It's only during these rare occasions that I can actually teach and the students can actually learn."

"I can't believe what I'm hearing! You go over there right now and wake that child up!"

"I'm sorry, but I'm not going to do that."

"Well, if you're not going to wake her up, then I will! That child needs to understand the reason why she's here!"

As the district lady made her way over to the snoring student's desk, Brenda suddenly felt someone tugging on her sleeve, motioning her to bend down.

"Ms. Connor, it ain't a good idea for that ole woman to wake Precious up."

The little boy was absolutely right. Although the snoring student happened to be named Precious, precious she was not. Although she was only thirteen years old, she stood nearly six feet tall and was built like a linebacker. She had beaten up almost everyone in the class and had been suspended more than any other student in the entire school. Everyone who knew Precious knew to keep his or her distance. Brenda knew it, and the students knew it—only the lady from the district didn't seem to know it.

"Look, Ms. Connor! That ole woman be pokin' Precious! Don't she know what gonna happen if Precious wake up?"

Clearly, the woman from the district had not given any thought to what would happen if Precious woke up. As she forcefully nudged the child with a ruler, the other students turned around, looked at Brenda, and waited to see what she would do. One of the kids pointed to the telephone, urging her to call security, but she refused to pick up the receiver. Why should she? Why should she go out of her way to help this woman? This woman certainly didn't go out of her way to help Brenda. Like everyone else from the district, this woman was a spectator on the sidelines, ever careful to maintain a safe distance, never willing to roll up her sleeves and help. But that was about to change. Someone had finally crossed over and stepped into Brenda's domain. Someone was finally going to walk in Brenda's shoes and experience the struggle that she experienced each and every day. Perhaps she should have stepped in and stopped this incident, but as far as she was concerned, it wasn't her place to interfere. After all, she was only a second-year teacher, and who was she to tell the people from the district what to do?

"Young lady? Wake up, young lady! This is a classroom, not a bedroom! You need to open up your textbook and follow your teacher's instructions!"

"Who da fuck are you?"

"My goodness! Such language! That's no way for a young lady to speak! Didn't anyone ever teach you any respect? Don't you have any manners? Now then, I want you to stand up and apologize for your behavior!"

Precious didn't apologize for her behavior, but she did stand up. She stood up, lifted her desk over her head, and then threw it directly at the district lady. The children sitting nearby had anticipated this display of rage and were able to get out of the way in the nick of time, but the poor old woman was not so fortunate. The desk knocked her out cold, and she started bleeding profusely all over the classroom floor. The other two ladies who had been sitting in the back of the room jumped out of their seats, ran over, and frantically began yelling out instructions to Brenda. One lady instructed her to call security, while the other lady instructed her to call an ambulance. The children, fascinated by the spectacle, left their seats to take a closer look. Precious, feeling no remorse at all, picked up her desk, placed it against the wall, and resumed sleeping. As everyone congregated around the fallen district lady, Brenda called security and then sat down at her desk. A year ago, she would have been terrified—fearful of being called into Mrs. Harrison's office—but now she no longer cared. Why should she? As far as she was concerned, she was on her way out. What did it matter whether she got fired now or later? The way she saw it, she had nothing left to lose. Mrs. Harrison had done everything humanly possible to terrorize her, but now everything was coming to end. Within a few short weeks, it would all be over, and Mrs. Harrison would never be able to hurt her again.

CHAPTER 23

With so much pressure in her life and no outlet for her stress, it was inevitable that Brenda would eventually fall apart. The beginning of her demise started with a cough; it was mild at first and then, over time, became more persistent. In due course, she lost her voice altogether and resorted to using a whistle to get her students' attention. Although her body ached and her fever ran high, she persevered, dragging herself to work and fighting hard to make it to the end of each day. She ignored her symptoms for as long as she could, but the day eventually came when she could no longer deny the fact that she was sick. One morning, she woke up and was shocked to discover that she could not get out of bed. Every time she tried to stand up, she felt dizzy and fell back down. She made herself some hot tea and took a decongestant, but nothing seemed to help. Months of abuse and far too many sleepless nights had finally taken a toll and caused her body to collapse. It was a terrible time for her to take off from work, but what else could she do? She had no choice but to stay in bed until her health was fully restored.

Like everyone else who worked in the school system, Brenda occasionally took a day off here and there, but she had never been out for an extended period of time. Because she was going to be out for at least a week, she needed to not only notify her supervisor but also find a substitute to cover her classes. Under normal circumstances, a teacher needed only to call the SubCentral hotline, and any substitute looking for work on that particular day would pick up the job. However, finding a substitute to cover her classes was no easy feat. With so many schools in the county, substitutes could pick and choose where they wanted to work. And because the hourly rate was the same regardless of where they went, most people opted to work in the higher—performing schools. Brenda never understood why compensation didn't vary from school to school. Why weren't substitutes paid more to work in the harder-to-staff schools? Why did everyone receive exactly the same pay no matter where he or she worked?

Substituting was a thankless job in general—one that most people did only until they found something better. It was convenient in the sense that a person could select the location and make his or her own hours; however, at less than twelve dollars per hour, the aggravation that came along with the job hardly seemed worth it. Unlike the teachers, substitutes were private contractors who were paid only for the hours they worked. The flexibility was certainly a plus, but the lack of benefits and the stress of the job quickly drove people away. Hardly anyone stayed for the long term, and the few who did quickly burned out. In Brenda's opinion, substituting was every bit as hard as teaching. The people who worked in substitute positions were expected to do everything a teacher did, but for much less money. Some schools appreciated the substitutes, but most schools treated them like second-class citizens; the children ridiculed them, and the administration avoided them. And although they were only part-time employees, their part-time status did not exempt them from being disciplined. Unlike Brenda, they could never be placed on a professional development plan, but one wrong move could get them blacklisted and bar them from ever working in the school system again.

Despite these difficulties, Brenda always managed to find someone to cover her classes whenever she called in sick. Many of her friends from college were still unemployed and had resorted to substituting to help make ends meet. It didn't take long for her to find somebody, and once the arrangements were made, she went back to bed and tried to get some sleep. Although she hated being sick, it felt wonderful to finally be left alone. For the first time in a long time, nobody was watching or documenting her every move. However, she knew that this respite was only temporary. Eventually, she would have to go back to work and face the music. As she lay in bed, she suddenly became pensive and began to reflect on everything that had happened to her since she had started working at the school. She had come into the profession believing that she could make a difference, but now all she could do was scoff at her stupidity. Why hadn't she listened to those around her who were more experienced? Mrs. Clifford had tried to warn her on her first day, but she had refused to listen. Countless others had since tried to point her in the right direction, but still, she had refused to conform. Even after witnessing what Mr. Morrison went through, she had still been resistant to change. Looking back, she wondered what she could have done differently to prevent all this from happening. Maybe if she had been more like Mr. Richard, she wouldn't be in this mess right now. Had she been more compliant, she might never have become a target for Mrs. Harrison. Unfortunately, it was too late to save her job now. Within a few short weeks, she would be called into the office and would have to either accept being placed on a professional development plan or else resign from her job.

Watching her career unravel before her eyes had been difficult, to say the least, but having to go through the experience all alone was almost more than she could bear. With the exception of Mr. Fisher, everybody she'd thought was her friend had abandoned her. Like Ms. Spencer and Mr. Morrison, she had become an outcast among her peers and had been left to fend for herself. Nobody wanted to risk being seen talking to her, and those who had the misfortune of crossing her path were careful to avert their eyes until they were a safe distance away. Even Mr. Simon, the one person she had felt she could always depend upon, had ceased to be her friend and no longer allowed her admittance to his classroom. However, the greatest betrayal of all had come from the union. This organization in which she had placed all of her faith had shamelessly taken her money yet had done nothing in return to save her job. After meeting with the union representative, Brenda had promptly discontinued paying her union dues and cancelled her membership. After all, what benefit was there in remaining a member? In her mind, she could better allocate her hard-earned money elsewhere or perhaps place it in safekeeping for an uncertain future.

Although nearly everyone at Brenda's job had shunned her, she was abundantly blessed to have family and friends she could depend on during her time of need. Once her friends and family discovered that she was sick, the phone rang incessantly, and loved ones took turns visiting her at home. It lifted her spirits immensely to see her parents and sisters fussing over her, and it touched her deeply when Michael and others from the skating rink sent her a bouquet of flowers with a card encouraging her to get better soon. Everybody she knew showed his or her support in some special way—everyone but the one person she needed the most. Much to her disappointment, Joseph neither called nor stopped by to visit her. Over the last few months, they had slowly grown apart, and they were no longer in communication. As Brenda reflected on the last year, it suddenly occurred to her that she had failed not only in her career but also in her personal life. As Brenda thought back, she recalled the endless fights, the confrontations with his mother, and his unwillingness to join her at couples' counseling. Yet more than anything, she thought about the death of their unborn child. The miscarriage, which had taken place only a short time ago, was still fresh in her mind and weighed heavily upon her heart. Although a part of her still grieved, another part of her felt relieved that she had not carried the child to term. It was clear to her now that Joseph would never be the man she desired. He would never be a provider or place his family's needs above his own. After all this time, he was still heavily in debt and reluctant to leave the safety and comfort of his mother's home. With such a man, Brenda could never have a future. And although it saddened her to see their union end, she knew that she needed to shake off the grief and find a way to move on with the rest of her life.

Brenda received many visitors during the course of her convalescence, but one visitor in particular took her by surprise. One afternoon, her dear friend and colleague Mr. Fisher showed up unexpectedly, and although she was sleeping at the time of his arrival, she forced herself to wake up. By the look on his face, she could see that he was severely distressed and was going to burden her with some bad news. Although she felt poorly and wanted to be left alone, she could not bring herself to turn him away. How could she when he had always been there for her? With that thought in mind, she pulled herself together, propped herself up with a pillow, and braced herself for what he had to say.

"I'm so sorry to drop in on you like this, Ms. Connor, but there's something that I need to tell you."

"What's wrong, Mr. Fisher? Did something happen at work?"

"You're never going to believe this! Mrs. Bonner called me into her office today after school and announced that she was going to place me on a professional development plan."

"She can't do that! It hasn't been two months yet! You still have a few weeks left to show improvement!"

"That's what I said! But now that I'm no longer a member of the union, she can do whatever she wants. She doesn't have to wait two months. She can put me on the plan right now!"

"Oh my God! What did you do?"

"What could I do? I had no other choice but to resign. Don't you remember what the union representative said? He warned us to quit before we were placed on the plan. You know that employers always do a background check. If they see this on my record, I'll never work in the state of Florida again!"

"How could this have happened? You did everything that they asked you to do. What more could you have possibly done?"

"You know the answer to that question as well as I do, Ms. Connor. Neither of us was ever meant to succeed. We were doomed to failure the moment Mrs. Harrison started documenting us. I know that you're sick and that this is an inopportune time, but as your friend, I felt that it was my responsibility to warn you. You need to be aware of what they're plotting and prepare yourself for the worst."

Prepare herself for the worst? How in the world did a person prepare for something like this? After Mr. Fisher left, Brenda lay back down in her bed and considered her options. If she went back to work, she would undoubtedly be placed on the plan. Like Mr. Fisher, she had quit the union prematurely and, as a result, was no longer under its protection. And without the union's protection, the administration was left unrestricted to do whatever they pleased. However, abandoning her job was completely out of the question. Like it or not, she had to go back to work and face Mrs. Harrison and Mrs. Bonner one last time. In order to find another job, she would have to procure a reference from these two women, and the only way to accomplish that was to conduct herself professionally and leave on the best possible terms.

After exhausting the last of her sick days, Brenda had no choice but to return to work. She tossed and turned most of the night and woke up the next morning with a pounding headache. Although she had been out for over two weeks, she still wasn't feeling like herself. For a while, it had appeared she was getting better, but Mr. Fisher's visit had caused her health to spiral back down. Grudgingly, she rose from her bed and surveyed the suits that hung in her closet. With great sadness in her heart, she selected the most comfortable suit she owned and dressed herself meticulously for what she suspected was her last day of work. Once she was properly attired, she got in her car and took her usual route to work. Although she had driven through this neighborhood countless times before, she drove slowly, eager to take in the sights one last time. Once she arrived at the school, she took her usual detour through the teachers' lounge, but Mrs. Harrison and her entourage of security guards abruptly stopped her before she could make it to the cafeteria.

"Hello, Ms. Connor. I'm sorry to detain you, but I'm going to have to ask you to follow me to the administration building."

"But I just got here! Why can't I go to my classroom first? Why can't you just give me a chance to settle in?"

"I'm sorry, but Mrs. Bonner insisted on seeing you right away. Now then, if you'll follow me, I'll personally escort you to her office."

Before Brenda could protest, Mr. Davenport and the other security guards cornered her against a wall and coerced her into following Mrs. Harrison. For a split second, she considered bolting for the parking lot, but she quickly came to her senses and passively did as she was told. She had already come this far; she only needed to go a little further. Therefore, she allowed them to lead her away like a lamb to the slaughter and watched as the teachers came out of their classrooms to bear witness to her shame. Unlike Ms. Spencer, she did not cry, nor did she put up a struggle. Instead, she walked with her head held high and carried herself with the greatest of dignity. Once inside the administration building, the security guards led her into Mrs. Bonner's office and then left her alone to await judgment from her superiors.

As Brenda entered the office, she couldn't help but feel like the biblical figure Daniel, who was thrown and then sealed into a lion's den. As she looked around the room, she saw people looking back at her, all waiting with great anticipation to tear her to pieces. To her left sat Mrs. Bonner and Mrs. Harrison. To her right were Mrs. Johnson and a lady she recognized from the district. Directly behind her stood the security guards, heedfully watching, ready to pounce if she made a wrong move. Only one seat was empty, so she sat down, anxiously waiting to hear what Mrs. Bonner had to say.

"Ms. Connor, on behalf of everyone in this room, I would first like to take a moment to welcome you back. I was very concerned when you called out sick. I'm so happy to see that you're feeling better."

"Thank you, Mrs. Bonner. I appreciate your concern. May I ask why I've been called into your office this morning?"

"Please don't be alarmed, Ms. Connor. You can rest assured that you're not in any kind of trouble. We've simply called this meeting to discuss the progress that you've made in your classroom since we last spoke. As you remember, we had some concerns about your classroom management skills."

"I understand your concern, but I also seem to remember that I was given two months to show improvement. Don't I still have a few weeks left?"

"I'm sorry, Ms. Connor, but you haven't even come close to meeting our expectations. Dragging this out any longer would only be a waste of everyone's time."

"So what happens now?"

"Although we appreciate all your hard work and effort, everyone in this room unanimously agrees that it's in your best interest to be placed on a professional development plan."

"In my best interest?"

"Yes, Ms. Connor. Don't look at this as a punishment but as an opportunity to better yourself as a teacher. Once you're placed on the plan, you'll not only be provided with resources but also with assistance from everyone sitting in this room."

"And if I don't pass the plan? What happens then?"

"Obviously, I'll have no other choice but to let you go."

So there it was. The moment she had dreaded for so long had finally come. In her usual discreet manner, Mrs. Bonner had laid it all out, and everyone in the room was holding his or her breath, eager to hear how Brenda would respond.

"I'm sorry, but I refuse to be placed on the plan. I sincerely appreciate everything that everyone has done to help me, but I feel like it's time for me to move on. If you have nothing more to say, I'd like to submit my resignation and politely request that you allow me to go back to my classroom and collect my things."

"Ms. Connor, I believe that you misunderstand our intentions. We don't want you to resign. We want you to stay on board and continue on in your capacity as a sixth-grade math teacher. Nobody here wants to see you lose your job. Everyone in this room is your friend. We all have a common goal, and that goal is to see you succeed."

"Is that right?"

"Absolutely! Now then, why don't you rescind your resignation and sign these forms?"

Mrs. Bonner slid the forms across her desk, and without even glancing at them, Brenda promptly slid them right back.

"Keep your forms. I'm not signing anything."

And with that, Brenda exited Mrs. Bonner's office in a most unceremonious fashion and began walking toward her classroom. She could hear the security guards following closely behind, but she didn't care. All she wanted to do was grab her things and leave as quickly as possible. Once she got to her classroom, she checked the time and saw that she had only fifteen minutes until the arrival of her first class. Because she didn't want to be bombarded with questions by her students, she made a quick inspection of the room and took only her most prized possessions. It saddened her to leave so many things behind, but she could see that the guards were growing impatient, so she gathered what she could and headed straight for the door. However, before she could leave, a guard stopped her abruptly and ordered her to turn in her keys and laptop. Although these things technically did not belong to her, she was reluctant to let them go. The administration had taken everything from her, but relinquishing these items was the greatest blow she had received thus far. As the security guards took the keys and laptop from her hands, she could feel herself choking up and had to fight hard to keep it together. It took everything she had to hold back her tears, but she was determined not to cry until she was in her car and off of school property. After she had handed over everything, she was finally free to leave. She took one last look at her classroom, sighed sadly to herself, and then proceeded to follow Mr. Davenport and the other security guards to the parking lot. Once there, the security guards escorted her to her car and then walked back to the cafeteria without even looking back or saying good-bye.

Once she had packed everything away in the trunk, Brenda sat in her car and began to cry. She had promised herself that she would wait until she got home, but she couldn't hold it in any longer. What was she going to do? How was she going to support herself now that she no longer had a job? She had some savings, but not nearly enough to subsist on for any extended period of time. After weeping for what seemed like an eternity, Brenda gradually began to calm down and see things in a different light. Why was she crying? Her current circumstances were certainly unfavorable, but was the alternative preferable? Did she really want to continue working in an environment that fostered hostility and abuse? Wasn't it better to go somewhere where she would be appreciated? As Brenda wiped away the last of her tears, it suddenly occurred to her that her suffering was finally over. Never again would she have to walk through those doors and face the horrors within. Neither Mrs. Harrison nor anyone else at Twin Palms Middle School would ever be able to hurt her again. How wonderful it felt to not be afraid! Now that she was liberated, she could do whatever she liked and go wherever she pleased.

But where was she going to go? Teaching was the only thing she was qualified to do. Perhaps she could go back to college, or maybe she could move back in with her parents until she sorted everything out. One thing was certain: until things changed within the public school system, she would never step foot in a classroom again. Until someone spoke up, she had no choice but to abandon the profession. Unfortunately, it was unlikely that anyone would ever speak up. Teachers all around the country were forced to remain silent, for fear of losing their jobs. However, as of today, Brenda no longer had anything to fear. Because she no longer had anything left to lose, she could now freely speak her mind. Her entire life, Brenda had dreamed of being teacher, but now she had a new dream. With no constrictions in her life, she could take a stand and devote her time and energy to bringing about change. She could share her experiences with others and make her story known throughout the world. With the power of her words, she would bring awareness into the educational community and make sure that what had happened to her would never happen to another teacher again.